The Kate Redman Mysteries

Books 4-6

Celina Grace

© Celina Grace 2013

Table of Contents

Snarl

A Kate Redman Mystery: Book 4

Prologue

ON THE LAST MORNING OF his life, Michael Frank forgot to kiss his wife goodbye. It was a simple omission, brought about by the worse than usual morning chaos and the knowledge that if he didn't get a move on, he'd be late for his nine o'clock meeting. Knowing that next year's research budget hinged on the successful outcome of this particular meeting, Michael was rather more harried than usual.

Mary Frank was preoccupied with unloading the dishwasher, trying to find the second of her older son's football boots and chivvying both her children into brushing their teeth, rather than watching the television, which was currently blaring out from the corner of the living room, in total disregard of the usual morning dictate of 'no TV before everyone's ready' rule.

"I'm off," Michael said, grabbing his briefcase and doing his best to straighten his hastily-tied tie with his one free hand. "Have you seen the car keys?"

"Wherever you put them last," snapped Mary, crashing the door of the dishwasher shut. "Kids! Would you get a bloody move on?"

Michael found the keys on the third hook by the front door; not the first hook, where they *should* have been. Muttering, he picked up his briefcase again, called a goodbye to his children, who were finally heading upstairs to the bathroom, and another to his wife before pulling the front door closed behind him.

Cut off from the tumult, he took a deep breath, savouring the momentary peace. The Franks had not long moved to the house in Polton Winter, shortly after Michael started his new job at the MedGen Research Facility. Michael walked down the drive to his car, next to a young beech tree, newly clothed in fresh, bright green leaves. Michael unlocked the car, flung his briefcase in the passenger seat and, catching sight of the time on his wristwatch, cursed. His lateness made him just a little bit less cautious than he normally was and he jumped into the driver's seat and jammed the key into the ignition, turning it swiftly on.

The explosion, as the device clamped to the underside of the suspension ignited, was the loudest thing ever heard in the sleepy little hamlet of Polton Winter. The car blossomed into a firework display of debris as the fireball tore through it, hurling twisted pieces of metal, lethal shards of glass and smoking body parts into the air. Michael's forearm was flung against the front wall of the house, as if knocking for entry. Fortunately, Mary Frank had bent down to continue unloading the dishwasher as the front windows of the house shattered into thousands of pieces, and she escaped the worst of the blast. The two Frank children were closeted in the bathroom at the back of the house, but as the explosion roared like an angry dragon, they dropped the foamy brushes from their mouths and screamed in utter terror.

As the noise faded to the crackle of the flames that remained, and people in the village began to stream from their houses, drawn towards the oily smoke and the tick-tick-tick of cooling metal, blackened wisps of the beech tree's leaves began to sift down from the sky, like the singed feathers of a million little birds.

Chapter One

Kate Redman faced her reflection in the mirror by the front door. Hair smooth and fringe neat – check. Jacket settled squarely on her shoulders – check. She was annoyed to find her hands were shaking a little and she flexed her fingers, straightening them out and trying to stem their trembling. She checked her bag: purse, phone and warrant card, all present and correct.

Kate wandered through to the living room, peered out the window and then let the curtain fall back into place. He was late, although not by much. She went back to her station by the front door, regarding herself in the mirror again. Her return-to-work outfit had been carefully chosen. She wanted to look composed, firm and no-nonsense, not a hint of the invalid about her. Automatically, her hand went to the small of her back, pressing against the raised ridge of the scar beneath her ribcage. Where the hell was he? He knew she'd be nervous so, just *for once*, why couldn't he be on time? Kate tried to slow her breathing, consciously bringing the air deep into her lungs, aware that her chest was tightening up.

As if on cue, the doorbell rang and she jumped. Grabbing her bag, she pinched the bridge of her nose, closed her eyes momentarily and took another deep breath. She adjusted her face – she wanted to get her expression and tone just right. Then she flung the door back with a beaming smile.

"Good morning, Detective Inspector Olbeck."

Olbeck smiled, a little sheepishly. "Morning. Sorry I'm late."

"I'm used to it, Detective Inspector."

"How are you feeling?"

Kate wondered whether she could push it a third time and decided, what the hell, she would anyway. "I'm fine, thanks, Detective Inspector."

"All right, all right," said Olbeck, grinning. "You've made your point. I don't hear any congratulations, by the way."

"I *said* congratulations when you told me," said Kate, locking her front door. Now that Olbeck was actually here, she felt better. It was always the way – anticipation was the worst thing, reality was never quite as bad. In almost all cases.

"Feel free to say it again," said Olbeck, ushering her to the passenger seat. "As many times as you like."

"Nope," retorted Kate, buckling up. "That's your lot."

"Oh well." Olbeck slammed the driver-side door and started the engine. "Thanks for the card, seriously. It was nice."

"You're welcome."

Kate watched the sunny streets of Abbeyford roll past as they drove on for a few moments in companionable silence. Kate watched the flicker of blue sky visible between the roofs and walls of the buildings flashing by the windows. It was late spring; warm, sunny, with the full glory of the spring flowers and tree blossom in evidence.

"How are you feeling?" Olbeck asked.

"Fine."

He glanced over at her. "No, how are you *really* feeling?"

"I'm fine," snapped Kate, her tone belying her words. Olbeck said nothing but hummed a little tune as he indicated to turn right onto the police station road. There was a moment of silence.

"All right," said Kate, giving in. "I'm feeling a bit nervous. It's my first day back, what do you expect?"

"I didn't expect anything," said Olbeck, mildly. He slowed for the entrance to the underground car park beneath the station. "You're bound to be feeling a bit shaken up. I don't blame you."

"Hmm." Kate realised she was clenching her fists and forced herself to relax her hands.

"Did Anderton call you last night?" asked Olbeck.

"No," said Kate. She shot a sideways glance at him. "Why – why, did he say he would?"

"I thought so. Perhaps he meant to and got caught up. Things are a bit hectic at the moment, as I'm sure you can appreciate."

"When aren't they?" murmured Kate.

The station itself hadn't changed. Built sometime in the late sixties, it personified that charmless, boxy style so characteristic of the era: small windows, flat red brick and no features of architectural interest whatsoever. But it was functional, large enough to cope with everything that the Abbeyford criminals could muster between them, and the team's main office had been renovated last year.

Olbeck parked the car and he and Kate got out. Now that they were actually on site, Kate felt her nervousness increasing. That remark of Olbeck's about Anderton phoning her – when he hadn't – had thrown her. She hadn't spoken to Anderton for more than a month, but she'd thought about him every day.

"Got your card?"

Kate groped for her handbag and then remembered. "It expired. I'll have to get Security to give me a new one."

"No probs." Olbeck passed his security card in front of the door scanner and the door lock clicked back. "In you go."

Kate stepped into the dingy corridor. It smelt the same; disinfectant, photocopier fluid, cooking smells from the canteen. She felt her hands go up, smoothing her hair again with fluttering fingers.

They walked past the door to the cells, up the stairs, past the door to the reception area, up another flight of stairs and along the corridor to the office. Kate let her feet guide her there automatically, her hand trailing up the banister of the stairs. Every so often, there was a little spike of surprise; *oh, that wall's been painted; oh, that poster's new.* She paused at the entrance to the office, unobtrusively, she hoped. Olbeck squeezed her arm and opened the door for her.

The whole team was in the office, it seemed. There was a moment of silence, as everyone clocked who was back, and then a cry of 'Kate!' from Theo, who leapt up from his desk and hurried over, flinging his arms around her. She blushed, pleased and embarrassed. Rav got up from his chair, smiling and waving. Kate's gaze flickered over the desk next to Rav's – she thought of it as 'Jerry's desk', but of course, Jerry was no longer here, having retired last year.

By now, Rav and Jane had come up to say hello and there were slightly awkward hugs and cheek kisses and rather facile chat about how well Kate was looking, how they'd missed her, how was she finding it and was she back for good? Kate said *thanks,* and *me too,* and *not too bad,* and *yes, I hope so*; noting Jane's new haircut, the bountiful red curls shorn off into a rather unforgiving pixie cut; that Rav finally looked a little bit older and not so much like a sixth-former doing some work experience; Theo's sharp new suit, clearly the proceeds of his recent promotion. That last thought struck her rather unpleasantly. Theo, once her subordinate, was now her equal and Olbeck... Olbeck was her superior. Kate smiled more widely to hide the jab that thought gave her, and caught sight of the biggest change yet. Someone else was sat at her desk.

Kate felt the fixed smile drop from her face. Her principal feeling was one of outrage. It wasn't just that there was someone else sitting at her desk. It wasn't just that this person had their chair – Kate's chair – tipped back and their feet propped on the surface of the desk, as if they were relaxing at home on the sofa. It wasn't just that this person was dressed as no detective should ever be dressed: in a filthy T-shirt and combat trousers, falling apart trainers with trailing laces and sporting matted dreadlocks that reached their shoulders. It was all of these things together.

Olbeck had followed Kate's intent gaze. "Ah, yes," he said, taking her arm and pulling her forward. "Come and meet the newest member of the team. Stuart Granger, meet Kate Redman."

Stuart flipped his dirty shoes off the desk and stood up, extending a large hand to Kate. "Hi," he said, grinning. "You probably shouldn't call me Stuart, though."

"What should I call you?" asked Kate politely, running through a few choice epithets in her head.

"Ah, yes," said Olbeck again. "Stuart's our undercover. He'll be working with the various groups we've got picked out as the possible suspects for the bombing."

Well, that explained the outfit. There was something about his expression, though, that made Kate's hackles rise. What was the word? Self-satisfied? Arrogant? God knows, Kate was used to working with cocky young men, but this Stuart Granger, or whatever the hell he was called, took the biscuit. Perhaps all undercover officers were like that, by nature of the job; she wouldn't know, she hadn't met one before.

Well, you think you haven't, Kate. If they were working undercover, how would you actually know?

"Nice to meet you," said Kate, in a tone barely above freezing. Stuart winked, clearly not upset at her frostiness. She supposed he was quite good looking, in a kind of broad-faced, sandy-haired, cheeky-grin sort of way. She bet he knew it, too.

"So, where am I sitting?" Kate demanded of Olbeck. It was bad enough having to come back after six months, knowing that everyone was wondering whether you'd be able to hack it again, without being booted off your own desk as well... She knew she was being prickly and defensive but somehow wasn't able to snap herself out of her mood.

"Tell you what," said Olbeck. "You can sit here." He gestured to the desk opposite Stuart.

13

Kate stared at it and then stared back at him. "That's yours," she said, waiting for the grin and the joke that she was sure was coming.

Olbeck looked a little embarrassed. "Ah," he said. "Not anymore. I'm over there now."

Kate looked at where he gestured. 'There' was a glassed-in cubicle at the end of the room. An office. Olbeck had his own office.

Quickly, before everyone could see, Kate resettled her face and said, in an arch tone "Ooh. Get you!"

"Fancy, huh?" said Olbeck. "I'll even give you the secret password, so you'll be able to enter its hallowed portals."

"You're too kind," said Kate, pulling out the chair from Olbeck's old desk. "Don't let me keep you, Detective Inspector Olbeck." For a moment Olbeck looked at her anxiously and she managed a grin and wink. Clearly relieved, he winked back.

Slowly, everyone settled back to whatever they had been doing before Kate arrived. Kate, left alone, stared blankly at her computer screen. She'd expected to be a bit unsettled, being back here with the team, but for a moment she was afraid that she'd actually start crying. Sitting there, she felt as if all her hard-won knowledge and experience were running away from her, pooling under the unfamiliar desk. What was left wouldn't be enough to sustain her. Sitting at this desk – Olbeck's desk! – with her erstwhile partner ensconced in solitary splendour at the other end of the room made Kate wonder how she was going to get through the rest of the *day*, let alone anything more. How was she going to talk over cases without Olbeck being right there in front of her? Instead, she would have to knock on his office door and request an interview. He's my superior now, she thought again, and her entire middle section felt hollow.

And where the hell was Anderton? Hadn't he heard she was here, and if he had, where was he? Kate continued to look blankly at her computer screen, seeing nothing. Anderton. Her boss. The enigmatic, energetic Chief Inspector, who she had slept with once during the serial killing case last year; an incident apparently relegated to the dim and distant past by both of them. It had never happened again. And I'm glad about that, Kate told herself stoutly. Shagging your boss was no way to progress in your career, despite what some cynics might say.

So it was a bit of a surprise that, when Anderton did finally appear, Kate's stomach seemed to drop floorwards and remain somewhere down by her ankles. On top of that sensation came an unexpected surge of fury. Why hadn't he telephoned her last night, as he had apparently said he would? Why hadn't he come to welcome her back, personally?

He crashed through the door of the incident room as he always did, sending the usual ripples of reaction through the room. People sat up straighter, put their phones down, and turned to face him.

"Morning team, morning team. How are we all, this bright, sunny morning?"

There were a few chuckles and murmurs of assent. Then Anderton caught sight of Kate.

His face flickered minutely, some kind of emotional reaction, gone too swiftly for Kate to interpret it. Then he was smiling, walking forward to greet her. "DS Redman, how long have you been here? You should have come and said hello. How are you?"

"Fine, sir," said Kate, smiling until she thought her face would crack under the strain. "Just getting this lot back into some sort of order."

"God knows they need it," Anderton said. There was an 'Oy' from Theo and a giggle from Jane. "Well, you're looking well. Fit and healthy again."

"I'm fine."

"I've no doubt. Anyway, we'd better get on. Come and see me after the debrief and we'll catch up properly."

Kate was sure her face was now permanently stuck in this

ridiculous smile. She nodded, unable to say anything. Anderton had already turned and was heading back to the front of the room, where the crime scene whiteboards were located. Kate hadn't even had a chance to look at them yet.

Anderton began pacing up and down as the team swung their chairs to keep him in view.

"Now, I'll do a brief recap, for Kate's benefit," he began. "Kate, I'll go into things more thoroughly later, but this is just to get you up to speed so we won't waste any time. As you no doubt know, we're investigating the murder of Doctor Michael Frank, the head of research at the newly opened MedGen Research Facility in Polton. He was killed by an explosive device attached to the underside of his car, which ignited when he started the engine. Your common or garden car bomb, in fact. We've got experts examining what was left of the device – and the car – and we're expecting the full report back in a couple of days. Suffice to say, they reckon it was made by an amateur, but one with a sufficient knowledge of explosives to produce a device that actually works. Which it undoubtedly did."

Anderton reached the far side of the office, turned on his heel and began to pace back again. Kate couldn't help a small smile. He didn't change; he still prowled about the room like a caged tiger. She wondered if you strapped Anderton in a chair and forced him to deliver his debrief completely stationary, whether he'd be struck dumb. Then she blinked and made an effort to switch her thoughts. The thought of Anderton strapped to a chair was provoking some highly unprofessional feelings.

"As you know, the opening of the MedGen research facility has resulted in a lot of negative press attention, protest groups and demonstrations. There's been the kind of civil disorder you'd expect from this kind of event, but I'm not sure we could have anticipated that the stakes would rise quite so highly or quickly. This is an act of terrorism, make no mistake. The people who did this will most probably attempt the same thing again, if they think it's been effective in fighting their cause. We need to make sure that they don't get the chance."

Anderton came to a halt by a convenient desk and hoisted himself onto it.

"I've been consulting with a few bods from Counter Terrorism Command, up at The Met, to get some background on the types of groups that might do this. I'm hopeful that one of them might deign to come down and give a face to face rundown of what we can do to track them down. In the meantime, we start to dig. Talk to the employees of the facility, talk to the neighbours and friends of the Franks. They've not long moved to the area – they moved here because of Frank's new job at the lab. As you also know, we've got Stuart here, who's about to become a protestor himself."

Kate saw Stuart draw himself up a little, putting his shoulders back. Anderton gestured to him. "Stuart, take it away. Give us the details of your assignment – those you can disclose."

Stuart waited until the room was completely silent, a smile that Kate interpreted as smug on his face. Look at him, revelling in the attention, she thought. Cocky so-and-so.

"Hello everyone," Stuart finally said. "Welcome back, Kate."

He flashed her a smile which she limply returned. Why was he welcoming her back as if he ran the place, when he didn't even know her?

"As most of you know, I'll soon be going undercover with the protest groups and activists who are currently targeting MedGen," Stuart continued. "I'll be there for a minimum of one month, reporting back regularly to see if we can uncover any evidence on the bombing. You may or may not know this, but in this type of situation, there's a distinct hierarchy to the groups, different... layers, shall we say." He spread his hands to demonstrate. "You've got the bottom rung; the mostly respectable protestors, the Guardian-readers, the lefties. Not normally much to worry about there, unless you're scared of petitions and badly made placards."

There were a few grins at this. Kate gritted her teeth.

Stuart went on. "As you get further up, in amongst the more... *serious* protestors — the more militant ones – that's where you start to get useful info. That's where you have to dig in deep, get yourself accepted, before people start opening up to you." He hesitated, looked as though he was about to say more, then clearly thought better of it. "Anyway, as I said, I'll be working in the field for a month, probably longer." He looked over at Anderton.

"Right, thanks, Stuart," Anderton said immediately. "Stuart will be reporting back regularly to myself. And, of course, if any of you run up against him in the course of the enquiry, you are on no account to acknowledge him as one of us. Naturally. I would hope that I wouldn't even have to say that."

"You didn't have to," said Olbeck, with a smile.

Anderton nodded. "Well, exactly. Right, now we're a bit more up to speed, we can get on. Mark, why don't you and Kate head to MedGen and continue the interviews there? Theo, you and Jane continue with the neighbours and friends of the Franks. Rav, you're on desk duty today, I'm afraid – I need someone manning the office. Anyone got any questions?" No one had. "Right, let's get on. Kate – come and see me in my office in five minutes' time?"

There was the usual sense, once Anderton had left the room, that a great mass of energy had suddenly dissipated. The team slowly returned to their work.

"Come and grab me after your meeting with Anderton and we'll head off," Olbeck said to Kate. He gave her a cheery wave and made his way down to the end of the office.

Kate watched him go. She was keenly aware that Stuart was watching her closely and she wouldn't give him the satisfaction of knowing she was upset. She blinked, bent her head studiously to the papers on her desk and pretended to read them. This was awful. She'd been looking forward to getting back to work for so long, and now she was here, she couldn't help but think longingly of her home; the sofa where she'd spent so many hours, the garden where she'd sat in the sun and breathed deeply and got better. She mentally counted down the seconds until five minutes had passed, casually pushed back her chair and made her way to Anderton's office.

"Come in," said the familiar voice at her knock. As she pushed open the door, Kate thought of all the times she'd stepped through this doorway into the office, remembering all the emotions that she'd experienced in this room. She took a deep breath and set her face to neutral.

Anderton waved towards a seat. "Shut the door behind you," he suggested and Kate did so. As she turned to take her seat, Kate remembered the last time she'd been in here with a closed door and what had happened. She wondered whether he did, too. Would that ever happen again or was he always going to be the one that got away? For a moment, she felt horribly bleak. Why was she even thinking that? What was wrong with her?

"So," said Anderton, flinging himself in the seat opposite her, his desk between them. "How's your first day back going?"

"Fine," said Kate, totally unwilling to let him know how hard she was finding it. "I'm easing myself back into the swing of things."

"That's good," said Anderton, hunting for something in one of the desk drawers. "Take it easy, though. No need to rush anything."

"No," said Kate. Was he trying to tell her something? She shifted a little in her chair and almost unconsciously, her hand went to the small of her back, feeling for the ridge of her knife scar.

"It's hard coming back after a long time away," Anderton continued. "Believe me, I know. But you get there, in the end. In a couple of weeks' time it'll feel like you've never been away."

"I'm sure you're right," Kate said. When was he going to stop with the platitudes and actually say something meaningful?

A silence fell. Kate cast about desperately for something to say, suddenly convinced that Anderton was doing the same. Their gaze met and there was a long, charged moment where the air hung heavy with everything that was not being said.

"Well," said Anderton eventually, looking down at his desk. "I won't keep you much longer."

"No," Kate said.

"I'm sure you've got lots to catch up on."

"Yes," Kate said.

"Let me know if you need any help with anything."

Kate sighed inwardly. "Yes," she said again, standing and pulling her hand back from where it was rubbing at the scar.

"Thanks, Kate. And seriously—" Anderton finally stopped fidgeting with his desk drawers and looked at her properly. "It's good to have you back."

"Is it?" asked Kate, unable to hide a smile. Anderton said nothing in response but winked. Kate left the office, struggling to keep her smile from becoming a wide grin.

Chapter Two

As she and Olbeck drove away in his car, Kate began to feel better than she had all day. Sitting across from her partner – former partner, she reminded herself – she could feel herself relaxing back into familiarity. This was how it used to be; the two of them driving from interview to interview, case to case, talking about the crime and the suspects and what they were going to do next. It was easy, it was comfortable; like putting on a pair of well-worn-in shoes. She had been worried that Olbeck would now treat her like a subordinate, someone to be talked down to and patronised, but of course he didn't. He treated her as normal. She felt a little ashamed that she'd even entertained the thought. You're getting paranoid, she chided herself.

"Did Anderton brief you?" asked Olbeck.

Kate shook her head. "Nope. Not a sausage."

Olbeck gave her a puzzled glance. "That's odd. I thought that was why he—" He didn't finish the sentence and Kate could hear him mentally shrugging. "Anyway, want me to run through things with you?"

"Please. I feel like I'm totally floundering at the moment."

"No problem." Olbeck shifted gears and settled back in his car seat. "Right, basically, the MedGen Facility is the brain child of two research boffins, Jack Dorsey and Alexander Hargreaves. They met at university – one doing chemistry or something like that, one doing something a bit less scientific. Dorsey's the boffin, Hargreaves is the businessman, as far as I can see."

"What is it that they research?"

"Oh, God, something totally esoteric, I don't understand a single bit of it; it's something to do with human metabolism – something like that. Anyway, the end result is that their original research got them into developing new methods of weight loss pills. That's partly why all these protestors are up in arms – all this animal suffering for something as frivolous as the diet industry. Something like that, anyway."

"Right."

"Made them both huge amounts of money. But we'll find out a bit more when we interview them. When I spoke to them before, it was just to check alibis and get first impressions, we didn't get a chance to go into the nitty-gritty of the business."

As he spoke, Olbeck flicked on the indicator. The car turned off into a smaller road that continued for about half a mile before ending in a formidable gate. The gate that blocked the road was topped with razor-wire and the glassed-in booth by the entrance had an impregnable look. Olbeck drew the car into the side of the road and approached the guard, sat impassively behind the screen. After a long and suspicious perusal of their warrant cards, he pressed the button that drew back the gate and they were able to drive through.

"They're obviously expecting trouble here," said Kate, noting the cameras and the high fences that surrounded the site. "They clearly value security. Why wasn't Michael Frank more careful?"

Olbeck shrugged. "He was new to the job. He was in a hurry. And, security or no security, they've never had a car bombing before. No one was expecting *that*."

"I suppose so," said Kate. She watched as the buildings of MedGen came into view. They looked as if they had once been some kind of government building, perhaps ex-council offices or something similar, but had clearly undergone a huge and expensive renovation.

Olbeck parked the car at the front of the main building. The two officers made their way through the automatic glass doors, into a reception area that wouldn't have looked out of place in a luxury spa. Behind the curving steel and glass of the front desk sat a polished young woman in a tight black suit. Her well-shaped eyebrows twitched upward minutely as Kate and Olbeck flashed their warrant cards but otherwise she preserved the neutral expression of a shop window mannequin.

Another glossy young woman, equally stone-faced, came out to usher them through to what was clearly the inner sanctum of the executive offices. Kate looked around as they waited. The glass-topped coffee table before them was scattered with a variety of glossy magazines and broadsheet newspapers; The Times, The Spectator, Tatler, Racing Times. The fittings were plush and expensive, with several vaguely medically themed objects d'art dotted about the room. An abstract painting on the wall, full of swirling reds and blues caught her eye. As she got up to take a closer look at the tiny label at the bottom of the frame, she realised it was actually a hugely magnified photograph of a cell from the smaller human intestine.

"Nice," she murmured to herself as the glass door to the office opened.

Both directors of the company emerged to greet them. Jack Dorsey was a man who missed being handsome by a mere whisker; he was just a shade too thin, his face a little too bony for true good looks. He, according to Olbeck's notes, was forty six – he looked older, partly because of his receding sandy-grey hair and the deep-cut wrinkles at the corners of his eyes. But there was still an element of freshness in his general demeanour; something of youth and vigour and keenness. Kate could imagine he was devoted to his job.

His partner, Alex Hargreaves, seemed to embody the opposite

qualities. Attractive, in a kind of coarse, slightly overfed way, Hargreaves was very much the businessman; well dressed in a Jermyn Street suit, thick black hair combed back, and the hint of a jowl developing above the collar of his expensive linen shirt.

When they were all seated in Alex Hargreaves' huge office, with coffee cups placed before them by the black-suited automaton who had shown them in, a small silence fell. Jack Dorsey sat forward in his leather chair, his bright blue eyes fixed on Olbeck's face. Alex Hargreaves lounged back in his seat, one leg crossed over the other.

Olbeck began by thanking them for their time. He was almost always courteous to begin with, Kate remembered.

"We're following up a number of leads in relation to the murder of Michael Frank," Olbeck continued. "What would be really helpful for us is to find out more about the victim himself. Can you tell us anything about him? What was he like?"

Both men went to answer, glanced at each other and half-laughed. Dorsey inclined his head in a kind of 'after you' gesture and Hargreaves nodded, leaning forward in his chair. "I interviewed Michael for the role – well, we both did, but I took the first interview. We're always on the lookout for new talent here, the brightest and the best. Michael was pretty well established in his old firm, but he was looking for more responsibility, something a bit more challenging."

Olbeck nodded encouragingly.

"Anyway," Hargreaves went on. "He got the job. He was far and away the best candidate, hands down."

"What was he like?" asked Kate, thinking she should speak, finally.

"Like?" Hargreaves looked confused.

"Yes. What did you think of him? Personally, as opposed to professionally, I mean."

"Well... I—" Hargreaves looked a little confused. "He was a nice bloke, I suppose. Bit quiet."

"He *was* quiet," broke in Dorsey. The others in the room looked at him and he went on, unruffled. "He was quiet but he wasn't shy. He had one of those personalities that grow on you. He had... character, I suppose you would say. To use an old-fashioned term."

Hargreaves looked at his partner with an expression that Kate couldn't quite place. It was half admiration, half something else. Impatience? Irritation?

"I see," said Olbeck, nodding. "Was Mr Frank well-liked in the company? Did he mix well, make friends?"

The two directors looked at one another. Hargreaves almost, but not quite, shrugged.

"I don't know," Dorsey said, after a moment. "I certainly don't think he was *dis*liked. Unfortunately, he wasn't here long enough for me really to be able to make a judgement on his popularity, poor man."

"Did you have a lot of contact with him, day to day? Both of you, I mean?"

Hargreaves nodded. "A fair amount. We had weekly meetings of the exec team – the executive team, I mean – and Michael was part of that. Ad-hoc meetings during the week, as and when were needed. Budget meetings once a month. Is that the sort of thing you mean?"

Olbeck nodded. "It all helps to build a picture. We'll need to speak to any of the staff who worked closely with him, who reported to him, worked under him, you get the picture. Would you be able to take us down to where he worked?"

Dorsey clasped and then unclasped his hands. "We can, Inspector. It's—" He hesitated for a moment and glanced across at Hargreaves. "These are the areas of... well, animal experimentation. If you get distressed by that sort of thing..."

Kate refrained from pointing out that they were here to investigate the brutal murder of a human being. She waited for Olbeck to answer and, when he didn't, said crisply "I'm sure we'll take it in our stride, sir."

"There's very little *actual* experimentation here," Hargreaves said quickly. "But that's what the media and the protestors are all over, of course."

"That's something else we'll need to talk to you about," Olbeck said. "I see you've got fairly good security on site but what with the bombing, this is clearly not enough. Is there someone we could talk to about that, as well?"

Dorsey nodded. "I'll ask our Head of Security to come up now. He'll be able to take you through the set up here, and you'll be able to ask any questions that you want."

"Fine," said Olbeck.

They were shown back into another plush meeting room, with a crystal carafe of water and two glasses placed before them on the table by the receptionist, who barely nodded in response to Kate's thanks. Olbeck's phone buzzed.

"Damn it," he said, checking it. "I need to head back after this meeting. Anderton wants me on a conference call."

"Oh?" said Kate. She was conscious of a spurt of something that felt suspiciously close to jealousy. Why did Anderton want Olbeck on a call and not her?

Because he's a DI, Kate. And you're not. She clamped down on the thought, telling herself it didn't matter.

"What about interviewing his co-workers?" she asked. "Want me to do that?"

"No, that can wait until tomorrow. You and Theo can come down and work them together. Okay?"

"Okay," muttered Kate. She didn't actually agree – wasn't time of the essence? – but she wasn't ready to start querying Olbeck's orders. Not quite yet.

There was a knock on the door and a tall, bald man walked in, introducing himself as Terry Champion, Head of Security. Thickset and muscular, with one of those protruding bellies which makes the owner look eight months pregnant, Champion was nevertheless helpful and forthcoming. Ex-army, Kate surmised.

She wondered why it was that security guards and chiefs were always bald? She went off into a mini-reverie whilst Olbeck asked the questions, fantasising that an excess of testosterone was responsible for both their choice of occupation and their hair loss, before bringing herself back to reality with a start.

"Oh yes, lots of threats, tons really," Champion was saying breezily. "We X-ray all the post as a matter of course."

"Any letter bombs or anything like that? Suspicious packages?"

Champion rubbed his chin. "Nothing that bad, to be fair. Occasional package of dog shit, but we take that in our stride."

"Not very pleasant," Kate said, feeling she should contribute something.

Champion looked at her with an expression she couldn't decipher. "No," he agreed. "But better dog shit than a car bomb, eh?"

"Not much you can say to that," Kate said to Olbeck, as they drove back to the office. He chuckled.

"I need to brush back up on my interviewing skills, I think," she continued gloomily.

"You're just out of practice. You'll get the hang of it again."

"I know."

"It's your first day back, woman. Take it easy."

Kate sat on her hand to stop it reaching around to her back. "I know," she said, again.

Olbeck glanced over at her and then patted her on the knee. "Chin up," he said, and Kate tried to smile.

Kate was just shutting down her computer, feeling more tired than she had in months, when her mobile rang. Andrew's name flashed from the screen. As always, there was a quick flash of something, a feeling she couldn't quite pin down and didn't exactly want to. Was it anticipation? Annoyance? No, that was too strong. It wasn't comfortable, though, and Kate didn't like that.

She didn't want to think about her visceral reaction to her first sight of Anderton today and how different it was to the reaction she had to her boyfriend calling her.

She answered the phone.

"How's the first day back going?"

As soon as she heard his voice, Kate felt better. She relaxed back into her chair. "I'm surviving. That's about all I can say."

"You must be buggered."

"I am."

"That's a shame." He hesitated for a moment. "I was hoping to take you out to dinner. But if you're really tired…"

Kate considered. She was hungry and she knew Andrew would pay – he insisted on it. But he also had a penchant for fine dining and very formal restaurants, with white linen tablecloths and attentive waiter service, and Kate just didn't have the energy for it today.

"Why don't you come over to mine?" she suggested. "We'll get a takeaway and chill out on the sofa."

"Really?" He sounded eager and, for a moment, she felt a flash of irritation. This time, it was easy to interpret. Just as quickly, she felt guilty. What was wrong with her?

"Definitely," she said, making her tone extra warm. "I'd like to see you."

Kate switched her computer off, stood up and pulled her coat on. She had the sudden absurd impulse to walk around everyone's desks, saying goodbye to each person individually. Of course, she wouldn't do that but… it was still too strange, too new for her to be able to just walk out, throwing a casual 'goodnight' over her shoulder. She wondered how she was going to get home. Olbeck was out, Theo had already left and she hadn't driven herself. Bus it was, then, or should she treat herself to a taxi, just this once?

Outside the station, as she stood vacillating from one choice to the other, a horn pipped and a second later, Andrew drew up in his BMW. She felt a welcome burst of pleasure at seeing him and climbed into the cool interior of the car, smiling broadly. Her greeting kiss was heartfelt.

"Well, you look better than I thought you would," said Andrew, brushing her hair back from her cheek. "Not quite as knackered as I was expecting."

"It's all a front," said Kate, strapping herself in. She let her head fall back against the headrest and sighed, closing her eyes. "Now I can relax."

"You certainly can. Sure you want to go home?"

Kate nodded fervently.

"Right you are, my sweetheart."

The traffic was heavy and it took them longer than normal to get back to Kate's house. When he was able to, Andrew rested a hand on Kate's thigh and she tried not to show the irritation that caused her. Then she felt guilty for feeling that. Why shouldn't he rest his hand on his girlfriend's leg? I'm just tired, she told herself. I don't want to be pawed about. Then she felt guilty again, even for thinking the words. She put her own hand on his leg and gave an answering squeeze and he turned his head and smiled at her.

It was Kate who unlocked the door of her house – she hadn't yet given Andrew a key. He'd offered to get her one for his place but she'd declined, knowing that she would then have to make a reciprocal offer. She wasn't ready for that, yet. Stepping inside the hallway, she was enveloped by the sense of pleasure that her house always induced in her; the calm, tidy, ordered interior that greeted her every day, the furniture and pictures and ornaments that she'd chosen with care and attention.

"Shall I cook?" asked Andrew, throwing his jacket over the newel post of the staircase.

Kate set her teeth for a moment and hung it on the hooks by the front door. She shook her head. "Don't bother. Let's get a takeaway."

Kate placed her shoes neatly in the shoe rack and put her hands to the small of her back, stretching. Her scar throbbed.

"No, don't worry about that," said Andrew. "I'll cook. I'd like to."

"Suit yourself," said Kate. She pulled herself up, realising how ungrateful she sounded. "That would be lovely. Thank you."

Andrew tipped her a salute and headed to the kitchen.

Kate made her way upstairs.

"I'm going to jump in the shower," she called. She prayed Andrew wouldn't want to join her. At that very moment, she wanted to be by herself again; just her, in her cosy house with the door locked and her phone switched off, licking her wounds and trying to see a positive way forward. Andrew, nice as he was, was a distraction. Kate rubbed her face, pulling her fingers over her closed eyes. She couldn't remember being this tired in a long time. Perhaps I'm not up to it anymore, she thought, and felt a cold thrill of fear. If she didn't have her work, what did she have?

Andrew called up to her to tell her he was making her a cup of tea and, this time, she felt grateful he was here.

Kate closed the bathroom door behind her, hesitated, and then locked it. So what if Andrew tried to come in? He'd have to learn that she needed her privacy, sometimes. There was nothing wrong with wanting to take a shower on your own, for God's sake. Kate came to with a start, realising she was arguing with a fantasy version of Andrew inside her head again. The real Andrew was downstairs in the kitchen, singing untunefully along to the radio. Kate rubbed her face. She was starting to think she should have turned his offer of company down tonight, made up a little white lie. But no – she did want the company, didn't she?

The shower was throwing clouds of white steam into the air. Kate dropped her clothes neatly into the hamper and climbed under the spray of hot water. Immediately she began to feel better. The sense of defeatedness, of hopelessness, that had surrounded her ever since she'd sat down at her new desk at the station, began to disperse. She poured a generous dollop of expensive shower gel into the palm of her hand, sniffing the perfume appreciatively. It would work out. She would be fine. She would slot back into her work as if she'd never been away. Her fingers went automatically to the ridge of the scar, sliding over it. The shower gel fell to the floor of the bath with a splat and Kate tutted with annoyance and yanked her hand away from her back. Just *leave* it, Kate. Think about something else, for a change.

Showered and dried, dressed in her slobbing-at-home clothes. Kate paused at the entrance to the kitchen. Andrew was clattering pots around, chopping herbs, whistling as he worked. Kate watched him for a moment, unobserved. He's good looking, he's smart, he works hard and he cooks, she thought to herself. You're lucky to have him. She smiled, but at the same time was suddenly aware of how tired she was. She leant her head against the door frame, closing her eyes.

"Whoah," Andrew's voice said and Kate felt his big arms close around her shoulders. She leant forward, resting her head against him without opening her eyes. "You're just about dead on your feet, aren't you?"

Kate nodded, too tired to even speak.

"Well," said Andrew. "My considered medical opinion is you should go straight to bed. Come on—" He lifted her bodily and she gave a tired giggle. His physical bulk was one of the most attractive things about him; when she was in his arms, she felt safe, enfolded, protected. Andrew carried her up to the bedroom and deposited her on the bed. Kate rolled gratefully under the covers.

"Shame," said Andrew softly, stroking her hair back from her forehead. "I was hoping for a little bit more than that. But hey, there's always first thing tomorrow, right?"

Kate grinned tiredly at him. Then she muttered something like 'thanks', pulled the duvet cover up to her nose and was instantly asleep.

Chapter Three

KATE WAS WOKEN THE NEXT morning by the shrill electronic peal of her phone, buzzing and skittering over the bedside table like a large black insect. She grabbed for it blearily, whilst behind her Andrew groaned and rolled over. It was Theo.

"Pick you up in an hour, right?"

"What?"

Theo sounded incredibly alert and wide-awake. Kate rubbed her eyes, looked at the clock. Seven ten am.

"What bloody time do you call this?"

"The early bird catches the worm, Kate. Rise and shine! I'll pick you up in an hour. See you then."

The bleep of a disconnected signal sounded in Kate's ear. She sat up, rubbing her eyes again.

"I've got to go," she said to Andrew, who was half buried beneath a pillow. He was working normal hours this week, which meant a nice, nine-thirty start. He grunted something.

Kate got ready, guiltily relieved that she had seemed to have got out of having sex with her boyfriend. That was the last thing she felt like, first thing in the morning, especially after an exhausting day before. She planted a kiss on Andrew's cheek, bristly with morning stubble, grabbed her bag and made her way downstairs.

Theo was dressed in another nice suit. It looked expensive and he looked altogether older, and to be taken seriously. Kate caught sight of herself in the passenger seat mirror. She really must get her hair cut. How old was the jacket she was wearing? Five years? She shifted a little in her seat and her scar began to throb. Surreptitiously, she tried to rub it.

"You all right?" asked Theo. "You look knackered."

Kate grimaced. "Gee, thanks. It's my second day back on the job, I'm amazed I'm even awake and coherent." She ran her hands through her hair, shook her head, made an effort. "Where are we going?"

"Back to the lab. Mark wants us to interview the co-workers, this time."

"Oh yes," said Kate, a little dazedly. "I remember."

"You and Mark spoke to the directors yesterday, right?"

"That's right. Jack Dorsey and Alexander Hargreaves."

"What are they like?"

Kate rubbed her face. "We'll speak to them again and you can see for yourself."

Again, they were shown into the plush waiting room. Theo whistled under his breath and paced around a little. Kate subsided into an armchair and fought the urge to put her head against the back of it and go to sleep.

Theo picked up the copy of the Racing Times and flicked through it.

"Didn't know you were a betting man," murmured Kate, as much for something to say as anything.

"Well, I'm not, really," said Theo. "Flutter on the National, that's about it. Few quid on the gee-gees, now and then. Nothing amazing."

Alexander Hargreaves opened the door to the waiting room himself. Kate saw his gaze go to the magazine in Theo's hand and the minutest flicker of some kind of emotion crossed his face, gone almost before she could register it. Then he was striding forward, his hand outstretched. "Sorry to keep you waiting, DS Redman. How can we help you today?"

Kate introduced Theo and asked whether they could have a chat with Michael Frank's colleagues. "Are you able to take us there, Mr Hargreaves?"

Jack Dorsey entered the room. Again, Kate was struck by the energy he brought with him, a sort of compressed vividness that he carried about.

After the pleasantries, Kate repeated her question.

"I'm free for the next half an hour," said Jack Dorsey. "I'm happy to take you down there."

"Great," said Theo, cutting across Kate who was just opening her mouth to reply. She smiled to hide her annoyance. "Thanks for meeting with us, Mr Hargreaves."

Alexander Hargreaves shook both their hands. His palm was smooth and warm against Kate's, the press of a large signet ring on one finger almost making her wince as his fingers closed around hers.

"Any help we can give you, any at all," he said, his tone serious. "Michael was a great scientist and he had children too... whatever we can do to help."

Jack Dorsey led them both along a series of corridors, down two flights of stairs, through numerous security doors and finally brought them to a halt in front of a glass panelled door, again with a security system fitted to it. Behind his shoulder, through the glass panel, Kate could see several people in white coats bent over microscopes and making notes on clipboards.

Jack Dorsey's manner changed a little. Up in the office suite, he'd been serious and calm, although still with that air of suppressed energy. Here, clearly his natural environment, it was as if that energy became apparent. His eyes noticeably brightened.

"This is the lab," he said, tapping in a code on the security panel of the door. They heard the *thunk* of a heavy-duty lock drawing back. Dorsey held the door open for them.

Kate was first struck by the warmth... and the smell. Underneath the antiseptic wash of disinfectant was the earthy, musty smell of mice. She could see a bank of stacked plastic cages over by the far wall. The two people who'd been visible through the door looked up curiously as the detectives and Dorsey approached.

"These are Michael's colleagues," Dorsey said. "Sarah Brennan and Parvinder Goram." He introduced the detectives and the two scientists turned looks of mixed comprehension and apprehension towards them.

Kate opened her mouth to ask a question but just as she was framing the sentence, Theo got there first.

"You worked closely with Michael Frank?" he asked, directing the question to Sarah Brennan as the older of the two women. She was in her late forties, with smooth dark hair and a pleasant, careworn face.

She nodded. She looked at Jack Dorsey with an expression Kate couldn't quite place.

"Don't worry, Sarah," Dorsey said smiling. "It's all perfectly straightforward. I'll leave you with the detectives."

The laboratory door *thunked* shut behind him. Kate raised her eyebrows in what she hoped was a pleasantly interrogative way. "You worked closely with Michael?" she asked Sarah Brennan again.

"Yes." Sarah tucked her hair behind her ears. She was wearing a rather lovely pair of diamond earrings. "The project he'd been hired for was something I'd been interested in for a while. I transferred over from another department when I heard he'd be working here."

Again, Kate began to say something and Theo cut across her. She hoped her annoyance didn't show on her face.

"You knew him well, then?"

Sarah nodded again. Kate's eyes dropped to her hands, noting the lack of a wedding ring, the short, blunt, practical nails.

"We'd worked together before he came here, actually," Sarah was saying. "We were both at the same lab back in Northumberland - this was back in the nineties. Quite funny that we ended up working together again, but not that surprising. His research background was in a quite a niche area and mine is the same. I suppose it was fairly inevitable that we would end up working together again."

"How about you, Doctor Goram?" Kate jumped in before Theo could draw a breath. Again, she was forcibly reminded of how different working life was going to be now. She and Olbeck had interviewed together seamlessly, years of knowing when to talk and when to keep quiet meaning they didn't even have to think about who was going to lead on the questions. Theo's style was obviously very different.

Parvinder Goram was probably younger than thirty-five. She had a thin, pretty face and eyes that were ringed with shadow that could have been exhaustion, but might have been genetic. Just glimpsed underneath the collar of her lab coat was a bright red fluffy jumper, which struck an oddly frivolous note.

She was less forthcoming than Sarah Brennan, or perhaps she had less to say. "Michael was my supervisor," she said. "I'm two years into my doctorate. So, technically, I'm a 'Ms', not a doctor, yet."

"Sorry," said Kate. "How was Michael to work for?"

Parvinder cast a glance at Sarah, a glance that was too quick for Kate to decipher. "He was fine," she said.

"Can you tell us anything more about him?" said Theo. He edged forward a little, his shoulder nudging Kate's, as if he were literally trying to budge her out of the conversation. She gave him an annoyed glance.

Parvinder took in Theo's handsome face and well-cut suit and her manner changed. She smiled a little flirtatiously. "He was a bit of a cliché, in some ways," she said, with something that was almost a giggle. Sarah Brennan's face flickered a little. Parvinder went on. "I mean, he was quite absent minded and he was always late for everything. He was always losing things. I can't remember how many times he'd shout out from his office, 'has anyone seen my... whatever,' and mostly we hadn't."

"He was very good at his job," broke in Sarah. She shot a look at Parvinder that Kate interpreted as repressive. "Yes, he was a little absent minded, now and again, but that's because he was always thinking about something more important than the minutia of daily life."

"I see," said Kate. "Well, I—"

"Can you tell me anything about Michael's personal relationships?" Theo cut across her again.

Kate couldn't help glancing at him in surprise. Where was he going with this?

"What do you mean?" asked Parvinder.

"His relationship with his wife, his friends," said Theo. "Did he have a good relationship with his wife, that you know of?"

Sarah Brennan was frowning. Parvinder looked mystified. "I suppose so," she said, "I don't really know."

"Where were you going with that?" asked Kate as they drove back to the office.

"What d'you mean?"

"The questions about Michael Frank's wife. What was all that about?"

Theo gave her a strange look; half indulgent, half annoyed. "Get with the program, Kate," he said. "We're assuming that this is a straight act of terrorism. Aren't we?"

Kate nodded, reluctantly.

"Well," said Theo, changing gears with a cocky flick of his wrist, "What if it's not? What if it's for some other reason? A personal reason?"

"A *car bomb*?" Kate tried to keep the scepticism from her voice. "What the f—" She cleared her throat and tried again. "I mean, what the hell are you talking about?"

"It's just an idea," said Theo, airily. "I'm just running with it.

What if it's not a terrorist attack at all? Perhaps his wife wanted him dead. Perhaps he's pissed another scientist off. I don't know, I'm just thinking out loud."

"Right," said Kate. "His respectable, middle-class wife and mother of his two children decides to forego the divorce court by planting an explosive device under his car. Yes. I can see how that might happen."

Theo reddened a little.

"I'm not saying it's *likely*. I'm thinking aloud, here."

Kate made a mammoth effort to stop herself casting her eyes up to the ceiling.

"Have you told Anderton your theories?"

Theo changed down gears as they approached a T-junction, this time with more of an annoyed shove. "No, I haven't. I don't have any *theories*. I'm just thinking aloud."

"All righty, then," said Kate, this time not bothering to keep the contempt from her voice.

"Feel free to chip in with any ideas of your own," Theo said snappily. She heard him mutter the rest of the sentence under his breath and despite pretending not to hear, heard the words clearly enough. *If you have any, that is.* She breathed in sharply through her nose, clamped her mouth shut, and looked out of the window. They spent the rest of the return journey in silence.

Chapter Four

KATE WAS GETTING USED TO these early morning wake-up calls. This time it was Olbeck, calling to tell her he was *en route* to pick her up.

"Sorry about the late notice. Tried calling you last night, but I couldn't get through."

That was because Kate had crawled straight to bed after getting home the night before, not stopping to wash, eat or check her phone. She decided not to mention that.

"Sorry," she said, sitting up in bed. "I didn't check my phone."

"No worries. Anyway, we're interviewing Mary Frank this morning and I need you along. Pick you up in an hour, okay?"

Polton Winter was a tiny village, saved only from being a hamlet by the presence of the ancient village church. The gateway of the Franks' house was visible from the churchyard – at least what was left of it. The stone wall that encircled the garden at the front of the house was nothing more than a pile of rubble and the young beech tree that had stood by the driveway was stripped of all of its branches on one side. Sap had run like blood down its blackened trunk.

The house itself was a small, pretty, Georgian cottage, built of what had once been golden Bath stone. The windows had already been replaced, but the front of the house was chipped and pocked with tiny pieces of metal, which had embedded themselves in the porous stone.

Olbeck parked on the driveway. As Kate got out of the car she felt herself shiver as she realised they had parked on the blackened piece of tarmac where Michael Frank's car had stood.

The two Frank children were at school. Mary Frank opened the door to the two officers and Kate was immediately struck by her haggard face and shaking hands. She managed a flicker of a smile – convention was obviously too strong for her not to be able to show some form of greeting – but as she led them through to the living room, she hunched her shoulders as if expecting a blow to fall upon her.

The two officers took seats. Mary Frank remained standing for a moment, clasping both arms across her body. "Could I get you tea – coffee?" she asked, faintly.

"No, nothing for me," Kate said immediately and Olbeck also murmured his polite refusal.

Mary Frank sat down rather too suddenly in an armchair. Kate eyed her uneasily. The woman was like a spring wound tight, every muscle clenched. A nervous system flooded with adrenaline. Post-traumatic stress disorder, was the phrase that sprang immediately to mind and Kate knew all about that.

Olbeck was very gentle with Mary, speaking softly and calmly. "I know this must be very distressing for you, Mrs Frank, but I was wondering if you could just take us through the few days preceding the – the incident." Mary Frank's shoulders jerked and she tried to cover the movement but shifting in her chair and re-crossing her legs. Olbeck continued. "It would be really helpful if you could tell us anything about anything strange you might have noticed. Any strangers. Anything slightly odd, perhaps."

Clearly, they had already had a preliminary interview with Mary Franks and this was a follow up. Kate sighed inwardly. She was coming at this case so behind it was difficult to know whether she was missing anything important.

Mary Franks was looking blindly down at the arm of her chair. The fingers of one hand pulled compulsively at the thumb of the other, over and over again. "I don't think so," she said in a low voice, after a moment's silence. "I can't remember anything. It was – it was just normal."

"Try and cast your mind back to the day before. What did you do?"

Mary Frank closed her eyes for a moment. Kate thought she was probably running through the memories in her head, watching the pictorial record of her life scroll past – the last moments of the life she'd known before it was blown to smithereens by eight pounds of plastic explosive.

"I don't remember, exactly," she said, in a quiet voice. "I was at work in the morning – I teach adults with learning disabilities, part time – but I came home for lunch. I did some housework, I think. I can't remember exactly, I'm sorry—"

"Not to worry," Olbeck said soothingly. "You didn't notice anyone hanging about the house or driveway? No strangers came to the door?"

"No. No, I don't think so."

"Did Michael mention anything to you that seemed significant, in the light of what happened?"

Mary's mouth cramped. She shook her head mutely.

Olbeck glanced over at Kate. She knew he was thinking what she was thinking: that this interview was pointless. Mary Frank was too traumatised, too broken to even think about what she was saying. She didn't want to remember anything about the days leading up to the bombing because she then had to accept that it happened, and she wasn't ready to do that yet – not by a long shot.

"Right," said Olbeck after a moment. "I can see that this is still very painful for you, Mrs Frank. Have Victim Support been in touch with you?"

"Hmm?" Mary Frank was staring at the floor, her fingers pulling compulsively at a fold of her jumper. "What's that?"

"Have you been offered any counselling by Victim Support?"

After a moment, the woman's blank stare focused a little. "Oh, yes," she said faintly. "They've been very kind. Everyone has been very kind."

Olbeck exchanged a glance with Kate. She shifted forward in her chair, preparing to get up.

"Wait," said Mary Frank suddenly. She was frowning slightly, her foggy gaze clearing. "There was something – it's probably nothing..."

"What was it?" Kate asked, trying not to sound too eager.

"It was one night, about a week before the – before it happened. Michael and I were just going to bed and he said 'that car's been parked out the front for ten minutes now. Do you think they're lost?'"

"You didn't recognise the car, then?"

Mary Frank shook her head. "It was dark and there's only one streetlight near the house. It was quite a big car. A dark colour, dark blue, perhaps?"

"Can you remember the make of car?" asked Olbeck.

Mary Frank frowned again, biting her lip. She was silent for a moment. "I'm sorry, I can't remember anything more about it," she burst out. Tears shone in her eyes. "Do you really think it might – might have had something to do with – with—"

"I can't say, Mrs Frank, I'm sorry. We'll have a look at the local CCTV for that night. What night was it, can you remember exactly?"

This time Mary shut her eyes. She clenched her hands together, pressing her fingers against one another until the knuckles went white. "It was the Tuesday... that's right... the Tuesday before it happened. Michael was late coming to bed because he'd had a call from his brother that went on for a while. They don't speak often." She tripped herself up over the tense she'd used and gulped. "I mean, they *didn't* speak often, so when Paul rings, they chat for a long time. That's right, I looked at the clock when Michael came up and it was past eleven o'clock. He twitched the bedroom window curtain as he walked past it and that's when he mentioned the car.

I had a quick look but I couldn't see much. Whoever it was drove off just after I looked out of the window."

Kate was scribbling quickly in her notebook. She didn't imagine there were many cameras in Polton Winter, if any, but it would be worth a try to see if anything had been picked up.

"Thank you, Mrs Frank," Olbeck said, putting a great deal of warmth into his voice. "That's really helpful. If you can remember anything else that might help, you will let us know, won't you?"

Mary Frank nodded fervently. She looked better than she had at any point since they arrived, but still, even as they said goodbye on the doorstep, Kate didn't want to leave her. She made a point of mentioning Victim Support again as they took their leave and made sure Mary had her business card.

"Poor woman," she said to Olbeck as they drove away.

"Yes, indeed."

They were both silent for a moment. Kate watched the sun-dappled beech woods roll past the windows of the car. She remembered Mary Frank's compulsive pulling of her thumbs as she sat in her chair and realised her own hand was creeping towards her back, almost stealthily. She put it back in her lap with an exclamation of annoyance and Olbeck looked over, surprised, but didn't say anything.

STUART WALKED BEHIND THE GROUP of protestors, far enough back so that they wouldn't realise he was there, close enough to get a good look at them. They were heading for one of few the pubs in the area that would serve them; Stuart had seen a handwritten sign on the door of one of the other nearby pubs that had said 'No Protestors'. He was determined that this would be the opening he was looking for.

The pub was a dive – sticky carpet, yellowed wallpaper, stench of old cigarettes embedded in the fabric of the seats. Stuart waited until the small group of protestors had been served, got his own pint and sat down unobtrusively in a corner, ostensibly reading the tabloid newspaper that had conveniently been left at the table, but really taking a closer look at the people he was tailing. He was looking for the weak spot, the one who would let him in.

There were two women and three men in the group. Stuart focused on the women – it was almost always easier to strike up a conversation with a woman. The two he was watching were both young, both quite pretty under the crazy dyed hair and facial piercings and crappy clothes. Which one? He chose the smaller, slighter one, the one who laughed a lot, looking up at the men in the group with a face that was slightly too eager.

Stuart waited until the girl of his choice made her way to the loo. He waited until she re-emerged and, seemingly on his way to the bar again, gently bumped into her.

"Oh, sorry!" she said in a surprised tone, even though it was technically his fault and that was when he knew he'd picked the right one.

Her name was Rosie and she was twenty-two, having just graduated from some no-mark university. Stuart bought her a drink, gave her his best cheeky-chappy grin and made sure she got a good look at his Plane Stupid T-shirt.

"Were you at the Heathrow protest?" she asked, gesturing to his chest.

"For sure. Were you?"

She shook her head. "Not that one. We went along to the camp, though. That was where I met James, actually."

Stuart followed her gaze to one of the other protestors; a rangy, tall, dark-haired guy who was casting curious glances back at them. Rosie waved him over and introduced Stuart.

"This is Mike," she said. Stuart inclined his head slightly and held out his hand. After a moment of hesitation almost too brief to notice – although Stuart did notice, that's what he was trained to do – James shook it.

"All right?"

"Yeah. Rosie was just telling me all about how you guys met." Stuart had stepped back a little, out of Rosie's personal space. Good decision, as the next moment had James sliding an arm around her waist and pulling her closer to him.

"You an activist, then, man?" James asked, with just the slightest hint of hostility in his voice.

Stuart knew how to counter that. Find the commonality, find the shared experience – something that will soften someone towards you. There was always something. With James, it was his accent. Stuart had spent some time in Newcastle and he could hear the faint intonation of someone who'd once lived there – for how long, he couldn't tell – but it was there, in James's voice. That was his opening.

"You know, man, I think I've met you before," Stuart said, getting a nice mix of doubt and delight into his tone. "Did you go to Newcastle?"

The faint suspicion clouding James face cleared. "Yeah. Yeah, I did. Did you?"

Stuart improvised a quick story about visiting a mate at the university and hitting some of the student bars there. He mentioned a few names – "John, John Richards, you know him? No?" and when James came up with the names of several other Johns who'd been students there, Stuart was able to feign recognition and claim a vague acquaintance with one of them. This, coupled with a few anecdotes centred around some riotous drinking at the campus bar, was all that it took. A few pints later and James was his new best friend, Rosie shunted off to the side and almost forgotten.

"You coming to the protest tomorrow?" James asked as they said goodbye at the end of the evening. Stuart was as sober as a judge, being a master in the art of seemingly drinking without actually doing so. The other activists were nine tenths drunk, falling against one another, laughing.

"For sure," said Stuart. "That's why I'm here, man."

"Cool. See ya, then. Oh, and there's a party tomorrow night, as well."

"Even better," said Stuart, grinning. He winked at Rosie, bumped his fist against James' and, raising a hand to the others, set off for the grim little bedsit he was renting for the duration of this job.

Chapter Five

Andrew's house had a very pleasant conservatory at the back of the kitchen, where one could sit drinking good coffee from a fine white china mug, toes snuggled into slippers, looking out at the pretty garden and distant hills beyond the back fence. Kate drew her dressing gown more snugly about herself and sipped her hot drink, watching the sparkle of the morning sunshine on the lawn, bejewelled with a million little beads of water.

Andrew was busy in the kitchen and the delectable smell of frying bacon soon filled the room. Kate smiled to herself. Here she was, dressed in a fluffy white dressing gown, with her good coffee and her feet up on the bar under the table. The Sunday papers were scattered over the tabletop. She could almost imagine herself to be in a glossy photo-shoot of a lifestyle magazine. How did someone like me end up here? She remembered chaotic mornings in her mother's filthy kitchen; the shouting, the hunt for a clean bowl, the rancid smell of the milk that hadn't been put away in the fridge overnight. Too many children, too much stuff everywhere. Trying to get herself ready for school, trying to find a shirt that wasn't too dirty. Kate shuddered and looked about her again, at the cleanliness and luxury, taking comfort in the beautiful view through the sparkling windows.

A hand appeared from behind her, bearing a plate loaded with food.

"Dig in," said Andrew. "If you manage to get through that lot, I'll be amazed."

"I'll give it my best shot," said Kate, smiling up at him. "Wouldn't want you slaving over a hot stove for nothing."

Andrew sank into a chair opposite her with his own full plate in front of him. He picked up the sports section of The Times, flapped it open and settled back in his chair with a loud sigh of contentment. Kate began attacking her breakfast with appreciative noises.

Andrew looked up after a moment. "I like seeing you at my breakfast table," he commented.

"I like being here. Particularly when I get a full English breakfast cooked for me."

Andrew smiled. "Perhaps we ought to make it a more permanent arrangement," he said, flipping the page of the newspaper.

Kate froze, laden fork halfway to her mouth. A piece of bacon fell back onto her plate. "Sorry?" she asked, after a second that felt more like a minute.

"Make it a more permanent arrangement," repeated Andrew. He was still perusing the newspaper and his tone was casual. "What do you think?"

Kate put her fork back down on her plate. "Well—" she began carefully, but was interrupted when her mobile rang, loud and insistently. She could feel it vibrating in her dressing gown pocket.

She fished it out. The shock of Andrew's words was nothing compared to the shock of seeing Anderton's name glowing on the screen of her telephone. She fumbled to answer it.

"Hello, sir."

She could tell something had happened even before he spoke. There was something heavy in the dead air humming between the satellite signals that brought his voice to hers.

"Kate. Sorry to interrupt whatever it is you're doing. I know you're not supposed to be working."

"It's fine," Kate said quickly. She could feel her pulse quicken. "What is it?"

"The usual. Worse than usual. I need you here right away."

"No problem—"

"I'm sending Mark over to get you. He can fill you in on the way."

"No problem," said Kate again. She felt a little winded. Worse than usual...what the hell did that mean? Then she remembered Anderton didn't know she wasn't at her own home. She explained.

"Stanton's place? Yes of course – Mark said something—" Anderton sounded... well, she couldn't quite put her finger on it. Pissed off? Amused? It was the merest trace of something, gone in an instant as he went straight back into professional mode. "I'll tell Mark to take a detour then. Does he know where your paramour lives?"

"Yes he does." *I've been seeing him for almost a year, you know.* "I'll be ready."

"Right. See you soon."

"Do we have an ID on the victim yet?" asked Kate quickly, before he could ring off.

Anderton was silent for a moment. "We've ID'd one of them," he said, eventually.

"*One* of them?" repeated Kate and Andrew looked up from his paper at her tone.

"This is a multiple murder, Kate. Didn't I say?" *No, you didn't.* "It's one of the co-directors of the MedGen Facility."

"Alex Hargreaves?" asked Kate, shocked.

"No, Jack Dorsey." Dead air hummed down the line again for a second. "That's all we've got at the moment. See you soon."

The broken line bleeped in Kate's ear. She put the phone back in her pocket. Andrew was looking at her from across the table, his mouth crimped.

"Was that work?" he asked. She knew he knew it had been.

"Yes. I've got to go."

"Oh, not today, surely?"

Kate tried to look sorry. "I have to. I'm really sorry, Andrew. You know what it's like."

Andrew looked down at the paper again and flipped another page with an irritated flick of his fingers. "Yes, I know what it's like," he said, quietly. "Oh well. If you have to, you have to."

"I'm sorry," said Kate, more sincerely this time. She quickly got up and gave him a kiss. "I'll let you know how I get on."

"Fine."

She kissed him again and then turned and made for the stairs and the bedroom, racing for her clothes and feeling that welcome sense of anticipation, tinged with a little fear, that she always felt at the start of a new case.

Within ten minutes, she heard the beep of Olbeck's horn outside. She grabbed her bag, kissed Andrew again as he sat, still in something of a sulk, at the breakfast table and left the house, shutting the door behind her firmly. She flung herself into the passenger seat rather breathlessly.

"Fill me in. Please, fill me in."

"Alright, alright. Keep your hair on." Olbeck reversed the car out of the driveway as Kate buckled herself in. "We've got plenty of time."

"I heard it's Jack Dorsey."

"You heard correctly. Dorsey, a currently unidentified male, and Dorsey's wife."

"Jesus." Kate was silent for a moment, looking ahead unseeingly through the windscreen. "What are the first ideas? A domestic? Or something else?"

"I don't know and can't speculate. I haven't even been to the scene yet. It's in Poltney Carver; village on the far side of Abbeyford."

"I know it. Well, vaguely. Isn't it the next village to Poltney Winter? Where Michael Frank lived?"

Olbeck nodded crisply. "That's right."

"Hmm," said Kate. "Well, I guess we'll know more when we get there."

It was a beautiful spring day: the kind of day where the British countryside looks its best. Its best is very good indeed, thought Kate, looking out of the car window. The trees were newly clothed in leaves of a bright fresh green and the sky was a clear, dazzling blue. Faint white wisps of cloud lay on the horizon. The hedgerows and fields were dotted with a profusion of colourful wildflowers, like dainty embroidery on a smooth, green blanket.

The car passed the sign for Poltney Carver. It was a small but clearly affluent place: the driveways of the pretty cottages that lined the few streets of the village housing large, expensive cars. Several of the houses of golden stone sported window boxes, filled with golden, dancing daffodils and the smooth upright heads of pink and white tulips. Ahead, Kate could see a police car and a couple of uniformed officers guarding the gateway to what was obviously Jack Dorsey's house. Olbeck slowed the car to flash his identification and they were waved through.

The drive was a long one, winding through sun-dappled woods where the first early bluebells could be seen in a faint, bluish haze under the beech trees. Olbeck slowed a little as they approached the next blind bend in the driveway. It was as well that that he did, because the second they rounded the bend, Kate yelled and Olbeck gasped as the broad white snout of an ambulance filled the windscreen of the car from side to side. The siren screamed as Olbeck yanked desperately at the steering wheel. The two vehicles passed each other with a sliver of space between them. Then the ambulance was past, blue lights flickering briefly over the interior of the car. Hedgerow twigs and leaves thrashed at the windows as the car juddered down the rough edges of the road, before burying its bonnet half in and half out of a hazel hedge. The engine stalled.

Kate and Olbeck remained motionless for a moment, Kate gripping the sides of her seat with both hands. As she realised they'd come to a stop and she was still in one piece, she released her grip, finger by rigid finger, and slowly sat back in the seat.

"Jesus, that was close," she said, when she could be sure of her voice.

Olbeck had gone pale. "You're not wrong. What a brilliant piece of irony that would have been; killed by a speeding ambulance..."

He fumbled his seatbelt open with shaking hands and got out of the car, holding onto the door like an old man. He groaned. "God, would you look at my paintwork."

Kate got up out of the car herself. She was feeling sick with the backwash of adrenaline, although the fresh air helped. "It's a mess," she agreed. "Still, could have been worse."

Olbeck was bent over the bonnet, tutting and flicking at the myriad scratches. "I've probably buggered the suspension as well," he muttered. "God Almighty..."

He swung himself back into the driver's seat and gingerly tried the key in the ignition. The engine turned over a few times, then sputtered back into life. "Move back a bit, Kate, while I try and get this out."

Kate moved back obediently. Olbeck nudged the car back out of the hedge and onto the open road again. He revved the engine a little. "Seems to be okay. Let's get on."

Kate hopped back in, feeling more normal. The same thought struck the two of them simultaneously and they turned to one another in the same instance.

"The ambulance—"

"Blue lights—"

"That means – that must mean—"

"One of them is still alive," said Olbeck. "Probably. Let's go find out, shall we?"

He drove very cautiously along the rest of the winding driveway, sounding his horn at every corner. They encountered no other vehicles. The driveway ended in a wide sweep of gravel in the front of a beautiful, four storied house of the gothic Victorian type, built in Bath stone with a multitude of glittering mullioned windows and a small fountain playing in the smooth green circle of lawn in front of house. There were several cars parked already and two uniformed officers guarding the half-open front door.

After the shock of the near-accident, Kate hadn't anticipated what they would soon be seeing at the crime scene. The beauty of the surroundings somehow made the fear of what was to come worse. She felt a twinge of pain in her back, deep within the scar. As Olbeck turned off the engine, she took a deep, shaky breath and unclipped her seat belt.

Chapter Six

THE SILENCE WAS THE FIRST thing that she noticed. The only noises she could hear were natural ones: birdsong, the rustle of leaves, the musical tinkle of the falling water in the fountain. Their footsteps sounded abnormally loud as she and Olbeck crunched across the gravel to the front door. Kate took another sweeping look around before they entered the house. There was a security camera mounted up on the front wall of the building, another trained on the step on which she stood. Alongside a car that she recognised as Anderton's, and two patrol cars, there was a large black four wheel drive vehicle, something that looked like a classic vintage sports car and another silver four wheel drive. Did those belong to Jack Dorsey and his family? Kate looked again at the front of the house, with its myriad windows. Behind the nearest window to the front door, she could see thick folds of expensive fabric held back by a glossy curtain tie. Against the wall of the house were flowerbeds planted with old-fashioned, cottage garden flowers: hollyhocks, larkspur, well-clipped rose bushes. There was money here – a lot of money.

Olbeck and Kate slipped on gloves and boots and stepped forward into a small inner hallway, wooden panelled and unfurnished except for a delicate little wooden table stood against the far wall. On its surface, a mercury glass vase held an arrangement of spring flowers. As she walked forward, Kate caught a faint breath of their delicate scent, obliterated a moment later by the heavy, metallic tang of blood. It should have been a warning but she still had to look twice as they walked out into the larger, inner hallway. The walls were painted a warm cream and the overhead lights were on. Kate thought for a moment that the hallway was tiled with glossy, wine-coloured tiles, a decorating choice that contrasted rather oddly with the rest of the interior. The illusion lasted a second, until she realised that the floor tiles were actually a conventional black and white, in a checkerboard pattern. They looked a glossy scarlet because they were submerged in a flood – a veritable lake – of blood.

A body lay in the middle of the red pool that filled the hallway from edge to edge. The body of a middle-aged man, tall and heavy, dressed in a dark tracksuit. His hair was cut brutally short and the bald spot at his crown shone under the overhead lights. He was waxen-white, the cleanly incised wound in his neck just visible.

The police officers regarded him in silence. Kate could feel her face freezing to a neutral expression automatically. It was partly a learned response – you realised early on not to show any sign of distress or emotion if you didn't want the piss ripped out of you by the male officers – but it was partly a defense mechanism, as well. Keep your face blank and somehow the horror of what you saw was reduced, just slightly. Just enough to cope.

"Is all the blood his?" Kate asked Olbeck, in a subdued monotone.

He was standing at the edge of the blood, staring intently at the body. Kate realised there was no way to get past the blood pool to the other side, without walking through it. Not a chance. Scene of Crime would kill them if they attempted it – she could already see two white suited technicians giving them uneasy glances from further down the hallway.

"Looks like it," said Olbeck. He raised a hand to the SOCOs to placate them. "We'll go round, guys. Don't worry."

They retraced their steps back through the first little antechamber and stepped back into the sunshine. Kate lifted her face to the warmth of the rays. The air felt incredibly fresh after the tainted stuffiness of the hallway. She closed her eyes briefly. The redness of the sunshine through her closed lids recalled the bloody lake inside, the body of the man spread-eagled within it, as if swimming.

They walked around the outside of the house, looking for a side entrance. Through a wrought iron gate in a box hedge, the path opened out onto smoothly manicured lawns, with a white iron conservatory before them. There were more cameras here, trained on the French doors that led into the conservatory. The doors stood open and the edge of a green curtain, made of what looked like heavy, lined silk, could be seen flapping gently in the breeze.

"Look at all these cameras," Kate said, gesturing. "Surely we'll have something from one of them?"

"Let's hope so." Olbeck had caught sight of Anderton and Theo, standing on the threshold of the house. At the same moment, their colleagues noticed them and lifted their hands in greeting. Theo looked as if he'd got up too early after a heavy session the night before. Anderton looked fairly normal, perhaps just a trifle pale.

"Good morning," he said, as Kate and Olbeck approached. Kate didn't smile in response – it felt inappropriate in the circumstances. "I suppose you've been through the front?"

"Tried to," answered Kate. "Couldn't get past the body."

"That's the security guard. His name's Darryl, not sure on the surname, yet."

"Not much of a guard, was he?" Olbeck said, a remark that from him that was quite remarkable in its unexpected callousness. Kate raised her eyebrows. Perhaps he was more unnerved than he was letting on.

"What else have we got?" she asked.

Instead of answering, Anderton gestured towards the house.

"Go on through. You'll soon see. Come back out and tell me what you think."

"You're not coming?"

Anderton gestured again. "Just go and get your first impressions," he said.

Theo sat down rather abruptly on a convenient garden bench and lit a cigarette. His hands were shaking slightly. Kate was going to say something, tease him a little about coming to work on a hangover, before deciding that she'd better keep her mouth shut. She and Olbeck exchanged a look and then stepped through the doorway, into the conservatory.

The same heavy green silk curtains they had glimpsed from the garden had been drawn over the panes of glass that made up the walls. The floor was tiled in the same checkerboard pattern as the hallway. Kate and Olbeck stepped cautiously through into the house. They came out into a large room; a sitting room, beautifully furnished, with pale green walls, a polished dark-wood floor and a large, cream rug. Antiques stood against the walls, too many beautiful things to take in at once. The lights were on, blazing from the overhead chandelier and the curtains were drawn back from the ceiling height windows.

The beauty of the room made what was in it worse. Jack Dorsey's body lay in front of the fireplace. Kate had to look twice to be sure it was him, he had been so savagely attacked. She looked once at the knife wounds to his face and chest and then looked away, swallowing. She groped for her neutral mask and tried to fix it back onto her face, which wanted to grimace and crumple. She could feel Olbeck at her side, his arm touching hers, and the warmth of his body momentarily brought a little comfort. She fixed her eyes on the rug, purposefully not looking at the body. Dorsey's blood had spurted in arcs and splashes and sprays, marking the pale rug in an awful abstract artwork. It was dry now, brownish red, stiffening the long fibres of the carpet. She realized now why Theo had looked so bludgeoned. Her gaze was drawn to another dark splash on the far wall, next to the huge, gilt-framed mirror that reflected the horror contained within the four surrounding walls. Something written in blood, in dragging, jagged letters a foot high. KILLER.

She and Olbeck remained at the edge of the room while the technicians did their work. Camera flashes went off at monotonous intervals, Kate trying not to flinch at every one. After what felt like an hour, but was probably only ten minutes, Olbeck turned to Kate and, with mutual appeal in their glance, they turned and left the room.

Once again, out in the open air, Kate drew in a shaky breath. The air outside tasted indescribably fresh and sweet after the abattoir inside. She and Olbeck walked over to where Anderton and Theo sat on their bench. Anderton looked up in silent enquiry.

"Jesus," Olbeck said eloquently. He sat down on a low garden wall that edged what looked like a kitchen garden.

"Exactly," agreed Anderton. "Butchered. I think that's the word I'd use."

"Was there another victim?" asked Kate, remembering the ambulance.

"Dorsey's wife, Madeline. She was lying next to him when we got here. Terribly injured but, incredibly, still alive."

"Alive?" asked Kate. She felt her pulse quicken. "Do you think she'll make it?"

"I don't know. I hope so. But – well, if you'd seen her..."

"What were her injuries?"

"Knife wounds, same as Dorsey. She looked like she'd lost a lot of blood."

"God," said Olbeck. He pushed himself up off the wall and began pacing around. "Was it – I mean, we're certain there was an intruder?"

Anderton looked pleased. "Ah, you're thinking it could be a domestic? It's possible, although from the fact that the security guard is also dead, unlikely. We'll obviously know more if Mrs Dorsey pulls through."

"Who reported it?" asked Kate.

Theo spoke up for the first time. "Cleaner," he said, a little thickly. Clearing his throat, he threw his cigarette butt into a flowerbed and went on. "She's currently in the kitchen with a WPC, having hysterics."

"Understandably," Anderton said, also getting to his feet.

Kate remembered something; a flashback from her interview with Jack Dorsey at MedGen. His desk, a silver-framed photograph: blonde wife, blonde children, arms interlinked. She felt a coldness spreading in the pit of her stomach. "The children," she said, feeling as if she didn't quite have control of her mouth. "The Dorsey children... are they – has anyone checked—"

Anderton looked at her properly for the first time since she'd arrived. A flicker of sympathy crossed his face. "They're at boarding school, both of them. Both safe. Thank fuck," he added, almost as an afterthought.

Kate sat down on the wall herself, feeling almost queasy from the wave of relief that spread over her. Then she thought about having to break the news to them. Sorry, kids, about your mum and dad... Resolutely, she turned her mind away from the thought.

"We've searched the rest of the house and we're spreading out into the grounds." Anderton had been speaking for a few moments before she became aware of what he was saying. She tried to concentrate. Anderton went on. "There's no sign of forced entry. We haven't yet had a look at the CCTV footage, that's obviously top priority once the SOCOs are finished here."

He stopped speaking and for a moment, they all faced each other, sharing an odd moment of solidarity. Kate, despite all the horror of the scene, felt a warm thrill of belonging, of coming home, back where she should be. It was the first time she'd felt it since she had come back to work and, for a moment, she luxuriated in the sensation. It was as if life had suddenly come back into focus.

"So," said Anderton quietly. "Thoughts?"

"Someone came to the door," said Kate. "The security guard let them in and he was walking back through the hallway when they attacked him."

"Given the position of the body, I'd say that was a fairly accurate guess," Anderton said. "And why would he let someone in through the door, given that he's supposed to be guarding the house?"

"Because it was someone he recognized," said Kate. "Someone he knew. Someone he didn't think was a threat."

"Exactly. Hopefully the CCTV will tell us exactly who that was."

"Is that likely?" asked Olbeck, in a cynical tone.

"Well, we won't know until we look. I agree, anyone who comes ready to kill three people is probably going to take some pains to conceal their identity." He raised a hand to his head, tousling his hair in a characteristic gesture. "You mentioned a possible domestic, Mark. I don't think we should discount that, out of hand. I don't think we can comfortably do that. We don't know enough about the victims, their relationship with each other – we know nothing about the Dorseys' marriage, their history. I agree with you, Kate, that this has all the hallmarks of an outsider, an intruder killing – all I'm asking is that we need to keep an open mind."

Everyone nodded.

Theo lit another cigarette. "The writing on the wall," he said. "What's with that?"

"Yes," agreed Anderton. "The literal writing on the wall. What's that telling us?"

"The most obvious answer is that it's a message, isn't it?" suggested Olbeck. "Telling us Jack Dorsey's a killer. It's a motive."

"Is it?" asked Anderton. "Perhaps it's a very mentally disturbed person, telling the world what he – or she – has done. It's a sign. 'I am a killer'."

Olbeck shrugged. "Yes, could be."

Kate rubbed her temples. "We don't yet know who the intended victim is, do we, sir?" she asked. "I mean, if there was *one* intended victim. I'm assuming it's Jack Dorsey – and maybe his wife..."

"That's a reasonable assumption," said Anderton. "But nothing is definite."

"It's just – the guard looked like – well, like that was a quick, almost clinical killing. To get him out of the way, perhaps. Whereas Jack Dorsey..." The image of his body flashed up in Kate's mind's eye and her voice faltered for a moment. "That was savage. That was *anger*."

Chapter Seven

Kate had had a clear picture of the cleaner in her head, especially after she learned her name was Mary Smith. Middle-aged, working class, overweight and homely – Kate chastised herself for the stereotype, but somehow, the mental picture persisted. It was something of a shock to find that Mary Smith was in her very early twenties, blonde, slim and with an impeccable accent. She was dressed casually, in a pink T-shirt and tight blue jeans, with her long hair pulled back into a low pony tail. Her good looks were apparent at a second glance, but at first sight were subsumed beneath the utter shock and terror distorting her face. Mary's pink T-shirt had a jarring pattern of red dots and jagged stripes, which Kate realised, after a moment, were blood stains.

The officers sat down. The WPC, Mandy – Kate knew her very vaguely – kept a comforting hand on Mary's trembling shoulder and handed her another mug of tea. Enough sugar in it to make the spoon stand up straight, Kate had no doubt. She had a sudden vivid flash of her grandmother saying exactly that, as an eight-year-old Kate handed her an afternoon cuppa. What was Nana's other tea-related phrase? Strong enough to trot a mouse on. Kate blinked and dismissed the memory, bringing herself back to the present and the interview at hand.

"Now, Miss Smith," began Anderton. "I'd like to thank you for talking to us. I appreciate what a dreadful shock this must all have been."

Mary Smith said nothing but her shuddering increased. A little tea splashed over the edge of the mug clamped in her hands. Mandy bent over and gently removed it, keeping her hand on Mary's shoulder.

"I'd just like to hear what happened when you arrived at the house," said Anderton. "Can you take us through what happened?"

Mary Smith had been holding herself rigid. At Anderton's gentle request, she gave a small nod and winced, as if that tiny movement hurt her. "It all looked totally normal from the outside," she said after a moment, in a tone so low she was almost whispering.

"You have a key?" Anderton asked, after it became clear that she wasn't going to say any more.

Mary swallowed and made a visible effort to pull herself together. "Yes, I've got keys to the front door and the alarm codes. I got here – I think it was about ten thirty, normal time. It all looked so normal."

"And then what happened?" Anderton prompted.

Mary swallowed again. "I unlocked the front door—"

"Wait," Olbeck interrupted. "The front door was locked?"

Mary nodded. "That's why I didn't realise – I didn't think anything was wrong... it would normally be locked."

"Right. Sorry – go on."

Mary pinched either side of her nose, shutting her eyes momentarily. "I unlocked the door and went into the hallway and I saw – I saw Darryl—"

She drew in her breath in a great sobbing gasp. For a moment, Kate was sure she would collapse again, but after a moment she went on, her voice shaking.

"The lights were off and it was dark – it's always quite dark in there, as there aren't any outside windows, so I put on the light and – Darryl was there, *dead*, in all that blood... I thought – I thought I was dreaming for a moment. It was like... like something from a nightmare. I stepped in the blood, I didn't even realise I had – I was frozen for a moment—"

Her voice failed and she drew in another whooping breath. Mandy patted her arm encouragingly.

"Go on, Miss Smith," said Anderton.

"I ran towards him, I – I could see he was dead, logically I could see he was dead, but I couldn't help it – I was going to feel his pulse but then I saw the cut in his neck and I couldn't touch him—" She looked pleadingly at the officers, as if they would take her to task for it. "I'm sorry but I couldn't, I was hysterical – I didn't know what to do..."

"You're doing really well, Miss Smith – Mary. What happened then?"

Another shuddering breath. Mary's eyes were closed, her chest rising and falling fast. "I was going to go on, go through the house to see if Jack and Madeline were there – I thought – well, I wasn't really thinking anything, I just was kind of blindly going forward – and then I thought 'suppose whoever did this is still here,' and that was it... I just ran, ran out the house and down the driveway. I – I don't remember much else."

As Anderton told them later, a woman from the village, walking her dog along the main road, had seen Mary come screaming out of the driveway, blood-streaked and hysterical, and caught her in her arms. She was the witness who'd called the emergency services.

"So, let me just check that we've got everything," Anderton said, very soothingly. "You arrived, as normal, at about ten o'clock this morning. You unlocked the door, which is what you would normally do, and you walked in and found Darryl on the floor."

Mary nodded.

"Would Jack Dorsey and his wife normally be at home during the day on a Friday?"

Mary took in another deep, shaky breath. "Jack definitely

wouldn't be. He's always at work. Madeline's sometimes in, but just as often she's out. That's why I had the key and the codes."

"I see. How did you get the job here?"

Mary looked confused for a moment before her face cleared. "Through the university. I'm a student at Bath Spa."

"How long have you been working here, Mary?"

"Um... not long. About six months."

"That's great. Could I just ask you to hold on one moment? I'm sure Mandy will make you another cup of tea."

Anderton drew his officers to one side for a moment. "Theo, can you take over here? I don't think there's much more she can tell us, other than what she's already said, but you never know. Kate, Mark, can you get on and see if you can find the CCTV? Quick as you can."

They all nodded. Theo sat back down next to Mary. Olbeck inclined his head towards Kate. "After you."

"No, I insist," said Kate, standing back. "After you, DI Olbeck."

"Just get on with it," said Anderton, half smiling. "I'm off."

"Where are you off to, sir?" Kate asked as they let the kitchen.

Anderton's face became grim again. "Hospital," he said, briefly. "To see if Madeline Dorsey's alive or dead."

Chapter Eight

"SO WHERE'S THIS PARTY, THEN?" Stuart asked as he helped the others dismantle the table and load it into the back of the dirty white van that they'd parked just outside the gates of MedGen. Stuart, along with James and Rosie, had been manning the leaflet table since he arrived at ten thirty that morning. The leaflets had a variety of gruesome pictures displayed beneath shouting black headlines. Stuart had seen several people, obviously out walking their dogs, stop, looking interested in what they were doing, catch sight of the pictures of bunnies clamped to tables and puppies punctured with needles, and recoil, walking on with a nervous glance back. He wondered whether to point out that these leaflets seemed to be totally counterproductive to their cause and decided not to.

"We're heading there now. Want a lift?" asked Rosie. She was struggling to lift a heavy box into the back of the van. Stuart lifted it from her arms and slotted it into place. "Oh, thanks. Why don't you come with us?"

"Sure, will do. It's not like I even know who's throwing it," said Stuart. "Whose house is it?"

Rosie had turned away to gather more boxes. James was already climbing into the front seat of the van. Seeing he wasn't going to get an answer, Stuart shrugged and went to help Rosie collect the last of the boxes. He wasn't dressed for a party, but what the hell – he doubted very much it would be a black-tie affair.

They drove for about twenty minutes, Stuart crouched uncomfortably in the back of the rattling, clanking van, with boxes of leaflets sliding into him as they drove around corners. He wiped some of the dirt off the back window to see if he could see where they were going. James was following the dual carriageway out of the town, heading for the outskirts on the north side, where the village of Armford had long been swallowed up by the creeping boundaries of Abbeyford. Stuart pushed a box away from him and noted the road sign that flashed past. They were driving into a housing estate built around the nineteen thirties, by the look of the houses, travelling along progressively narrower roads until they drew into a cul-de-sac where the gardens of the houses backed onto a scrubby piece of woodland. The van stopped with a jerk. Stuart opened the back doors and clambered out, wincing at the bruises on his thighs inflicted by the sliding boxes.

It was about six o'clock, not yet quite dark. They had parked outside a run-down detached house, the front garden paved with concrete. Stuart followed James through the open door of the house and was immediately met by a wall of heat and a fug of cigarette and spliff smoke so thick it felt like a physical barrier. Trying not to inhale, he followed James's denim-clad back through to what turned out to be the kitchen, although Stuart was fucked if he would dare eat anything produced in the fetid little room. There wasn't any food anyway, merely a sink full of beer and a table crowded with wine bottles and cans. People were everywhere; smoking, talking, shouting, waving to one another. Most were young, most were clearly activists – there were a lot of piercings and tattoos and interesting hairstyles. Stuart had tied his dreadlocks back this evening. One thing he was looking forward to, after this assignment finished, was getting the whole bloody lot cut off. That would be first on his list of things to do once he was back in the real world.

He, James and Rosie grabbed beers and made their way out through the crowds to the garden beyond the kitchen door. It was just a square of lawn and a tumbledown fence, but the evening air was beautiful; soft and warm in a way that English spring nights so rarely were. There was an outside light which, despite the dingy shade, had attracted a fluttering cloud of moths and insects forming a moving corona.

"Whose house is this?" asked Stuart.

"Dunno who it *belongs* to," said James, "But we know a few of the guys who live here. It's a squat."

Stuart should have guessed. He thought longingly for a second of his own flat back in London; minimal furniture, many gadgets. "Who's that, then?"

Rosie was crouched awkwardly on a low brick wall that ran partway along the length of the garden boundary, rolling a joint. She gave the papers a final, expert twist.

"Angie lives here, doesn't she?" she asked, of no one in particular. "And Rizzo. I don't know really, people just seem to drift in and out. I stayed here for a bit myself, when I first came down."

"Before you met me," said James.

"Right."

She lit the joint, took a deep drag and handed it to Stuart. He lifted it to his lips. As he could spend the evening seemingly doing some serious drinking while actually remaining as sober as a teetotal judge, he could also do a credible impression of a man toking hard without actually doing so. The Bill Clinton Method, he thought, with an inner grin.

Quickly as he decently could, he passed the joint on to James. He needed to know more about the loosely knit group he'd infiltrated, and this party was the perfect opportunity to do some tentative preparatory digging. He'd tried, subtly, to find out a little more about James and Rosie's immediate friends and fellow activists but, for people single minded about a certain cause, they were frustratingly vague about their colleagues and mates. Perhaps here at this party, he could start to ascertain his next move, who he should be taking a deeper interest in.

He went back inside to fetch more beers, an exercise designed to continue the good impression he was making on James and Rosie and to give him the opportunity to stake out a few of the fellow partygoers.

He walked slowly; it was impossible to do otherwise, given the crowded space, but he wanted to keep his ears open to the possibility of overhearing something interesting. He reached the kitchen. For a moment, the press of bodies in front of him opened up a little and that was when he saw her.

She was standing under the harsh strip light, bathed in a strident white light that would have been utterly unforgiving to nine out of ten women. She was the tenth. The brilliant white light turned her face to a beautiful blank mask, bleaching out all the little imperfections that you saw in normal skin. Her hair was jet black and very short, almost a sculpted cap that hugged the contours of her perfectly shaped head. All Stuart could see for a moment was a sulky red mouth and two huge dark eyes, as her gaze met his. A challenging stare. For a second, he was aware of a surge of anger, almost as strong as the opposing one of desire.

The challenging, almost aggressive look was gone in the blink of an eye. Stuart wondered whether he'd imagined it. Now she was looking over at him with the tiniest trace of a smile, her face softened and open. He made up his mind.

"Hi."

She looked up at him from under her long lashes. "Hello."

"I'm Mike."

"Hi Mike. I'm Angie."

His ears pricked up a little at that. "This is your gaff, isn't it?"

She nodded. Up close, he could see faint freckles on her pale skin, the merest dusting of them, like gold glitter spread over her little nose. She wore a slash of black eyeliner and that red lipstick, but no other make-up.

"It doesn't belong to us. We're squatting here. It was empty and unloved so – we took it on."

Stuart looked around at the squalid room surrounding them. Angie followed his gaze and laughed. The laugh transformed her face, from beautiful but chilly sculpture to a more appealing, boyish gamine. Stuart could feel the faint warmth of her body from a few inches away, they were standing so close.

"Yeah, I know," she said. "It's pretty shitty. But beggars can't be choosers."

She had an unexpectedly deep voice for such a delicate looking girl, rather husky, as if she were just getting over a bad cold. She confirmed the reason why after a moment of silence between them. "Coming for a smoke?"

"Lead on," said Stuart, who sighed inwardly at the thought of another fake toking session. Still, if that was what it took...

They passed James and Rosie on their way through the garden and Angie stopped when she saw them. She and Rosie greeted one another with a kiss on the lips, which inwardly raised Stuart's eyebrows. James didn't seem to mind, looking on with a slightly lecherous smile. The four of them stood and smoked and talked. Stuart tried to quell his impatience. He wanted to talk to Angie on her own.

"Who's 'we'?" he asked Angie, in a break in conversation.

She looked at him with those large dark eyes, eyelids made heavy with dope. "What?"

"You said 'we' took it on. The house."

"Oh, yes," she said. She passed the joint to Rosie and hoisted herself onto the brick wall, kicking her heels against the bricks. "There's a few of us here. Rizzo and Charlie, mostly. People come and go."

"Seen Kitten lately?" asked James.

Stuart had his eyes fixed on Angie's face and he saw the tiny ripple of some kind of emotion go over her face, gone in an instant. She pushed her hair back from her forehead.

"Not lately," she said, a trifle coolly.

There was a moment's silence. Then Rosie started talking

about the protest, how she was sure it was having an effect, *they must be getting pissed off with us by now...* Stuart kept his eyes on Angie. The mask had come back down over her face and, after a moment, she slid off the wall.

"Getting a drink," she said. She gave Stuart a look he couldn't quite decipher and after a moment, she walked away.

Stuart hesitated. He wanted to follow Angie and he wanted to know more about this Kitten.... He made up his mind in a split second, no time to dither and walked off after Angie, miming a 'getting a beer' motion to James and Rosie. He heard Rosie's derisive snort behind him and took a moment to wink at her before quickening his pace to keep Angie in view.

She walked straight past the table of drinks in the kitchen, through to the hallway and turned up the stairs. He saw people, men mostly, turning to stare at her as she passed. He followed her up the stairs, looking at the smooth white skin at the nape of her neck where her hair grew in twin dark points. There was a second, smaller staircase on the landing and Angie climbed that, Stuart following her. The stairs ended in a blue-painted door at the top and beyond the door was what was obviously Angie's bedroom.

Stuart paused for a moment in the doorway, getting his bearings. It was difficult because, as he quickly realised, the walls and ceiling were covered in tiny, glittering shards of mirror glass, hundreds of them; a mosaic of reflections, lit only by the candles that stood in the tiny iron heath in the chimney breast. Stuart turned slowly, watching an infinite number of tiny Stuarts turn with him, moving in the mirror pieces. There was hardly any furniture in the room, just a small chest of drawers, a bookcase stuffed with books and a double mattress on the floor, covered with a patchwork quilt. There was a large amount of computer equipment arranged on a desk against the wall, the oversized screen dominating the room. Several video cameras were arranged neatly next to the keyboard. Angie sat cross-legged on the quilt, a small wooden box in her lap, watching him with a small, amused smile.

"Far out," said Stuart. He put a finger out to the nearest wall, feeling the individual edges of the mirror pieces. "How long did it take to do?"

"About ten years," said Angie absently, occupied in a hunt for something within the wooden box. "No, not really. About three weeks. I was almost blind by the end of it, fiddling with all those tiny little pieces."

"Amazing." Stuart realised what she'd been hunting for as she withdrew it from the box – a small plastic bag half filled with white powder. She looked up and saw him watching.

"Want some?"

Stuart didn't hesitate. "If you can spare it."

"Wouldn't have offered if I couldn't'." Angie patted the mattress beside her and Stuart sat down carefully.

He watched as she shaped the powder into two lines, neat snowy drifts on the top of a CD case. Even after years in the field, he still felt that tremor of anxiety at the thought that he, a police officer, was about to do something illegal. He would still do it, of course, as small a line as he could. The last thing he needed now was to arouse Angie's suspicion.

She offered him the CD case and he shook his head. "Ladies first."

She grinned and ducked her head and while she was still head down and rubbing her nose, he took the case, whisked the majority of one line off of the surface with his thumb and quickly inhaled the miniscule amount that was left.

He was hoping that the coke would make Angie open up a little, but when she turned to him with glittering eyes and parted lips, he could see that she had a more wordless activity in mind. He had a second of hesitation, training too strong in him to be able to ditch it without a qualm, but then her lips were on his and her hands on him, and all his thoughts of ethics and morals were swept away in an instant of reckless abandonment.

Chapter Nine

KATE AND OLBECK BEGAN A preliminary check of the building. The house was beautiful, but the horror of what had happened within it somehow tainted its elegance and charm. Kate, climbing the main staircase, was reminded of too many horror films where the victim climbed unknowingly to their doom. The heavy silk and velvet drapes that hung at every window seemed to bulge unpleasantly, as if concealing someone within their folds, waiting to jump out. The rooms and hallways seemed full of too many shadows, even with the bright sunlight outside. She shook herself mentally and told herself not to be so stupid, but ridiculously, she found herself hurrying to stay close to Olbeck as they moved from room to room.

"Anderton said it's been searched already, right?" she asked, as they entered what was obviously the master bedroom. It had a four poster bed within it, draped in white linen. The covers were bunched messily at the foot of the bed.

Olbeck nodded absently, as he surveyed the room. An empty mug stood on one of the bedside tables, beside a stack of books. Kate went over to see what they were. No fiction at all; a pile of learned scientific works and what looked like several PHD theses. Kate checked her gloves were intact and picked one up, flicked to the front page, read a few paragraphs in increasing confusion and put it down again.

"See, that looks like English but it can't be, because I can't understand one word of it."

Olbeck grinned. "Well, he's a boffin, isn't he? Dorsey, I mean."

"Was," corrected Kate.

The grin fell from Olbeck's face. "Yes. Was." He walked over to the matching bedside cabinet on the opposite side of the bed. Here was a top of the range Kindle, encased in a pink leather case, a half full water glass and a box of tissues. Olbeck opened the cabinet. Shoes, handbags and scarves were thrust in a piled heap within it. He began removing them, piece by piece, placing them neatly on the carpet.

"Some nice stuff here," he commented.

Kate took a look and nodded. "Well, they weren't exactly short of money, were they? They were loaded, in fact."

"Yup." Olbeck sat back on his heels and looked up at Kate. "Was that the reason for the security guard? Or was it because of MedGen?"

"Probably the latter. Don't you think? Lots of rich people around here and I don't think many of them have on-site security."

She held out a hand and pulled Olbeck up onto his feet.

"Thanks. We'll have to check."

"There's another thing," said Kate as they moved onto the next room. "Mary said the door was locked when she arrived, right?"

"Yes."

"But she didn't mention anything about turning off the alarms. She said she knew the codes, but I'm sure she didn't say anything about turning off the alarms."

Olbeck paused in the doorway to the room next to the Dorseys' bedroom.

"Yes, I think you're right. She didn't mention that, and she would have done, wouldn't she? I mean, if the alarms weren't turned off, they would have gone off after a few moments once Mary had entered the hallway, wouldn't they?"

Kate nodded.

"I would have thought so. So either they weren't turned on – why? – or they were disabled in some way, or someone who knew the codes turned them off."

"I'll flag that up to Anderton. What else? Should we try and track down the CCTV footage now, leave this search 'til later?"

Kate was touched that he was still deferring to her opinion, just as he had when they were true equals. She squeezed his arm. "I think we should. Just imagine if we can get a clear look at the perp. We could have this wrapped up by the end of the day."

Olbeck laughed a cynical laugh. "You know how much I would love to believe that. Let's go, then."

They retraced their steps back to the first room they'd come to, the conservatory at the side of the house. They could still hear the flash and whine of the cameras in the drawing room as the SOCOs continued their work.

"Where would they keep the equipment?" Olbeck asked, as he stood, hands on hips, and stared up at the ceiling, as if it would give him the answer.

Kate tapped her chin with her finger, thinking. "We should ask Mary Smith. She might know."

"Good idea."

But when they went back to the kitchen, Mary Smith had already left, carted away to the police station by Theo to make a statement. Kate shrugged when they were told by one of the uniforms.

"Well, back to looking." She looked around the room at the few people remaining. "Does anyone know where the CCTV equipment was kept?"

There were blank looks, shrugs and 'don't knows'. One dark-haired officer, who looked as if he was barely out of Hendon, volunteered the information that there were two doors in the corridor outside that might contain what they were looking for. They thanked him and made their way in the direction he'd indicated.

The corridor was tiled in ancient red floor tiles and the walls were scuffed and marked. There was a rack for wellington boots and a coat stand piled with coats and hats. Kate and Olbeck walked to the end of the corridor which terminated in a small room, stacked with cardboard boxes and odds and ends of furniture, clearly used as nothing more than a store room.

"This was probably the servants' hall, in olden times," said Kate. "Don't you think? Just off the kitchen."

"Probably." Olbeck glanced around once more and retreated back into the corridor. "How about these doors, here?"

The first door, when opened, led to a wall cupboard, but when Olbeck opened the second, he gave a satisfied chuckle. "Here we are. Good for that PC, he was right."

It was a tiny room, almost a broom cupboard, bare of furniture except for a desk on which stood a bank of blank CCTV screens. Various pieces of equipment were assembled on the top of the desk, all with a suspicious lack of electrical activity.

"Hmm." Olbeck peered over the back of the desk and then looked at Kate with a wealth of expression on his face.

"It's turned off at the plug?" asked Kate.

"Got it in one."

"Okay..."

They looked at each other and then both suddenly laughed.

"What did I say about solving the case by the end of the day?" Kate giggled.

Olbeck pushed a hand through his hair. "Oh God, you know you jinxed it as soon as you uttered the words. If you hadn't said anything, we would have walked in here and found everything working perfectly..."

Kate looked at the blank row of screens and grew sombre again. "Wait a minute," she said. "Why the hell *are* they turned off? Why would you run a top-notch security system and not bother to switch it on?"

"Well, that's easy," said Olbeck. "Our perp turned it off. I bet he took the tapes, too."

"Tapes? Surely it would be digital?"

"Well, yes...I suppose. We'll have to get Tech to look at it. Get your mate over here, what's his name, Sam. He'll soon be able to get hold of anything, if it's there to be got."

Kate stood looking at the screens, rubbing her finger along her jaw. "The murderer knew this place," she said. "He must have done. It took us forever to find this little... cupboard. He must have known where to go."

"Not necessarily," said Olbeck. "We have no idea about times, at this point. He could have been here all night, searched the whole house...although—" He stopped for a minute. "You're right, in a way. It's a hell of a risk to come all this way, with this many cameras, on the off chance that you *might* be able to disable them."

"Exactly."

They both stood looking at the dead equipment in front of them for a moment longer, as if it would suddenly, spontaneously, spring into life again. Then, almost as one, they turned and said, "Let's get going, then," half laughed at their timing, and left the room, Olbeck shutting the door firmly behind him.

Chapter Ten

Stuart was back at the protest the next morning and was unsurprised to see that neither James or Rosie, or even Angie, had made it. Sleeping off massive hangovers, probably. He introduced himself to the middle-aged lady who was behind the leaflet table, whose name was Jane. It was a cold day, with intermittent spitting rain, and no one came along to question or harangue them. After twenty minutes, Stuart decided that he'd be better off, chasing up his new friends.

Back at his car, he mused over which direction to take. Almost without hesitation, he decided on the direction of the squat. As he drove there, he was uncomfortably aware of just how much he wanted to see Angie. He reflected on what had happened the night before in some disbelief. He would never have thought that he would go that far, actually sleep with someone he had under observation. He was half proud of himself, half aghast. He wanted to tell someone, just to share the secret; that particular secret amongst all the secrets he was having to keep, but he knew that he couldn't. Who would he tell, anyway? Anderton? His boss? Aloud, he scoffed, shook his head and dismissed the thought. By the time he parked the car outside the scruffy house, he was firmly back into character.

He wanted to walk straight in but caution made him ring the doorbell and, when that failed to work, knock on the peeling paint of the front door. After a wait of a few minutes, it was opened by a man – a boy, really – someone who Stuart had never seen before, with curly auburn hair, a half-asleep expression and dressed only in a dirty T-shirt and boxer shorts.

"Is Angie in?"

"What?" said the boy, scratching his neck. Then his expression cleared. "Oh, you're Mike, aren't you? Angie said you might be coming."

Stuart felt a tremor of something: anxiety, or was it anticipation? "She's in, then?"

"Yeah. Upstairs." He said nothing else but stood back to let Stuart into the house.

Stuart climbed the stairs to Angie's glittering cave. He expected to find her lolling in bed, possibly naked, but she was standing in the middle of the room, dressed in a white vest and black combat trousers, feet in laced up black plimsolls. She looked... *alive*, that was the first word that sprang to mind. To Stuart's eyes, the air around her shimmered for a moment and the casual cocky grin he was wearing dropped off his face within seconds.

She fixed him with her gaze, her face back to its beautiful blank mask again. Then she smiled and the odd moment of tension was broken.

"Hello, you," she said, quite casually.

"Hi." Stuart hesitated for a second, crossed the room and took her into his arms. She returned his kiss briefly but voraciously.

"Were you going out?" he asked, when he could breathe again.

"I was," said Angie. "It can wait, though."

This shouldn't be happening, thought Stuart, even as their clothes fell to the floor. This shouldn't be happening. I have to stop it. But still he was on the bed with her, under the covers with her, even while he was saying that to himself. I have to stop it, this can't go on... but then it was useless, the words dropped away and there wasn't room for any thought at all.

Afterwards, she lay face down with her head turned from him. He ran a hand down her back, marvelling at the perfection of her skin, that whiteness dusted with golden freckles. He thought she'd fallen asleep and was surprised when she spoke.

"Where do you live?"

"London," Stuart said, briefly. Always stick as closely to the true facts as you can. Angie made an indeterminate noise. "Have you lived here long?" he asked.

"'Bout six months." Angie turned her head to look at him and he was struck anew by the perfection of her features. She could be a model, he thought, opened his mouth to tell her and then firmly shut it again, cringing at the thought. What was the matter with him?

"Where did you live before?"

Angie shrugged with one shoulder. "With a friend."

She said it in a neutral tone but Stuart was surprised at the sudden spurt of jealousy he felt. Better get over that, and quickly...

"So, when you're not protesting, what do you do?" he asked, changing the subject

"I'm an artist."

Inwardly Stuart rolled his eyes. Of course she was. "What kind of art? Paintings, you mean?"

Angie smiled. "All sorts of art. Multi-media, mostly. Digital and video, and sound combined with physical media."

"Right," said Stuart, none the wiser.

Angie's mouth quirked up at the corner. "This room is one of my works, you know."

Stuart looked around him. The curtains were shut and the mirror pieces glittered dimly through the half-darkness.

"It's a piece of work, all right." He raised an arm slowly and lowered it, watching the infinite tiny reflections in the mirror pieces. Angie rested her head on her arm and watched him, still smiling.

"You know they say that you shouldn't get between two mirrors," she said. "It's bad luck."

"Why?" asked Stuart, still watching his arm in the mirrors.

Angie rolled onto her back. "I don't know. Perhaps because it drags out a piece of your soul."

"Right," said Stuart, grinning. "I'll risk it."

"Well, you have to have a soul in the first place."

"Is that right?" asked Stuart. "Are you saying I don't?"

She shook her head, smiling that closed, secretive smile again. "No, you're all right," she said. Then she said, in the same voice, "I don't have one."

"One what?"

"A soul." She rolled to face him. They were eye to eye for a breathless, hushed moment while her words reverberated around the silent room. Then Stuart laughed and Angie laughed and the tension was broken.

"So," said Stuart, keeping his tone very casual, "How did you get mixed up with all the protests, then?"

Angie kept her eyes fixed on him. She smiled a little. "Mixed up?"

"Yeah. I mean, how did you get into it in the first place?"

Angie's smile grew wider. "I think you're labouring under a bit of a misapprehension," she said and giggled a little. "I'm not part of the protest. I don't – I'm not into that sort of thing."

"You're not?" Stuart could feel the half smile on his face sag into non-existence. "So how come—"

"I know James and Rosie? I just do. We have a lot of parties."

"Oh, right. So protesting's not really your thing, then?"

Angie rolled onto her back again and yawned. "No. I don't care enough about it. All I care about is—" She stopped for a moment and brushed away a strand of hair from her face. "I just want to make art. That's all that really matters to me."

"Good for you," Stuart said automatically, while his mind sifted through this new information. Topmost was the thought, sudden and inescapable, was that if this were true, he had no need of Angie's company, anymore. He was disconcerted by the sudden jump of anxiety, of grief almost, that that engendered in him.

Get a grip, Stuart. You're playing a dangerous game, here.

"I could show you my portfolio, if you like," said Angie. The diffidence of her voice touched him.

"I'd like that," Stuart said. Then, wanting to escape the clamouring voices in his head, telling him to leave, get out of there, try something else, he pulled her closer to him and kissed her.

EN ROUTE TO THE HOSPITAL, Kate felt her phone buzz and jitter. A text from Andrew, asking if she was coming back to his house later. She realised, with a guilty jump of the heart, that she hadn't spared him a second's thought since she'd left him that morning. Could it really still be the same day? It felt as though a week had passed since that peaceful breakfast in his conservatory. It was only then that Kate remembered his suggestion that she move in with him. She swallowed, put the phone back in her bag without answering it and turned her mind from the problem.

On arrival at the hospital, they were directed up to the Intensive Care Unit. There, they found Anderton pacing up and down in the reception area. He raised his eyebrows as they walked towards him, but Kate couldn't read his expression. Did that mean Madeline Dorsey was still alive?

The smell of the hospital, a nostril-flaring mix of disinfectant, old sweat and worse, brought Kate back to that time last summer, after the incident. She tried to think of it as *the incident*, not *the time I almost died*; it helped, somehow. It reduced its importance in her mind. She remembered those first confused and pain-filled weeks and then the long, slow process of recovery; endless physiotherapy appointments, counselling sessions, too many afternoons spent on her sofa watching crappy romantic comedies and anything that didn't involve violence or bloodshed. Too many nights waking up with a sodden pillowcase, coming back to consciousness with a start, clasping her chest and gasping for air.

She never dreamed directly about her attacker; instead she was attacked by birds with long sharp beaks, impaled by metal poles, or she fell endlessly towards spiked railings.

"Kate?"

She realised she'd come to a standstill in the middle of the room and blinked, bringing herself back to the present. Anderton and Olbeck were both regarding her with curiosity, tinged with a little concern. She forced a smile. "Just thinking," she said. "Is there any news?"

Anderton looked sombre. "Nothing definite. The docs are not holding out much hope, though, from what little I've been able to glean."

Nothing of the ward could be seen through the opaque glass panels of the swing doors. Kate could picture Madeline Dorsey though, flat on her back on a hospital gurney, tubes and pipes and needles festooning her body. Hanging by her fingernails from a precipice, oblivion in the abyss underneath. *Hold on, Madeline.* Would she drop to join Jack Dorsey, or cling on for her children? Which would it be?

Occasionally, a harassed-looking doctor or nurse would hurry through the doors or past the windows of the ward. Kate knew her job was stressful, but it didn't compare to the working conditions of these people. No wonder Andrew had opted for pathology; not for the physically squeamish, true, but you didn't have to confront the kind of messy human emotions that a doctor to the living would have to deal with on a day to day basis. Thinking of Andrew, she checked her phone, reading his message again. Even as she was contemplating a reply, another text came through from him, repeating his former question. For the first time, Kate was conscious of a surge of annoyance. After a moment, she texted back *sorry, still on case, will be totally shattered so will head to mine. Call you later.* After another moment, she added a kiss to the end of the message and sent it. Then she turned her phone off and put it away.

After another hour's wait, there was still no news. Anderton began to mutter about getting back to the office. Kate volunteered to stay.

"Sure?" asked Anderton.

Kate nodded. Olbeck opted to go back with Anderton. As the two men left, they passed a woman in the doorway, a blonde, dressed in a white linen shirt and blue jeans, with long legs that ended in feet tucked into jewelled sandals. Her face was pretty but terribly drawn, her eyes red and her mouth pulled in tight. She was breathing fast, as if she'd been running. Kate watched her walk to the doorway of the ICU and hover, clasping her arms across her body. Then the woman turned, saw Kate watching her and came towards her.

"I don't know what's happening," she said, her voice ragged with panic. "Why won't somebody tell me what's happening to Madeline?"

Kate got up immediately. "You know Madeline Dorsey?" she asked.

The woman nodded, a quick bob of the head as if her neck were stiff. "I'm her sister. Harriet Larsen." She eyed Kate with confusion. "Who are you?"

Kate introduced herself and Harriet blanched. For a second, Kate was sure she was going to faint and quickly grabbed Harriet's arm, steering her over to the bank of chairs at the side of the room.

"Thanks," said Harriet faintly, when she was safely seated. "I'm sorry, I just don't know what to think – I can hardly take it in. Is it – is it true that Jack's *dead*?"

Kate hesitated. Then she said, "There's been no formal identification just yet, but yes, I'm afraid he is."

Harriet drew in her breath in a whooping gasp. She put one hand up to her trembling mouth, pearly painted nails pressed against her lips.

"Dead..." she whispered, half to herself. Then she cried, big ragged sobs, dropping her head so her blonde hair fell forward in a long, fair curtain.

Kate sat down next to her and kept a hand on Harriet's arm. She let her cry for a few minutes and then gave her arm a comforting little squeeze. It was hard, she supposed, to question someone in the depths of extreme emotional torment, but the truth was that, when someone was emotionally vulnerable, it was sometimes when you could learn some very valuable things. And time, naturally, was always of the essence. She waited for a slight cessation in Harriet's tears and then, after murmuring a few words of condolence, she said "This must be terribly hard for you, Harriet, I'm so sorry. But if you could talk to me now, tell me about Jack and Madeline, it would really help. We need all the information we can get, if we're going to catch the person who did this."

Harriet sobbed harder. Kate said, slightly more firmly. "Do you understand?"

After a moment, there was a bob of the head. Then Harriet raised her tear-stained face. "Yes, I understand," she said, hoarsely. "What – what do you want to know?"

"Well," said Kate. "Let's start at the beginning. You're Madeline's sister, right? Older or younger?"

"I'm the oldest. Madeline's two years younger than I am."

"Do you have any other siblings?"

"No. It's just us."

"What about your parents?"

Harriet gave another gasping breath that was almost a sob. "Mum died about ten years ago. Oh, thank God she's been spared this, thank God... she couldn't have coped. Dad lives overseas. I've spoken to him, he knows... he's trying to get a flight over here—"

"Where does he live?"

"Denmark. Copenhagen. He's half Danish, you see, and after Mum died he went back to live there."

85

Kate nodded, thinking that explained the sisters' fairness and height. "Did you grow up there?"

Harriet shook that long fair mane of hair again. "No, no we always lived in England. Up North, actually, near Harrogate."

"Where did Madeline meet Jack?"

A little colour was coming back into Harriet's face. She sat up a little. "University. They met at Oxford. Madeline was doing English and Jack was doing something very scientific. Particle physics, or something like that. Well, maybe not physics. I never actually understood it and he tried to explain it to me about three times." Harriet was almost smiling. Then memory obviously returned and her face fell apart again. She raised a trembling hand to her mouth. "I can't believe he's dead, I can't *believe* it. Who would have hurt him? Everyone liked him..."

Her voice was dissolving. Kate said quickly, "So Madeline and Jack met at Oxford. That's where Jack met his business partner too, isn't it?"

"Alex? Yes, that's right." Harriet cleared her throat. "They were in the same halls in the first year, had the rooms next to one another." Something seemed to strike her and she turned to Kate, wide-eyed. "God – *Alex* – has anyone told him? Does he know? He'll be devastated, he was Jack's best friend..."

"Don't worry about that," said Kate, patting Harriet's arm. "We'll keep everyone informed, as well as we can. So you've known Jack and Alex since they were at university?"

Harriet nodded. She took a deep breath. "Yes, we've all known each other a long time. Almost like family, you know?" She was on the verge of saying more when they were interrupted by the appearance of an exhausted looking doctor. Harriet jumped up, her face grey.

"Is she – oh my god, is she—"

"Madeline's in a critical condition, Ms Larsen, but we've done what we can for her." The doctor looked at Kate with raised eyebrows and she introduced herself quickly, flashing her card.

He gave it a cursory glance and then turned his attention back to Harriet. "As I was saying, she's as stable as she can possibly be at the moment. I won't pretend to you that her condition is not very serious, very serious indeed, but at the moment, she's holding on."

Harriet sat back down on the plastic chair abruptly. She looked up at the doctor, her face working, hope and despair battling it out for control of her features. "Will she – will she live?"

The doctor half smiled. "She's doing as well as she can, Ms Larsen. You must – you must prepare yourself, though. I simply can't give you that reassurance at this time. I'm sorry."

Harriet dropped her head, nodding minutely. Kate caught the doctor's arm as he was turning away.

"A quick word?" She drew him a little away from Harriet. "I have to ask you to restrict access to Mrs Dorsey," she said. "No admittance to anyone apart from medical staff, okay?"

"Naturally," snapped the doctor. He was a grey-haired man of about fifty and he looked rather outraged, as if Kate were trying to tell him his job. "That goes without saying, Officer."

"Fine," said Kate. "I'll have a uniformed officer here when I leave."

"As you wish. Now, if you'll excuse me..."

Kate watched him walk back into the ICU. Then she returned to Harriet, who was staring blankly at the floor. "Let me get you a cup of tea, Harriet," she said. "And you can carry on with what you were telling me."

Chapter Eleven

"Morning, team," Anderton said the next morning, crashing through the door in his usual ebullient fashion. Kate, Olbeck, Theo, Rav and Jane were ranged around the office, talking amongst themselves. Kate, noticing the empty chair that stood at her old desk, wondered what Stuart was doing and whether he was making any progress. For a moment, she considered what it must be like to work under cover. Having to pretend to be someone else, day in and day out. I'd be a natural at it, she thought, with a wry inner grin. That's what I've been doing since the start of my career.

Her thought process was derailed by Anderton slapping another crime scene photograph on the whiteboard. It was a hugely magnified shot of the word left written in blood at the scene. Kate read it again, remembering the room and the heavy, wet scent of blood in the air. *Killer*. She wondered what Anderton had to say.

"Firstly," he began, hoisting himself onto the edge of a spare desk. "You'll be glad to know that Madeline Dorsey continues to hang on. She's still in intensive care and she's in an incredibly bad way. I don't think we'll be taking any witness statements from her any time soon, but she *is* still alive, so we'll just have to wait and see. Kate, you spoke to her sister at the hospital, didn't you? Anything there we should know about?"

Kate pushed her fringe back from her face. "Her name's Harriet

Larsen and she's the older sister by two years. No other siblings, their mother is dead and their father lives abroad in Denmark. He's been informed and I think he's probably already in the country, by now. Harriet's known Jack Dorsey and Alexander Hargreaves since they – Jack and Madeline – met at Oxford, over twenty years ago. She was too distressed to tell me much more than that, but as far as she was aware, the Dorseys had a good relationship. She wasn't aware of anything out of the ordinary, in terms of strange visitors, odd happenings, etcetera etcetera, but she doesn't live locally, she's London-based and she hadn't seen her sister for a couple of months."

Anderton nodded. "Did she say they were close? Did they talk a lot? Would Madeline have confided in her?"

Kate shrugged. "I'm going back to talk to her again, later today. Hope to get a bit deeper this time."

"Okay, good." Anderton jumped from the desk and began pacing in front of the whiteboards. "Now, we're still waiting on a lot of the forensics and the PM on Dorsey won't take place until tomorrow. I think your beau might be doing that, Kate." He grinned, as did Theo and Olbeck. Kate tried to smile, but was conscious of a spurt of something much like humiliation. Why did Anderton think it was such a bloody big joke that she had a boyfriend? "Anyway, Mark, can you pop along and see what's what when that goes ahead?"

Olbeck nodded. Anderton reached the wall and turned on his heel to retrace his steps. "Kate, I want you to come with me while I go and see young Mister Hargreaves. I want his alibi checked."

He raised a hand. "Standard procedure, people. Don't go jumping to conclusions. The same goes for Harriet Larsen, Madeline's father, the cleaner, and any other staff in the house." Anderton came to a halt and a brief silence fell. "I'm not sure about this one," he said quietly. There was an odd, loaded hush in the room. Every eye was fixed upon him. "There's a few too many undercurrents here for my liking. Is this another terrorist attack?

Or is there something else going on? I don't know. And I know you lot don't know, but that's what we have to find out. I know we can do it. I know *you* can do it."

Kate was suddenly conscious that she was sitting up straighter, shoulders back, like a soldier on parade. How did Anderton *do* that? Look at us all, she thought, watching the others. We'd go into battle for him. I know I would.

Anderton clapped his hands together and the sharp noise broke the spell. He crooked his finger at Kate and she nodded and jumped up, grabbing her coat and bag. She gave Olbeck a wave and then followed her boss from the room.

It wasn't until she was sitting in the passenger seat next to Anderton that she realised that, essentially, this was the first time she and he had been alone together since... well, since that night. Immediately, memories and images recurred and she fumbled with the seatbelt, keeping her head down while she clicked it into place to hide the blush that wanted to surface on her face. Then she smoothed her hair back and sat up, in control of herself again.

"Well, Kate," Anderton said as he accelerated away from the station. "Here we are. How are you feeling?"

He couldn't know what she'd just been thinking of, could he? Was he remembering the same thing? Kate coughed.

"Sorry," she said. "I'm fine. I'm back in the swing of it, now."

"Well, it's certainly back in the deep end, isn't it?"

"You're not wrong. Still, I may as well start as I mean to go on."

Anderton smiled. They waited to join the traffic on the dual carriageway.

It was a day of oddly contrasting weather; brilliant sunshine one moment, spitting rain and scudding grey clouds the next. The car windscreen wipers went on, then off, then on again. By the time they reached the driveway that led to Hargreaves' house, the grey clouds had closed completely overhead, the sky like a dingy flannel blanket that sagged ominously with oncoming rain. The driveway led through pine woods, the trees in regimented lines, obviously an old plantation. Now and again, Kate could see patches of sandy heath in the distance with the spiky shapes of the gorse bushes and the softer outline of heather. The road plunged back into the dimness of the pine forest again, wound gently through the trees, and eventually came out in front of a large and unusual looking house. Part of it looked much older than the other, a square stone building that had been absorbed into a much more modern construction of wooden frames, cedar cladding and large glass windows. The windows ran in a long, unbroken line of glass that stretched around the side of the house, and onto a large wooden jetty and decking area which skirted the edge of a lake.

It looked deserted, although a silver BMW was parked near the front door. Kate and Anderton got out of their own car. The wind gusted through the pine trees on the edge of the shore and Kate could hear the faint lapping of water against the jetty. Overhead came the shrill shriek of some sort of bird of prey. These were the only sounds she could hear and she was reminded of arriving at Jack Dorsey's house on the day after the murder – how silent it had been. For a moment, she felt a ridiculous jump of panic. Were they going to open the front door to find Alex Hargreaves' body, face down in a pool of blood or stabbed so viciously he was unrecognisable?

She told herself not to be so stupid, but she could see Anderton was a little uneasy, too. He glanced towards the silent house, with its blank, shuttered look.

"They like their out of the way retreats," he murmured. "Look at it. You couldn't be much more isolated."

"I know," said Kate. "I guess if you can afford it..."

"What I don't understand is—" Anderton began, and then they both started a little as the front door swung open. For a moment, the doorway showed only blackness and then the tall figure of Alexander Hargreaves moved into the light. He was wearing dark glasses and his expression could not be discerned. After a minute glance at one another, Kate and Anderton approached him.

"I know why you've come," he said in a flat voice.

"You've been informed of the death of Jack Dorsey?" Anderton said and Hargreaves winced.

"The people who broke it to me the first time were a bit more tactful," he said, but in the same flat voice, with no real heat in the reproachful words. He turned away from them and walked back into the house, almost plodding, leaving the door open behind him. Kate and Anderton followed him through the doorway and Kate shut the door behind them.

The interior of the house was large and airy, the wooden beams supporting the roof used as an architectural feature. The floor was tiled in slate, the furniture uncompromisingly modern. There was a lot of leather and glass about, and quite a variety of modern art. Kate's eye was caught by a sculpture that looked like an elongated robot, all twisted silver limbs and square protrusions. Then she noticed a framed painting on the far wall which looked like, and quite possibly was, a genuine Jackson Pollock.

Hargreaves had slumped down on one of the large leather couches. On the glass table in front of him was a square cut-crystal glass, half full of an amber-coloured liquid.

"I don't suppose either of you want a drink," he said, a statement more than a question. Kate and Anderton confirmed his presumption with a shake of their heads. He gave the ghost of a nod and went on, "Well, I'm sure you won't mind if I have one. I need one, by God."

"This must be very distressing for you—" Anderton began and was interrupted by Hargreaves' gasp, a half sob that shook his rigid shoulders. He put a hand up to his mouth, as if holding himself back from retching. As Kate watched, tears began to slide out from under his dark glasses and, a few moments later, Hargreaves removed them, throwing them down on the table next to his whiskey glass. His eyes were red-rimmed and puffy.

"I can't take it in," he said after a moment, in a ragged voice. He rubbed the tears away from his face. "I never thought... Jack – and Madeline too... I can't – I can't bear it..."

Kate cleared her throat, glanced at Anderton for permission. "Mrs Dorsey is still alive," she said quietly.

Hargreaves head snapped up. A variety of emotions chased themselves over his face. "Is that true?" he breathed, as if talking louder would draw a negative response from Kate. "Seriously? She's still alive?"

Kate nodded. Anderton said "She's alive but she's still extremely ill. There's a good chance that she won't make it. I'm sorry."

Hargreaves' eyes filled with tears again and he dropped his head into his hands. "Why would you say that?" he muttered. "Why give me that hope and then take it away again?"

"She's doing as well as she can, sir," said Kate, feeling a wrench of pity. "The doctors are doing all they can do. Her sister and father are with her."

Hargreaves raised his head again. "Harriet's here? I must call her – she must be devastated, poor girl. They were close..."

There was a moment's silence. After another glance from Anderton, Kate leant forward a little. "We'd like to talk to you about Jack and Madeline, if we may, sir. You might be able to give us some more information that could be very valuable."

"Me?" Hargreaves rubbed his face again. "I don't know what I can tell you."

You were only his friend and partner for twenty years, thought Kate impatiently. If you can't tell us anything, then we're really in trouble.

Anderton had clearly been thinking the same thing. He said, with a slight edge to his voice, "The first thing you can tell us, sir, is where you were between the hours of eleven pm and two am on the night of Thursday the ninth of May."

Hargreaves blinked his sore-looking eyelids rapidly. "You want to know where I was that – that night? Why, for God's sake? You can't seriously suspect me of killing my friend?"

His tone was verging on panic-stricken. Anderton raised a placatory hand. "Standard procedure, sir. We ask everyone. It's a process of elimination, nothing more."

Hargreaves continued to blink rapidly. "I was – I was – where the hell was I?" He still sounded panicky. "I'm sorry, my nerves are shot to pieces... that's right, I was at the pub. In the village." Relief flooded his voice. "There's a good gastro-pub in the village, I eat there quite a lot. I was there most of the night, ran into a few buddies, played some pool after dinner. The Haverton Arms, in the village."

"I see," said Kate, writing down the name. "And what time did you leave?"

"Late... I don't know exactly. It's got a late licence. I don't know – maybe one o'clock? One thirty?"

"Did you drive there?"

"I never drive there," said Hargreaves, in a virtuous tone. "Always want a drink, you see, and it's not too far. I can cut back across my land."

"Were you alone?"

"Yes." Now he sounded offended. "What do you mean?"

"I don't mean anything, sir. Do you have a partner? A wife?"

"I'm divorced," said Hargreaves heavily. "Not that I can see the relevance of that to this situation. I got divorced about five years ago and I've been fancy-free and single ever since."

"You've known Jack Dorsey a good few years, isn't that right?" Anderton asked.

Hargreaves nodded. He reached out, picked up his drink with one hand and his dark glasses with the other. He took a sip of whiskey and swung the glasses by their arm.

"Jack and I met at university," he said. "Oxford. We had rooms side by side and somehow we just – well, we just clicked, really.

Chalk and cheese, you know – don't know why we clicked but we did..." He trailed off into silence.

Kate took up the questions. "Had you or Mr Dorsey ever received any threats?" she asked. "Any direct threats, or even implied ones? By letter, or email or in person?"

Hargreaves gave her an incredulous look. "Are you serious?" he asked. "We were threatened *all the time*. We never opened any of our post, it all went through Security and was X-rayed. We've both got unregistered numbers, both careful... but – I don't know – until that car bomb, it never felt very real, if you know what I mean. Just a load of animal rights nutters and old biddies. We never actually felt like they'd actually do us any harm."

"Both you and Mr Dorsey live in extremely isolated conditions," said Anderton, in a neutral tone. "For people who were worried about security, that does strike me as rather strange."

Hargreaves half laughed. "Really?" he asked. "It makes perfect sense to me. It did to Jack. Hide yourself away and you won't be bothered. We've both got serious security systems, I mean, really top notch ones."

Kate and Anderton exchanged glances.

"That didn't seem to do Mr Dorsey much good, in the end," Anderton said eventually.

Hargreaves winced again and dropped his head. "I don't know," he said. "I don't know what happened there. Jack had a security guard, for God's sake—"

"Who is also dead," Anderton went on, remorselessly.

"I don't know," repeated Hargreaves. He was shaking his head from side to side, as if to clear his thoughts. "I don't know how it could have happened."

They left him pouring another glass of whiskey while they took a short walk around the outside of the house, ostensibly to check on his own security arrangements. Kate and Anderton stood side by side on the decking looking over the surface of the lake, its waters ruffled into a multitude of little wavelets by the wind. It was beautiful, undeniably, but there was something lonely, something almost sinister in the landscape, empty of any sign of human activity. Kate thought of being here in the dark, alone, with the night pressing heavily against that great expanse of glass and almost shivered. The lapping of the water against the pillars of the decking was almost hypnotic. Kate found herself staring at a bobble of floating litter trapped against one of the pillars; several screwed up balls of pink paper, a crumpled plastic bag and an empty juice bottle. She focused her eyes on the up and down movement as her mind ticked over what they'd just heard.

"Let's check his alibi on the way back," said Anderton. "We might have a spot of lunch there, if the food is as good as Hargreaves says it is. What do you think?"

They easily found the pub in the village. Part of it was obviously the original building, probably dating back to Tudor times, judging from the broad black beams that ran through the walls, and when they entered it, the pitted stone floor and low ceilings. The windows were mullioned and small. A larger, modern extension had been built onto it, to house the restaurant. Kate had expected Anderton to quiz the staff about Alex Hargreaves' presence on the night of the murder, but he shook his head when she asked and directed her to a table.

"Let's eat, first," he said, with a grin. "I get nervous when I have my food prepared by someone who knows I'm a copper. You never know when they might hold a grudge."

Kate smiled. They found a table by the fireplace which held a vase of silk flowers. Kate relaxed back into her easy chair. Looking around, she realised that this was exactly the sort of place she liked to eat: comfortable, quietly decorated, people dressed casually, talking and laughing without much reserve. The waitress was a large young woman, with a cheerful face and spiky blonde pigtails. A secondary thought followed the first; she really didn't much like the formal restaurants she went to with Andrew – all those hovering, deferential, attentive waiters, the hush that fell over the room that seemed to muffle any attempt at a normal conversation. She was always worried about spilling something on the white linen tablecloths. Kate looked across at Anderton who was reading a menu and commenting enthusiastically on various dishes. Shit, this really did feel like a date. She dragged her own attention back to the menu, her appetite deserting her.

"So," said Anderton, once their food had arrived and they were eating; Kate without much enthusiasm. "How's it feel to be back at work?"

Kate chewed, giving herself time to formulate an appropriate answer. "Fine."

"You're not finding it a bit much? Straight back into a serious murder investigation?"

"No," Kate said, a bit annoyed. She was getting a bit tired of being treated like some fragile, porcelain doll. "I don't find it a problem at all."

"Okay. Just asking."

"Sorry," said Kate. "It's just – oh, I don't know – I get a bit fed up of all this solicitousness."

"I thought you'd be glad people cared," said Anderton.

Their eyes met across the table and Kate was transported back to that one night, a year before, instantly. Damn it, when was she going to get over that? The worst thing was that she could see Anderton was thinking along much the same lines.

There was a moment of loaded silence. Kate was very aware that they were eating in a pub that offered accommodation as well. We could do it, she thought. We could book a room here, just for the night, and stay a few hours. No one would know. She felt giddy with the possibility, almost faint with the longing. I just need to say it and he'll agree.

Oddly, it was the thought of Olbeck's face, if he ever found out, that stopped her. She pictured his shock, her shame and embarrassment... Andrew's face came into her mind a few moments later and then, of course, she was swamped by guilt at him not being the first thing that stopped her.

She stood up abruptly. "Want another drink?"

Anderton indicated their half full glasses. "What's wrong with yours?"

Kate blinked and sat down again. "Oh. Yes. Sorry."

"Are you all right?"

He sounded merely concerned. Perhaps she'd imagined that look in his eyes. Thank God she hadn't done anything about it. Kate realised something – that there couldn't be any more of these cosy little meals together. Not alone. She wouldn't always be able to be strong.

The plump waitress came to see if they wanted anything else and Kate could have kissed her. Anderton replied in the negative to her enquiry, but then followed it up with "But you could help us with something else, if you don't mind."

Anderton pulled a print out of Alexander Hargreaves' headshot from the MedGen website and held it out.

"Can you tell me if you know this man?"

"Alex?" said the waitress. "Seriously, are you, like, joking? He's in here all the time."

"You definitely recognise him?"

"Oh yeah. He's often in here to eat and play the fruit machines."

"Was he here last Thursday night? The ninth of May?"

The waitress narrowed her eyes in suspicion, which then widened as Anderton showed her his warrant card. "Oh," she said. "Right. Yeah. Yeah, he was here then."

"Do you know what time he left?"

"Not sure. Quite late. Sometimes he stays behind for a bit, after we close up. It's like a private party," she added, hastily, as if they were going to arrest her for breaking the licensing laws.

Anderton nodded. "You have CCTV here?" he asked.

The waitress looked positively scared now. "Yeah, we do. Above the front door."

"Could we perhaps speak to the manager?" asked Kate, smiling reassuringly. "What's his name?"

"Tim," the waitress said, one finger up to her pierced lip. "Tim Jones. I'll go and get him, shall I?"

She hurried off before they could speak. Anderton gave a tiny shrug and turned his attention back to his plate. Kate stared after the girl for a moment. The ring in the waitress's lip had reminded her of someone.

"How's Stuart getting on?"

Anderton looked up in surprise. "Stuart? Fine, as far as I know. We'll pull him in for a debrief soon, but he's been reporting in regularly."

"Hmm."

Anderton finished the last mouthful on his plate and pushed it away from him with a satisfied sigh. "You don't like him, do you?"

Kate half-laughed. "I don't even know him."

"Well," said Anderton. "We none of us really know him. I know he's good at his job, and that's exactly the sort of person I needed."

Kate placed her knife and fork together neatly in the centre of her plate. "Who is he, really?" she asked.

Anderton met her gaze steadily. "SO15, Kate. You know that, I don't need to spell it out."

"Why? Why go that far?"

"I had to, Kate. We're out of our depth, here. I need someone on the inside and my team aren't – you people aren't trained for it and you're too well known around here. I needed an outsider, someone with experience." He pushed his chair back a little and added "Someone who knows what he's doing."

Kate smoothed back her hair. "We were out of our depth last year," she said. "You said that. We still got a solve."

"*You* got a solve," said Anderton. "No one's forgetting that."

Kate forcibly restrained her hand from reaching around to rub her back. She saw Anderton's eyes flick downward at the sudden, stilled movement of her hand and was sure he knew exactly what she was trying to stop herself doing.

"I'm fine," she hissed suddenly, as if he'd just told her the opposite.

"I—"Anderton began, but they were interrupted by arrival of the manager of the pub; a tall, gangly young man with anxious eyebrows.

Tim Jones looked barely out of his teens but he grasped what they wanted with speed. After leading them to a viewing room, which reminded Kate a little of the one at Jack Dorsey's house, they could see for themselves a grainy black and white image of Alex Hargreaves entering the pub at eight thirty five pm on the ninth of May and leaving it again, slightly unsteadily, at one forty one am that night.

"Well," said Kate as they drove away. "He's out. What now?"

"Dorsey's PM is tomorrow. We need to interview Harriet Larsen and I need an update from the hospital, see if our Madeline is still holding on."

"I'll do Harriet," offered Kate.

"Good, okay. Take Theo with you."

"Okay," Kate said, suppressing a groan. She looked at Anderton's profile. That moment of weakness back in the pub dining room seemed even more like madness to her now. She pulled out her mobile and texted Andrew; *miss you, shall I come round to yours tonight?* She signed it off with three kisses.

Chapter Twelve

STUART PUT ANGIE'S DRINK DOWN in front of her on the scarred top of the pub table. She was busying texting someone on her phone and was so intent on the task that she barely looked up.

"'Thanks, Mike,'" Stuart said ironically when she finally slipped the phone into her pocket.

"Thanks," Angie said, not rising to the bait. She took a deep swallow of the whiskey and said nothing more.

Stuart sipped his pint. This was the first time he and Angie had been out together, to a pub of her choice. Stuart didn't think much of it – it was scruffy, down-at-heel, with a variety of rough looking men congregating at the bar. Angie didn't seem to notice the squalor. She sipped her drink, looking out the grimy window by the table, her eyes fixed on something that Stuart couldn't see. Again, she was dressed only in black and white.

"Don't you ever wear any colours?" asked Stuart, if nothing else but to break the silence.

Angie seemed to come back to life. She turned to face him, smiling. "Why do you ask?"

"I only ever see you wearing black and white clothes. Is it deliberate, or—"

"Yes, I suppose you could say it's deliberate," said Angie, slowly, as if she'd not considered the matter before. She tapped the side of her head. "All the colour's up here, you see. It's all there and it only comes out in my work."

Stuart didn't know why but he felt awkward when she mentioned anything to do with art. It was pretentious, that was why; it was something that felt phony, unreal. Listen to yourself, he chided himself. Who are you to talk about being false?

He felt impatient – at her, at himself. He was supposed to be on a case, he was supposed to be gathering information. Instead he was sat here, in a shit pub, with someone who wasn't even really part of the scene he was supposed to be investigating. And if he was just going to sit here in silence with Angie, with her occasionally waffling nonsense about 'art', then he'd quite frankly rather be in bed with her, not talking...

He stamped down on his impatience.

"Where did you grow up?" he asked, leaning forward and taking her hand. She had small hands, unvarnished nails edged with occasional rainbow rims of paint.

Angie looked at him. Some indefinable emotion passed over her face in a flicker too quick to gauge. "Guildford," she said briefly.

"I know it," said Stuart. "Do your parents still live there?"

"They don't live there."

"But—"

"I said that's where I grew up. That's not where my parents lived."

"So," said Stuart, confused. "What are you say—"

"I grew up in care," said Angie. She withdrew her hand from his.

"Well," said Stuart in a hearty tone that even he despised. "There's nothing wrong with that."

"There's plenty wrong with that," said Angie. "My mother died when I was little and when I was ten, my father remarried. My stepmother hated me and my father took her side."

"Oh," said Stuart. "That must have been hard." He felt like hitting his forehead sharply. What a stupid thing to say...

"Yes," said Angie remotely. She swallowed the rest of her drink.

"Want another?"

"Yes."

Stuart went to the bar and got another couple of drinks. When he got back to the table, Angie had gone.

Flabbergasted, he stood for a moment with the drinks in his hands. Then he spotted her through the grimy window. She was pacing up and down, talking on her mobile. The walls were too thick and the wind outside was too strong for him to hear what she was saying. As he watched, still clutching his glasses, she ended the call and turned back to the door of the pub. Quickly, he sat down at the table.

She sat down again without comment, picked up her fresh drink and drained it in three gulps. She didn't thank him.

"Are you all right?" asked Stuart.

She gave him a brief, chilly smile. "I'm fine," she said. "I've got to go. See you later."

"Wait—" Stuart said, but his only answer was the pub door banging shut behind her. He sat there for a while, finishing his own drink. What on Earth was that all about? This is stupid, he told himself. Why are you even bothering with her? He tossed the last remaining mouthful of his drink back and jumped up. Sod her, then. It was time to get back to work.

MADELINE DORSEY CONTINUED TO CLING to life. Kate had phoned the hospital before she went to see Harriet Larsen. The prognosis remained the same but, for now, she was alive. Kate swung the car into the car park of the hotel that Harriet was staying in, one of the nicest ones in Abbeyford. She'd called round for Theo but he'd already taken off to re-interview the security guard at the MedGen facility. Kate supposed she should be feeling aggrieved, rather than relieved.

Kate walked into the foyer of the hotel. As old and stately as it looked on the outside, the inside was almost aggressively modern in décor, with a lot of leather, glass and chrome in evidence. Kate was briefly reminded of Alex Hargreaves' house. She found Harriet Larsen in one of the sitting rooms, at the back of the hotel, where a long glassed-in enclosure got the best of the morning sunlight. It was a peaceful place, with comfortable chairs dotted about low tables, gentle jazz music playing on some kind of sound system and a view of the lovely gardens through the conservatory windows. Harriet Larsen sat alone in one of the chairs by the window, an untouched cup of coffee steaming beside her on the table. She was looking out the window but Kate would have sworn she saw nothing of the beauty there.

She greeted Kate with a ghost of a smile and a colourless 'hello'.

"How's your sister?" asked Kate, sitting down opposite Harriet.

Harriet shrugged. "She's holding on. There's no change... she's not better but she's not worse. The kids wanted me to take them to see her yesterday but... I didn't think it was right, they would have been so distressed..." She trailed off, her blank gaze returning to the garden.

"Are the children still at school?"

"No, they're with Jack's parents. I don't know whether that's the best thing - they're all so distressed - I don't know, maybe it's good that they can all be together? They were always close to their grandparents—"

Harriet's voice shook into silence. She put a hand up to her face, pinching either side of her nose. "I don't know what to do," she said after a moment and Kate heard simple bewilderment in her tone.

Did they ever think, these perpetrators, of the utter devastation their actions left behind? Did they ever think about the people left to pick up the pieces? Of course they don't, Kate, you idiot, she chided herself. The surge of anger she felt was welcome, it was that which propelled her to become a detective in the first place.

She brought herself back to the task in hand. "Can I get you some more coffee, Harriet?" she asked, seeing that the cup already on the table had cooled.

Harriet shook her head. "No, thanks. I can't seem to eat or drink anything at the moment, it just makes me feel ill."

"Of course," said Kate, in a sympathetic tone. "Try and eat something though, won't you? Otherwise you really will get ill."

Harriet gave her another pale smile. "Was there something you wanted?" she asked.

Kate became brusque. "Yes, there is. I need you to tell me about Jack and Madeline. I know it's going to distress you, but I'm afraid it's too important to wait."

Harriet sat up a little in her chair. "What do you mean? Tell you *what* about Jack and Maddy?"

Kate pulled out her notebook. "I need to know about their relationship. Their marriage. Did they get on? Was it a good marriage?"

A small white dent had appeared on either side of Harriet's narrow nose. "A good marriage?" she said, tightly. "What the hell has any of that got to do with this... this awful thing?"

Seeing Harriet bristle, Kate held up a placating hand. "It's background we need," she said. "We need to know everything we can about the - the victims of the crime. Often that's more important than the information we get about the perpetrator. Do you understand?"

Harriet still had that pinched look of fury on her face. "No. No I don't understand. I don't know why you need to know all the gory details of someone's private business when it's perfectly obvious that this is someone who's come from outside the house, a stranger, some psychopath. What the hell does it matter whether Jack and Maddy got on? Why does that make any difference at all?"

"So, they didn't get on, then?" asked Kate.

"I didn't say that!"

"You mentioned 'gory details'. Where there any?"

"I didn't say anything of the kind," snapped Harriet. She pushed her chair back, preparing to get up.

"Harriet," Kate said, in a tone that was such that the other woman froze in a half crouch. "Please sit down."

Slowly, glaring at Kate, Harriet lowered herself back into her chair.

"Now," said Kate calmly. "I know you're upset. I know you're functioning under an enormous amount of stress. I can sympathise with that. But the longer you push me away and storm off in high dudgeon, the further and further away we get from catching whoever attacked your sister. Who *killed* your brother-in-law. I'm assuming you don't want that, no matter how much you don't want us digging into your sister's marriage and relationships."

Harriet remained silent for a moment, sitting rigidly upright. Then she blew out her cheeks and slumped back into the chair. Tears ran from the corners of her eyes. Kate guessed that their confrontation had just drained what little emotional energy Harriet had had left and while she felt for her, she was glad that the severity of the situation had been recognised.

After a moment, Harriet wiped her face and sat up again. She leant forward and took a sip of the cold coffee, grimacing. "There's not that much to tell," she said, in a low voice. "Nothing too scandalous, I mean. The weird thing is that Jack and Maddy were always a bit of an odd couple. Jack was always so clever, I mean really intellectual and Maddy - well, she wasn't stupid, not at all, but academia was never her thing. She was always more about having fun, if you see what I mean, although don't get me wrong, she's no ditsy airhead, not at all."

"They met at university?"

"Yes. I'm sure I mentioned that before. Anyway, they got together at uni and stayed together. Got married in... when was it? 2002 and had Alicia a year later. Harry was born in... um... 2005."

Kate was busy scribbling. "Would you say it was a happy

marriage?" she asked, looking up to gauge Harriet's reaction. The other woman half smiled.

"Yes. Yes, it was. It wasn't perfect, of course. What marriage is?"

"Well," said Kate, "I'm sure you're right."

There was a minute of silence broken only by the scratching of Kate's pen on her notepad. Then she looked up. "And?"

Harriet looked at her, warily. "What do you mean?"

"I said, 'and'? What are you keeping back?"

"What—"

"All you've told me is that Jack and Madeline had a good, uneventful, happy marriage. If that's the case, why get so defensive with me when I start asking about it?"

"I - I didn't—"

Kate raised an eyebrow and Harriet collapsed back into her chair again, throwing up her hands. "All right," she almost shouted. Then she sat forward, propping her forehead on her hands. "Jack - he - last summer—" She took a deep breath and said "Last summer, they did go through a bit of a rough patch. Okay?"

She clammed up and Kate raised her eyebrows again. "You'll have to be a bit more specific, Harriet."

Harriet bit her lip but the anger had gone out of her face. She looked sad. "All right. Jack - he had an affair. Last summer."

"Can you tell me anything more than that?"

Harriet pushed her hair back from her face. "I don't think it went on for long. Maybe a couple of months. Maddy - she knew something was up for a while before she found out, but she just thought Jack was really stressed out, about the business."

"So, she did find out?"

"He told her. Apparently he and his lady friend decided that they couldn't live with themselves, broke it off and then Jack told Maddy." Harriet's tone was scathing. "Why he couldn't keep it to himself and spare her the pain, I don't know."

"Perhaps he wanted to make a fresh start?"

Harriet snorted. "Yes, maybe. Or maybe he knew he'd get found out eventually and thought he'd better make sure she heard it from him, rather than from anyone else?"

"Like whom?"

Harriet sat back again. "I don't know. I'm just thinking aloud, really."

"Who did Jack have the affair with?"

Harriet had a lock of hair between her fingers and was twirling it between her finger tips, as if examining it for split ends. Displacement activity – Kate did the same when under pressure.

"Someone he worked with," said Harriet. Then she snorted again. "Of course. Not his secretary, or anything like that. I have to say that Jack wouldn't be that clichéd. It was one of the other scientists, Sarah someone."

"Sarah Brennan?"

Harriet's eyes narrowed. "I think so, yes. I don't remember her surname." She paused for a moment and then said in a rush, "Maddy was, well, *incredulous* when she found out. It wasn't like Jack, he was never a Jack the Lad or anything like that." She smiled faintly. "Jack wasn't a Jack the Lad. He never seemed that interested in women."

"But you've only ever known him as your sister's boyfriend and husband, right?"

Harriet sighed. "Yes. Yes, I suppose so."

Kate flexed her aching hand. "So you were surprised, too? Did Madeline confide in you?"

Harriet nodded unhappily. "She'd been telling me something was wrong for a while. Not that she knew what it was, but... she just had a feeling something was wrong."

"So, what happened when Madeline found out?"

Harriet blew out her cheeks and slumped back into her chair again. "She went crazy. Screamed and threw things. Broke a lot of very expensive ornaments. Could you blame her?"

Kate nodded. She paused for a second because she wasn't sure how she could tactfully ask the question she needed to.

"Did Madeline...um... did she take her anger out on Jack?"

Harriet raised an eyebrow. "Yes. Who else? That Sarah woman?"

"No, I mean... did she express it physically?" Kate sighed inwardly and stopped beating around the bush. "Did she attack him, try to hurt him?"

"I doubt it. Well, she might have thrown something at him—" The penny dropped and Harriet sat bolt upright in her chair. "What are you implying? You can't – you can't think that Madeline did this? You can't think that, you can't!"

People at neighbouring tables were beginning to glance over. Kate raised a soothing hand. "I'm not implying anything, Harriet, certainly not what you seem to think I am. I'm just trying to get the bigger picture, that's all."

"You must be crazy if you think that," said Harriet. Angry tears shone in her eyes. "I'd laugh if it wasn't so – so bloody *tragic*. How dare you?"

Kate soothed and murmured and adopted the least aggressive body posture that she could. For all her outrage and overemphasis, she could see that Harriet was genuinely flabbergasted at the prospect of her sister being thought a suspect. Which, despite their marital difficulties, meant it hadn't even occurred to her. That was interesting.

Once Harriet had calmed down a little, Kate decided on a new tactic. "You've told me about Madeline's reaction to Jack's affair. How do you think Jack felt about it?"

"What do you mean?" Harriet took another sip of her cold coffee and almost gagged. "What do you mean, how did Jack feel about it?"

"You've said that he told his wife that he ended the affair. What reason did he give for doing that?"

Harriet shrugged. "Maddy said he said he knew it wouldn't

work. He didn't want to lose his children and he didn't think Maddy deserved to be a single mum."

"So he was basically renouncing his affair for them?" Kate scribbled down notes to hide her thoughts. That sounded suspiciously noble to her. What if there was another reason? Did Jack Dorsey just not fancy what would no doubt be a whopping divorce settlement if the marriage had broken up? But then, why take the risk of telling your wife, if that were the case?

Harriet had gone back to staring out of the window. "I suppose so," she said, after a moment.

Kate tapped her pencil on her pad. "Did they ever split up, after Jack came clean?" she asked. "Did he ever move out, for example?"

Harriet shook her head. "No. No, that never happened. I suppose after a while it just got – got swept under the carpet."

Kate made a noise of assent. There were still so many questions she wanted to ask but, before she antagonised Harriet any further, she wanted to run a few things past Anderton first. And she knew who else she needed to talk to as a matter of priority. Sarah Brennan.

Chapter Thirteen

KATE HAD ARRANGED TO MEET Sarah Brennan at her home. It was a conversation that was probably better conducted in private, although Kate had been careful not to give any hint of what she wanted to talk to Sarah about when they made the arrangement. Sarah probably thought Kate wanted to talk to her to find out more about Michael Frank. Kate thought about Michael as she drove to Sarah Brennan's house. Were they coming at this from entirely the wrong angle? Could Michael Frank's death really be unconnected with the murder of Jack Dorsey? Was it just horrible coincidence? No, I can't accept that, Kate thought as she found a parking space. She checked her hair was smooth, pulled the shoulders of her jacket straight and got out of the car.

Sarah Brennan lived in a nondescript semi-detached house, built sometime in the nineteen fifties. It wasn't an attractive house but it was well maintained, the small front garden neat, if not particularly interesting to look at; merely a square of well-cut lawn and some shrubs around the borders. The front door was one of those unattractive plastic ones. Kate rang the doorbell and waited. She realised she had absolutely no idea what a scientist like Sarah earned for a living. Presumably working in the private sector, rather than the National Health Service, would be slightly more lucrative...?

Kate had met Sarah before and was therefore, slightly ridiculously, expecting her to be dressed in her usual white lab coat. Of course, at home, Sarah wore casual clothes; jeans, a plain blue T-shirt. She wore no makeup and her dark and plentiful hair was loose around her face. As she made coffee for herself and Kate in the open-plan kitchen and dining area, Kate observed her. Sarah must have been in her late forties, perhaps early fifties. She was slightly overweight, but in an attractive way, with a clearly defined waist, heavy hips and a large bust. Kate thought back to the photograph she'd seen of Madeline Dorsey; blonde, petite, slim and sexy. Why had Jack jettisoned his ostensibly more desirable wife for this no doubt clever but much more homely woman? Kate gave herself a sharp mental slap for thinking such sexist thoughts, but it was true, wasn't it? Why had he done it?

The coffee that Sarah gave her was good, hot and strong. The other woman sat down at the pine kitchen table, opposite Kate. She had shown no sign of emotion, anxiety or upset as yet; the soft edges of her face were placid in repose. There was a kind of restful quality about her, Kate noticed; she gave the impression that she would rarely be hurried, or upset. Was that what had attracted Jack Dorsey?

Kate swallowed her mouthful of coffee and began. "Thanks very much for seeing me, Sarah. I'd like to talk to you about Jack Dorsey."

Sarah's face flickered for a moment but the movement was soon gone. "Oh yes?" she said, a trifle coolly.

Kate took a deep breath. "You and he had quite a long affair, didn't you?"

The histrionics that such an accusation would normally invoke in a suspect weren't forthcoming. Sarah's well-shaped eyebrows twitched upwards for a moment. "Who on Earth told you that?" she asked, in a fairly normal tone.

"Harriet Larsen."

"I don't know who that is, sorry."

"She's Madeline Dorsey's sister."

The calmness flickered again. Sarah's eyes met Kate's and then looked away.

"I see," was all that she said, after a short silence.

"Is it true?"

Sarah placed her empty cup back on its saucer and the chime of china against china rang out into the room. "Oh, yes, it's true," she said.

"Can you tell me—" Kate began and then stopped as Sarah's face suddenly crumpled and collapsed inwards. The other woman began to cry, silently at first and then with harsh, tearing sobs. After a minute, she put her head on the table, hiding her face from Kate with shaking hands.

Kate waited. After an uncomfortably long time, Sarah Brennan's crying tapered off. Eventually, there was nothing left of the storm of emotion but the occasional gasping hitch in her breathing.

Sarah sat up slowly. "I'm sorry," she said. Her voice was steadier than Kate had expected. Sarah looked at her with wet eyes. "I loved him, you see," she said simply.

Kate nodded. She fished a clean tissue from her bag and held it out to Sarah.

"Thanks." There was a pause while she mopped her face and blew her nose. "It was wrong, of course it was. He was married with children. That's why it had to end."

"Really?" said Kate, trying to keep the cynicism from her voice.

Sarah half smiled, not fooled. "I know, it sounds ridiculous. But the thing about Jack—" Her voice shook and she cleared her throat. "The thing about Jack was that he had integrity. I know that sounds stupid, given he was cheating on his wife. But, he really did have integrity. And morals. That's why we – our relationship – couldn't carry on. It was tearing him apart. And he couldn't stand the thought of not living with his children."

Kate clamped down on what she wanted to say, which was

if Jack Dorsey was so concerned about day to day life with his children, why the hell had he sent them away to boarding school?

"How did your affair start?" was what she asked instead.

Sarah looked away, towards the kitchen window. "It was about a year ago." Her gaze was far away, obviously remembering. "It was one of the new formulas, we were working on it together." She transferred her gaze from the window to Kate. "We understood each other. We worked well together."

Kate raised her eyebrows encouragingly and Sarah went on.

"He didn't talk much about his marriage. He and Madeline had met at university and I think – well, I think when he met her he was a bit bowled over that someone like her would go for someone like him. You know. Jack was wonderful but he wasn't – he wasn't glamorous. Not like Madeline."

"Do you think they had a happy marriage?"

Sarah's gaze fell. "I don't know. But - he was lonely. I know he was lonely. I'm lonely myself, sometimes – who isn't?" Her steady brown gaze met Kate's and Kate was unable to look away this time. "We're all lonely sometimes, aren't we? But I tell you, being lonely in a marriage is worse, I think. You're there in life with someone who's supposed to understand you and be with you, and when you don't have that, well, it's a terrible thing really, isn't it?"

"You and Jack talked a lot about work, I presume?"

Sarah half smiled again. "That's right. We're both – we were both passionate about our work. Jack liked to have someone to talk to about it. He doesn't get that – I mean, he didn't get that with Madeline. Even with Alex. Alex is very clever, of course, but I always get the impression that the important thing for him is the money, not the science itself." She was screwing the damp tissue into a ball in her hand. "Actually, it's funny... that's reminded me..." She tailed off.

"Yes?" Kate prompted, after a moment.

"Nothing. It's nothing. It's just that Jack said something about money, once. I know he was worried about it. I just can't remember exactly what he said..."

"Jack Dorsey was worried about money?"

Sarah transferred the tissue ball from one hand to the other. "I don't know, I can't remember. We didn't always talk..."

She smiled a smile that held all kinds of secrets. It was gone in a flash and a heavy look of sadness settled back over her face. Kate tried pushing her for more details on what she'd just mentioned, but Sarah insisted that she couldn't remember anything more. "It was just a throwaway remark. I can't remember any more. I'm sorry."

Kate nodded. There was a short silence before Kate broke it. "I may need to talk to you again, Sarah. If I give you my card, can you call me or contact me if you remember anything else that you think might be important?"

Sarah nodded. "Are you any further with the investigation into Michael's death?"

Kate looked up from closing her handbag after extracting one of her business cards. "Michael Frank? We're following up several leads. That's about all I can say at the moment."

Sarah nodded again. "He was an amazing man, too. I always had a bit – God, this sounds awful telling you now when you know about Jack." She coloured and cleared her throat. "I always had a soft spot for Michael. Nothing happened. He wasn't interested in me, not like that. But... oh, it's hopeless, isn't it?" She didn't appear to expect an answer. "The good die young, don't they? That's what they say."

Tears were forming in her eyes. She didn't see Kate to the door, but remained at the kitchen table, looking off into space again. Kate let herself out, closing the horrible plastic door behind her softly.

Chapter Fourteen

"Well, that's interesting."

Anderton paced up and down the office floor. Kate, momentarily distracted, wondered whether he'd actually wear a path in the laminate, one day. She dragged her attention back to what he was saying.

"Let me recap, Kate. You're saying that Sarah Brennan had a fairly lengthy affair with Jack Dorsey and you're also telling me that she had a thing for Michael Frank."

"Well, that's what she said." Kate brushed her hair out of her eyes. "She also told me that Jack Dorsey was worried about money, or said something of the kind."

Anderton rubbed his chin. "Sarah Brennan, sexually involved with Jack Dorsey, who is now dead. Sarah Brennan, apparently emotionally involved with Michael Frank, who is also dead. Could it be—" He didn't finish, but started pacing again. The others watched him.

"Oh, this is insane," Anderton said, stopping suddenly. "It can't possibly be her. Could it?"

Olbeck shook his head. "Her alibi checks out for both deaths. And why would she kill Dorsey so savagely, anyway? She said she loved him."

"'Hell hath no fury...'" Anderton said absently. He rubbed his chin and looked at the crime scene pictures. "But no, I agree with you. It doesn't make much sense. But, you know, I would swear that there's a woman involved here, somewhere. I can't say why, I can't quite put my finger on it. There's a sexual motive here, sure as eggs is eggs."

"Why do you say that, sir?" asked Theo, frowning.

"I don't know. I can't say. Call it a feeling?"

"So the terrorism's out, then?" said Kate, trying to keep the impatience from her voice.

"No, I'm not saying that, either."

Kate remembered her first impressions of the Dorsey house, when she and Olbeck had arrived after their near miss with the ambulance. Anderton might think that there was a sexual motive underlying the crime, but Kate wondered whether it might be even more prosaic than that. What had her exact thought been? There's a lot of money here...

"I think I should talk to Sarah Brennan again, see if she can elaborate more. Perhaps she can give us some more on Michael Frank," she suggested.

Theo rocked his chair onto its back legs. "What's going on with our undercover guy?" he asked. "Has he got anything at all?"

"Now that," said Anderton, "is a good question. He's bringing me up to speed, later today. I'll be able to debrief you on any developments tomorrow. Now, what else? We're still waiting on a lot of the forensics." He paused again, staring intently at the crime scene photographs. "I'm hoping that throws something up. Well, if no one else has anything earthshattering to impart, let's break it up and get on with it."

The team drifted back to their desks. Kate sat down, adjusted her keyboard and rolled her chair back and forth. She felt impatient, not content to do paperwork. She wanted to be out there, questioning, digging, tracking down suspects. She looked across the table at the empty desk opposite. For a moment, she envied Stuart. He wasn't stuck here, in a stuffy office, trawling through reams of data. He was out there in the field; active, a real participant in the hunt.

Olbeck, *en route* to his office, made a detour to come and

perch on Kate's desk. "That's just reminded me," he said, gesturing towards Stuart's empty chair. "Stuart's coming round to ours for dinner tomorrow. Fancy joining us?"

"Stuart?" Kate said. "Why?" She realised how rude that sounded and rephrased. "Why are you having him round for dinner?"

"Well, it's not like he can just join us down the pub, is it? And it's lonely work, being undercover. I just thought he might enjoy it, get to know us a bit better, you know. That's why you should come. The more the merrier."

Kate tapped her pen on her jaw, thinking. She felt like hugging Olbeck – he was so *kind*. Always looking out for the underdog, for those on the bottom of the heap. Must be why he likes me so much, she thought gloomily.

"Nothing fancy," said Olbeck. "But Jeff's cooking, so it'll be good. Few beers. You know."

"Who else is going?" asked Kate. She could not help the slight quickening of her pulse at the thought that Anderton might be there.

"Oh, the usual. You, me, Jeff, Stuart, of course. But if you're busy…"

"No, I didn't say that," said Kate, quickly. "I've just got to check with Andrew. I have a feeling we're supposed to be doing something."

When Olbeck had gone back to his office, she reached for her phone and scrolled back through her text messages. Yes, here was the message Andrew had sent about their plans for tomorrow night. Dinner with Kirsten Telling and her husband. Doctor Telling was a pathologist who worked with Andrew; Kate knew her briefly through work and liked her as far as she knew her, but… sitting around a dinner table with two pathologists talking shop wasn't the most appetising social engagement she could think of. She hadn't yet replied to Andrew and did so now. With a quickly suppressed stab of guilt, she declined the invitation.

Then she emailed Olbeck. *Am too lazy to walk over, but count me in for tomorrow night. K x.*

STUART ZIPPED UP HIS HOODY and pulled the hood up over his dreadlocks. It was cold for early summer, the blue sky blotted out with threatening grey clouds. As he walked towards the protest table, he was unsurprised to see only two people staffing it and a little cheered to see that they were James and Rosie. Before he could draw near enough to shout hello, he became aware of the angry stance the two of them were taking, squared up to one another, with gesticulating arms and jabbing fingers. Even as he watched, James delivered what was clearly his final hissed remark and stalked off, leaving Rosie behind the stall, flushed and angry, biting her lip.

Stuart's pace slowed to a saunter. He stuck his hands in his pockets, wondering whether to pretend he'd seen nothing or make a suitably tactful remark to Rosie. As he drew level with the table, saying a cautious 'hello', he could see she was close to tears. "You all right?" he asked, throwing discretion to the winds.

Rosie sniffed and swiped her hand across her cheek. "Oh, I'm fine," she said crossly. "Actually, I'm not fine. You probably saw what just happened."

"Well..."

"James and I had a bit of a row. He's so bloody *stubborn*—" She clamped her mouth together, as if she wanted to say a lot more, turned away and busied herself with tidying the leaflets into a pile.

"Do you need a hand?" Stuart offered.

Rosie exhaled. She shoved a pile of leaflets away from her, put her hands into the small of her back and stretched. "You know what, Mike?" she said. "I'm sick to death of it all. All of it. I have had enough today, I really have."

Stuart's heartbeat picked up a little. The mood she was in, he might be able to get more information that he'd ever managed before. "You know what?" he suggested. "You're right. Let's leave it for today. Come for a drink."

Rosie took her hands away from her back and looked at him in surprise. She had clearly not been expecting him to say that but, after a moment, she lifted her chin and said "Yeah, you're right. I'd love a drink."

"Let's go, then. I'm buying."

They went to the same pub they'd visited on the night they met. Rosie made a beeline for a table at the back while Stuart bought the drinks. When he brought them to the table, she was staring into space, chewing her lower lip.

"Sorry," she said as he sat down. "I'm still angry, I guess."

"Want to tell me about it?"

"There's nothing really to tell... he wants one thing and I want another. Humph." She downed half her pint in three large gulps. Stuart watched her long, smooth throat ripple and reminded himself to keep his mind on the job. Inevitably, his thoughts went to Angie. Three days now, without any contact. It worried him how much he missed her.

"Seen Angie lately?" he asked, before he could stop himself.

Rosie, who'd been in the middle of a monologue about James' shortcomings, looked surprised. Then she frowned. "Why'd you ask?"

"I just wondered. I thought you guys were friends."

"What's James been telling you?"

"Nothing," said Stuart, startled at her tone. "I haven't – I haven't heard anything."

Rosie knocked back the rest of her drink in one go. "Well, we are *friends*," she said, wiping her mouth with a gasp. "But that's it."

"Right," Stuart said. Thinking he'd better change the subject, he asked her what she wanted to drink and went up and bought another round.

After another few pints, Rosie's mood changed again. Stuart was being as attentive and charming as he could be, pulling out all his best activist anecdotes and making her laugh and shriek with recognition.

"All4One, I remember them. I used to go out with a guy who was with them. He was this mad painter, used to do these huge junk sculptures, like robots made out of cars and things."

"Yeah, I know," said Stuart, nodding. All4One were a radical group, half creative types, half anti-globalisation activists who'd come to national attention when they'd turned a huge empty Hampstead mansion into a commune and art studio before being violently evicted, two months later. "I saw his stuff at Glastonbury, I think," Stuart went on. He tipped his empty pint glass back and forth, in what he knew would be a vain prompt for Rosie to buy her round. "Did you ever live there?"

"At the HQ?"

"The Hampstead place, yeah?"

Rosie shook her head. "No, never lived there. We had a few parties there. Then, I don't know, it all got a bit weird..."

There was a subtle shift in the atmosphere that made Stuart sit up mentally. "Oh yeah?" he asked, careful to keep his tone casual.

Rosie had drunk enough to throw caution to the winds. She propped her chin on one unsteady hand, looking at Stuart intently through her fringe.

"Yeah, weird. When I was there it was all about art and creativity, all that life force stuff – used for good, you know. But then Kitten came and suddenly it was all about—"

She broke off suddenly and went to tip up the last of her fourth pint. Stuart drummed his fingers on his leg under the table, unsure of whether to break the sudden bond that had appeared between them in order to get her another drink. He knew as well as anyone that when you broke up a two-some, it was sometimes impossible to regain that fragile connection.

He stayed put.

"Kitten?" he asked, with just the right amount of curiosity in his voice. He hoped.

Rosie was staring into the depths of her empty glass. She turned it round and round, watching the last few dregs spiral at the bottom of the glass. "Yeah," she said eventually. "He's a bit of a nutter."

"Who is he?"

Rosie shrugged. "One of Angie's friends. Huh, *friends*." She smiled cynically for a moment and Stuart was surprised at the stab of jealousy he experienced as he got her meaning. "He used to be in the army, fought in Iraq. He's really into animal rights; I remember him saying that human beings were the worst things on the planet, once. I think he likes animals a lot more than he likes people. He hates people."

Stuart was listening, holding his breath. He knew he'd heard that strange name before – where had it been? After a moment, it came to him. The party at the squat, James saying with a loaded voice to Angie – 'Seen Kitten lately?' And she'd turned and said coolly, 'Not lately, no...'

Rosie had taken out her phone and was scrolling through her photographs. She held the screen out to Stuart. "Here's HQ. Look at it, isn't it massive? Bloody obscene, something that big belonging to one person."

Stuart looked. There was Angie, sexy in a tight black dress, incongruous against the graffitied wall that stood in the background. She was looking at the camera, the man beside her was looking at her. Again, Stuart felt that jump of jealousy and stamped down hard on it. He looked more closely at the man. Tall, well-built, balding. One muscular arm bore a sleeve of blue and red tattoos.

"Who's that beef-cake?"

Rosie giggled. "That's Kitten."

Under the table, Stuart clenched his fist in a jump of exhilaration. He wondered whether he'd be able to steal Rosie's phone without her knowledge. Probably not...

Stuart made interested noises and Rosie scrolled through a few more photos. The man called Kitten appeared in several more; in one he was smiling at the camera, the maw of a broken or missing tooth visible far back in the right hand side of his mouth, crows-feet around the dark eyes. Dead eyes – there was nothing there, in the depths. Stuart could feel the first prickle of anticipation as he looked at the man in the photograph. He'd seen eyes like that before. You're it, mate, he thought. I've got you.

"Kitten's a weird name for a bloke," he said, still with a casual note in his voice. Rosie was still scrolling through her pictures, chuckling, occasionally shaking her head.

"Yeah, well, it's not the weirdest thing about him by a long shot, take it from me."

"What's his real name?"

"Guy. Guy Something. Guy Ward? Something like that. Don't know, really."

Rosie tapped the screen of her phone. She was casting suggestive glances at her empty pint glass. Stuart knew he should keep questioning her, but he was already late for Anderton. Besides, get her any drunker and she'd be incoherent anyway.

"Listen, Rosie, I've got to go. Got to see someone about a dog."

She smiled lopsidedly at that. He took pity on her and handed her a ten pound note.

"Get yourself another drink. Only one more though, okay? Get yourself a taxi home."

She pouted but took the money. He had a moment's qualm that he was leaving a vulnerable girl to drink by herself in a not-too-salubrious pub. There was an older woman behind the bar though, and he thought she'd probably keep any eye out. He chucked Rosie under the chin and left, the name running through his head. Guy Ward. Guy Ward. I've got you.

Chapter Fifteen

WHENEVER KATE AND OLBECK GOT together outside of work, they had a kind of informal rule that they didn't talk shop. If Jeff was there, being a polite man who was interested in other people, he'd sometimes ask Kate about her work and she'd happily tell him what she could. But, most of the time, the three of them talked about other things: art and music, films and politics, and funny anecdotes from their past. Kate was unsure of what was going to happen tonight, with Stuart there as well. Would he even be able to talk about the case, given that what he was doing was so secretive?

He was the last to arrive and although he was smartly dressed, in a suit and white shirt, accompanied by a really good bottle of wine, Kate was quite shocked at the look of exhaustion on his face. His eyes were ringed with shadow and his cheeky grin, that had so annoyed her on first meeting him, was nowhere to be seen. It must be tiring, she thought, having to pretend to be someone else all the time. Never able to let your guard down. Not knowing who you could trust. No wonder she'd heard that undercover officers tended to burn out quickly. A few years and they were out of the game. Perhaps that wouldn't be such a great career move for her, after all.

Mark and Jeff were charming hosts and Kate could see Stuart gradually relaxing as he was plied with food and drink, and kind attention. She took a back seat, maintaining a civil silence while the men chatted. She wanted to do full justice to Jeff's excellent cooking, too – Kate really did hope Mark appreciated his good fortune in having a partner who was so skilled in the kitchen. Andrew is too, she reminded herself, dutifully.

After a short period of inattention, Kate came back to the present, realising Stuart was actually addressing her directly. He was asking her about the serial killing case last year, asking her about her injury. She felt a flash of annoyance that, for once, she'd actually managed to forget about that for half an evening, only to be rudely reminded.

"I'm fine now," she told him, trying not to sound too cool.

"It's not easy though, is it?" said Stuart, actually sounding rather humble for a change. "I got shot once. That took years to get over."

"Well, it would, wouldn't it?" said Kate, trying not to let her eyes widen. She struggled for a moment, not wanting to indulge her curiosity – she was sure he was just saying it to show off – and then gave in. "What happened?"

"It was a drug-ring case. Only my second job. Working alongside a lot of bad people and I ran into the wrong one, one night."

"Bloody hell," said Olbeck, topping up Stuart's glass. "Where did you get shot?"

"We were down on the docks—"

"No," said Olbeck, laughing. "Where physically?"

"Oh, right." Stuart smiled, a ghost of his previous grin. Kate assumed that it was a memory that probably wasn't a great deal of fun to recall. "In the chest. Shattered my collarbone on this side." He indicated with his hand. "I was lucky, though. He was going for my heart."

"You must have been out of action for a while," said Kate, thinking of her own long, slow recovery.

Stuart nodded. "I was. It was worth it, though. We smashed the ring. Good job too – these people were scum."

He looked grim, suddenly, truly forbidding. There was a short silence and Jeff got up to clear the plates.

"It's why I joined the force," Stuart said suddenly. He was looking down at the table, his brows drawn together. "My brother was a heroin addict. He died young."

"Oh, I'm sorry," Kate said. She felt a sudden and genuine surge of sympathy for him. One of her older siblings had died in a car crash at eighteen. Kate had barely known her half-brother, born years before she was, but she still remembered the devastation that his death had caused her family. That was when her mother's drinking had taken a distinct turn for the worse, not that it had ever been very good. Kate hadn't spoken to her mother in almost two years. They were estranged, she supposed, and despite her awful childhood, despite everything, she was swamped by a sudden wave of depression.

She and Stuart were briefly alone at the table as Jeff took plates into the kitchen and Olbeck went to find more wine. Their eyes met and Kate was shocked again by the sudden connection she felt with Stuart – not a sexual feeling, but a brief flicker of emotional closeness. It only lasted a moment, before his gaze dropped away and Olbeck came back with an opened bottle, but the small glow of warmth remained.

They all talked about other things and police work wasn't mentioned again until right at the end of the evening, when Olbeck asked if there was any progress. Stuart nodded. "We've got a name. A name with a history. I expect Anderton will brief you all tomorrow."

"Well, that's great," said Olbeck. He was helping Kate on with her jacket. "Does that mean you're back with us, again?"

Stuart half laughed. "I wish. Not yet. There's still a lot of work to do, so..."

Kate picked up her handbag. "Just as well the boys had you over for dinner tonight, then," she said, smiling. "Sounds like you won't be joining us for after work drinks, any time soon."

"No, that's right. And thanks," said Stuart holding out a hand to Olbeck. Jeff was lounging in the kitchen doorway, a tea towel slung over his shoulder. "Thanks very much, guys. I enjoyed it."

"Our pleasure," said Jeff.

Kate and Stuart left the house together, waving to Olbeck and Jeff, who were framed in the doorway.

"Can I give you a lift?" asked Kate and caught herself, realising that she wasn't even supposed to be seen talking to him in public.

"No, I'm good," Stuart said, absently. "My car's just up here. Listen, Kate..."

He trailed off. Kate waited and then said, "Yes?" in an encouraging way.

"Doesn't matter. Forget I said it. Thanks, Kate, good night."

And with that, he was gone. Kate walked slowly to her own car, pondering. What had that been all about? She got the impression that he'd wanted to confide in her. Was that possible? Confide in her, a virtual stranger, because of that odd little moment of connection they'd experienced? He might have been about to ask you out, she told herself; but that was vanity talking. It wasn't the impression she got. Dismissing her inner musings, she unlocked the car, got in, re-locked the doors and drove away.

YOU FOOL, STUART TOLD HIMSELF as he unlocked his own car. For a second, he'd almost told Kate about Angie; how much he missed her, why he had no idea how she had so strong a hold over him. The words had come surging up his throat and, for a moment, he'd actually thought about saying them. You fool. Why would Kate even be interested, anyway? He liked her, although he got the impression she didn't think much of him. In a funny way, Kate reminded him of his kid sister, Charlotte – Charlie. Physically they weren't much alike, but Kate had that same sort of doughty scrappiness he associated with Charlie – a kind of 'screw you, world, I can take care of myself' type aura that shone out over her neat exterior. It was clear to see that she'd been pretty shaken by that knife incident last year, but that wasn't surprising. Theo had told him the whole story, the second day he'd joined the Abbeyford team, and then when Kate had finally made it back to the office, Stuart could see the vulnerability that lurked under her cool manner. Of course, it was hard getting back on the job, he really did know that.

He drove back to his bedsit slowly, tired after a long day and somnolent with Jeff's good food. That Mark Olbeck was a lovely guy, too. It was funny, but he'd never had a gay mate before; not that he was homophobic or anything like that, it just hadn't happened. Stuart wondered what it would have been like for Olbeck, declaring his sexuality to the rest of the officers in the station. Pretty nerve-racking, and that was from someone who'd put their life on the line on more than one occasion.

Stuart parked the car, switched off the engine and sat for a moment, rubbing his eyes. He was bushed. He wearily climbed the dank little staircase to his room and opened the door, realising a second too late that it was already ajar. He stopped dead, nerves singing. There was someone in his bed.

A second after the adrenaline kicked in, the bedside light snapped on. It was Angie, resting on one pale arm. He could see she was naked. She said nothing, but looked at him with a heavy-lidded gaze, that incredible face wearing that same indefinable look of challenge that he'd first noticed about her.

"Evening," said Stuart, his tone belying the thudding of his heart. "How did you get in?"

Angie smiled. "Your neighbour was kind enough to help me out."

"My neighbour?" Stuart had barely seen any of the other occupants of the adjoining rooms. And how the hell did his neighbour have a key to his – Stuart's – room?

Angie's smile grew. "Okay, he didn't. I picked the lock. It's only a Yale one – quite simple, really. You really ought to get a stronger one fitted."

"So I can see." Stuart hadn't as yet made any move towards the bed. That faint warning bell was ringing louder this time, like an increasingly loud siren in his mind. *Danger ahead.*

Angie twitched the covers a little and he could see a little more of her. He swallowed. He thought he'd missed her, but up until this moment, with Angie present before him, he hadn't quite realised the depths of his longing. It was visceral.

"Come on, then," said Angie gently, almost maternally. As he stumbled towards the bed, Stuart's last coherent thought was of his dead brother, lost back there in the past. I miss him, he thought, and then Angie's arms were around him and he didn't think of much else for what seemed like a very long time.

Chapter Sixteen

THE SUNLIGHT WOKE HIM, STREAMING through the curtains that didn't quite meet in the middle, lancing through the gap like a spear of molten gold. Stuart lay there quietly, watching the dust motes spin and dance in the beam of light. He was conscious of Angie, breathing quietly beside him. It was the first time they'd slept together, in the literal sense of the word. Perhaps he hadn't so much fallen asleep as much as passed out, exhausted by the long day and by Angie's voracious demands.

Moving quietly, he eased himself out of bed. He'd spotted Angie's handbag over by the chair against the wall. Stamping down on the last remnants of conscience that still remained, even after years of undercover work, he extracted her phone and, keeping a wary eye on her sleeping form, scrolled through the large list of names and numbers stored in the Contacts section. He went straight to the 'Ks' and, despite knowing he'd find it, there was still the drop and twist of his stomach as he saw Kitten's name and a mobile number underneath it. Quickly, he scribbled it down. Angie made a muttering, sighing sound from the bed and Stuart, heart thumping, put the phone back, noting as he did so that the top contact in Angie's phone was a number stored with no corresponding name. He had no time to investigate further – Angie was waking up. He moved swiftly away from her bag, busying himself at the little table where he kept an electric kettle and instant coffee.

"Morning," said Stuart casually, handing her a mug of coffee. He realised he had no idea how she liked it, but guessed she would drink it black with no sugar. She took it from him with no comment but a smile. She sat up in bed quite unselfconsciously to drink it. Stuart tried not to be distracted by the sight of her breasts, something he was still unused to.

Angie drank her coffee in several fast gulps, put the cup to one side, yawned and stretched like a cat.

"I wondered what had happened to you," said Stuart, trying not to sound accusing. Angie smiled.

"I've been busy. I'm working on a big piece at the moment."

"Piece?"

"A new multi-media project. It'll be the best thing I've ever done." She went far away for a moment, her eyes looking at something that Stuart couldn't see. "It's *consumed* me."

Stuart felt embarrassed when she talked like this. It sounded, what? Pretentious. Phony. She believed it, though, and that was somehow more embarrassing than anything else.

"That's good," he said, rather limply.

Angie came back to life. "I can't show you anything yet," she said. She smiled. "Soon you'll be able to see."

"Can't wait," said Stuart, grinning. "Will this be the piece that makes you famous?"

"Oh yes," said Angie, seriously. She cocked her head on one side for a moment. "I can't show you *that* at the moment, but have a look at some of my early work."

Oh God... Stuart pinned an interested look in his face whilst Angie scrambled out of bed and hunted in her bag. He could feel the scrap of paper with Kitten's number on it burning a hole in his pocket.

If he had put the phone back in the wrong place, Angie didn't seem to notice. She retrieved her phone and flung herself back on the bed next to him. He kept that interested look on his face as she scrolled through a variety of photographs. He didn't know much about art – and I don't know what I like, he finished with an inner grin.

Angie's stuff was a mixed bunch; some sculpture, some paintings, an enormous collage that seemed to incorporate a television screen that showed the same loop of film over and over again, a woman riding a bicycle with a large fish in the front basket. Stuart said 'fantastic', 'that's incredible', 'I like what you've done there' and other such inanities. He had the feeling that Angie was barely listening to him anyway; she was absorbed in her pictures.

"This is my last but one project," she said eventually.

"Oh yes?"

"Yes."

She held the screen in front of him. It was another collage, with an integrated screen, but this time, the film shown was – Stuart blinked – a montage of scenes of animal cruelty. A fox disappearing under a yapping flood of beagles. A cow, stun-gunned, its freshly cut throat glistening as the blood pumped away. A blurry shot of someone beating a cow at what looked like a market.

"Far out," he said faintly. He could tell Angie was looking slyly sideways at him, wondering whether he was going to react. "That's... um... powerful."

"It is, isn't it?" said Angie, with satisfaction. "Really makes you look twice. I got some very interesting reactions to that one."

"I'm not surprised."

"That was a commissioned piece."

"Really?" said Stuart, unable to hide the surprise in his voice. Before he could stop himself, he blurted out, "So, people actually *buy* your stuff then?"

A chill settled upon the room. Stuart mentally kicked himself and tried to make amends. "It's fantastic, though," he said hastily. "Really powerful."

Angie said nothing. She slid her finger across the screen of her phone in one slow, deliberate swipe, hiding the pictures from view.

Stuart knew when to stop. This was a bad time to ask what he had to ask, but he had the feeling that it wouldn't make much difference now, anyway.

"Listen," he said. "I'm trying to get hold of someone and I think you might know them."

"Oh yes?" she said, indifferently. Her features had settled into a beautiful but stony mask.

Stuart swallowed, trying to get some liquid into his dry mouth. "His name's Guy, but everyone calls him Kitten."

The pause was there; infinitesimal, but there. His heart sank. Then Angie said coolly, "Kitten? I haven't seen him in months. What do you want him for?"

It was an innocent enough question, but there was something in her inflection that made Stuart's heart spike again.

"Nothing much," he said, as casually as he could. "I knew him a long time ago, at HQ. Just wanted to catch up with him, if he's around."

"HQ? What's that?"

His heart dipped again. He remembered Rosie's photograph of her, with Kitten by her side.

"Just a place. So, you haven't seen him, or anything? I used to have his number, but I lost it."

Angie got up and started pulling on her clothes, the same white vest and black combat trousers that he'd seen her wear before. "He changes it all the time," she said. There was a tiny mirror hanging by the door and she took a brief, assessing look into it, smoothing her flat cap of hair back into place.

Stuart knew when to not push things. "Thanks for coming over," he said. "Your art is fantastic."

She gave him a brief smile, which he saw in her reflection in the mirror. Then she snatched up her bag and was out the door, closing it behind her in a movement that wasn't quite a slam.

KATE INTERVIEWED SARAH BRENNAN AT the laboratories the next day. Expecting her, Sarah ushered her into a small office that stood off the corridor from the main laboratory and shut the door.

"Parvinder's ears are on stalks," Sarah said, pulling a swivel chair forward for Kate to sit in. "I thought we could probably do with some privacy."

"Yes, indeed." Kate settled herself and began. "Sarah, when we met before, you mentioned something about Jack Dorsey and money – specifically that he was worried about money. Can you tell me anything else about that?"

Sarah hadn't sat down, possibly because there wasn't another chair. She rested against the edge of a desk, her arms folded across her chest. She was composed today, no sign of tears, her voice quiet but firm. "I already said, it was just a throwaway comment. I don't really know what I can tell you. It was just one conversation we had, and not much of anything of significance was said."

"I'll be the judge of that," Kate said, as nicely as she could. She leant forward a little. "What exactly did Jack say?"

Sarah frowned. "I can't remember it word for word."

"Just tell me what you can remember."

Sarah's gaze dropped. "We – we were in bed. Just talking, you know, lying next to one another. Jack went quiet and I – God forgive me, I thought he was thinking of Madeleine – but when I asked, he said something like 'Sorry love, it's just work. There's something not quite right at work.' And of course, I said, 'What do you mean?' thinking he'd run into difficulties with the new formula and I was feeling a bit miffed that he hadn't said anything to me before, you know, professionally. And then he said something like 'No, it's money. Just money stuff.'"

Kate paused in her scribbling. "That's it?"

Sarah shrugged. "That was pretty much it. Oh, and he said something about auditing, or auditors, or something like that."

"He never mentioned this again?"

"No."

"When was this? Can you remember?"

Sarah shifted her position and re-crossed her arms. "I can't be sure, exactly. Since you asked me last, I've been thinking about it and it must have been a few months ago. It wasn't that long ago, I know that."

Kate paused. Something wasn't adding up here. "Sarah," she said slowly. "You told me that your affair with Jack Dorsey finished last autumn. So what were you doing, making pillow talk a few months ago?"

She held Sarah's gaze until the other woman's eyes wavered and dropped.

"Sarah?"

Sarah raised a hand to her face, dropping her head forward. "Things sort of started up again," she said, in what was almost a mumble. "We just – we just couldn't seem to stop ourselves."

"So, tell me exactly, were you and Jack still seeing each other when he died?"

Sarah continued to hide her face and Kate repeated her name sharply. The other woman's head snapped up sharply. Her eyes were brimming with unshed tears. After a moment, she nodded, causing the tears to spill over. She swiped at her own cheeks angrily, wiping them away.

Kate sighed inwardly. "Did Madeline know?"

"I don't think so."

"You don't *think* so? What did Jack say?"

"What do you mean?"

"I mean," said Kate, unable to keep the sarcasm from her voice this time. "Was there going to be another heroic casting aside of his lover for the good of the family? Or did he learn from the last time and decide discretion was the better part of valour?"

Sarah flushed and bit her lip. "He didn't say," she said after a moment.

Kate could see her trying to get angry and decide that it

possibly wasn't the brightest thing to do. "What were you doing on the night of Thursday the ninth of May?"

Sarah blinked. "What do you mean?"

"Can you tell me what you were doing on the night of Thursday the ninth of May, specifically between the times of eleven pm and two thirty am?"

Kate knew Sarah's alibi had already been checked, for the times of both the crimes, but she wanted to see what she said. Sarah told her more or less exactly what she'd said before in her statement; she'd visited her elderly mother and stayed the night, the two of them having dinner at home and watching television, before bed at eleven pm. Kate nodded, satisfied. She knew from reading the CCTV reports that Sarah's car had remained outside her mother's address all night.

"I need to talk to Alex Hargreaves," Kate said, getting up. Sarah moved back a little. She was holding herself rigid, her face hard with the effort of appearing composed. "Do you happen to know if he's here?"

Sarah cleared her throat. "He's not, as it happens. He's taking a few days' leave."

"Perhaps you should do the same," said Kate. She said it gently, but the other woman flinched, still raw with revelations. Kate said goodbye quietly and left the office, shutting the door behind her and leaving Sarah Brennan inside, silent and staring off into space.

Chapter Seventeen

"Morning, team," Anderton bellowed, crashing through the door in customary style. "I hope you're all feeling bright-eyed and bushy-tailed this morning, as we have a lot to get through. Wake up, young Theo—" he caught the new DS in a huge yawn. "Late night, was it? Chuh, you young things. Anyway, settle yourselves and let's get started."

Kate sat up keenly. Again, she felt that welcome sense of enthusiasm, of excitement, almost; that things were finally moving and she was part of it.

Anderton indicated a large pile of cardboard folders on his desk. "Right, PM results are back, as well as various forensic reports from the crime scene – the Dorsey crime scene. Take a while to familiarise yourself with what's in them, but I'll summarise for you; Dorsey died of multiple stab wounds, inflicted by a right-handed person. He had defence wounds on both hands and forearms, indicating he was facing his attacker at the time. Darryl Timms, the security guard, died of a single incision to the neck, also from a right handed person. No defence wounds. He was attacked from the side."

"What about Madeline Dorsey?" asked Kate, for the benefit of the team. She and Anderton had already discussed it beforehand.

"The doctors have indicated that there's a possibility that her injuries could be self-inflicted. *Could* be."

There was a brief silence in the room. Anderton gestured to

Kate. "Kate also has some information that might be pertinent. Take it away, Kate."

Kate cleared her throat. "Sarah Brennan's affair with Jack Dorsey wasn't over when he was killed. She confirmed to me yesterday that they were still seeing each other."

Theo whistled softly. "So, did his wife find out? Is that what you're saying?"

Anderton hoisted himself onto the edge of his desk. "I'm not saying anything, I'm just putting the facts out there. Madeline Dorsey found out her husband was having an affair in the late summer of last year."

"He told her," Kate broke in.

"Yes, he told her. Now, we have her sister's statement that Madeline reacted very badly to this unwelcome news. And what's more interesting, is that there didn't seem to be any sort of long-term fallout from Dorsey's revelation. By that, I mean there wasn't any divorce, or talk of divorce, or Dorsey moving out, or anything like that, that we know of."

Jane raised a hand. "Could that be because Madeline Dorsey was afraid of losing her husband? Might she have just turned a blind eye or told herself that it didn't matter because now it was over?"

Anderton nodded. "Could be. God, I wish that woman would get better, we'd have all the answers we need, then... " Kate raised a censorious eyebrow at his apparent callousness and he caught her eye and grinned. "Of course, we hope she recovers for her own sake, as well. Happy, Kate?"

Kate half-smiled. "Sir, can I just clarify something?" she asked. Anderton nodded. "Am I right in thinking that you're inferring that if Madeline Dorsey found out that her husband was having an affair again that... well, she could have – might have – reacted violently?"

"It's possible," said Anderton. "In an infinite universe, everything is possible."

Olbeck was shaking his head. "I'm not buying it," he said. "Attack her husband, okay, maybe. But to then kill the security guard at the same time? It doesn't make sense. The timing's all wrong. Darryl Timms died *first*, according to the reports. I just cannot see a nice, middle-class mother of two cold-bloodedly deciding to murder her husband and getting rid of the only possible witness first." He strode up to the photograph of Timms' body and pointed. "Look, look at that incision. That's almost, well, professional."

"Exactly," said Anderton. "We are still mired in confusion here. We've got motive for Madeline Dorsey, but there's too many conflicting factors for us to comfortably be able to point to her as our prime suspect. And you're forgetting something else."

Everyone looked at him expectantly. He jumped off the desk and joined Olbeck at the whiteboards, tapping another crime scene photograph. "What about that?"

His finger rested on the photograph of the word written on the wall of the Dorsey's drawing room in blood. *Killer*.

"A bluff?" suggested Rav, tentatively.

"Mmm... possibly." Anderton didn't look convinced. "If we accept Madeline Dorsey is the killer, then surely that means the bombing of Michael Frank's car is actually unrelated to this crime. Does that sound likely to you all?"

There was another silence.

"Anyway," said Anderton, as they all stayed close-mouthed. "I've got something else for you, on that. We have a name from our man in the field."

He held up a print out, an arrest report with the usual mug shot in the top left corner.

"Guy Wade, AKA Gerry Ward, AKA 'Kitten'. He's an ex-soldier, served in Iraq and Afghanistan. Dishonourably discharged from the army in 2010. Has been arrested numerous times for violence at demonstrations. Strong links with the Animal Liberation Front.

Most definitely someone we want pulled in for interview, under caution if necessary. Now, we just have to find the bugger."

There was a noticeable stir of excitement in the room. Anderton smiled, conscious of it. "All right, team. Top priority – find Guy Wade and bring him in. I want Sarah Brennan to make another statement. If anyone else has anything to add, let me know. Got it?"

There was a flurry of nods.

"Great," said Anderton. "Off you go, then."

The room hummed with that concentrated, silent busyness of a group of people intent and focused on their roles. Kate took the print out on Guy Wade and began to scour the multiple entries documenting his arrests and cautions on the relevant databases. At last, she felt like she was actually doing something positive. She found a name and address that she knew would be useful and tapped keys to print out the details, muttering "Yes, yes, yes," under her breath.

She looked up as someone paused by her desk.

"Got a last known address," said Theo, waving a sheet of paper in front of Kate's nose. She batted it away.

"Fine, I'll top that with the army contact who headed the regiment that Wade used to be belong to."

"We'll do mine first, right?"

Kate sighed inwardly. "If we must."

"Come on, let's go, then." Theo was almost bouncing on his feet. Despite herself, Kate was amused.

"I'm driving," Theo warned.

Kate sighed. "Of course you are."

She waved at Olbeck as they left the office, squashing down the wish that he were coming with her, rather than Theo. As well as being a cocky little so-and-so, Theo liked to listen to rap and RnB as he drove, which gave Kate a headache. Would it be rude, she wondered, to wear her iPod on the journey?

The traffic was fairly heavy on the way out of Abbeyford – the council were engaged in their seemingly interminable plan of digging up every available road to cause maximum inconvenience to all with the resulting roadworks. Theo said as much to Kate, except in words that were somewhat shorter and rather more Anglo Saxon in tone.

"Yes, I know," said Kate. The car inched forward another foot. "Where are we actually going?"

"Swindon. The landlady of the flat that Wade used to rent lives there. He skipped out owing a few months' rent, apparently."

Kate was flicking through the file they'd already amassed on Guy Wade. "This guy has a serious arrest record. GBH, ABH, civil disorder, resisting arrest..."

"Yeah," said Theo, finally pulling onto the motorway. "I know. Person of Interest, yeah?"

"Mmm." Kate watched the green banks of the motorway roll past. If Wade was the man they were seeking, they needed to find some hard evidence to link him to both or either crime. Just being a criminally violent thug wouldn't be enough, unfortunately.

Chapter Eighteen

THE HOUSE WHERE THEIR SUSPECT used to live was in the middle of a tired estate of mid-century houses, most of which had probably been built as social housing after the Second World War. Here and there were pretty front gardens and a brave – and in the context, somewhat pathetic – attempt to smarten up the exterior of a house. These few well-kept houses stood out in contrast to the dirty pebbledash, broken windows and rubbish-filled front gardens of most of the others. Kate had grown up on an estate not too dissimilar. She felt the same wave of depression wash over her as she had when she used to visit her mother. At least their estrangement meant she didn't have to do that anymore. Silver linings, and all that...

The landlady, Mrs Grenson, was a fat, blousy woman, with greying blonde hair scraped back into a scrappy ponytail and a lit cigarette dangling permanently from her fingers. The building in which she lived had once been a three bedroom house; she now occupied the ground floor, renting out the rooms upstairs as bedsits. Guy Ward had apparently lived there for six months, before disappearing eight weeks earlier.

"What was he like?" asked Kate, trying not to breathe in any more smoke than she had to, a hopeless task.

Mrs Grenson shrugged. "He was quiet, I'll give him that. Didn't make much trouble. Only thing I had to take him up on was the pets. I said no pets, see, and he still brought them in. A kitten and an effing great rabbit. Made a right mess of the carpet, chewed it all up."

"Did he ever have any visitors, people to stay?"

"Not that I ever saw."

"Do you know if he had any family?"

"Nah."

"I don't suppose he left any forwarding address or anything like that?"

Mrs Grenson laughed a cynical laugh. "Nah," she said, again.

"Do you have any tenants now?" asked Theo, as Kate was overtaken by a coughing fit. Mrs Grenson looked at her in disgust, as if she were putting it on.

"Just one. 'E's up there now, if you want to talk to 'im. Number one."

They escaped the downstairs flat thoughtfully and climbed the stairs. The smell of smoke gradually lessened, but was replaced by others just as unpleasant. Kate took a quick look into the bathroom and wished she hadn't.

The tenant of room number one took a long time to answer the door. When he did so, he looked at the police in sleepy confusion, which swiftly became panic as he realised who they were. Noting his bloodshot eyes and the reek of marijuana smoke that came from the room, Kate raised her hand in a placating gesture. "We're not going to arrest you for having a spliff," she said. "So you can calm down. We need to talk to you about Guy Wade."

The tenant, who turned out to be called Paul, looked to be about twenty two; he was skinny and pale, like someone who hadn't seen much daylight recently. He claimed firstly not to know who they were talking about, but after being shown Wade's photograph, foggy comprehension dawned.

"Oh, *that* guy. He was a nutter. Seriously weird eyes, like, I dunno, *dead* or something."

"Were you friends? Did you spend any time with him?"

"That guy didn't have any friends, I'm telling you. No one ever

143

came to see him. He just used to spend his time watching these well loud films or porn. I'm telling you."

"How do you know?"

"These flats are so shit, you can hear everything through the walls, man."

"Did you ever hear him talk on the phone, perhaps?"

Paul sniffed. "Dunno. Oh yeah, maybe a couple of times. He was mumbling though, couldn't really hear what he was saying."

They persisted for a few more questions, but it was obvious that neither Paul nor Mrs Grenson could help them any further. Returning to the car, Kate sniffed her shirt sleeve, grimacing.

"Come on," said Theo, "That wasn't the worst house you've ever been in, not by a long shot."

Momentarily, the bloodied drawing room of the Dorseys' house recurred to Kate.

"No," she said, after a moment. "There have been worse."

Their next destination was Royal Wootten Bassett, the scene of so many sad homecomings of soldiers who'd paid the ultimate price for the service of their country. As Theo drove along the main street, Kate remembered the crowds who turned out to line the pavements, the solemn onlookers, the tearstained faces of the grieving families. Had Guy Wade's experiences in the army turned him from patriot to misanthropist, or did his apparent hatred of the human race go deeper than that?

Guy Wade's once commanding officer, Peter Wentworth, was a distinguished looking man of about fifty, still with a thick head of hair scarcely touched by grey, except at the temples. He reminded Kate a little of Anderton, except without the latter's unceasing energy. Captain Wentworth had a clipped but calm manner, and courteously offered them both refreshments before they got down to business.

"Guy Thomas Wade," said the captain. "Yes, I remember him. He was a troubled man."

"Really?"

"He came from a very lowly background. Born the wrong side of the blanket, no real father figure. Rackety kind of childhood. I only know this second-hand, of course, from his fellow soldiers."

Kate tried not to resent the words used. She'd been 'born on the wrong side of the blanket', stupid term. She'd had a rackety kind of childhood. *We can't all have a privileged upbringing, mate.*

The captain went on speaking. "I often see it in the ranks," he said. "Plenty of men and women join the forces because they're looking for order and stability, and the comfort of having someone else tell you what to do."

Again, Kate was pierced by his words. It was true. Why else had she wanted to be a police officer? Catching the bad guys, of course, that was the conscious reason. But the unconscious one was to bring more order to the chaos of life. She remembered her first week at Hendon, settling in with her dorm-mates. She even remembered the first night there; lying in a strange bed in a strange room, in a building filled with strangers. She should have been homesick – instead, she remembered feeling an overwhelming relief. She remembered Stuart at Olbeck's dinner table, head down, clutching his glass. *That's why I joined the force...*

She brought herself back to the present with an effort. Theo had obviously just asked a question and the captain was frowning.

"There were – incidents," he said. "There were several fights, both with other soldiers and with civilians. It culminated, as you know doubt know, in a discharge from the services."

Kate recalled the notes of the case. "He was involved in the serious beating of an Iraqi citizen, who later died from his injuries," she said. "So, he was court-martialled?"

Captain Wentworth looked uncomfortable. "No. No, it never actually came to that. There was a lack of evidence – one of the key witnesses' testimony was very unreliable. The family of the victim eventually dropped the charges."

"Why?"

Captain Wentworth sat back in his chair, one thumb running along the edge of his jaw. "Let's just say that they probably didn't want too much close attention paid to their... situation. The victim was – well, let's just say he was a person of interest to our side."

Theo looked puzzled. Kate felt like giving him a poke in the ribs.

"They were insurgents?" she asked and watched Theo's face clear.

"Possibly."

"Was it—" Kate looked down at the notes on her lap. "What was Guy Wade's motive for the attack? Did he have one?"

Incredibly, Captain Wentworth chuckled, a single dry cough of a laugh. Then he cleared his throat. "Forgive me. I actually remember what Wade said, after we'd arrested him. He said he did it because the victim had been flogging his donkey."

For a moment, Kate thought that was some kind of sexual euphemism. Then she realised it was the literal truth. Guy Wade had killed a man for being cruel to an animal. She and Theo exchanged a glance.

"One more thing, captain. Did Wade ever work in bomb disposal, or with explosives in any way?"

"No. No, not that I'm aware. We do, of course, have such units in each of our battalions, and it's possible that Wade had some friends or contacts in those units. He was a fairly quick learner. He was a violent, troubled man, like I said, but he wasn't without intelligence."

"SO, WHAT DO YOU THINK?" Kate asked as they made their way back to the car.

Theo glanced over at her. "Sounds like our guy, doesn't it?"

"Yes, it does. So now we just have to find him."

Chapter Nineteen

THOSE WERE ANDERTON'S SENTIMENTS WHEN they arrived back at the station for the debrief.

"I need Stuart back here," he said. "Things are moving quickly, now. Someone go and get him in – pretend to arrest him, if you have to."

There were a few grins at this and Kate could see that several people quite fancied the novelty of 'arresting' one of their colleagues. Let's hope we never have to do it for real, she thought.

"Anyone got anything else to add?"

Something had been nagging at Kate, something to do with the whiteboards. As she swept her gaze along them, it snagged on whatever had been nudging her. Someone, Anderton probably, had drawn a couple of pound signs and circled them, right by the crime scene pictures of the Dorsey house. She raised her hand.

"Sir, I'd like to go and interview Alexander Hargreaves. I've got several questions for him."

"Fine. Do that. Take someone with you."

"I'm fine—"

"No buts, DS Redman." Kate fought down an angry blush. Patronising git. "I'm not having my officers wandering around that isolated spot without back-up."

"I'll come," said Theo, helpfully. Kate tried to look grateful.

At least this time Kate could insist on driving, as she'd been there once before and Theo hadn't. Her radio station had been tuned to Classic FM, which came on automatically when she started the engine but she turned it off rather pointedly.

"Cor," Theo said as they drew up beside the lakeside house. "Nice gaff. I'd love something like this."

Kate made an agreeing noise as she parked the car. Theo was craning to see out of the windows, shielding his eyes against the glare of the sunlight.

"I think I saw this on *Grand Designs*, once. I love that show. I'm going to have a place like this, one day."

"Really?" asked Kate, trying not to sound too surprised – or too cynical. She thought of pointing out to Theo that even if he rose to become Chief Superintendent, the likelihood of him being able to afford a multi-million pound house was nothing but a faint, distant dream; but why stamp on the poor bloke's aspirations?

Once they were out of the car, Kate once again became aware of the sense of isolation. It was a warmer, sunnier day than the time she and Anderton had visited, but there was still a pressing sense of solitude as they stood in the driveway. She could hear the faint lap of the lake waters against the posts of the jetty. The pine trees stood by the lakeside like needled sentinels. A car that Kate vaguely recognised as the large BMW that had been parked here on their previous visit was parked inside the open garage.

"Looks like he's home," she said, and Theo nodded.

But no one answered their knocks on the door and rings of the doorbell. After five minutes, Kate gestured to Theo and they began to walk around the decking that ran along the back of the house. Theo exclaimed over the view.

"I know, it's nice but—" Kate began and then stopped dead.

The long wall of glass at the back of the house was currently in shadow, and the interior of the house was clearly visible. Kate's heart leapt into her throat. Within the dim interior, she could see a figure, slumped in one of the armchairs around the glass coffee table, and there was a dark stain on the fluffy white rug on the slate floor. She clutched Theo's arm.

"Oh, fuck," said Theo, taking it in. "Shit. Is it him?"

"Alex Hargreaves? I think so." Kate pressed her hands up against the glass, trying to see as much as she could through the twin barriers of glass and low light. "Oh my god. Theo, we've got to get in."

"I know." Theo sounded as shaken as she was. She knew what he was thinking – was this another murder? "I'm going to call it in right now, and then we'll get that door down."

They ran back around to the front of the house, Theo already talking to Dispatch. After he'd hung up, he tried Anderton, terminating the call with a curse when he obviously got his voicemail. Kate was already calling Olbeck.

"Oh, Lord," said Olbeck. Kate pressed the phone to her ear, grimacing – he sounded like he was walking down a wind tunnel. "I'm just leaving the office – I'll be there as quick as I can. Are you okay?"

"Fine, we're fine. Just worried about what we're going to find."

"Maybe you should wait 'til the patrol get there."

"We'll be fine," said Kate, trying to keep the impatience from her voice. "Can you get hold of Anderton?"

"He's with the Chief. I'll grab him as soon as he's done."

Kate didn't have faith that the two of them would be able to break the front door down, despite Theo's youth and strength. If he'd had any sense at all, Hargreaves would have built himself an impregnable fortress. But, primed with adrenaline, it only took three shoulder charges before the frame splintered and a gap appeared. Theo kicked the door fully open in just thirty seconds.

Kate braced herself for the peal of an alarm, but there was nothing. After the splintering and crashing of the door break, the silence rolled back in. Kate found herself holding her breath. She was a little ashamed that she let Theo go in first, although he would have probably stopped her if she'd tried to be the one to take the lead. As it was, he held out a protective arm as she stepped forward, which she found simultaneously touching and annoying.

As they stepped over the threshold, Kate was assailed with fear. This was stupid, we're not armed, we have no idea who might be here... Over their quick, high breathing, she caught the faint sound of sirens and relaxed a little. Theo edged forward, Kate following him closely, until they were standing in the huge, atrium-like space in the centre of the house.

As soon as she saw the body, Kate felt her fear dissipate. Alex Hargreaves sat in one of the leather chairs, his head rolled forward onto his chest, his eyes closed. Both arms were loose at his sides, the sleeves of his white shirt rolled up to above the elbow. Blood had run from the wounds in his wrists and pooled on the floor beneath him. In front of him, on the glass coffee table, was an empty bottle of whisky, the dregs of which were dried into a sticky amber film in the bottom of a glass. There was a square yellow Post-It note stuck to the glass of the table, with an object placed on top of it. Kate and Theo edged closer. The scrawled writing on the note said the simplest and saddest goodbye of all. *I'm sorry*. The small object was a memory stick. Kate looked closer. Balled-up pieces of pink paper were scattered around Hargreaves' feet and she remembered seeing the same kind of paper bobbing in the lake outside on her previous visit. She leant a little closer, trying to see them in more detail.

"What are those?" she whispered to Theo. It felt wrong to speak in a normal tone.

Theo bent forward to take a closer look. "Not sure," he said after a moment. "Nothing sinister. I think they're betting slips."

"Oh."

There didn't seem to be anything more to say. There was no jagged undercurrent of fear left in the room, no taint of horror as at the Dorsey crime scene. There was nothing, simply absence. Kate and Theo kept looking, standing side by side and staying quiet, as the sound of sirens became louder and eventually they heard the crunch of tires over the gravel outside.

THE BANK OF WHITEBOARDS IN the Incident room had grown. Two days after the discovery of Hargreaves' body, Kate and Olbeck stood in front of it, looking at the photographs from the victim's house. There was something even sadder in the juxtaposition of Hargreaves' slumped body, drained white, against the luxurious backdrop of the house itself, with its expensive furnishings and dramatic artwork. Kate looked more closely at a close-up shot of the suicide note. Something about it reminded her of the jagged letters written in blood on the wall of the dining room at the Dorsey crime scene. The handwriting and the meaning were completely different but, like the other, it was a message. But a message to whom?

The door crashed open and Anderton bowled through with a laptop in his arms, the lead trailing behind him like the ribbon on a kite.

"Morning, team. Can someone help me get this set up?"

Once the equipment was sorted out, the police officers arranged themselves around the room in a way that they could all see the projection screen. Anderton opened a file on the laptop and adjusted it on the screen. It was an Excel spreadsheet, filled side to side with a mass of (to Kate) impenetrable numbers.

"Know what this is?" asked Anderton.

Olbeck raised his hand. "I'm hazarding a guess that it's something to do with MedGen's accounts."

"You hazard right. We've had the analysts go through the files which were on the memory stick left by Hargreaves at his suicide. I'm not expecting you lot to understand this – you're not accountants, thank God – but you can possibly hazard another guess at why Hargreaves left this for us, or someone, to find."

Kate scanned the spreadsheets, frowning. The numbers still

didn't make much sense, but she could guess what Anderton was inferring.

"He was embezzling funds," she said, quietly. "That's why Jack Dorsey was worried about money. Remember, Sarah Brennan said he'd been talking about getting the auditors in, to look at the accounts, or something like that?"

Anderton nodded. "Quite right, Kate. It turns out Alex Hargreaves not only had expensive tastes in houses and clothes and artwork, he also had quite a gambling addiction. Had accounts with all the bookies in Abbeyford, the respectable ones as well as the not-quite-so respectable ones. So he needed money and, as one of the directors of MedGen, he had access to a lot."

Kate found herself nodding in dawning comprehension. She remembered the trip to MedGen with Theo, how they'd been talking about betting and horse-racing in the waiting room. Theo holding the Racing Times magazine and Hargreaves coming in, noticing it, his face briefly registering a flicker of emotion. She remembered the bobbing pink betting slips in the lake by Hargreaves' house.

Olbeck rubbed his chin. "So, Hargreaves was taking the money, Dorsey found out about it – or was on the verge of finding out about it. So that meant... what? Did Hargreaves have to stop him?"

Theo was flipping the case notes back and forth. "Hargreaves has a rock-solid alibi for the night of Dorsey's death, guv," he said. "A pub full of people have confirmed that he was there for most of the evening."

"Yes, thank you for that illuminating fact, Theo," said Anderton. "I'm quite aware of that."

"He would make sure he had a rock-solid alibi if he was going to pay someone to do his dirty work for him," Kate said impatiently.

There was a moment's silence, broken by the door to the office opening. They all turned to see Stuart making his way towards them. He was dressed in his activist gear, in stark contrast to how

Kate had last seen him, although he looked as tired as he had that evening at Olbeck and Jeff's house. He raised a hand in slightly self-conscious welcome as he joined them at the whiteboards. "All right, everyone?"

"Glad you could join us," said Anderton. "I hear the patrol had a fun time dragging you in for questioning."

Stuart grinned. "I didn't resist arrest, if that's what you're saying, sir."

"Not at all. Come into my office for a moment, I just want a quick word."

The tension in the team was broken as Anderton and Stuart left the room. Kate continued to run her eyes over the photographs and the files on screen, wondering whether she'd missed anything important. Theo took the files back to his desk and began to read through them, muttering something under his breath. Rav and Jane went to stock up on coffee.

Kate was still standing there, unsure of what to do next, when Stuart appeared at her shoulder. "All right?" he said amiably.

She smiled up at him in greeting. It was funny, but since that odd little moment at the dinner party last week, she didn't have that same sense of irritation and annoyance around him as she used to do.

"These the Hargreaves photos?"

Kate nodded. Stuart moved along the row slowly, looking at each in turn.

Kate, having seen all of the sad images that she wanted to see, looked around the room. Theo still had his head bent over the file – she could imagine that patronising little comment of Anderton's had smarted and he was trying to find something in the file to help him regain a little ground. She sympathised. She thought about going to get a cup of tea and turned back to Stuart to ask him if he wanted one. "Fancy a c—"

One look at his face stopped her sentence in mid-flow. He was staring intently at the photographs and his face was literally draining of colour before her eyes, as if a plug had been pulled somewhere in his throat and all the blood were running away down the plughole. She had a sudden, horrifying flashback to last summer, watching Gerry suffer the heart attack that put him in Intensive Care; here in front of her was the same greyish pallor, the same stare of utter shock and dread. She took an involuntary step towards him.

"Stuart..."

"Where are the toilets?" he asked, in a faint, faraway voice.

Surely he knew? She told him and he turned at once and walked quickly to the door, holding himself stiffly, as if he were hurt and trying not to show it. Kate watched the office door swing closed behind him, one hand up to her mouth. What on Earth...?

"Kate, can you come with me and—"

Olbeck had appeared at her shoulder. She turned to him and grasped his arm.

"Go and see if Stuart's all right, will you? He's in the men's loos."

"What?"

"Oh, never mind," said Kate impatiently and hurried through the door after Stuart. Outside the grey painted door to the men's toilets, she hesitated for a second and then knocked and pushed it open.

Stuart was sitting on the floor of one of the cubicles, clearly oblivious to the filthy floor, his head in his hands. The room stank of vomit. Trying not to breathe, Kate squatted down by him and put a hand on his shoulder. "You all right?"

He raised his head and she saw with alarm that he was almost crying. "I'm fucked, Kate. I'm so fucked. Oh God, help me, I didn't know – I didn't know..."

She didn't waste time asking what was wrong. She had to get out of this fetid room but she couldn't leave Stuart. The door to the room opened and Olbeck walked in.

"What's the problem?" He caught sight of the state that was Stuart. "Oh, God. What's wrong?"

"Help me get him up."

They hoisted Stuart to his feet between them. He was crying openly now, and Olbeck looked across his bent head at Kate in alarm.

They manhandled him out of the loos and across into an empty office. Olbeck shut the door.

Stuart had his head in his hands again.

"What's going on?" asked Kate, gently.

There was no answer. She could hear Stuart's high, terrified breathing.

"Stuart!"

He dropped his hands from his face, rubbing the tears away. She could see him make an effort to collect himself. "I'm so *fucked*," he said, again.

"All right," said Olbeck. "Why?"

Stuart took a deep, shaky breath. "In the photos – the photos—"

"Of the Hargreaves crime scene?" asked Kate. She sat down next to him and took one of his large hands. He clutched it gratefully.

"Yeah, that scene. There's a sculpture in one of them, a big silver thing, a bit like a robot..."

"Yes?"

There was a moment's silence in the room, broken only by Stuart's ragged gasp. "I know who made it."

There was another silence. Kate and Olbeck exchanged a glance.

"Yes?" asked Kate, careful not to sound impatient. "And?"

Stuart put one shaky hand up to his eyes. "I know it – I know what happened. I can see the links now. I can see it all."

"So what happened?"

"I need to talk to Anderton. Oh Christ, he's going to kill me."

"Stuart," said Kate, fighting the impulse to take him by the shoulders and start shaking. "What the hell are you talking about?"

Stuart took a deep breath and got up, releasing Kate's hand. He looked at her and then looked at Olbeck and smiled a smile that was nothing more than a grimace. "I've been fucking a murder suspect," he said and then walked out of the room, leaving Kate and Olbeck with their mouths ajar.

Chapter Twenty

THEY DIDN'T TALK MUCH IN the car on the way there. Rav was driving and Stuart sat next to him. Kate, who was by herself in the back, looked at Stuart's face, which was set tight, as if it had frozen stiff. She wished Anderton were there, or Olbeck, but they were both busy elsewhere and Stuart had specifically asked if she would accompany him.

"This is going to blow your cover," she'd said as they walked to the car. He'd laughed raggedly.

"You think that matters now? My career in Undercover is *over*, Kate. I'm probably off the force for good."

Kate thought of that grim note to his voice as he'd said that. She leaned forward and squeezed his arm. "Stuart, do you think – do you think this is a good idea? Should I make the arrest, instead?"

"No," said Stuart, that same note in his voice. "I want to see her face."

"Is it this turn?" asked Rav.

They swung off the main road into a cul-de-sac. The houses were pre-war; nineteen thirties construction, not particularly attractive but well-built and large, set back from the road with long driveways and front gardens. The house they sought was right on the edge of the estate, its boundary abutting a scrubby bit of woodland. Stuart, exiting the car, thought of the first time he'd been there and how he'd first seen her, spot lit under that harsh kitchen strip light.

The three of them stood for a moment, looking up at the

silent house. There was a large, battered estate car parked on the crumbling concrete driveway that Stuart couldn't recall being there before. All the dirty curtains were drawn, although that wasn't so unusual, Stuart recalled. He wondered how many people were in the house.

"Well," said Rav. "What are we waiting for?"

"You're right," replied Stuart. "I'm going in."

There was a sharp crack and Kate felt the sudden sting of something in her upper arm and a buzzing noise. She looked down, expecting to see some kind of insect. Instead, there was a blooming patch of red on her bicep, the sleeve of her shirt torn open as if ripped by a tiny hand. She was still staring at this, the implications not reaching her brain quickly enough, when there was another crack and Rav gave a kind of grunt before folding up next to her, literally crumpling to the ground as if his legs had been dynamited from under him.

Within the next ten seconds, and how she didn't know, she and Stuart were behind the parked car on the driveway, with Rav on the floor beneath them. She was still so dazed it took her a second to realise that she'd been shot, the bullet grazing her arm. Rav had been shot in the stomach. Had Stuart picked him up bodily whilst hurrying her under cover? She supposed he must have, but it was as if the last few moments of her memory had been burned away.

"What the fuck—"

"Shut up! Keep down!" said Stuart in a hissing shout. Kate heard Rav groan and dropped to her knees beside him. His face was an awful sepia tone, grey bleaching out the brown. He looked incredibly young. She put a hand on his chest and he clutched at her fingers. She had a sudden, piecing flash of memory; her brother Jay, when he was teething as a toddler. Kate, at eleven years old, would take him into her bed when he cried and he'd lie beside her, cuddled close, clutching her fingers. She did the same to Rav as she'd done then to Jay, lying close beside him and shielding him as best she could while she put her forehead against his clammy cheek and murmured to him just as she'd murmured to little Jay; *it's okay my darling, it's okay my sweetheart, you'll be okay...* She was conscious that any second could bring a final bullet to them both and the terror was so overwhelming that her comforting murmurs were as much for herself as for poor Rav. She was dimly aware that Stuart was pressed against her back, his arms around her, shielding her as she shielded Rav.

"It hurts, it hurts..." Rav moaned and Kate helplessly kissed his face and stroked his head, not knowing what else she could do. She daren't put any pressure on the wound, not knowing how badly his insides were injured. She had a vague recollection of Stuart shouting for an ARU, for an ambulance but that seemed a long time ago now. Was Rav dying, under her hands? Another shot pinged and ricocheted off the car and both Kate and Stuart flinched, huddling even closer to the ground.

"What's happening?" she asked Stuart, almost sobbing, as if he would know.

"I'm sorry, I'm sorry—"

His voice shook so much she almost couldn't make out the words. His arms tightened around her and she pressed back against him, feeling a tiny measure of comfort from his physical bulk.

Rav started to fit beneath her. She gasped and tried to hold him, feeling his muscles jerk and twitch beneath her hands. She tried to put her hands under his head to stop it banging on the concrete.

"Rav, oh hold on, hold on, sweetheart – hold on, darling – I've got you—"

She was crying properly now, her tears falling on Rav's grey face. *Don't die, oh please don't die...* Distantly, just as she had at Hargreaves's house, she heard the sound of sirens. Her heart leapt in hope within her.

"They're coming, Rav, they're nearly here, you'll be all right sweetheart, hold on..."

Then they heard it, even over the sound of the approaching

emergency vehicles. There was another shot but from within the house, a gunshot that somehow sounded more final than any of the ones before. Stuart and Kate remained frozen for a second. Had they heard what they thought they'd heard? Rav calmed and his body stilled beneath Kate's hands. Terrified, she bent to put her head on his chest and exhaled sharply in relief, not even knowing she had been holding her breath, as she heard his heartbeat beneath her ear, faint and erratic but there all the same.

"What was that?"

"I don't know. Don't move. Don't do anything until the ARU get here."

All the cars and teams seemed to arrive at once .There was a confusion of screeching tyres, shouts, blue lights pulsing, running feet, more shouts. Kate stayed crouched down, her arms around Rav, until she was pushed aside by a paramedic, a burly middle-aged man with a beard. She fought the urge to kiss him. Almost before she could say anything, another female paramedic crouched beside her, talking calmly but forcefully.

"Officer, are you hurt? Are you shot? Can you tell me?"

"I'm fine, I'm fine." Kate looked around, dazed. Rav was being loaded onto a stretcher, the bearded medic bent over him. Where was Stuart? Was it safe to sit up?

"That arm looks nasty, I'll have to treat that."

Ignoring her, Kate flung herself floorwards again and looked across the driveway from beneath the car. She could see a semi-circle of police cars, several armed officers with their guns trained on the house. Almost as she looked, she heard the front door go down with a splintering crash amidst shouts of "Armed police! Armed police!"

"Officer, you need to come with me for a moment. We'll be safe over here…"

The female para was gently pulling her away to the shelter of an ambulance, parked behind the fence that marked the boundary.

Kate craned her neck, trying to see where Stuart was. Had he gone inside?

"Officer, *please*. You need to come with me."

Another ambulance's siren started up, loud enough to make Kate jump. She watched it drive away, bearing Rav with it. She muttered a quick, open-eyed prayer as she watched its tail-lights recede into the distance. Please God, let him be okay...

"Officer—"

Kate relented. She followed the paramedic into the remaining ambulance and allowed them to shut the door.

Stuart stepped through the broken front door frame of the house. Fragments of wood lay scattered across the hallway's dirty floor tiles. ARU officers thronged the rooms downstairs. In so far as he was able to wonder about anything, Stuart wondered whether anyone else had been in the house – that curly-haired Charlie, or the one with the funny name, Rizzo or something. He hoped not.

He climbed the stairs, watching the treads move in and out of his vision. His chest ached and his jaw; he'd been clenching it for so long. Up to the first floor, where rooms had been checked and cleared. He paused at the beginning of the final staircase. How strange that he was climbing upwards when his life was in an uncontrollable spiral downwards. There was no escape now, nothing to stop his descent. He walked slowly up the narrow wooden stairs, hand desperately clutching the banister. The door at the top of the stairs was open, leaning drunkenly on its hinges. They'd broken that one down, too. There were two uniformed officers by the doorway, staring into the room. As Stuart approached them, one turned to him and said something, but he was too far gone now to understand. He moved into the room of glittering mirrors and again, he was reminded of the first time he'd been there. Again, he watched himself in miniature, a million tiny reflections of himself, a million tiny images of his haggard, aghast face.

The body of Guy Ward lay face down on the floor, one side of his head a ragged mess of blood and bone. A shotgun lay by one outstretched hand and there was another gun lying on the floor between the body and the bed. Angie was stretched out on the bed with two officers restraining her, pinning her to its surface. For a frozen moment, Stuart thought she was dead too and then realised her face was turned towards him, her eyes fixed on him, unblinking. She wasn't struggling. He looked once at her beautiful statue's face and then his gaze rose to the large computer screen on the desk by the wall. He swallowed.

There was the Dorsey drawing room, the beautiful antiques, the velvet curtains. For a moment, Stuart thought he was looking at a photograph of the room and then there was a flicker in the corner of the screen and he watched Wade advance on Jack Dorsey, who was turning, open-mouthed. Where was Angie? Behind the camera; he answered his own question a second later. Stuart watched up until the moment the knife first went in and then he looked away, feeling sick. He remembered Angie showing him that other multi-media collage on her phone – the same time he'd seen her silver sculpture. Was this to have been her next project? A living snuff film, if that wasn't a contradiction in terms. He had to get out of this room. He remembered her telling him about her latest artwork. *It's consumed me...*

Anger and nausea rose up in him and, to stop himself from attacking her even as she lay prone and flattened on the bed, he rushed for the door. The walls flickered, a million little Stuarts running with him.

Chapter Twenty One

WHEN KATE HAD FINALLY GOT back to the incident room, Olbeck had said nothing but simply thrown his arms around her and held her tight for a long time. Then he'd stepped back and touched the bandage on her upper arm. He'd traced a line across from the bandage to the centre of her chest. "God, if that had been four inches further across…"

"Oy, hands off the boobs," Kate had said.

"Well, it's the only pair I'm ever likely to get my hands on," Olbeck had replied. Then his mouth had twisted and he'd pulled her back into a hug.

It was seven thirty in the morning, the day after the shooting, and they were all waiting, pacing the floors, biting their nails, drinking cup after cup of the rank instant coffee that was all the station could offer. Most of the team hadn't slept at all. They were all fixated on the door and when it finally crashed back, admitting Anderton, there was an audible intake of breath heard.

He didn't waste time keeping them in suspense. "He's alive, he's okay," said Anderton.

That in-held breath rushed out. Jane burst into noisy tears, sobbing, "Sorry – sorry, everyone," and then cried again. Theo put his arm around her and she leaned into him, hiding her face. Kate sat down suddenly, the nervous energy that had propelled her through the rest of the night suddenly dissipating. Olbeck sat down next to her and put his head in his hands for a moment, rubbing his eyes. Kate heard him murmur something like *oh, thank God.*

Anderton's eyes were pouched with shadow and his skin had that grey tinge of exhaustion. He held up a hand. "I should qualify that a bit. Rav's not *okay*, he's very badly hurt. But he'll live. I know you're all dying to see him, but he's in Intensive Care. He's not allowed visitors at the moment and obviously his parents and his sisters will be first in the queue when he is, all right?"

They all nodded. Jane wiped her face and sat back up again.

Kate opened her mouth to ask about Stuart, and then shut it again. She had a feeling she wouldn't like the answer.

"Now," said Anderton. "Now, those who want to can go home and get some sleep. I've got our prime suspect to interview. Anyone want to sit in on that with me?"

"I will," Kate said, immediately.

"Me too," said Olbeck.

Theo opened his mouth for a second and then shut it again.

"Right," said Anderton. "Let's go then."

THE WOMAN'S FACE REMINDED KATE of a statue, one of those ancient marble Greek sculptures. The same strong lines of the face, the same absence of expression. The woman's eyes had that same blankness, too. She was beautiful but it was the beauty of a distant supernova or the sinuous curves of a poisonous snake; something lethal, best appreciated at a distance.

Too fanciful, Kate. She turned her attention back to Anderton and what he was saying.

"So, Angie," said Anderton, pleasantly. "We've been having a look at your records. What made you choose the name Angela Sangello?"

Angie looked at him with no expression. "She's an Italian artist of the twentieth century," she said, in a bored tone. "Don't worry. *You* won't have heard of her."

"I'm afraid I haven't. But then I don't know much about art."

The contempt in Angie's face was now visible. Kate clamped down on a smile. She knew Anderton had a variety of ways of softening up a suspect and knew that his line in self-deprecation would be just the thing to get through to this arrogant, chilly girl.

"That's not your real name, is it though?" asked Anderton. "Not according to our records. You were born Clara King, firstborn daughter of Damien King, or should I say Lord King, hereditary peer. Ring any bells?"

"I'm estranged from my family," said Angie, coldly.

"How very sad. I wonder why that could be?"

Angie remained silent.

"Now, let me see, your mother died when you were seven. I'm sorry. And your father married again when you were ten. Am I right, so far?"

The solicitor next to Angie, a grey-haired, middle-aged man, shifted slightly in his seat. No doubt he, as well as Angie, was wondering where this was going.

"Now, your new stepmother and father had another child, didn't they? Another girl. Can you tell me anything about your sister, Angie? Or should I call you Clara?"

Angie's face tightened a little, but she still said nothing. Anderton continued.

"Now, it seems that your younger sister was tragically killed in an accident when she was two. She fell from the top of a quarry near your house at the time, near Guildford. What an awful thing. That must have been extremely traumatic for the family. Was it very traumatic, Angie?"

Angie's face had settled back into blankness. She didn't respond to Anderton's question.

"Now, it seems that after this dreadful event, your father actually had you taken into care. Why was that? Could you not cope with your sister's death?"

Angie looked at him with contempt. "My stepmother hated me. She was just looking for an excuse to get rid of me."

"Oh, is that why?" Anderton shuffled the papers before him into a little more order. He went on, the gentleness of his tone belying the devastation of his words. "It wasn't because your father and your stepmother thought you were actually responsible for your sister's death?"

The solicitor made a sound of protest but Angie cut across him. "You can think that, if you like," she said, her eyes narrowed. "I don't give a shit. If you've got access to my notes, you'll see there was no charge."

"No, that's true, that's true," said Anderton. "There was no actual *charge*. Father pulled some strings, did he? Or was it that he knew, deep down, exactly what his daughter was, but just couldn't face up to it?"

Angie scoffed. She leaned back in her chair, looking away ostentatiously.

"Well," continued Anderton. "We've also had a look at your medical notes. Diagnosed with a personality disorder at sixteen, I see. In and out of various therapies, expelled from your boarding school..."

He waited a moment.

"What I find remarkable," he said, in the same quiet tone, "is that you've managed to make such a name for yourself, despite such, well, difficult beginnings. Your art, your relationships... quite remarkable. And it helps that you're beautiful, too. That must really help."

Kate kept her face neutral as he elaborated on this theme for some minutes. It was working, though. She could see Angie gradually thawing, becoming more animated. The more Anderton heaped praise upon her, the more she responded. Anderton had a lot of charm, when he wanted to use it – God knows, Kate knew about *that* – and he was laying it on thick, here.

"So," said Anderton eventually, smiling genially. "How did you and Alex Hargreaves meet?"

Angie fell into his trap. "At a poker game," she said. Then she smiled and laughed a little cruelly. "I thrashed him. Alex was obsessed with gambling - shame he wasn't any good at it."

"He was an admirer of your work?"

"Of course."

"And you were lovers?"

Angie's smile dimmed a little. "Occasionally."

"So, you wouldn't say it was a serious relationship?"

"No, not really."

"I see," said Anderton. "Well, that's strange. We've been going through his personal belongings and he seems to have all sorts of pictures of you, including several obviously taken at social events. If we asked Alex's friends, do you think they might give us a different answer?"

Angie shrugged, seemingly unconcerned. "They might. It depends what he told them. He was always much more keen on the relationship than I was."

"Is that right?"

"Yes," Angie said. Her gaze slid from Anderton's face to come to rest on Kate's. "You know what men are like."

Angie smiled a slow smile directed at Kate, her eyelids falling slightly. For a moment Kate, incredibly, felt it – whatever had snagged Stuart, and Wade, and Alexander Hargreaves. She found herself smiling back, leaning forward, almost eagerly. Shocked at herself, she sat back sharply in her chair and snapped the smile from her face. Angie's smile changed, from conspiratorial to triumphant. Kate thought of those Sirens from Greek mythology, who'd lured sailors to their deaths by their sweet singing. I need to stop my ears with wax, she thought.

"Did you know that Alexander Hargreaves was embezzling funds from his company, MedGen?"

Angie's eyes widened. "No," she said and Kate could have

congratulated her on the feigned shock in her voice. For the first time since the arrest, Kate started to think that perhaps they might have bitten off more than they could chew.

"You had no idea?"

"Of course not."

"Did he ask you for help in any way?"

Angie looked at him coolly. "I have no idea what you mean."

"You didn't introduce Alex Hargreaves to your other lover, Guy Wade? They didn't arrange the killing of Jack Dorsey between them?"

Angie was shaking her head, seemingly horrified. "I don't know what you're talking about. Guy was – Guy was a brutal man. I was terrified for my life."

Anderton sat back and regarded her. She looked at him, her eyes big and dark. "So, tell me what really happened, Angie," he said, softly.

The silence stretched on and on. Kate could even hear the faint ticking of the clock up on the wall, an ancient model which hadn't yet been replaced by a digital one. From outside, came the sounds of normal life; car engines, bird song, slamming doors.

"Well," said Anderton eventually, seeing Angie wasn't going to speak. "Here's what I think happened. Perhaps you'll correct me if I'm wrong."

Silence. Angie's face had changed again, from a beautiful stony mask, to the hurt expression of a young vulnerable girl. Oh, she was good – Kate would give her that.

"You and Alex Hargreaves were lovers. You were also the lover of Guy Wade, a violent and revengeful animal rights militant. How did you meet him, by the way?" Anderton waited a second for Angie to answer and then went on, clearly knowing she wouldn't. "You made a piece of art for him, Angie, didn't you? The multimedia piece, with the footage of all the animal cruelty? What made you decide to go even further? Was it his idea, or yours, to film the death of Jack Dorsey?"

Angie's face had stilled again. Kate could see a distant spark in the depths of her dark eyes, as if her thoughts were there, ticking over, the only outward sign of her search looking for a plausible explanation. When she spoke, it sounded as though it was something she'd been preparing for some time. No doubt, she had.

"Guy threatened me," she said. Her voice quavered a little and Kate inwardly cursed, knowing the effect that would have on a jury. "He was obsessed with animal cruelty. He said if I didn't help him, he'd *kill* me. You have to believe me."

"So what did he ask you to do? Did he plant the bomb that killed Michael Frank?"

Angie nodded, her head down.

"Did you help him with that?"

"No."

Kate spoke up, unable to help herself. "Did you *film* it?"

Angie looked at her and for a moment, Kate saw the snake, down there in the darkness, stirring. "No."

"Really?" said Kate sceptically. "So I guess when we wade through all the footage on your computer, Angie, we won't find anything like that? I wonder."

Angie's mouth tightened a little and Kate felt a little spark of triumph. She was pretty sure that once they'd searched through all the evidence, they would find exactly that.

Anderton gave her a glance and she sat back, letting him take up the reins.

"You're a pretty persuasive person, Angie, from all I've heard. Men become quite obsessed with you, don't they? Did you suggest to Alex Hargreaves that you could introduce him to someone who could do his dirty work for him?" Angie said nothing, staring at him blankly. "Did you suggest to Guy Wade that you could give him access to one of his targets?"

"I don't know what you're talking about," said Angie, coldly.

"No? How did Guy Wade know the alarm codes to Jack Dorsey's

home? How did he know where Jack Dorsey's home was? How did he know to locate and wipe the CCTV onsite?"

Angie shrugged.

"He knew, Angie, because you told him. Hargreaves told you, and you passed the information on to Wade. You were there at the scene, holding the camera, Angie. And, in fact, I think you were the way in. Darryl Timms opened the door to you because you were no threat, were you, Angie? Is that right? He saw a frightened, tiny young girl on the doorstep and opened the door to you. That's why he was facing away from the door when he was killed, because he was leading you into the house. That's when your lover, Guy Wade, came up behind him and killed him."

Angie crossed her arms across herself. "I was being *threatened*," she said, as if Anderton was unbelievably dense. "Guy told me he'd kill me if I didn't do what he said. He *forced* me. He forced me to film it."

"Well," said Anderton. "As he's dead, we can't really ask him, can we? How did he die, Angie?"

She stared back at him. "He shot himself in the head."

"Did he? You didn't shoot him yourself?"

"There's no evidence of that," interjected the solicitor, sharply.

"Exactly," said Angie. She flashed Anderton a tight smile. "I was being held *hostage*, in case you'd forgotten."

"When the officers who were first on the scene found you, you were sitting calmly at your editing suite, working on the footage of Jack Dorsey's murder. Does that sound like someone who was in terror for their life?"

"I told you, I wasn't in my right mind, I was terrified. I can't account for every single thing I was doing."

Anderton sat back in his chair. "Forensics can tell us a lot, Angie. I wonder what we'll find on the gun that killed Guy Wade? Your fingerprints overlaying his, perhaps?"

There was a beat of silence. Then Angie raised her head a

little, turning her face so it could be clearly seen by the recording camera. Her mouth quivered.

"I moved the gun after he was dead," she said, almost choking the words out. "I was so frightened he wasn't dead and he was going to get up and kill me."

With half his head missing? Kate held down a cough of disbelief. The trouble was, Angie's performance was all too convincing. She was aware of a slowly creeping unease, a discordant note, something that they'd missed.

It didn't take long to surface. The grey-haired solicitor stirred himself, pulling himself upright.

"Am I to understand, Chief Inspector, that my client is being held on suspicion of murder? I see nothing you've put forward in this interview to show that my client can be held responsible for any of the terrible crimes you seem to be accusing her of. There is simply no justification for holding her on this charge."

"I can hold her on plenty more," snapped Anderton. He pushed his chair back from the table. Both Angie and the solicitor regarded him; the solicitor with a cynical smile and Angie with the same hurt, vulnerable look she'd worn before. Kate's palm itched to slap her.

"A short break," said Anderton. "I'll leave you to confer with Miss Sangello. Or should that be Miss King?"

He, Kate and Olbeck huddled in the corridor, far enough away so their whispered conversation couldn't be overheard.

"Fuck," said Anderton. "I was hoping he wouldn't pick up on that."

"You're joking, right?" said Kate. "We can't hold her on a murder charge?"

"Look, I'm doing my best, here. But we've got no evidence that she had anything to do with the car bomb – yes, there might be footage, but all she needs to say was what she's been saying about the Dorsey case. She did it under duress. We actually have the murder of Jack Dorsey *on tape* – it's irrefutably Wade."

Kate's chest felt tight. "What about Wade? Surely we can prove that she handled the gun. The angle, the fingerprints..."

Anderton half smiled. "Well, you see how quickly she threw out an excuse for having her prints on the gun. We can pin our hopes on forensics, but..." He shrugged.

Olbeck put both hands up to his temples as if he had a sudden headache. "You're not telling me this – this sociopath – is going to just walk away?"

Both Anderton and Kate gave him an old-fashioned look.

"How many years have you been a detective, Mark?" said Anderton. "For Christ's sake, she's not getting off scot free. She's an accessory to murder, for one thing. Concealing a crime. There's plenty there to be going on with—"

"But not what she's truly guilty of," Kate said, quietly.

The three of them stared at each other for a moment.

"Look, let's not go giving up yet," said Anderton. "We've got hundreds of pieces of evidence to go through. There'll be something there that can help. And even if there isn't..." he trailed off for a second. "Something will come up. You'll see."

They walked back into the interview room together. Anderton conferred with the solicitor, letting him know with a kind of quiet intensity that they would be detaining Angie for further questioning, murder charge or not. The solicitor nodded a crisp assent and briefly murmured in Angie's ear. Kate watched her face closely but the stony mask had slipped back down again.

Kate waited until Anderton had left the room. Olbeck was preparing to leave. She flashed him a quick glance and then walked over to the table. Angie looked at her sullenly.

"Oh, and by the way," said Kate, quietly. "You're not an artist."

Angie said nothing for a moment. Then, frowning, she opened her mouth to reply.

"Yes, I—"

"You're not, you know," Kate went on, cutting her off. "Artists create. That's what they do. You don't create, you destroy. You're not an artist."

Angie's face contracted. Now, as Angie's pupils shrank down to tiny, glittering pinpoints of fury, Kate was reminded of another figure from Greek mythology. *Medusa*. If looks could kill... but Kate knew she'd got through. The barb had struck home. That's for Stuart, you bitch – and Mary, and Madeline, and Harriet, and Jack, and the children. Take that. The solicitor was looking at her with a look she couldn't decipher, his mouth slightly twisted. Inside her, she felt a delicious leap of self-righteous glee.

Kate stepped back. "Yes," she said, infusing her tone with just a hint of pity. "You're *not* an artist. You might want to mull that thought over, in prison. You'll have a nice long time to really think it through."

Behind her, Olbeck stifled a laugh. Kate kept her face in the same rueful, pitying smile and she didn't clench her fist in triumph until they were both safely out of the room.

"Nice one," said Olbeck, as they reached the corridor. "I'm only surprised you didn't cough 'whole life term' under your breath as you left the room."

"I would have done, if I'd thought about it."

They both looked at each other and collapsed, bellowing slightly hysterical laughter. Kate knew Angie would be able to hear them from inside the room. *Good*.

They walked back to the office, half-supporting one another, still wheezing. Theo looked up in surprise as they staggered through the door.

"What's up with you two?"

"Oh, nothing," Kate said, wiping her eyes. "Just a bit of a delayed reaction, I think."

"Right," Theo said, in a mystified tone. "Anyway, I've got some good news. Madeline Dorsey's regained consciousness."

Kate and Olbeck looked at each other, sobering up completely.

"That's brilliant," said Olbeck. He sat down at a nearby desk, running his hands through his hair. "That's great. Do they think she'll recover?"

"As far as I could tell. They were being cautious, but I gather that's the gist."

"Fantastic," Kate said. She pinched her nose and heaved a deep sigh. "What did Anderton say? Something will turn up."

"Well—" Olbeck began.

"Come on, this could be it! Hopefully all the additional evidence we'll need."

Olbeck looked sombre. "Come on, Kate. You know as well as I do that she might not be able to remember a thing. Traumatic amnesia and all that."

"Yeah," said Theo. "We might very well end up with nothing."

"Oh, I know." Kate reached out and shook them both gently, one hand on each. "But let's hope for the best, eh?"

The two men smiled reluctantly.

Kate went back to her desk to collect her bag and coat. She was so tired that even moving felt like wading through slowly setting concrete. She dropped her head on her desk and sighed.

Olbeck paused on his way past. "Are you all right, really?"

Kate nodded, head still down. Then, with an effort, she lifted it.

"I'm all right," she said. "You know what? I was just thinking I might have a pop at the Inspector's exams."

"Why not? You'll breeze through them, I'm sure."

"I'm sure I will," said Kate. "After all, if *you* can pass them..."

Olbeck snorted and Kate grinned tiredly.

On the steps of the station, Kate felt her phone vibrate. Another message from Andrew, to add to the multiple calls that she'd let go to voicemail. Standing there in the sunshine, too exhausted for her usual denial to kick in, Kate faced the fact. She didn't love him. Surely the first person you'd normally want to see after a traumatic experience would be your boyfriend? She didn't want to see him; all she wanted to do was go home, on her own. Olbeck passed her with a pat on the shoulder – she could see Jeff in the car down on the road, waiting to collect him. That was what a relationship should be. You know it, Kate. You know what you have to do.

She sighed a little.

"You all right?" asked Theo, passing her.

"I'm fine." When were people going to stop asking her that?

"Need a lift home?"

She smiled at him. He was a good lad, really. "Yes. Please. Thanks, Theo."

As she got into his car, she sent Andrew a text. *I'll call you later and tell you everything. Don't worry.* She didn't put a kiss on the end of it.

THE END

Chimera

A Kate Redman Mystery: Book 5

Prologue

THE NIGHT SKY OVER ABBEYFORD was spangled with a million little explosions of light; red, blue, gold and green lit up the dark clouds before falling and fading into oblivion. In the town below, the crowds thronged the pavements and the open space of the fairground that lay to the north of the town park gardens. Along the high street came a fantastic beast, jointed in three places; a giant, scaled snake with huge yellow eyes. Children yelled and pointed, and adults clapped and cheered at the sight. Beneath the snake costume, fifteen sweating men held up the frame that supported its body. The night air carried the acrid tang of cordite from the fireworks and billowed with smoke from chestnuts cooking on braziers. It was thick with the greasy smell of the fast food vans offering chips and hot dogs and candy floss. Thumping bass music blared from the funfair on the park ground itself, pierced by the shrieks and delighted yells of those on the fast rides and the bumper cars. Abbeyford was enjoying its annual pagan festival; for one night in late September the town celebrated the myth and legend of the Abbeyford Wyrm, a giant snake-like creature once rumoured to have lived in the woods and forests surrounding the town.

Olly Chandler had something more than the festival on his mind. He and his girlfriend, Mia Smith, strolled through the fairground, hand in hand. Mia wanted to go on the Ghost Train but Olly scoffed. "Got something even better than that," he said, pulling Mia close. "A quiet place just for us and some decent weed. How about that?"

Mia looked at him, pouting. Then she giggled. "Let's get stoned and *then* go on the Ghost Train," she said, close to his ear. Her warm breath and the way she licked his neck after she spoke made him even more anxious to get her to where they were going.

"Come on," he said and pulled at her hand. They ran, Mia a little awkwardly in her high heels, over the dusty, bruised grass of the park towards the dip of the hill and the river beyond it.

"Where we going, Olly?" Mia asked as they left the lighter area of the park and walked into the darkness, relieved only here and there by dim streetlights.

"You'll see. We used to go there when we were kids. It's private – no one ever goes there."

"Okay." She sounded doubtful. Olly found the footpath somehow – it was much more overgrown that it used to be – and pushed aside tree branches and brambles.

"Down there?" said Mia. She actually sounded nervous now. "What is it?"

"S'alright," said Olly, conscious of a little spike of uneasiness himself. "It's a row of little houses. They're empty now, been like that for years." The two of them pushed through the last of the undergrowth and came out onto a little back road. There were no lights but the moon had emerged from behind a cloud and cast a silvery radiance over the tumbledown buildings before them.

"Are you sure this is safe?" Mia looked down at herself, strewn with leaves and bits of undergrowth, and tutted. "Look at my top. This had better be worth it."

"It's fine," Olly said impatiently. The desire he'd felt at the fairground was ebbing away, down here in the darkness and silence, not to mention the faint unpleasant smell that hung in the air. Maybe this wasn't such a good idea after all. But where else did they have to go? He thought resentfully of his older brother, who'd recently gained his driving license. Only another year to go before Olly could take his test. He couldn't wait.

Mia was still hanging back, and Olly felt protective. He pulled her close to him and kissed her, and she responded enthusiastically. "Come on, it'll be fine," he said. "You want to, don't you?"

"'Course." Mia took his hand trustingly and he led her through a space in the front garden wall of the first house in the row of three, where a gate had once hung.

Olly chose the first house because it was the nearest. If he remembered rightly, the door looked closed but could be opened with a shove. Though the house on the end had no front door at all...perhaps they should go there? No, they wanted a bit of privacy. Definitely this one, Olly thought to himself, a decision that would prove to cost him years of therapy.

They stumbled up the garden path to the front door, black in the moonlight. Olly put a hand out to the peeling paint and gave it a shove. The door creaked open and he felt a quick moment of triumph before the smell hit them in the face.

"Ugh, ugh, that's *disgusting*," shrieked Mia. "I'm not going in *there*."

"It's okay, it's going, it's going." A night breeze whipped up and carried the worst of the stench away. "Come on," said Olly, desperately. He couldn't have said himself why he was so hell bent on getting into the cottage now, though his family would have told him it was because he had a stubborn streak a mile wide running through him.

He almost dragged Mia into the darkness of the cottage. Once inside, the smell returned and Olly almost gagged. Mia made a small, choked noise behind him. The inside of the cottage was pitch black, so black that as Olly inched forward, fumbling for his phone in order to use its pale screen light as a torch; his feet collided with something hard and he tripped and fell.

His phone went flying and he put both hands out to break his fall. Both hands connected with something that, while ostensibly solid, broke open under the impact of his body. Olly felt his hands sink into something peculiarly liquid and the smell, which had already been terrible enough, intensified to something so repulsive it felt almost like a physical force.

Behind him, Mia held her phone aloft and it cast a pale, ghostly light over the room, showing Olly what he'd actually fallen into. Mia began to scream, but he hardly heard her because, by that time, he was screaming himself.

Chapter One

"THIS IS FREAKIN' AMAZING!" JAY shouted in Kate's ear. "I can't believe you've lived here for four years and never *once* been to this festival."

"I know, I know." Kate was thinking the same thing herself. She'd never seen the normally fairly quiet streets of Abbeyford so busy, packed with a shouting, laughing, gesticulating crowd; from tiny babies in prams to pensioners gamely tottering on their walking sticks or regarding the festivities from wheelchairs. "I always thought it was – well – a bit – a bit..."

"A bit what?" asked Hannah, Kate's best friend who was visiting from Brighton. Hannah's husband, Dan, was standing with his hands in his jeans pockets, a bemused expression on his face. Kate knew how he felt.

"I don't know. A bit...fuddy duddy. Like Morris dancing and the W.I."

"Jesus," said Jay, grinning. "I would have thought something like the Women's Institute was right up your street. You're hardly rock and roll, are you, sis?"

Kate slapped his arm. "Compared to you, no. But then compared to you, the most debauched of the Roman emperors aren't very rock and roll."

That wasn't actually very fair, as she knew full well that Jay had calmed down a lot over the last few years. But he was her little brother - teasing was her prerogative.

The main reason for Jay's newfound sense of responsibility came up and linked her arm with his. "He's like a toddler," said Laura Murray, Jay's girlfriend of the last two years. "He gets overexcited, especially if he's had sugar. I knew that candy floss was a bad idea."

Jay growled and bent his girlfriend over in a backwards wrestling hold. She shrieked and flailed at him until he pulled her back upright, the two of them giggling.

"Come on," said Hannah. "Let's go and get a drink."

"Yes," said Dan in a fervent tone. "All these giant worm things are weirding me out."

They wandered along the crowded streets in a loose group, one or the other of the couples straggling behind or moving ahead. Kate tried not to mind that she was the only single person amongst them.

"There's a really nice pub down by the river," said Jay. "Let's head there. It's off the main drag so we'll ditch the crowds, at least."

"Sound good to me," said Kate. "The Boathouse, right?"

"Yep. We need to take the first right up here and go past the fairground."

The fairground was still heaving with people, showing no signs of slowing down for the night. The air was thick with the greasy smell of fried food, with the odd waft of sweetness from the clouds of candy floss being whirled into existence through the machine.

Kate found herself walking next to Hannah. Dan was up ahead, talking football with Jay. "How are you doing?" asked Hannah, linking her arm with Kate's. "I was so sorry to hear about Andrew."

"Oh, that's fine," said Kate, a little uncomfortably. "We just weren't right for one another, that's all."

"But he was lovely!"

"I know," said Kate, "But he wasn't my kind of lovely. Anyway, I'm fine. Don't worry about me. How's my beautiful godson?"

"He's fine. But insane in the way only a two year old can be. He's developed a scream that the army could use as a sonic weapon and he deploys it whenever he doesn't get his own way."

Kate laughed. Hannah always did have a way of putting things. "I must come down and see you soon."

Hannah gave her arm a squeeze. "Yes, do. A few days at the seaside...it'll do you good."

"Mmm." Kate always forgot that to almost everyone else, Brighton was a nice, hip, seaside town. To her, it was one of the hunting grounds of the person who'd almost killed her. She felt her hand moving towards the scar on her back, as it did every time she started thinking about it, and consciously stopped it. Hannah, who must have felt her flinch a little, gave her a quick glance but said nothing, giving her arm another quick, friendly squeeze.

"How's gorgeous Mark?" asked Hannah, after a short silence.

"He's fine, as far as I know. I haven't seen him for a few weeks – he and Jeff have been living it up in the Caribbean for a fortnight."

"Coo, nice. All right for some."

"He deserves it. He works hard. Mind you," Kate paused, considering, "so do I."

"Your Inspector exams are coming up, aren't they? Are you nervous?"

Kate shrugged. "A bit. I've been revising like hell, though. It's just...I don't know what to anticipate, really. It's been ages since I've done any kind of written exam."

"Well," said Hannah comfortably. "I'm sure you'll be fine. You always did better than me at college, that's for sure."

They walked on. The lights and noise of the fairground retreated a little as they moved away from the main part of the town park gardens and onto the wide footpath that led down the river and the footbridge that crossed it. Stately iron lamp posts, a nod to the park's Victorian heritage, stood at intervals along the footpath, casting a faint orange glow over the group as they made their way down the gentle slope of the hill.

Hannah and Kate had outpaced the others by about fifty feet, Kate's usual fast walking pace having swept her friend along. They had almost reached flat ground down by the banks of the river, and the iron railings that spanned the footbridge could dimly be seen up ahead in the street lights.

"Jay's grown up a lot, hasn't he?" Hannah said quietly as they walked along.

Kate looked at her in surprise. She'd noticed that about her little brother but it was heartening to see that someone else had too. Mind you, Hannah had known her and Jay since they were fourteen and five respectively; she was almost as close as family. Come to think of it, Kate thought, remembering several family members, Hannah was closer.

"He has," she agreed. "It's Laura's influence, I think. God, I hope they never split up."

Hannah smiled. "Well, they might not. They might even get married, one day."

The thought gave Kate a jolt. She smiled to hide the small tremor that Hannah's remark had given her. She didn't want Jay to get married before her. I'm much older than him. It should be me first. But...fat chance of that happening anytime soon.

Hannah was saying something else but Kate held up a hand to stop her, frowning.

"What is it?" Hannah asked.

"I'm not sure – shush for a moment. I thought I heard something..."

They both listened. For a moment, there was nothing, just the busy silence of the landscape around them and then the wind changed and they both heard it – the faint sound of screaming.

"Wait here!" Kate called, catching a glimpse of Hannah's astonished face as she pelted off, running flat out towards the sound of the screaming. She let her feet take her pounding down a smaller footpath, then onto an unlit lane. Adrenaline spiking, she ran just as she had when she was training with Olbeck for the half marathon two years ago, steadily but quickly, trying to see through the gloom. Up ahead she could just about make out two figures, one staggering about, one crouched by the side of the road. The screams came from the crouching figure. The staggering shape was uttering sounds that were almost worse; guttural, choked cries and moans.

"Are you hurt?" gasped Kate, skidding to a stop by the crouching shape – a teenage girl; she could now see even in the darkness. The girl had both her hands clasped in her hair and her mouth was an open, vibrating hole. "Can you hear me? Are you hurt?"

The girl didn't answer but her screams faded into whimpering gasps. Kate turned to the other person, who was still staggering from one side of the lane to the other, weaving like a drunk, holding his hands out in front of his body in a peculiarly stiff-armed way.

As Kate got nearer, she became aware of the smell. She stiffened, nostrils flaring. The teenage boy with his arms held away from his body stopped and looked at her, panting. She could see the whites of his eyes through the darkness of the street.

"What's wrong? Can you tell me what's wrong?"

The boy's voice was hoarse. He almost whispered. "In there. It's in there. I – I didn't realise... I fell..." He started to cry.

Kate turned at the sound of running footsteps behind her; Jay and Laura arrived at the scene, panting.

"What's going on, sis?" Jay asked between puffs. Laura said nothing but immediately headed towards the crying girl and crouched beside her, putting an arm around her shoulders and talking to her comfortingly. God, that girl is good in a crisis, that's for sure. Kate had a fleeting thought that she might try to recruit her.

"I don't know yet. You wait with him," she said, indicating that Jay should stay with the boy.

He nodded and approached him, flinching a little when he got close enough to smell him, but managing to keep his voice calm and even. "You all right, mate? Don't worry, don't worry, you'll be fine..." Even as he spoke, he was reaching for his mobile and dialling. What a difference a few years made, thought Kate. Back when Jay was in his teens, he wouldn't have called the police if he'd been kidnapped by Jeffrey Dahmer. Now Kate could hear him steadily relaying what little information they had to the dispatcher on the other end of the phone line. Good lad; Kate was proud of him. She reached for her keys and the little pen-sized torch she kept on the key ring.

The smell got steadily worse, invading her nostrils as she approached the open door of the derelict cottage. What on Earth were these kids doing down here? Kate tried not to breathe as she nudged the door open with her elbow, shining the little beam of the torch in front of her. Even though she was expecting it, the state of the body was still a shock. What was left of what had once been a person – it was impossible to tell whether it had been a man or woman – lay in the middle of the floor, surrounded by a lake of dark fluid. Had the poor kid actually fallen into the body? The poor bastard. Kate had to take a quick breath to fill her bursting lungs and almost retched. She retreated back out of the front door, leaving it slightly ajar, not wanting to touch anything with her bare hands.

WITHIN HALF AN HOUR THE lane was transformed; strobed by blue flashing lights on the attending police vehicles and the ambulance that had been ordered for the traumatised teenagers. Kate had sent her little group home, not without some grumbling from Jay that he was missing all the action. She stood waiting for Anderton, reaching for her phone every so often to call Olbeck before remembering with a curse that he was sunning himself on a beach in Barbados, the jammy git.

Scene of Crime officers arrived. Kate nodded to Stephen

Smithfield, who headed the team and she'd worked with several times before. She was more pleased than she thought she ought to be at the sight of Anderton's car drawing up and pulling in to park at the side of the lane.

"Evening, sir," she said, as he made his way over to her. He was dressed more casually than she was used to seeing him, in a rather nice shirt and jeans, and had the air of a man pulled reluctantly from an enjoyable social engagement. Had he been at the Great Wyrm festival? Surely not. "Sorry to interrupt your evening."

Anderton rolled his eyes. "Par for the course, Kate. Par for the course. What have we got?"

Kate told him as they walked towards the cottage. When she got to the part about the male teenager, Anderton whistled. "He fell *in* it? The poor little bugger. He'll not get over that in a hurry."

SOCO had set up powerful lights that illuminated the scene with a brilliant white glow. The body looked diminished, even more pathetic than it had been in the dark. Anderton, observing from the doorway, didn't say anything but his eyebrows rose. "The paths will have their work cut out for them," was his only remark.

Kate hadn't thought of that, and it was then she realised that her ex-boyfriend, Andrew Stanton, would probably be doing the post mortem. Her heart sank. Would she be able to get Olbeck to go instead of her? Then she remembered, again, that he wouldn't be back from Barbados for another couple of days, the jammy *git*.

"It may not even be a suspicious death," Kate remarked, as she and Anderton watched the SOCOs do their work. Camera flashes momentarily dyed the air in the room an even brighter white. "Could have been a homeless guy who just died naturally."

"Yes, that's true," agreed Anderton. "We won't know anything more tonight."

Just as he said that, there was a sudden flurry of interest in the room. One of the technicians held up something in an evidence bag. Kate squinted. "What have you got?" she called.

"Syringe," the woman holding the bag called back. "Several syringes, actually."

Kate and Anderton looked at one another. "There you go," said Anderton. "Common or garden overdose. Not for us."

"You can't know that for sure," protested Kate.

Anderton blew out his cheeks in a sigh. "No, I know that. But I was dragged up here from a very nice dinner engagement that I would really rather like to get back to. Stick around for another hour or so if you want, Kate, but I don't think there's anything for us here."

Dinner engagement? With who? Kate was aware of a rather unpleasant prickling sensation, a swoop of her stomach, as if she'd stepped into a plummeting life. Dinner engagement with *who*? Not that it was any of her business, but...

Anderton said his goodbyes and left the cottage. Kate muttered a goodbye in response and turned her eyes back to the scene, barely comprehending it. She and Anderton had had a one night stand, several years ago, and she couldn't avoid her powerful attraction to her boss. Nothing else had happened between them since, but Kate wondered – far too often for comfort – whether Anderton's feelings for her were in the dim and distant past or, like hers for him, merely under the surface, waiting for the perfect chance to erupt again.

She sighed and made an effort to focus on what was happening in the here and now. After another half an hour, Stephen Smithfield came over, pulling off his gloves. "Hi, Kate, you still here?"

"Someone's got to be."

"What happened to Anderton?"

Kate shrugged. "He had to get back somewhere. Can you give me any more info on the body?"

Stephen nodded. "This is all very preliminary, you understand. You'll have to wait for the PM for the details. But based on the clothing and the size and shape of the body, I would estimate that it's a man, probably middle-aged. He's been dead for several weeks. In fact, judging by the insect activity, we could be talking months."

"He's been here for months? Undiscovered?" Kate raised her eyebrows. "You're sure about that?"

"Call it two months," said Stephen. "But don't quote me."

"Cause of death?"

"Again, this is just ballpark. There's no obvious signs of violence. No blunt instrument lying nearby, no ligatures, no knives. And you know we found those syringes. I think you're looking at a natural death."

"Well," said Kate, "far be it from me to do myself out of a job, but let's hope so."

"If it turns out to be a heroin overdose, which is looking likely, we might be able to narrow down the time of death. Amazingly, you know, certain drugs can actually significantly affect the rate of larval development. Fascinating, really."

"Is that right?" asked Kate, hiding a grimace. "Well, I'll guess we'll see what the PM throws up. Thanks, Stephen. I'm going to head off now."

"Enjoy the rest of your evening," said Stephen, without evident irony. Kate grinned to herself as she walked away. Techs were a little weird, you couldn't get away from that. Nature of the job, she supposed. She pulled her jacket a little more firmly around herself – a chilly wind had suddenly sprung up – and made her way back to the main road.

Chapter Two

"Morning, team," Anderton said, clearly in ebullient mood as he crashed into the office. "Hope there aren't too many sore heads from the festivities last night. Kate, I know *you'll* be all right. What's the latest on our very, very dead body?"

Kate snapped her mouth shut in the middle of a yawn. Yes, she wasn't hung over – she didn't really drink – but she'd still only managed about four hours of sleep. Needless to say, Jay, Laura, Hannah and Dan had pounced on her the second she'd walked through the door of her house, wanting to know every gory detail. She'd not been able to tell them much but they had still insisted on staying up late into the night, hashing over the events of the evening and wondering who the poor man or woman had once been. Kate, conscious that the smell from the corpse had permeated her hair and clothes, had finally pleaded for mercy and jumped in the shower, only to find that Jay had drained the hot water tank in his own frantic ablutions. Eventually, she boiled the kettle and had a very unsatisfying strip wash in the bathroom before everyone eventually succumbed to weariness and she could finally get to bed.

She hauled herself into a straighter sitting position. "There's no ID as yet – it seems likely that they'll have to go off dental records, or even DNA, which means we'll have to wait for the PM."

"And that is taking place...?"

Kate fought back another yawn. "Tomorrow."

"Fine. Hopefully we'll have an answer then and we'll also know whether we're even taking on the case. If it's an accidental death, nothing suspicious, then that's not our department. God knows we've got enough to do without worrying about careless junkies."

There were a few smothered grins at that but Kate was conscious of a twinge of annoyance. They didn't yet know for certain whether this was a suspicious death, did they? For the first time, she wondered whether Anderton's mind was completely on the job. He seemed, well, a trifle hasty to dismiss this case.

She realised Anderton was still speaking to her. "Kate, would you mind doing the PM tomorrow, seeing as you're already involved with the case?"

Kate was all set to protest. She knew very well that it would probably be her ex-boyfriend, Andrew Stanton, conducting the post mortem and that would be rather awkward. On the other hand, nobody else seemed at all interested in taking this on. She should be responsible for it, if only to make sure that nothing was missed.

"Yes, I'll do it," she confirmed, with a small inner-sigh. It might not be be Andrew conducting the examination, after all.

Anderton nodded, apparently satisfied. "Anyone else got anything?"

Theo raised his hand. "We've done some preliminary interviews with the neighbours, not that there are really any neighbours to the cottages. There's a few houses fairly nearby though, on the other side of the river, and we've had a couple of reports that the cottages were used by vagrants, homeless men. One in particular was spotted there several times a couple of months ago. Nothing hugely conclusive though, no names or anything."

"Okay, fine. Thanks, Theo. Anyone else?" Silence fell across the room. Anderton shrugged. "Okay, well, let's break it up. If anyone needs me, I'll be in my office for the next hour."

Everyone drifted back to their desks. Kate spent a moment conferring with Theo and getting a description of the man the 'neighbours' had mentioned. Armed with that information, she spent an hour scrolling through the records of the various homeless people who'd made it onto the database for one reason or another, before she stopped, annoyed with herself at not immediately realising that without knowing the age or the sex of the body they'd found there was no point in printing off any records for comparison. She'd just have to wait for the post mortem tomorrow before doing anything else. She swung her chair back from the desk a little, frustrated and a bit bored.

By this time it was lunchtime and she made her way to the canteen. Normally she ate with Olbeck, or occasionally with Theo and Jane, but today she didn't feel much like being sociable. Having a house full of visitors meant that she was feeling the need for a bit of solitary peace and quiet. She bought a salad and a carton of orange juice and took it away from the hubbub of the canteen, deciding to eat it in the little park just over the road from the police station.

She passed through the main entrance and reception of the station on her way out and paused for a second by the main desk, checking she'd put her pass in her hand bag. There was a man standing by the front desk on the visitor's side; a non-descript man, short and rather slender, and with the kind of thin moustache that hadn't been fashionable since the 1940s. Kate only noticed him because of his air of nervousness and the way he was shifting from foot to foot.

"What was that again, sir?" asked Sergeant Brown, who was currently manning the reception desk.

"I *said*, I wish to report a robbery," the little man replied. His voice was high with nerves, or perhaps naturally that way.

"Can you give me a few more details?" asked Sergeant Brown.

The little man hesitated for a second. "*Here*? Give you the details here and now?"

"Well, just so I can see how best we can help you—" began the sergeant, but the man made a sound that was almost a squeak and then began backing towards the door, shaking his head.

"I changed my mind – it doesn't matter – I don't... I changed my mind—" he stuttered and then turned and fled.

In the silence that followed, Kate and Sergeant Brown exchanged meaningful glances. Then, rolling his eyes to the ceiling, the good sergeant sat back down again and Kate smiled and made her way outside. On the steps, she caught sight of the little man, almost running, turning a corner down a side street before he scurried out of sight.

Kate had forgotten all about the incident by the time she returned from her lunch break. She checked her emails, noting with pleasure that she had one from her friend Stuart, once a colleague and now a private investigator, suggesting lunch next week. She replied to him in the affirmative and made a note in her diary. It would be good to have someone to run this latest case by, seeing as Olbeck wasn't around.

The phone on Theo's desk rang. Concentrating on her emails, Kate just about registered that he'd answered it. After a moment, the tone of his voice pierced her consciousness and she raised her head, looking across the desk to where he held the phone wedged between his ear and his shoulder, nodding and making notes.

KATE HESITATED, LISTENING. SHE COULDN'T have put her finger on what exactly was being conveyed from the other end of the phone, but her copper's sense was tingling. Something had happened.

She waited until Theo had put the phone down and raised her eyebrows questioningly at him across the desk.

Theo winced and stretched his neck. "What?"

"What was that? And you shouldn't take a call with the phone like that, you'll bugger your neck."

"You're telling me," Theo said with feeling. "Anyway, it's nothing much. Couple of bodies found but – wait a minute—" he cautioned as Kate tried to interject. "Doesn't look suspicious at all. Common or garden overdose."

Something about the phrase made Kate sit up a little. Who had said that? She remembered then – it had been Anderton, at the scene last night. And here it was again. More overdoses?

"So who was that?" she asked.

"Uniform. They're just reporting."

"*Two* bodies found?"

"Yeah, I know. That's the only thing that's a bit strange. Why are you so interested, anyway? Do you want to go and see?"

"Yes, actually, I do," Kate said slowly. "Are you coming?"

Theo shook his head. "Nope, you can have this one. It's probably nothing, anyway."

"Well, maybe," said Kate. She picked up her bag and said goodbye, rummaging for her car keys as she left the office.

Her al fresco lunch had done her good; she felt more awake. Kate lowered the car window to get the full benefit of the lovely weather. She hoped the Indian summer would continue for a good few weeks yet. She thought, with a touch of slightly malicious enjoyment, that it would be rather good if it held *right* up until Olbeck and Jeff touched down at Heathrow tonight and then broke into torrential rain. Then she'd have the pleasure of telling them what they'd missed whilst they were swanning around Barbados.

Chuckling to herself, Kate swung the car into a side street in the suburb of Arbuthon Green. She could clearly see which house she should be heading to – there was a uniformed officer standing outside, fending off enquiries from curious passers-by. Blue and white crime scene tape had been stretched over the front of the driveway. Kate parked the car and locked it. She showed her badge to the officer on guard and ducked under the tape. She didn't recognise him but that wasn't unusual; Abbeyford had recruited a lot of new personnel in the last year. The house itself was a charmless sixties box made of pale yellow brick with a red-tiled roof. The small front garden was badly overgrown, the white trumpet-shaped flowers of bindweed twining their way through the uncut privet hedge. The front door, covered in peeling pale blue paint, stood open. Kate poked her head tentatively around the frame. Through the cluttered hallway, she could see more officers standing in the living room, observing something that was currently out of her sight.

"Hello?" Kate walked further in. She recognised one of the uniformed officers, Sergeant Bill Osbourne, and shook his outstretched hand. "Hi, Bill. What have you got?"

Osbourne indicated with a nod of his head. "Two bodies. Not sure it'll be for you, though, Kate. Looks pretty unsuspicious to me."

Kate followed his gaze. The bodies of two young men sat opposite one another, in a rather eerie mirroring of each other's posture. Both were sat upright but slumped, each with a tourniquet around their left arm and a syringe deeply embedded within the crook of their elbow. Both had their eyes closed, both were pale as milk, the skin of their faces already beginning to blotch with decay.

"Well," said Kate. She bit her lip, pondering. "I have to say you're probably right. Overdose."

"Aye," said Osbourne. "Pretty straightforward."

"It's a bit odd that they both died at the same time," said Kate. "Isn't it?"

Osbourne shrugged. "Not if the drug was unusually pure. If they shot up together at the same time, it would have been quick. Neither of them would have been aware of the other, I would have thought."

"I suppose you're right," said Kate. "I guess there's nothing else..." She looked about, hoping for inspiration. "A gas leak?"

Osbourne chuckled. "You're clutching at straws, lass. The PM will confirm what we suspect, but I'd be stunned if it was anything other than a straightforward overdose."

Kate sighed. "Yes, I'm sure you're right." She looked again at the bodies, feeling a queasy pity. "Who are they?"

Osbourne consulted his notebook. "Pete Hardew and Wayne Potter. Known addicts, petty criminals, no great loss to society."

"Right." There didn't seem to be much more to say. "Well, I guess there's not much point me hanging around then, is there? Could you let me know if anything surprising does turn up?"

"Aye, will do, Kate."

"Thanks, Bill." Kate said goodbye and turned to leave the fetid little room.

Chapter Three

OLBECK WAS BACK IN THE office the next day, ridiculously tanned and relaxed looking. He handed around bottles of rum and hot pepper sauce – Kate took the sauce – and suffered half-teasing, half resentful remarks about 'glad you decided to finally come back', 'beach got too boring for you, did it?' and all the usual clichés. After everyone had finally settled down and got back to work, Olbeck came over and perched on Kate's desk, swinging one leg.

"So, what have I missed?"

"Not a lot, actually," Kate admitted. She turned her chair to face him. "God, you're *so* brown. We've had several dead bodies but nothing too untoward, apparently."

"*Several* bodies? Tell me more." Olbeck listened as Kate outlined the last few cases. "It's a bit weird that they've all started popping up now, isn't it? Or could it just be coincidence?"

"You tell me," said Kate. "The thing is, Anderton's not interested, which means that it's not top priority. He's kind of just chucked it at me to keep an eye on."

"Right." Olbeck rubbed his tanned chin and got to his feet. "Well, keep an eye on it then, and let me know if anything untoward actually turns up."

"Aye-aye, captain." Kate threw him an ironic salute. "So when am I going to see the photos, then?"

"When I put them on Facebook, of course."

"I don't do Facebook."

"I know you don't, you Luddite. Tell you what, I'll have a grand cinema screening over at our place sometime soon and you can see them then."

"Marvellous."

Olbeck cautiously scratched at his nose, which was peeling. "What are you up to today?"

Kate grimaced. "I've got the PM on the body from the cottage."

"What fun for you."

"Indeed." Kate got up herself and began to gather her things together. "And guess what's even *more* fun? Andrew's doing the PM."

Olbeck winced. "Ouch. Awkward."

Kate hoisted her bag onto her shoulder. "Don't suppose you want to do it for me?" she asked, cheekily.

Olbeck gave a cynical laugh. "Nice try, but no."

"Oh well." Kate gave him another salute. "I'll go and face the music then. See you later."

Driving towards the pathology labs, Kate's expression of false cheer collapsed and she groaned. Seeing Andrew was just *so* awkward. Doctor Stanton was still obviously very hurt by Kate ending the relationship on such spurious – at least from his perspective – grounds and, whilst he was too much of a gentleman to go so far as to make pointed and cutting remarks, there was a stiffness to his manner, a marked contrast to the easy flirtatiousness that used to characterise their interactions. Kate fervently hoped that the scheduling of the post mortem had been changed, or – even better – that Doctor Telling had replaced Andrew as the one performing the procedure, but it was not to be. Kate checked in at reception and made her way to the theatre, swearing under her breath.

As it happened, Theo was already there. Kate was left relieved that there was another person there to temper the frosty atmosphere but also annoyed that he'd beaten her to it. Theo had been promoted to Detective Sergeant last year, and whilst he and Kate worked better together now than they had at first, their partnership had nothing of the easy familiarity that Kate used to enjoy with Olbeck. Kate took a deep breath, greeted Andrew with as nice a smile as she could, and vowed that she would spend the evening hard at work studying. She was due to take the exams for her Inspector's certificate in three weeks' time, and – *please, God* – if she passed them then she and Olbeck might be back working together again.

Once the PM was actually underway, some of the tension in the room eased a little. Andrew had always had a rather terse, abrupt way of working, which meant that any undercurrent of resentment went virtually unnoticed. Kate could concentrate on the job at hand, watching as the sad remains of what had once been a human being were probed and weighed and measured and the mystery of their death hopefully cleared up.

"Your victim is male," Andrew said, bending over the table. "I would say late forties, perhaps older. Early fifties maybe."

Kate nodded. "Any chance of fingerprints?"

Andrew risked a glance at her. "Not a hope. I think your best bet will be dental records, although we'll be able to do DNA tests as well. There might be a match."

Kate nodded again and fell silent whilst Theo asked a few more questions. She normally found post mortems hard, particularly if the victim had been young, but this one was turning out to be less emotionally draining than normal. The body was so badly decayed it was almost unrecognisable as a human being, and detachment came surprisingly easily.

Eventually Andrew stood up, easing his shoulders back with a groan. Kate was uncomfortably reminded that she used to give him back massages when he came home from work. She swore, yet again, never to get involved with anyone else she might be likely to have to work with in future. It never ended well. Inevitably, her thoughts flew to Anderton. Something was different about him lately. He seemed...younger, somehow. More *invigorated*. Kate frowned, and concentrated on what Andrew was saying.

"...not possible to ascertain a definite cause of death," he continued. "There's a plethora of further tests to be run though and I'm hopeful that one of those will have the answer. You can read up about it in my report."

"Thank you," Kate said hurriedly. He gave her a stony-faced glance and merely nodded before leaving the room. Kate sighed.

"Dear, oh dear," Theo said with a tinge of malice. "You're not very popular here at the moment, are you, Kate?"

"Oh, sod off," Kate said, picking up her bag. "How's *your* love life these days, anyway, Theo?"

Theo looked smug. "Doing nicely, thank you. Why, want to join the harem?"

Kate laughed, despite herself. "It's tempting but...no."

"You don't know what you're missing," Theo said as they left the building together.

"Oh, sod off," said Kate again, but this time she was grinning as she said it.

"WELL?" OLBECK ASKED AFTER KATE returned to the office. "Get a name?"

Kate shook her head. "Nope. We'll have to wait for dental records. We don't even have an official cause of death yet."

"Drugs overdose," Anderton said over her shoulder, making her jump. She hadn't heard him come up behind her which, given Anderton's usual mode of conduct, was something of a miracle. "I keep telling you. Mark, have you got five minutes?"

Olbeck got up. Kate watched them both walk out and slowly went back to her desk. She felt uncomfortable; frustrated, a bit bored, unsure of what to do next. Unenthusiastically, she began to deal with the paperwork that had accumulated over the past couple of days. She checked her emails, noting that she had one from Bill Osbourne, which made her perk up a little until she realised he was just letting her know about the post mortems for the two bodies found in Arbuthon Green. Well, she wouldn't be going to those. One session with Andrew's unspoken resentment was enough for her, thank you very much.

She became aware of the growling of her stomach and realised that it was nearly two o'clock and she'd not yet eaten any lunch. She considered the canteen but it was a lovely day and perhaps a quick sandwich in the nearby park would restore her enthusiasm. Kate picked up her bag and made her way out of the building, passing through the main station reception area as usual. There was a man standing at the front desk, but the only reason Kate noticed him was the phrase he used, identical to the one used by that funny little man who'd changed his mind about reporting a crime.

"I want to report a robbery."

The moment Kate heard that, she recalled the earlier occasion. She stopped and listened.

"A robbery, sir?" asked the desk sergeant.

The man nodded. He was tall and broad-shouldered, with curling black hair and a rather rakish goatee. Kate, moving closer, thought he would make an excellent pirate.

"Yeah," he was saying. "Definitely a robbery. I'd rather not give you all the details right here, though. That a problem?"

"That's fine," said Kate, stepping smartly up to the counter. Both the man and the sergeant looked a little startled. "I can take this, Sergeant. If you'd like to come with me, sir?"

The man grinned, showing a lot of healthy white teeth. His gaze swept from Kate's face to her chest, down to her feet and up again. "Hell yeah, officer. Lead on."

Kate knew she should be offended but instead she felt like laughing. He was just so obvious it was almost a refreshing change from the usual sly ogle. She led him to a vacant interview room and shut the door, gesturing for him to sit down.

"Now," she said, taking the chair opposite him. "I'm Detective Sergeant Kate Redman. What can I do for you?"

The man's grin grew wider. Wolfish, Kate thought to herself. The big bad wolf. It made what he had to tell her even more strange.

"I need to report a robbery," he said, quite easily, as if he were commenting on the weather. "It feels kind of strange to be telling a woman this, though. Not that I'm complaining," he added hastily. "I never thought I'd be one for the whole 'doing my duty' thing, but it kind of feels like that's what I'm doing, you know what I mean?"

Kate was lost. "Sorry, sir, you'll have to start from the beginning. You were robbed?"

The man nodded. "Yeah. I'm Jack, by the way, Jack Harker. Yeah, I was robbed. It's kind of a strange story though."

Kate smiled brightly. "Well, why don't you try me?"

Jack Harker looked around, as if there were someone else in the room, and then leaned forward conspiratorially. "I was at this bar, in town, last night. Twenty One. You know it?" Kate nodded as if she did, and he went on. "So, I'm having a few drinks, having fun, you know what I mean? These two chicks rock up. Sexy girls, young – you know?" Kate raised her eyebrows and he said hastily, "Not *too* young, early twenties, or something. Foreign. Think they were Eastern European or something. Had that really sexy accent. Anyway, we get talking and drinking and we end up back at my place."

KATE NODDED ENCOURAGINGLY, ALTHOUGH SHE wondered where this story was going.

Jack Harker continued. "Anyway, we're getting down to it and I pick up my drink – that's about the last thing I *do* remember – and the next thing I know, it's dark and I'm cold and I'm all alone in my living room, tied to a chair."

There was a moment's silence. Kate re-settled herself into her chair and cleared her throat. "You were tied to a chair?"

She would have sworn that Jack Harker was one of those rare human beings incapable of blushing, but a faint rosy hue became visible beneath the dark stubble of his cheeks.

"Yeah," he said awkwardly. "Seriously, they drugged me and left me tied up in a chair. I was fucking freezing, surprised I didn't die of exposure."

"Okay," said Kate, after a moment. "You believe you were drugged – something in the drink, presumably? – and then robbed. What did they take?"

"My wallet, credit cards. A bit of cash I had in the house. My iPad, my laptop. Everything, really."

Kate let her eyes fall to the notebook she was ostensibly making notes on. "Would you recognise these women again, if we managed to make an arrest?"

Jack Harker frowned. "I don't know. They were dark. Long haired, small, sort of thin. A bit thin for me, actually, but, you know..."

"What were their names?"

Jack Harker grinned a little sheepishly. "I can't remember."

Kate folded her lips, trying to hide her own smile. "It's probably not important, sir. They almost certainly gave you false names anyway, if they were planning to rob you."

"Right. Yeah."

"Have you seen your doctor? Or been to hospital?"

"No. No, I'm fine. Just a bit of a headache."

Kate leant forward a little. "I really would encourage you to get checked out. Just in case."

"Okay." His eyes flickered upwards for a moment and she knew he had no intention of doing what she suggested. Oh well, his loss.

She whisked through the rest of the formalities, gave him a crime identification number, and handed Jack Harker back to the desk sergeant. He tipped her a wink as he was led away to another interview room and she was unable to stop herself smiling back in response. Then she chastised herself as she turned away. Keep your mind on the job, Kate. The rumbling of her stomach made her realise she really did need some lunch now. She collected her handbag and made her way out of the building, dismissing the handsome Mr. Harker from her mind.

Chapter Four

KATE ARRIVED AT THE OFFICE earlier than usual the next day. Bathed in a glow of righteousness, she was somewhat annoyed to find that Olbeck had beaten her in by some time, judging by the multiple empty coffee cups lined up by his keyboard. She flung her bag under her desk and switched on her computer. While waiting for it to warm up, she wandered over to Olbeck's office and leant against the door frame. "Want a coffee?"

"Already had three." Olbeck was hunched over his keyboard, typing furiously. Kate watched him for a moment. There was something different about him, but infuriatingly, she couldn't quite put her finger on what it was. New haircut? She dismissed the idea. New suit? No, not that either. What was it?

Olbeck came to the end of whatever sentence he was typing and looked up. "What's up?"

"Nothing," Kate said, straightening up from her slouch. "Just wondering what you're doing?"

Olbeck looked surprised. "Nothing exciting. Why?"

"No reason..." Kate said nothing more as Olbeck's phone rang.

He picked it up with his customary greeting. "DI Olbeck here."

Kate watched. From the nature of Olbeck's comments, she gathered it was something serious. She saw his eyebrows raise at one point. She should be starting work but she didn't move. She had the feeling something important had just happened.

Eventually, Olbeck put down the receiver. Kate looked at him expectantly.

"Okay, okay," said Olbeck. "You know what that was, don't you?"

"Suspicious death," Kate said; a statement rather than a question.

"Got it in one." Olbeck hesitated a moment and then added "It's Trixie Arlen."

Kate's eyes bulged. "Seriously?" she managed, after a moment.

"So patrol says." Olbeck and Kate looked at each other for a moment in mutual shock. "That's what they said. They're at her house now."

Kate found her voice. "Wow. Seriously, Trixie Arlen?" She was silent for a second and then asked "What happened?"

Olbeck was gathering up his coat and keys. "Nothing tangible, as yet. They just called in to say Trixie Arlen's been found dead at her home, that's all." He looked up. "Will you come with me?"

"Er – yes," said Kate. "Of course I will."

ON THE DRIVE THERE, KATE tinkered with her phone, trying to bring up the Wikipedia page that covered Trixie Arlen's career, both the early glory years in her days as a Nineties 'It' girl and the most recent times with her reinvention as fertile earth mother, *Good Housekeeping* columnist, and luxury kitchen products designer. The signal out in the deep countryside where Trixie Arlen's farmhouse was situated was terrible and Kate, kept tutting and swearing as the page failed to load and then reload.

"Don't worry about that now," said Olbeck eventually. "There's probably nothing there that's particularly accurate anyway."

Kate conceded and put the phone away. "I remember her being on that chat show," she said. "Do you remember? *Wicked Weekend*?"

Olbeck winced. "God, the nineties..."

"I was about fourteen," said Kate, grinning. "How old were you when that was on?" she asked, mock-innocently.

Olbeck looked pained. "I was precisely four years older than you," he cleared his throat and went on, with dignity, "as you well know. And yes," he continued, looking a little more sober. "I do remember that. And when she lost her first husband and lost the baby..."

Kate's smile fell from her face. "Oh," she murmured. "I'd forgotten about that."

"Well, she bounced back," said Olbeck with an ironic grin. "Didn't she? I remember all the papers from that time. All about the phoenix rising from the ashes and all that bollocks."

"I'd totally forgotten about the baby," Kate said, and although she said it quietly, there was something in her voice that made Olbeck look over at her momentarily.

They drove on in silence for a few minutes. They followed a route into the deepest Somerset countryside, the roads gradually narrowing from A roads to B roads, and then to a road that was barely a farm track, hemmed in both sides by the sun-bleached cow parsley, brown bracken and the spreading tentacles of brambles, heavy with berries ripened in the September sun. Up ahead, Kate could see police tape cordoning off the entrance to another lane, crumbling brick columns standing sentinel on either side of the tarmac.

Olbeck showed his ID to the uniformed officer guarding the entrance to the gateway and they were waved through. Olbeck proceeded cautiously, mindful of the time he and Kate had almost been obliterated by a speeding ambulance on the way to a crime scene. They proceeded on this journey without mishap, passing an orchard, a pond and a field of waving wheat, before drawing up in front of a comfortable, shabby sort of house that nevertheless managed to convey an air of wealth, despite its peeling paint and Bohemian aspect. The farmhouse itself had been much extended, and a large silver Range Rover was parked at one side of the circular driveway. There was a building which had clearly once been a stable block, now converted into a garage, which held another black Range Rover and a new model Mini. Thick ropes of wisteria hung over the front of the house, framing the front doorway in drooping fronds of green.

Olbeck and Kate made their way inside, nodding to the constable who guarded the front door. The hallway was tiled in slate, the walls painted a soft green, an antique console table by the front door. A wire basket held children's shoes and wellingtons, and a canvas shopping bag, printed with a fashionable mid-century design, was hung from the peg rack up on the wall.

Kate and Olbeck followed the murmur of voices and the click and whirr of the crime scene cameras through the house. They glanced into the kitchen, where Kate saw more uniformed officers; a man in an expensive suit sat at the kitchen table with his head in his hands, a blonde woman, red-eyed and sniffling, sat beside him. That was all she could take in in a swift glance before they continued on through a comfortable and understatedly luxurious sitting room and then a playroom crammed with every conceivable toy, finally ascending a flight of stairs to the first floor.

The bedroom they found themselves in was large and square, dominated by a huge bed with a black iron frame. A grey silk counterpane had slipped to the floor and the bed itself was unmade. Trixie Arlen's body lay on top, half on her side, one arm dangling from the bed, almost brushing the soft pile of the carpet. Kate and Olbeck paused in the doorway, silently regarding the scene. Doctor Telling had already arrived and was leaning over the body, her deft, gentle fingers already measuring, probing, testing. Kate sent up a silent prayer of thanks that Andrew hadn't been the pathologist on call and then chastised herself for being so unfeeling.

Several Scene of Crime officers were already working the room and Kate and Olbeck stepped forward a pace or two and then remained still, to allow them to work undisturbed. Doctor Telling noticed them and nodded a silent greeting before turning back to the body.

"It *is* her, isn't it?" Olbeck asked in a murmur.

Kate nodded uncertainly. She could see it was Trixie Arlen; that face was instantly recognisable from a thousand different television and press appearances, but she could understand Olbeck's hesitation. Trixie looked...diminished, somehow; shrunken, reduced. But that was understandable. Death was the great leveller, and Trixie's beauty had always depended heavily on her natural vivacity. She had been cute rather than sexy; rather gamine, the girl-next-door type – *a nice girl, attractively wholesome, good clean fun* – in the media's stereotypical clichés.

Kate looked at Trixie's dead face. More so than usual, the scene felt unreal; a stage set of a crime scene rather than a real one. Was it because the victim was so famous? Kate recalled her first reaction to Olbeck's news – violent disbelief. Celebrities led charmed lives, didn't they? Things like this didn't happen to them – not to the ones who didn't walk on the wild side.

Kate let her gaze rest on the body, trying to take in as much information as possible. Trixie was dressed in grey marl leggings and a loose pink T-shirt. Her hair – that famous mop of bouncy brown curls – tumbled around her face, partially hiding it. Kate could see the wink of something sparkly in an earlobe, but she wore no other jewellery that Kate could see, except the huge diamond solitaire engagement ring and the plainer wedding band on the hand that dangled from the bed. The tips of her fingers on that hand were already purple with lividity.

There were no obvious signs of violence; no stab wounds, no ligature marks, nothing to indicate a violent death. Was this even a suspicious death? Kate tried to think back on what little she knew of Trixie Arlen from the papers. Had she had any health problems that she'd shared with the media? Kate thought she could recall something about Trixie having fertility treatment; how in God's name had she managed to retain that bit of trivia?

She didn't even *read* gossip magazines. That was everything she could recall. Momentarily, she remembered the lost baby that Trixie had suffered after the death of her first husband, musician Ivo Wright. A miscarriage at eight months – wasn't that technically a stillbirth? Kate winced inwardly. Poor woman, what a trauma that must have been.

She came back to reality with a start, realising that Olbeck and Doctor Telling were already conferring. Kate hurried over to join them by the bedside.

"Can you give us any indication at all?" Olbeck asked.

Doctor Telling peeled the surgical gloves from her long, thin fingers. She placed them neatly inside the pocket of her overalls and turned to pick up her medical bag.

"I'm not quite yet ready to give a definitive answer," she replied quietly. Doctor Telling always spoke quietly; Kate wondered, irrelevantly, if she and Mr. Telling ever had a really good, flaming stand-up row. Doctor Telling continued. "There are several indications as to a probable cause of death but I really don't want to commit myself before there's been a proper post-mortem. I'm sorry," she added, as Olbeck opened his mouth in protest, "but in a case that is bound to be as high profile as this one, I really can't be seen to get anything wrong."

"Fine," Olbeck said, clearly annoyed but able to understand her point. "Can you tell me whether you think it's a suspicious death or not, at least?"

Doctor Telling paused in the doorway. She shook her head. "I'm almost certain that it isn't, but that's all I can say at this point. I'll be doing the post mortem tomorrow and I hope to see you and DS Redman there. We can discuss it all thoroughly then."

They had to be content with that. Once Doctor Telling had left to arrange procedures for transporting the corpse to the pathology labs, Kate and Olbeck turned back to look at the body. It still had that same sense of surrealism about it. Kate fought the urge to reach out and touch it, just to check it was real. She stepped back a little and let her gaze swing around the room. Again, it was comfortable, well furnished, all in expensive but conventional good taste. A large wardrobe at the side of the room held seemingly enough clothes to fill a department store. There were several framed photographs on the dressing table, a family shot of Trixie, her husband and three young, cherubic-looking children. Several other individual shots of the children, twin boys and a younger sister from the looks of it.

Kate's fingers itched to start searching, burrowing through drawers and belongings and under the huge bed, but of course she couldn't. Olbeck was gesturing that they needed to leave the room to the SOCOs and Kate concurred. They made their way back down to the kitchen.

"Who found the body?" Kate asked as they walked down the stairs.

Olbeck ducked his head to avoid a low beam. "Her husband. He was away last night, on business apparently. He got home very early this morning and found her. The children were still asleep, thank God."

Kate stopped walking. "The children were *here*? All along?"

Olbeck nodded, his face grim. "I know. Imagine if they'd gone into her room and found her..."

"God," Kate closed her eyes momentarily. "Thank God her husband came home in time. Is that him in the kitchen?"

"Yes. Shh, we're almost there." Olbeck opened the door to the kitchen, which had been closed since they passed it earlier.

The black-suited man had raised his head by this time and was staring across the kitchen table, his face a blank, stony mask. The blonde woman beside him had stopped crying. She sat quietly, occasionally giving an exhausted gasp, as if she'd suddenly run out of air.

"Mr. Jacob Arlen?" asked Olbeck, quietly. The suited man stood to face them. Olbeck held out his hand and Arlen shook it automatically. "I'm Detective Inspector Olbeck and this is my colleague, Detective Sergeant Redman. I'd just like to convey our sincere condolences for your loss. Do you feel able to answer a few questions? It can wait, if you don't feel up to it."

Arlen hesitated. Then he shook his head and said in a low voice, "No. No, it's fine. It may as well be now."

"Thank you. Do you mind if we sit down?" At Arlen's nod of assent, Kate and Olbeck seated themselves at the scrubbed pine table, Kate facing Arlen, Olbeck facing the blonde woman. Arlen introduced her as 'Kyla Mellors, a good friend of ours.'

"Are your children still here, Mr. Arlen?" Kate asked. She devoutly hoped they'd already been removed to a safe and familiar place.

"My parents came and got them," Arlen said, and Kate inwardly sighed with relief. "I don't know how much they – I mean, I don't know how much they know. I was in such a state of shock I think I... I think I just said that Mummy was ill and they could see her later—" His voice broke. He put his fist to his mouth, as if his clenched fingers could stop the tears that Kate could sense were just below the surface of his ostensible control. Kyla Mellors reached out a tentative hand and Arlen, after a moment, took his fist down from his face and clutched at her fingers. "I'm sorry," he said after a few moments. "I know that doesn't help. I'll try not to – to break down again."

Olbeck murmured the usual soothing platitudes and Kate added hers. Kyla Mellors was visibly wincing at the strength of Arlen's grip on her hand, and after a moment he seemed to realise it, releasing her with a 'sorry – sorry, Kyla'. She nodded and smiled wanly but Kate saw her slip her hand beneath the table and thought she was probably rubbing away the pain with her other hand.

"If you could just take us through what happened, Mr. Arlen," Olbeck said. "I understand you were away on business last night?"

Arlen nodded. "Yes, that's right. I often have client meetings after normal office hours and last night I knew I'd be so late home that it wasn't worth me travelling back. I booked a hotel and left very early the next morning. This morning, I mean."

"Your office is in London?"

Arlen nodded again. "Yes, in the city. On Cheapside."

"Were you due to go back to work today?" asked Kate. "It seems an awful lot of travelling to be home for a few hours."

Arlen frowned. "I just wanted to see my children for a few hours, I see them so infrequently during the week that I take the opportunity when I can. My first meeting today wasn't until eleven am, so I knew I'd be able to be home for an hour or so, to help with the children's breakfasts and getting them ready for nursery." A thought seemed to strike him. "My God, I haven't told the office yet, I didn't think... I'd better call my assistant."

"That's fine, Mr. Arlen," said Olbeck. "I suggest you do that sooner rather than later. But I would strongly suggest you don't go into too much detail as to why you're unable to get to work. Unfortunately there's going to be considerable press interest and it would be good to head them off for as long as we possibly can."

Arlen looked shaken, as if that reality had only just occurred to him. "Yes. Yes I can see that."

Olbeck gave him a moment and then gently prompted him again. "You arrived here very early this morning."

"Yes, about six o'clock. The traffic can be appalling later on and I wanted to miss it if possible. Thank God I did come back so early...if the children had woken..." Arlen trailed off and there was a moment's silence.

"And what happened when you arrived home?" Olbeck asked patiently.

Arlen closed his eyes momentarily. "I unlocked the front door and let myself in. I was as quiet as possible – I didn't want to disturb anyone. I can't remember exactly what I did first – oh, yes, I put on some coffee. Then I went upstairs to change, and I walked into the bedroom and found – found Trixie. I...I gasped, I think, or made some sort of sound. I could see she was dead straight away. I – I was so shocked. I didn't really know what to do—"

"Did you touch the body, Mr. Arlen?" asked Kate.

Arlen winced. "Yes. Yes, of course I did. I had to check whether she was – whether I'd made a mistake." His head dropped forward and his voice lowered. "I knew I hadn't, though. She was so cold – I knew I was too late."

"What happened then?" asked Olbeck.

"I think I – yes, I called the police then, or an ambulance. I dialled nine nine nine. After I put the phone down I...I panicked a bit – I remembered the children and I thought for one awful second—" Arlen shut his eyes again and shuddered. "I thought for one awful second they were *all* dead, they'd all been killed or somehow died together." He shuddered again, leaning forward and Kyla took his hand once more. "I ran to their rooms and they were okay, thank God, thank God. Manon woke up then, and I took her downstairs and put her in her high chair." Kate blinked a little at the daughter's name. *Manon?* Arlen continued. "I locked our bedroom door so the boys wouldn't go in when they woke up. Then I – I just waited for the police to get here. They were the ones who suggested I call a friend."

"So he called me," said Kyla, speaking for the first time. She had a low, attractive voice. Kate wondered whose friend she had been; Trixie's? Arlen's? Or a true mutual friend? Kate studied her a little more attentively. Kyla looked to be about thirty-five, although she could have possibly been older. She had long, highlighted blonde hair, well-shaped dark eyebrows and good cheekbones – the striking looks of an ex-model. She too wore a wedding ring and a large multi-jewelled engagement ring.

Olbeck jotted down a few notes and looked up. "May I ask how long you've been married, Mr. Arlen?"

"Five years. We met a few years after Trixie's first husband died."

"Did your wife suffer from any health problems, any medical issues that you were aware of?"

Arlen frowned but after a moment, he answered. "No, nothing that I'm aware of."

"When was the last time you spoke to her?"

"I called her yesterday, at about five o'clock, to tell her I wasn't coming home. There'd been some uncertainty as to whether I'd be able to make it home that night or not, and I wanted to let her know that I wouldn't be able to make it."

"How did she sound?"

Arlen's eyes closed again briefly. "She sounded fine. Absolutely normal. I asked her if she had any plans – sometimes she went to the gym or to yoga in the evenings if she had a babysitter – but she just said she was going to have a quiet night and probably go to bed early."

"So everything seemed absolutely as normal?"

"Yes."

Kate had thought of something. "Mr. Arlen, your wife is a very famous person. Is she active on social media at all – Facebook, Twitter, that sort of thing?"

Arlen nodded. "She loved Twitter, she was on it all the time. She always used to laugh and read me the tweets that amused her."

"Thank you. If you could give me the details of all of her social media accounts, that would be very helpful," Kate said and Arlen nodded.

Olbeck turned to Kyla Mellors. "Mrs. Mellors, you might be able to help us as well. Did you speak to Mrs. Arlen at all yesterday?"

Kyla shook her head. "No, not yesterday. We met up for coffee the day before. Just a quick catch up, you know."

"Did you often do that?"

Kyla withdrew her hand from Arlen's once more. Kate watched her fingers twist together. "Quite often," Kyla said, with a break in her voice. "About once a week or so. I've got a daughter the same age as Manon – that's how we met, at an ante-natal class – and we often used to get the girls together for play dates." Her voice shook quite badly now, tears trembling on the edge of her eyelids. "I can't believe this has happened, it doesn't seem possible." She fell silent with a gasp and put her trembling fingers up to her mouth.

Feeling cruel but pushing on anyway, Kate asked her a question. "So, you were close friends? Would she confide in you?"

Kyla Mellors struggled for a moment. "I suppose so," she said eventually, with another gasp. After another moment, she appeared to regain some control. "We used to talk about all sorts of things. She'd had an interesting life."

"Indeed," said Kate. "Could you have said whether there was anything worrying her? Did she seem concerned or anxious about anything?"

Kyla appeared to give the question serious thought. "I don't *think* so," she said eventually. Her hand went up to her mouth again and she bit her thumbnail.

Kate's eyes narrowed. Something about Kyla's last statement didn't ring true. She sat up a little, wondering whether to push the questioning, but Olbeck was already talking. Kate sat back. She decided that asking more probing questions now would probably be counterproductive. There would be time enough for that later. And besides – maybe this would all be cleared up after the post mortem. Briefly, her thoughts went to Bill Osbourne; she must get in touch with him and find out what the findings of the post mortem on the two young men were.

For a moment, Kate experienced that sudden sense of surrealism again. She couldn't really be sat in *Trixie Arlen's* kitchen, could she? She, Kate Redman, couldn't really be questioning Trixie's bereaved husband? Her gaze slowly tracked the room as she listened to Olbeck asking Arlen for details of his firm and the hotel he'd stayed in last night. It was a large kitchen, the units obviously made to measure by an expensive firm, the floor slate-tiled, every accoutrement well made, costly and suitable. But for all that it was a homely place, full of family clutter and a refreshing lack of pretension. Kate recalled the first case she'd ever worked in Abbeyford, the kidnapping of the Fullman baby and the murder of his nanny. She remembered that house – that hideous, vulgar, new-money house – with no expense spared but no taste either. This house was very different. There was mess; toys everywhere, paperwork scattered over the kitchen countertops. Kate could see crumbs on the floor, muddy footprints by the back door that were too small to have been made by an adult, an overflowing kitchen bin in the corner. Her eyes went to Jacob Arlen. It was funny; he didn't look like the kind of man who would relish living in domestic chaos. He was clean-shaven and good-looking in a stern, ascetic way, trim for a man who had to be well into his fifties. Was this his first marriage? What must it be like for a middle-aged man to have a relatively large young family? He was a hedge-fund manager, or something like that, Kate recalled – something deadly dull but extremely lucrative. Had Trixie Arlen out-earned him or was he the breadwinner?

Olbeck wrapped up the questioning. He and Kate handed over their cards and took their leave. They walked back through the hallway and out into the space in front of the house. The sun blazed overhead, bright enough to make both of them screw up their eyes. Kate was amazed afresh at how nature just went on doing what it did, no matter what small, petty human dramas were being played out on the stage it provided The sun would travel slowly across the sky and set in the west, and night would fall and then the sun would rise again, and it would be the day after Trixie Arlen died. The day three children lost their mother would be over and gone, never to come again. She blinked several times and reminded herself to get a grip.

"Come on," Olbeck said. "Let's have a look around."

Kate followed him as he crunched over the gravel, round the side of the farmhouse. A flash of reflected light caught her eye and she looked over the gently rolling fields to the lane where cars were gathering. Figures with cameras were emerging and clustering at the gates. The paparazzi were here. Corpse flies, Kate thought with a scowl as she followed Olbeck around the corner of the house.

Chapter Five

KATE HAD SEEN MANY TERRIBLE things at various post-mortems. She'd seen bodies with ragged, gaping knife wounds; bodies with skulls crushed like empty egg shells; bodies burned so badly that they were barely recognisable as the remains of a human being. She'd been sickened and disgusted and angry in turn. But until Doctor Telling looked up from the body of Trixie Arlen and told Kate how she believed the woman had died, Kate realised she'd never been truly shocked. Not until now.

"A *heroin* overdose?" Kate was so flabbergasted for a moment that she couldn't think of what else to say. "You're…you're *kidding* me."

Doctor Telling, who rarely smiled, flashed her a slightly ironic one. "That surprises you?"

Kate put her hands up to her head and dropped them. "It surprises me? It bloody *stuns* me. Trixie Arlen, a heroin user?"

Doctor Telling stood upright, easing her back from the tension of several hours of stooping over the body. She slowly peeled the rubber gloves from her hands and dropped them into a yellow hazardous waste bin over by the sink. She nodded. "I had an inkling that that was how she died when I first saw her at the scene," she commented. "I noticed the puncture mark on her inner elbow straight away. Of course, I didn't want to say anything then and there. It could have been that she was on some other form of injectable medication or that she'd had a recent inoculation."

"I am absolutely *stunned*," Kate repeated. She looked at Trixie Arlen's blank face on the gurney. Doctor Telling was skilled at making a corpse appear as lifelike as possible; it was somewhat uncanny, but Trixie Arlen looked less dead here on the post mortem table than she had done lying on her own bed. For all that though, she didn't look as if she were sleeping. Whatever it was that had made her human had gone, and this outer shell was all that was left.

"You're absolutely certain it was heroin?" asked Kate, still without taking her eyes off of the body.

"No. No, not at all. I can't say that with any certainty – you'll have to wait for the results of the toxicology tests. But there were old injection marks on the body, between her toes and within the groin area."

Kate grimaced. "It just seems so incredible. She's – she *was* a mother of three. I know she was a bit wild in the nineties but...it just seems incredible."

There was a knock on the glass panel of the theatre door and they both looked up. Olbeck was waving at them, in a 'can I come in?' type of gesture. Doctor Telling raised her own hand in acknowledgement and he pushed open the door.

"Morning, ladies. Sorry I'm late."

Doctor Telling nodded. "Good morning, DI Olbeck. I've just been telling DS Redman the findings of the PM."

"And?" Olbeck adjusted the sleeve of his jacket. "Anything concrete?"

Kate was dying to be the one to tell him but it would be the height of bad manners to override Doctor Telling in her own workplace. She clamped her lips shut, watching Olbeck's face as Doctor Telling delivered the news, and saw the expression on his face mirror that of her own as she'd been informed.

"Bloody hell," said Olbeck, which was as close as he ever came to swearing. "I must say I'm surprised."

"You and me both," said Kate, unable to keep quiet any longer. "The press will have a field day."

Olbeck frowned. "Which is precisely why we're going to inform them that the results were inconclusive. Right, doctor?" Doctor Telling inclined her head in acquiescence. "There's no point stoking any more wild rumours until we get the results of the tox tests back, right?"

"Right," said Kate. They all looked at Trixie Arlen in silence.

"Oh," Doctor Telling said suddenly and the two officers looked at her quickly. "There's one more thing that struck me. She had some quite serious bruising on her upper right arm, almost as if she'd been gripped very hard. I thought that might be significant."

Olbeck's eyebrows rose. "Indeed. You think it was inflicted by someone else?"

"Yes. It's quite distinct. Have a look for yourselves." The two officers watched as the doctor lifted the sheet covering the body and indicated the bruising. Kate could see for herself the pattern of purple-blue blotches on Trixie Arlen's slender arm.

"I see," said Olbeck. "Well, that's something to take into consideration."

IT WASN'T UNTIL THEY HAD said goodbye to the doctor and were walking down the corridor towards the exit that the implications of what Doctor Telling had told them suddenly hit Kate, as if from a great height. She actually gasped under the impact and stopped dead.

"What is it?" asked Olbeck, turning back to her.

Kate looked at him, wide-eyed. "If Trixie Arlen died of a heroin overdose, then why didn't we find any drugs paraphernalia on or near her body?"

Olbeck's face looked as though he'd just walked into something. "Bloody hell." His face flickered again and Kate knew he was just realising that he should have seen that straight away. She couldn't help a small inner stab of triumph that she'd clocked it before he had. "You're absolutely right, Kate. I should have seen that."

Kate began walking again, a little faster than before. Olbeck hurried to keep up. Kate spoke to him over her shoulder. "We're not mistaken, are we? There was nothing there, nothing at all. Just the body."

"No, nothing. Well, if there had been it would have been obvious, wouldn't it? We would have known how she died straight away."

"I know, I was just wondering if we'd forgotten it." Kate remembered the two bodies at the house at Arbuthon Green, mirror images of one another, sat there with the syringes still in their arms. She felt, just for a moment, a tremor of something too insubstantial to put a name to – some tiny flicker of comprehension that slipped away almost before she noticed it. She came to a halt at the car, shaking her head in frustration.

"You all right?" Olbeck asked as he drew out his own car keys.

"I'm fine," Kate said impatiently. "We've got to get back and let Anderton know."

"I'll let him know," Olbeck said, and although his tone was neutral, Kate thought she heard something of a warning in it, a reminder that Olbeck was, in fact, her superior officer. She was conscious of a spurt of shame and then something very much like anger. It wasn't like him to pull rank. She pressed her lips together and got into her car.

"WELL, WELL, WELL," SAID ANDERTON, pacing the floor as was his habit. "We finally have a crime scene, ladies and gentlemen. Typical that it has to be the most high profile celebrity that we've ever had to deal with. The press will be trying to get everything they can on this one, so I'm sure I don't need to remind you that you speak to nobody without my say-so, and you don't discuss anything – anything at all – with your nearest and dearest."

"Trust nobody," said Olbeck, with a grin.

Anderton looked at him without smiling. "That's right, Mark. And if I find anyone leaking anything to anyone, they'll be out the door so fast their arse won't touch the ground. Do I make myself clear?"

Everyone nodded, grim-faced. Kate, momentarily distracted, thought that Anderton was looking particularly handsome today. His thick grey hair had obviously recently been trimmed and he was wearing a well-cut new suit. She blinked, bringing herself back to listen to what he was saying.

"Now I'll recap quickly for those of you who weren't at the scene. Trixie Arlen, former TV presenter and 'It' girl of the nineties – most of you younglings will only know her from her cookbooks and kitchen products range – was found dead at her home yesterday. No sign of forced entry, no sign of violence, no sign of foul play. The doctor at the scene thought it was a non-suspicious death and the PM seemed to confirm that. We're still waiting for results from the labs for the toxicology tests, but it seems likely that Trixie died of a heroin overdose. That's not yet been made public." Anderton reached the wall and pivoted on his heel. "Now, the problem with that is that we found nothing with the body that indicated that she'd been injecting. No syringes, no actual drugs, no paraphernalia, nothing. Can anyone tell me what that might mean?"

Kate raised her hand. She'd spent most of the night going over one scenario after another and Anderton could have them all if he wanted. "She might have been shooting up with somebody else. When she overdosed, they panicked, cleared everything away and fled."

Anderton nodded. "That's a very likely possibility. Anyone else?"

Kate opened her mouth to go on but Theo got there first, as he often did. Kate gritted her teeth. "She could have been alone when she died but someone found her and took the stuff away. Her husband, probably," said Theo.

Anderton had paused in his pacing and was scribbling frantically on a whiteboard. "Right, another good possibility. So we've got X, the unknown who might have been with Trixie when she died. We've got Y, the unknown who found the body and cleared away the stuff. Anything else?"

Kate raised her hand hurriedly before Theo could speak. "Someone could have been with her and left her *before* she overdosed."

Anderton was still scribbling. "So, this Z might be innocent of clearing any drugs, etc. away but could have still been with Trixie that night?"

Kate nodded. "Say that's how it happened and then, in the morning, her husband comes home, finds her dead and for whatever reason clears away the evidence of what killed her."

"Right," said Anderton. "Could be, could be. Anything else?"

There was a moment's silence. Then Kate said slowly, "Trixie could have been with someone who left before she died, as I said before. That person or someone else could have come back later, or even earlier in the morning than her husband, and cleared everything away. So her husband might not be implicated."

"Phew," said Anderton. "The plot most definitely thickens. Right, well, all of this gives us a firm starting point." He began to tick points off on his fingers. "We need a thorough search of the farmhouse. We need forensics on who's been in that bedroom and whether anyone can be eliminated. We need to know how quickly after injecting Trixie died and whether she could have moved to her bedroom from somewhere else in the house. Sod it, we need forensics from all over the house. And we need to start digging at alibis. I want Jacob Arlen re-interviewed as a matter of urgency."

People were standing up, preparing to move. The room began to hum with that slight sense of urgency and bustle that the beginning of a case could induce. Kate adjusted her shirt sleeve, which was slightly twisted, and recalled that something else that needed to be mentioned.

"Sir?" She had interrupted Anderton mid-flow and he frowned. "What is it, Kate?"

Kate reiterated what Doctor Telling had said about the bruising on Trixie's arm. "She said it looked quite distinctly as if someone had grabbed her there."

Anderton was still frowning. "Which arm?"

For a moment, Kate groped to remember. "The right one," she said, thankfully.

"And she injected into her left arm?"

"I think so. I'd have to re-read the report to be certain."

Anderton had stopped writing. He let his gaze sweep over the room. "Could you find out, Kate? Quickly?"

"Yes, of course," said Kate, slightly confused by the seriousness of his tone.

"Because," he went on, as if reading her mind. "If someone had hold of her by the arm which she was using to inject herself, could it be that she was actually forced to do it?"

The buzz of activity in the room stilled. Kate felt a small chill at the thought. If someone had forced Trixie Arlen to inject herself with a lethal dose of heroin then that would make her death...murder.

She could see by the expressions on the others' faces that the same thing had just occurred to them. Anderton cleared his throat. "Now, I'm not saying that that's what *did* happen. It's another possibility, that's all. But we mustn't discount it."

He began allocating various tasks to various people. Kate half listened, distracted by an image in her head; a large hand on Trixie's arm, strong fingers clamping a full syringe into her hand, forcing the needle into her skin, making her depress the plunger. Then nothing; oblivion. Could it have happened like that? Did that make more sense than thinking that a respectable, middle-aged, *famous* woman would actually voluntarily inject herself with a lethal street drug while her young children slept in the next room?

Kate came to with a start, realising that the room had emptied of everyone but Theo. He was busy pulling on his coat and fiddling with his phone.

"Am I with you?" asked Kate, walking over.

"Ha, ha," said Theo. "You almost had me there."

"No, seriously," said Kate with a shamefaced grin. "I was away with the fairies for a moment. What am I supposed to be doing?"

Theo rolled his eyes. "Of course you're with me, you dozy mare. We're doing the farmhouse search. Come on."

"Oh, right," said Kate. She tried to hide her disappointment. She knew Anderton and Olbeck would probably be doing the interview with Jacob Arlen and she would have much rather sat in on that. She thought she had a talent for interviews, for sniffing out when a suspect was lying or, at the very least, concealing something. Searching was all very well but... She let her train of thought trail away as she followed Theo out to his car. A secondary thought occurred to her - that she really *must* get some studying done. Her exams were coming up in less than a fortnight. Pass those, and she wouldn't be relegated to digging through farmhouse bedrooms, that was for sure.

THE CROWD OF PAPARAZZI AT the gate of the Arlen farmhouse was so dense that Theo had to slow to a crawl and eventually sound his horn several times to make any kind of progress. The two uniformed officers who were guarding the gate opened it for them to pass through and, looking back as they drove through, Kate saw them physically repel a particularly bold photographer trying to sneak it after them. She didn't envy them their job – she could just imagine the kind of remarks they were being subjected to as they stood there guarding the gate.

The house was empty. Arlen and his children were clearly staying elsewhere and Kate didn't blame them. It had only been three days since Trixie Arlen died but already a kind of grimness was settling on the house, along with a fine film of dust. The colours of the furniture and the pictures and ornaments seemed dulled, the gleam of glass and metal muted, and as Kate and Theo walked towards the stairs, their footfalls seemed more muffled than the carpets warranted.

They began in the bedroom. Kate took the bedside table first, a little delicate white-painted thing. On the top of it lay the latest issue of Vogue, a magazine that Kate had never seen the point of. Fashion bored her rigid, although she was clearly in a minority. Shaking it out, she laid it on the bedclothes, which still bore the imprint of Trixie Arlen's body. Kate felt a moment of nausea that was unusual. She turned back to the bedside cabinet, opening the drawers and unearthing a set of high-end sex toys that made her raise her eyebrows.

"Blimey. Theo, look at this." She held up a vibrator that could almost have been a work of art, a modern sculpture, perhaps.

Theo laughed. "Well, you never know, do you? I always thought that sort of shit stopped when you got married."

"Well, what would *you* know about that?" said Kate, suddenly annoyed at his tone. She laid the toys on the bed next to the magazine. She suppressed the little voice inside her that told her *she* didn't know anything about being married, either.

The cabinet didn't yield anything else of interest. Kate knee-shuffled over to the chest of drawers that stood against the far-side wall. That too was clearly expensive, a lovely mahogany antique. Kate began to work methodically from the top down. She could hear Theo open the wardrobe door behind her and the clank of hangers as he began to sort through the clothes inside.

The drawers held a lot of underwear, most of it surprisingly functional, given the discovery in the bedside table; Kate had expected to find scraps of black lace and little silk nothings, but most of what emerged was sturdy white cotton. The brassieres were mostly the type that enabled breastfeeding. She pulled each drawer fully out, searching right to the corners. She made sure to check underneath each one – sometimes people taped things to the bottom, a surprisingly effective hiding place for something thin enough to be concealed there – but her efforts yielded no results. Kate worked her way through the rest of the drawers, finding nothing more exciting than cashmere jumpers, multiple pairs of black and grey leggings and skinny jeans.

She and Theo rolled back the rug beside the bed, looking for trap doors or secret hiding places beneath the floor boards. Kate moved backwards slowly, on her hands and knees, scanning the boards for barely visible openings. She found none. They stripped the bed of its coverings and checked the mattress, and then the springs of the bedframe. It was a bed made of black wrought iron, sham-vintage, made to look old.

"There's nothing here," said Theo, eventually. "Let's move to the en-suite."

Kate had been tapping her fingers against the black bars of the footboard. "Wait," she said, suddenly aware of the hollow sound emanating from beneath her hands. "Wait a minute."

She looked carefully at the top of the footboard, which was actually a long rail which ended in the two posts which held up the foot of the bed. Each post was topped in a kind of curling iron flourish. Biting her lip, Kate tested one of them, twisting it gently left. It resisted for a moment and then yielded, unscrewing smoothly. Once it had come off in her hand, Kate held her breath and looked down into the hollow space that was revealed.

It was right there, near the top of the bed leg, stuck to the inside of the tube with sellotape. She reached it with her gloved fingers and drew out a small plastic bag, half full of brownish powder. She and Theo looked at each other.

"Well, well," said Theo. "So she was a junkie after all."

Something about his tone flicked Kate on the raw. "You don't know that," she said crossly. "We don't even know what's in it yet."

"Oh, come on."

Kate held the plastic packet pinched between two gloved fingers. She dropped it into an evidence bag and sealed it. That brief moment of anger flickered and died. She felt sad. "Well, you're probably right," she said quietly. "Let's check the other one."

Theo did that while Kate fetched a torch to look further down the exposed pipe of the bed leg. She didn't find anything else there. Theo also found nothing in the other leg. They renewed their search of the room with more enthusiasm but found nothing else suspicious.

They scoured the en-suite bathroom next, Kate starting with the mirror-fronted bathroom cabinet on the wall over the sink. She found several bottles of prescribed anti-depressants with Trixie's name on the pharmacist's label. There was an enormous quantity of luxury skincare and make up – literally boxes of it – in the only other cupboard in the room. Perhaps Trixie had been given some of it for free? Kate couldn't imagine how anyone would manage to get through this amount of makeup in a lifetime. She caught sight of the own face in the mirror and rubbed at her cheeks, frowning. She looked pale and tired. There were a pile of glossy fashion magazines in a rack by the toilet and topmost was one that made Kate stare and then extend a hand to pick it up. Trixie Arlen – yes, she hadn't been mistaken –was the cover star. Kate looked at her picture; the bouncing glossy curls, the glowing skin, the flash of white teeth. A memory of Trixie's body on the pathology table popped into Kate's head and there was something obscene in the juxtaposition. How could someone who looked this vital, this healthy, actually be a heroin addict? Was it possible?

Searching the children's bedrooms was somehow worst of all. Kate tried not to wince as her gloved fingers lifted out piles of neatly folded clothing, leaving them in brightly coloured heaps on the striped rug in the middle of the floor. The twin boys shared a room, two cot beds facing one another with matching duvet cover sets. Blue and white bunting hung on the wall and a little nightlight, shaped like a boat, stood on a small table between the cots. Kate didn't like to think of a mother, a parent, hiding drugs in their pre-schoolers' room, but you couldn't deny that it sometimes happened. She found nothing though and, relieved, went through to the little girl's nursery to search. What was her name again? Something weird. *Manon*, that was it. Kate paused in the doorway blinking, taking in the excess of pink. It was as if a giant ball of Disney princesses had exploded. She took a deep breath and began the search, again finding nothing.

After several more weary hours she and Theo called it a day, the single bag of powder the only thing that resulted from a whole day's search. They locked up the house, setting the alarm. They crawled their way back through the crowd of paparazzi; still as many, if not more, as had been there that morning. When would they get fed up of waiting? Kate thought of the headlines still to come, of the moral outrage that would result once the reality of Trixie's death was known. She winced inwardly and put her head back against the headrest of the car seat. Theo put his finger out to turn the stereo on and then seemed to change his mind, sighing a little. They drove back to the station in tired silence.

Chapter Six

THE NEXT MORNING, KATE REGARDED her desk with something akin to dismay. The surface had all but disappeared beneath a teetering pile of cardboard folders, slippery plastic envelopes, dirty coffee mugs and veritable strata of loose paper. She thought of everything she had to do and fought the urge to push her chair back and flee the room for good. Instead, she squared her shoulders, attempted to push the toppling piles of paperwork into some sort of order, and gave thanks that she'd actually treated herself to a 'good coffee' for once.

Theo, who sat opposite her, kept interrupting his own work to seize his mobile phone and swipe at the screen. Kate, whose own concentration was interrupted every time he did it, gritted her teeth until she couldn't hold back a barbed comment any longer. "Waiting for the football results, are you?"

Apparently, the bitchiness went straight over Theo's head. "No," he said absently. "I'm just checking the headlines. I want to see what they're reporting on Trixie Arlen's death."

Kate felt a little ashamed of herself. "Oh," she said. She got up and went round to his desk, leaning over to look at the little screen herself. "Anything interesting?"

"Nah. The usual sentimental guff, family's heartbreak, bringing up her tragic life, you know the kind of thing."

"Her tragic life?"

"Yeah – you remember, her first husband died, didn't he, and she had that miscarriage."

"Oh, yes," said Kate. "What *did* he actually die of?"

"Drugs overdose."

Kate's eyes widened. "Seriously?" She was silent for a moment, thinking. "That actually might strengthen the case that Trixie was a drug addict herself. I mean, suppose her first husband introduced her to drugs?"

Theo nodded. "But suppose it was the other way round? If you'd lost a loved one to heroin, why the hell would you start taking it yourself?"

Kate got up and went back to her own chair. "That's a good point," she admitted, sitting back down. "I don't know enough about addiction, really – the psychology of it, I mean." Briefly, she recalled her mother's struggle with the bottle. Perhaps she knew more than she realised. "I'll look into it," she said, half to Theo, half to herself.

The phone rang when she was halfway through a Google search for drug and alcohol treatment centres in Abbeyford. Impatiently she snatched it up. "DS Redman here."

"Oh, hello." She recognised the quiet tones of Doctor Telling. "I have some information on your John Doe. We've received the reports back from the dental lab."

Kate's head was so full of Trixie Arlen that for a moment, she had to struggle to recall who on Earth Doctor Telling was talking about. Then she remembered – the first body they'd found, in the abandoned cottage.

"Oh, yes, thanks," she said. "Do we have a name?"

"Yes, the dental records brought up a match. His name really was John, John Henry Miller, born in 1960 in Aberdeen. Should I send over the files?"

"Oh, please do," said Kate. She felt a little glow of satisfaction in the news. She hated the cases – and there were always a few – when a body went unidentified, unclaimed, unmissed. What an awful way to end up, with literally no one on Earth to mourn you. "Thank you very much, Kirsten."

"It's no problem," the pathologist replied in her quiet tone, but Kate thought she could detect an answering measure of satisfaction in her voice. Doctor Telling was gentle and empathic, like all the best doctors. Kate felt a moment's regret that; because of her break up with Andrew, she'd lost the chance of getting to know Doctor Telling better. She'd always felt that she would be a nice woman to be friends with.

"Is there anything else back from the labs with regard to the Arlen case?" she remembered to ask, but the answer was negative. Kate hadn't really expected a result yet – these things always took more time than anticipated.

The morning's work took on a more upbeat feel after the call. Kate flew through a load of outstanding paperwork, arranged an appointment with one of the directors of Outreach, Abbeyford's largest drug and alcohol treatment centre, caught up with her emails, and realised with a start at twelve o'clock that she was supposed to be having lunch with Stuart. She had to grab her coat and handbag and make a run for the café where they were supposed to be meeting, arriving five minutes late and looking more dishevelled than she would have liked.

Stuart was already there, at a table by the window. He caught sight of Kate as she hurried through the door and gave her a grin. She puffed up to the table, panting apologies.

"It's not like you to be late," Stuart said, leaning over to kiss her cheek.

Kate dropped into a chair, trying to smooth her hair. "I know. I've been flat out. Sorry."

"I remember." Stuart had worked as an undercover officer for the Abbeyford team before a catastrophic series of events had led to his resignation, and he now worked as a private detective. Although he put a brave face on it, Kate knew that he missed working for the police, but she'd learned by now not to mention the possibility of Stuart reapplying for the force.

It was funny, she thought as she took a menu from the hovering waitress, how differently she felt about Stuart now than when she'd first met him. She'd almost hated him on first sight, thinking him arrogant, pushy and rude. Of course, he could still be all of those things, she thought with an inner smile, but somehow it didn't seem to bother her anymore. He was clever and funny and good company. Olbeck kept muttering about how she and Stuart would make the perfect couple and why wasn't she doing anything about it, but Kate knew he was wrong. She appreciated Stuart's friendship and that was all; she hoped he felt the same way about her.

They gave their orders and then settled back in their chairs.

"So," said Stuart. "What's new?"

Kate told him what she could about the latest cases, the three heroin overdoses and the Trixie Arlen case. She mentioned that she'd made an appointment to talk to a drugs counsellor, to try and get a bit more insight into what made an addict do the things that they did.

"I can't help feeling that I should understand a bit *more*," she said, stirring her leek and potato soup. "I keep thinking that there might be a connection to these overdose cases. Well, of course there must be. How could there not be?"

Stuart swallowed a mouthful of food. "Yeah," he said. "You're on the right track. First thing you should do is pull some stats, don't you think? Get the analysts to do some digging. Find out the rate of overdose deaths last year – last month, even – and do some comparisons with the most recent cases."

Kate brightened. "That's a great idea. Thanks. I'll do just that."

"No charge," said Stuart, grinning. "You've got a name for the first body, right?"

Kate nodded. "Yes, we have. That's something I'll be looking into when I get back." She finished the last mouthful of soup, pushed her bowl away a little, and relaxed back into her chair. She looked across at Stuart. "It's funny, but I can't help thinking about Trixie Arlen." She opened her mouth to mention the one suspicious packet that she and Theo had found, and then recalled Anderson's warning. Of course, Stuart didn't know, and he *couldn't* know either, not from her. "It's so sad, isn't it?" Kate said hastily, covering herself. "It's always more sad when there are children, don't you think?"

"I suppose so," said Stuart. He appeared to be thinking about something. He reached out to spin his water glass in a slow circle. "It wouldn't surprise me..." he began and then stopped.

"What?" asked Kate.

"Well," said Stuart. "It wouldn't surprise me if the Trixie Arlen case is connected to these heroin deaths. It wouldn't surprise me at all."

"Really?" said Kate, as casually as she could. "What makes you say that?"

"Oh, you know. Sudden death of a healthy, relatively young woman. A woman known to have associated with heroin addicts in the past – her first husband, for one. She was pretty wild back in the nineties, wasn't she? All those rumours." Kate was uncomfortably aware that he was keenly watching her face. He was too good at reading people, damn him; it was his undercover training. "I don't suppose the PM threw anything like that up?"

"No," said Kate, truthfully. "It was inconclusive."

"So you're waiting for toxicology results, right?"

"That's right."

Stuart sat back in his chair and stretched. "I bet you a tenner I'm right. No, wait. If I'm right, next time we have lunch, you're buying."

Kate smiled reluctantly. "You know I don't gamble, Stuart. But I don't mind shouting you lunch."

Stuart laughed and, thankfully, Kate could see him dismissing the subject. "Can't believe you don't gamble. Don't you have Irish heritage? It should be in your blood."

"That's why," said Kate, standing up to leave. "Thanks, anyway. Let's meet up soon, yes?"

"You got it."

They hugged goodbye and Kate made her way back to the office, thinking about what Stuart had said. He was right. Why had she been so shocked by Doctor Telling's findings on the pathology table? Her, a seasoned police officer? With a pang, she recalled that Stuart had lost a brother to heroin addiction, years ago. No wonder he was more attuned to the possibility. She wished she'd remembered that at the lunch so she could have talked to him about it. But perhaps that would have been too painful.

Kate ran over the details of the case in her head. Even if Trixie had been an addict, it wasn't that straightforward, was it? What about the bruising on Trixie's arm? Kate pondered the questions as she walked back to her desk. Who had cleared away the syringes, the drugs, the tourniquets? She wondered whether Anderton had interviewed Jacob Arlen yet and whether anything interesting had come to light. She had a flashback to sitting at the Arlens' kitchen table, watching Arlen's face as he recounted his journey up to the bedroom, through the silent house, to find his wife's dead body on the bed. Kate remembered the blonde neighbour, the friend – what was her name? Kyla Mellors – and the slight hesitation in the woman's answers. There was something there, something to be further investigated. It could be nothing, but then again... Kate added *interview Kyla Mellors* to her ever-growing checklist of things to do.

DOCTOR TELLING HAD EMAILED THROUGH the information on John Henry Miller and Kate spent the rest of the afternoon reading through it. He'd been born in 1960, had gone to school in London, and joined the army at sixteen. Reading between the bare facts, Kate could see a man who'd lost his place in the world once he left the Armed Forces – a sad fact that was more common than people thought. There were several reports which detailed his arrests for vagrancy, for being drunk and disorderly, for possession of a class A substance. She flipped forward to the photo that Missing Persons had forwarded. A non-descript man, weathered by years of rough living, brown eyes, greying hair. Someone had obviously reported him missing at some point, for MISPER to have his details, but who? And did it really matter? Kate did a quick calculation and worked out that his parents were almost certainly dead, given his age. Was it worth trying to find out? This wasn't even their case anymore.

After a moment, she slowly clicked the mouse to close the PDF and exited the email, with a faint feeling of guilt. She wondered how long Miller had lain dead in that cottage. Had he actually died from the overdose or had he succumbed to exposure, lying there comatose in the filth and the cold? It was horrible to think of, almost as horrible to think that there was no one left to mourn him. She made a resolution that she would go to his funeral. She would probably be the only one there, apart from the celebrant, but that made it even more important. Kate made a quick mental note to find out when the council-funded funeral would be.

Miller's grizzled old face kept recurring to Kate that night as she relaxed at home. She had lit a fire, the first of the season, as the warm autumnal weather had suddenly given way to a chill. Her living room was neat, as usual, and filled with objects of comfort and sentimental value. She should have been happy, or at least relaxed, but somehow the image of the derelict cottage kept intruding, Miller's remains in a nauseating puddle on the filthy floor. *Unwept, unhonoured and unsung...* Kate poked up the fire, lit an expensive scented candle that she'd kept 'for best', and wrapped herself in a woolly throw. The crackle of the burning logs sounded too loud in the silent house and she felt the weight of the empty rooms above her. She tried putting on some music but it seemed to just make things worse – an echo in the void.

Oh, get a grip of yourself, woman, she told herself, but in the background, all she could hear was the same word, repeated over and over again. *Alone.*

She passed a bad night and got up the next morning feeling as though she hadn't slept. Olbeck, by contrast, almost bounced into the office, tousling Kate's hair as he passed her desk, which made her swat him away in annoyance.

"What's up with you?" she asked grumpily, sliding out of her chair and following him to his office.

"Nothing," said Olbeck, grinning. "Just full of the joys of spring."

"It's October."

Olbeck dismissed her comment with an airy wave of his hand. "Full of the joys of autumn, then. Hey, you doing anything next week? Thought you might like to come for dinner."

Kate felt a pang of anxiety, despite her tiredness. "I've got to study, actually. My exam's coming up soon."

"When?"

"On the fourteenth." Kate felt a stronger pulse of nervousness. She'd hardly done any studying at all. What had she been thinking? She straightened up a little and vowed that studying and only studying was what she would spend every spare waking moment doing.

Olbeck rummaged in his desk. "Right, right," he said. Kate wondered whether he was even listening. "No problem."

"Let's make it a date after my exams," Kate said, feeling that at least that would be something to look forward to afterwards.

"Hmm?" Olbeck looked up and blinked. "Oh right, yeah. Let's do that."

Kate rolled her eyes and went back to her desk.

"You look knackered," Theo observed, busy at his computer.

"Gee, thanks," said Kate. She rubbed her face and tried to get her work head on. "Did Anderton interview Jacob Arlen yesterday?"

"Nope, don't think so."

"Anything else I should know about?"

"Don't know. Haven't even seen the boss yet."

Kate sighed. "Anything from forensics?"

Theo reached for a pile of folders. "Now, that I can help you with. Here you go."

Kate opened the first file and did her best to follow it but the scientific jargon blurred in front of her tired eyes. She made herself and Theo another coffee and tried again, making notes of her own. She murmured the names under her breath.

"Fingerprints found in the master bedroom of the farmhouse were those of Trixie and Jacob Arlen, their children, Kyla Mellors, another child's and an unknown female." Kate read through the list again. The unknown child could well turn out to be Kyla Mellors' daughter, although that would have to be checked. But the unknown female...?

She really needed to talk to Anderton but, as before, he seemed to be absent from the office again. Had he ever been so hard to get hold of? His office was empty and his mobile went straight to voicemail. Kate emailed him and left a post-it note on his computer, hoping to cover all bases. She grabbed a salad from the canteen and ate it back at her desk, still wading through all the forensic reports from the Arlen case.

That night, Kate attempted to study. She cleared the small dining room table and set up her books, folders and study notes. She set her kitchen timer for forty minutes and sat herself down at the table, bending her head industriously to her books. She conscientiously read for five minutes, wielding her highlighter pen – the lazy person's way of making notes, she had always thought. After five more minutes she slumped back in her chair. Nothing was going in; nothing. She might as well be reading Swahili for all the sense it was making.

Kate got up and made herself a cup of tea. You're just tired, she told herself; but she knew it was more than that. It was Miller, long-lost to his family. It was Trixie, vibrant and beautiful and loved, and that still not being enough to save her. It was Olbeck, because just what the hell was going on with him and why hadn't he confided in her? It was Anderton and the sudden air of mystery that now surrounded him. It was Andrew Stanton, who'd loved her; why hadn't she loved him? What the hell was wrong with her? I'm alone, thought Kate, staring blankly ahead of her. If I died here, tonight, how long would it be before someone noticed?

She told herself to stop being ridiculous. Of course someone would notice. She tipped the cold cup of tea down the sink and tried again to concentrate on her studies. *I'm alone.* The thought kept recurring, like some kind of mordant song reverberating around her head. In the end, in utter frustration, she slammed the text book shut and gave up and went to bed, to stare up at the ceiling, trying not to listen to the two-word sentence that kept repeating in her head.

Chapter Seven

JOHN HENRY MILLER'S FUNERAL TOOK place on the following day. Kate dressed in a black suit and stopped on route to buy a small bunch of white roses. As she pocketed her change, she wondered why she was making the effort. Miller had been a vagrant, a petty criminal, a drug addict. Perhaps he'd caused harm to someone, even serious harm. Why was she doing this? We've all caused harm to someone, she reminded herself as she drove towards the crematorium.

It was a shabby little place; the entrance hall, with a swirly-patterned carpet, clearly hadn't been redecorated since the late seventies. Kate took a seat in the small hall and was unsurprised to see that, apart from the person conducting the service, she was the only one there. The pang that the realisation gave her took her by surprise. She found herself blinking hard as the vicar began the words of the service. She observed the coffin, which lay at the front of the room, and with another sharp pang saw that it was the first coffin she'd ever seen which looked too big. At every other funeral she'd ever been to, the coffin always looked too small, but this one was the opposite. It was because Kate could recall just how pathetic the remains it held were, how diminished, how reduced.

The vicar paused for a moment, and in the silence that followed, Kate heard footsteps behind her, the ring of high heels on the linoleum floor of the chapel. She turned and was astonished to see someone else taking a seat at the back of the room; a teenage girl, very young, barely sixteen. She was dressed top to toe in black, with her long hair piled up on top of her head and her eyes heavily outlined in kohl. Kate blinked. Was she John Miller's daughter? A granddaughter, even? The girl caught her gaze and quickly looked down at the floor. Kate turned back to face the front of the room as the vicar resumed his short speech, her curiosity piqued.

Once the ceremony was over and the too-big coffin had disappeared behind a pair of faded purple curtains, the vicar nodded at Kate and then left by a side door. Kate hurried to intercept the teenage girl, who was moving quite slowly towards the main entrance in her high heels.

"Hello," said Kate as she reached her side. As soon as she did so, she recognised the girl. It was the girl who, along with her teenage boyfriend, had actually found Miller's body. Kate was so flabbergasted that for a moment she stopped walking. The girl walked on, her head bowed. Kate quickly caught up with her again. "Thanks for coming," she said. Then, just to be sure, she asked, "It's Mia, isn't it?"

Mia nodded. "Yes."

She hadn't stopped walking, although her pace had slowed. Kate hesitated for a moment, unsure of what to ask. "Did you – did you *know* Mr. Miller?" she demanded. Surely that had to be too much of a coincidence?

Mia shook her head. "No. No, I didn't. I just – I wanted to come because – well, I just couldn't stand the thought of no one being here, and I thought that's what might happen. Because he didn't have anyone, did he? He was all alone."

All of a sudden, Kate found herself absurdly near to tears. It was the thought of this young girl – this *child* – being so sensitive, so decent, to want to give a total stranger a dignified goodbye. If that didn't warm your heart, nothing would.

"That was very good of you, Mia," she said, when she was able to speak. "Very good and kind of you."

Mia half-smiled. "It's awful to think that no one would miss you, isn't it?"

"Yes, it is," Kate said honestly. "It's very sad. How did you know where to come?"

They had reached the driveway in front of the chapel now and a blast of wintry air caught them both unawares. Mia clutched her black jacket to her neck, shivering. "The lady – the officer who talked to us afterwards – she rang up and told me."

Kate nodded. "How have you been, anyway?"

"I'm okay." Mia said it in a stout sort of way that made Kate smile inwardly. "Olly's not doing too good."

"I'm sorry to hear that," said Kate, unsurprised. You didn't fall into a decomposed body – literally – and expect to brush that off lightly. "Is he having counselling? Are you?"

They made small talk for a few more minutes before the cold wind forced them to say goodbye. Kate watched Mia walk off towards the bus stop. When she walked back to her car and drove off, she felt a little bit better about things. Not much, but a bit.

.

Chapter Eight

THE FINE WEATHER RETURNED THE next day. Kate drove through a golden morning, the leaves on the trees seeming to absorb and send back the rays of the sun, shining out in tints of red, amber and chestnut. The roads were fairly clear and Kate enjoyed her drive so much it was almost with regret that she drew up outside Kyla Mellor's house and parked the car.

It was a large house, but much newer than the Arlens' rambling old farmhouse. Almost aggressively modern, the outside was mostly cedar cladding, tinted glass and blocks of stone. Kate looked around, taking in the landscaped gardens, the covered swimming pool and the expensive sports car parked carelessly on the gravel drive. Plenty of money here, but that was true of most of the neighbourhood wasn't it? Did Kyla even work?

Kate rang the bell and a second later the door was pulled open by Kyla, who had obviously been watching for her approach. She was dressed in a navy and white striped top and dark blue skinny jeans, and Kate, who never worried about her weight, felt quite chubby next to her. Kyla's long blonde hair was pulled up into a messy ponytail and she had the kind of effortless style that Kate associated with those who had modelled for a living. She chanced a guess and asked if that was what Kyla did.

Kyla smiled a rather embarrassed smile. "How did you know that? I used to be a model. I haven't done anything since Gaia was born."

Kate managed not to guffaw at the name. "Gaia's your daughter? How old is she?"

Kyla's smile fell away. "Two and a half, almost the same age as Manon. Trixie and I met at an NCT class."

What was the NCT? Kate tried to look as though she knew. She had come prepared to dig a little into Kyla's relationship with Trixie, but she realised that it might be more worthwhile to let Kyla talk naturally about her friend. However Kate had thought that Kyla might be more of a natural talker than she was turning out to be.

Kyla made coffee, which was lukewarm and too weak. Kate took one sip and abandoned it. "Would you say you and Trixie were close friends?" she asked.

Kyla's gaze flickered then dropped to her coffee cup. She hadn't drunk much of it either. "I suppose so."

"Would she confide in you? If she had any worries or problems?"

Kyla was still looking down. "I guess so."

This was frustrating. Kate knew that Kyla was holding something back, but what? Was it important? "Were you aware that Trixie took drugs?"

"No," Kyla said, too quickly and too loudly. "I was horrified when I found out. I couldn't believe it."

"Hmm," Kate said and watched the other woman flush. "So you never took drugs with Trixie?"

"No!"

"Never?"

"I told you, no. I don't do drugs. Particularly not when I'm around my *children*." Kyla's high cheekbones were stained with red, but Kate wasn't sure if it was with anger or embarrassment. "Trixie and I used to have a drink together sometimes, when the kids were in bed. That was all."

"Okay," said Kate.

Kyla noticed her still-full cup. "You haven't touched your coffee. Shall I make you another?"

"No thanks," said Kate quickly. "I'm sorry if these questions are upsetting you, Mrs. Mellor, but it's useful for me to find out more about Trixie – from the people who knew her best."

Kyla was looking down at the table again, her face serious. She nodded, her blonde fringe catching on her eyelashes.

Kate pressed on, taking advantage of the silence. "Would you say that Trixie was happily married?" she asked.

Kyla looked astonished, then embarrassed. "I – I don't know. I think so. Well, I'm not sure."

"Can you elaborate?"

Kyla looked as though she was regretting saying anything. "Oh, I don't know. She used to tell me when she and Jake had had a row, now and again. But that's normal in a marriage, isn't it?"

"So you don't think she and Mr. Arlen were having any kind of marriage difficulties or anything like that?"

"No. No, I don't think so."

Kate pondered, wondering where to go next. Kyla got up and cleared their full cups away, putting them down on the kitchen counter near the sink. Kate watched her, just for something to do, and realised that Kyla's hands were trembling. She looked closer. Yes, they were shaking. Kyla was either terrified or she was badly hung over. Kate didn't think it was that – there was no smell of stale alcohol around her and she looked great, glowing skin and clear eyes. So why was she so nervous?

"Mrs. Mellor, can I ask you if you've got something to tell me?" asked Kate, taking the bull by the horns.

Kyla threw her a quick, nervous glance. "What do you mean?"

"Is there anything you want to tell me?" That was always an effective question. It was amazing how people spilled the beans if they thought you already knew something.

It didn't appear to work on Kyla; she had closed herself off. Kate could see her face become blank, smoothing into a neutral expression. "No," said Kyla. "I don't have anything to tell you, other than what I've already said."

"Can I ask you your whereabouts on the night Trixie died?"

That red stain once again graced Kyla's sharp cheekbones. "Why do you need to know?"

"It's standard procedure, Mrs. Mellor. I'm not accusing you of anything. Where were you on the night Trixie died?"

"I was here. At home."

Kate nodded. "Can anyone confirm that? Your husband, perhaps?"

Kyla looked away. "No, he wasn't here. He was working abroad all of last week."

"Did you talk to anyone on the phone at all? Use social media?"

"I don't do social media. I think I might have spoken to my mother early in the evening. She rang about dinner time."

DRIVING AWAY AFTER THE INTERVIEW had concluded, Kate found herself tapping the steering wheel lightly with irritation. That woman knew something. Was it possible that she was the person who'd been with Trixie the night she died? Kate considered the idea and then dismissed it. She wasn't sure she believed Kyla when she'd said she'd had no idea that Trixie took drugs, but she had sounded a lot more convincing when she'd said she herself didn't take them. Of course, being a former model, she'd probably partaken in the past, but that wasn't to say that she still indulged. Kate shook her head, irritated with herself. This was all hot air, conjecture, supposition. She made a mental note to check whether the tests on the drugs found in Trixie Arlen's bed had come back with results. Then, at least, she'd know what they were dealing with.

Chapter Nine

THAT NIGHT, KATE BENT TO her books again and felt a little better about her chances of passing the exam. It's not the end of the world if I don't, she told herself as she sipped camomile tea and made careful notes on one of her many lined note pads. I can always retake them. But the humiliation of failing... Kate didn't *fail* at things. Relationships, yes; but never *work* things. She took a deep breath and tried to focus back on the text that was blurring before her tired eyes.

She called it a day at midnight and went straight to bed, not stopping to shower as she normally did at the end of the day. Despite all her anxieties, she passed a dreamless night and awoke refreshed the next morning. So much so that when her phone rang before she'd even switched on the kettle, she managed not to groan. It was Olbeck.

"Fancy coming with me to re-interview Arlen?" he asked. Kate could hear traffic noise faintly in the background and hoped he was using the hands-free if he was driving.

"I thought you and Anderton were doing that?"

"He's bailed on me. Something about a meeting back at the station. Will you come?"

"Of course," said Kate, pleased to be asked. She flew around getting ready and was waiting on the doorstep, bag in hand, when Olbeck pulled his car into the kerb outside her house.

"By the way, Jeff says can you do the night of the fourteenth for dinner?"

"That's my exam day," said Kate. She felt another jump of anxiety and vowed that she would spend the whole of the evening studying, no matter how tired she was after work.

"Oh," said Olbeck. "Right. No matter. We'll do it another time."

"Actually," said Kate, thinking aloud. "I'd like to come over. It'll be something to look forward to after the horrors of the day."

Olbeck grinned. "That's the spirit. Great – that's settled then. Dinner at ours on the fourteenth." He seemed about to say something else, but clearly changed his mind. Kate was aware of the sense of suppressed excitement that she'd noticed before. She opened her mouth to ask him outright and then closed it again. If he wanted to tell her, he would.

The crowd of paparazzi at the Arlens' farmhouse had depleted to a solitary car parked by the entrance gate, with a man leaning disconsolately against the bonnet, a camera dangling from his hand. He perked up a little as Olbeck drove closer and indicated for the farmhouse lane but slumped when he realised that the car didn't contain anyone famous. He still took a few shots of them as they drove past him. Kate fought the urge to give him the finger as they went by.

"Paparazzi have thinned out a bit," remarked Olbeck as they drove nearer the farmhouse, stating the obvious.

"A week's a long time in show business," said Kate.

"Wait until the funeral next week. You can imagine what that's going to be like."

Kate made a noise of agreement. She thought of the thronging crowds that would no doubt be there, the famous names and faces, the attendant media, the footage that would no doubt make it onto the BBC. What a contrast it would be to the funeral of John Miller. Yet Trixie and John had died of the same thing, disparate as their lives had been. It was strange.

"It's so strange," she muttered to herself.

"What is?" asked Olbeck.

Kate shook herself back to reality. "Oh, nothing."

OLBECK PARKED THE CAR NEXT to the black Range Rover that had been parked there on their previous visit. Jacob Arlen opened the farmhouse door before they'd even locked the car and stood on the doorstep, as if guarding it, his arms hugged across his body. He was dressed in a sombre grey suit and looked much older than he had on the day he'd found his wife's body.

"The children are still with my parents," he said as the officers approached him. "I didn't want to talk with them around."

Did that mean he had something significant to impart? Kate wondered as she followed Arlen and Olbeck through to the kitchen. Possibly not. She would have to wait and see.

Arlen didn't offer them any refreshments. Kate imagined that he had an assistant who took care of that side of things in his office, and he didn't look like the kind of man who knew his way around his own kitchen. He sat down in the chair at the head of the table too quickly, as if the strength had left his body without warning.

Olbeck always started this type of interview with an expression of condolence. Arlen didn't say anything but nodded almost impatiently, as if wanting to dispense with the pleasantries and get straight down to business.

Olbeck didn't beat around the bush. "Were you aware that your wife was taking heroin, Mr. Arlen?"

Arlen visibly winced. He was silent for a long moment and then said slowly, as if the words were being pulled out of him, "I was – I became aware that she was doing that."

"How long have you known?"

"Not long. A matter of months, if that."

"It didn't worry you?"

Arlen looked up, incredulous. "Are you insane? Of course it worried me. It worried me *sick*. When I found out she was using again, I – I – she swore it was a one-off. That she'd just got so bored being at home all the time, that it was an impulse thing."

Trixie Arlen took heroin on impulse? Kate tried not to let her scepticism show. That was a lie, but was it Trixie's or Arlen's?

Olbeck probed Arlen for more details. "You first found out she'd taken heroin when, exactly?"

Arlen briefly closed his eyes, as if in pain. "It was a couple of months ago. Things hadn't been – we hadn't been getting on very well, and I'd been away a lot. I found a box of syringes at the back of her bedside table drawer and an empty plastic bag." He looked away. "She swore blind it was a one-off."

"Did you believe her?" asked Olbeck.

"I don't know," Arlen replied, again slowly and painfully. "I wanted to believe her. I hadn't ever known her when she was – was involved in that kind of world. Trixie said that when Ivo – her first husband – died, she never touched the stuff again. Ever."

"So why would she start using it again, do you think?"

Arlen was shaking his head. "I don't actually know that she *was* using it again. Not regularly." He paused and his brows drew down in a frown. "I searched the bedroom a couple of times. I didn't tell her that's what I was doing. But I didn't find anything."

Probably because Trixie had got better at hiding it, Kate thought but didn't say. Was it likely that Trixie had told the truth? The reality was that she had taken heroin again at least once more – the night she died. But had there been other times?

Arlen was still speaking. "A couple of times I came home and she was – well, there was just something a little off about her. She didn't really drink much but it was sometimes as if she was, well, a little drunk. But I couldn't smell it on her or anything like that." He looked directly at Kate. "I was worried, very worried, because she was on her own a lot with the children."

"Did you address this with her again at any time?" Kate asked.

Arlen's gaze dropped to the table. "There wasn't really anything I could say. I couldn't find anything to actually accuse her of."

"Did any of Trixie's friends, like Kyla Mellors for example, ever mention any concerns to you?"

Arlen's eyelids flickered minutely. He cleared his throat. "No, not that I can recall. No one said anything to me."

There was a hint – just a hint – of evasiveness in his reply. Kate frowned, wondering whether to take him up on it. But even as she was wondering, Olbeck asked Arlen something else, moving on to another subject.

"We've eliminated most of the fingerprints that our scientists found in the bedroom, Mr. Arlen. There's one though that you might be able to help us with."

Arlen looked faintly alarmed. "I would?"

Olbeck gave him the rundown from the fingerprint report. "So you can see, it's this unknown female we're looking for. Would Trixie's friends ever go up to your bedroom?"

Arlen's cheeks were faintly mottled. "That's rather presumptuous, Detective Inspector, isn't it? What are you implying?" Before Olbeck could answer, Arlen's face suddenly cleared and he went from looking mortified to looking relieved. "I'm sorry, how stupid of me. I didn't even think – it's almost certainly our cleaner. Rosa. She comes in every week."

Of course the Arlens would have had a cleaner, thought Kate. No doubt a gardener too, a dog-walker, an ironing service. It was only surprising that there hadn't been a nanny, but that particular bit of domesticity hadn't appear to have been outsourced. Again, Kate found herself doubting the evidence of her own eyes. Was it really likely that Trixie Arlen, earth mother and domestic goddess, would have risked being under the influence of a class A drug when she had the responsibility of three small children? Wasn't it more likely that someone – some unknown someone – had forced her to inject herself? But why? What possible motive would there be?

Olbeck asked Arlen for Rosa's details. Kate could have advised him to save his breath; there was no way that a man like Arlen would have been involved in hiring or supervising a domestic servant when even making coffee for visitors appeared beyond him.

As expected, Arlen didn't have a clue where Rosa lived, what her surname was, or even if she worked for an agency.

"Would you expect her to come to work again?" asked Kate quickly. "Considering what's happened? When does she normally come here?"

Arlen looked more confused than the simple question warranted. "I'm not sure. I was never really here when she was here. Wait a moment—" He got up and walked over to a noticeboard, thickly plastered with children's drawings, takeaway leaflets, school notices and business cards, on the opposite wall. He peered at it more closely and then carefully pulled a drawing pin free. Several other pieces of paper fell to the floor but he didn't bother to pick them up. "Here you are," he said, handing the little card to Kate. I knew I'd seen something before – that's the agency Rosa comes from, I think."

"Thank you, Mr. Arlen," said Kate, who looked at it briefly before tucking it away in her bag. It was pink, with the logo of the company in a flowery black script spelling out *Home Angels, Domestic Cleaning*. "It will be very useful to be able to eliminate another person from our enquiries."

Jacob Arlen nodded, looking serious. Kate glanced at Olbeck, wondering if he was going to bring up the most serious point of the interview. He gave her a minute nod, tacit permission to go ahead.

"There's something else that we need to discuss with you, Mr. Arlen," Kate said. "As far as we're aware, bearing in mind we're still waiting for the results of the toxicology tests, it seems fairly clear that your wife died of an overdose of diacetylmorphine – heroin, in other words." Arlen was watching her face intently, utterly focused on her words. Kate continued. "The problem is that despite that, we found no drugs, no drugs paraphernalia, no syringes, nothing at all with your wife's body."

There was a moment of silence. Kate watched Arlen's expression keenly. She could have sworn that the revelation came as an utter surprise to him.

"My God," Arlen said softly. "How - how is that possible?"

Kate cleared her throat before she spoke again. "It's possible, Mr. Arlen, because someone removed all evidence of drug use from the scene."

"What are you saying? It couldn't – Trixie couldn't have moved it, hidden it or whatever before – before she died?"

Both Kate and Olbeck had considered that possibility. They'd had the benefit of advice from Doctor Telling on the likelihood of just that happening. Kate explained to Arlen what Doctor Telling had told them.

"I'm afraid not. Your wife would have died very quickly after the injection – a matter of minutes. She wouldn't have been physically able to move far, let alone go to the trouble of hiding drugs and syringes in a place where we've not been able to find them."

Arlen's head had lowered and he was staring at the table again. "That means there was someone else here with Trixie. Doesn't it?" he concluded, looking up at them both. "Do you know who?"

"Our enquiries are continuing," Olbeck replied. "But there's another possibility, Mr. Arlen."

"There is?"

Kate and Olbeck exchanged glances. If this guy was lying, he was pretty good. "You could have removed whatever was there yourself, Mr Arlen," said Kate. She paused for a moment to let it sink in, watching Arlen's eyes widen with shock, and then went in for the kill. "Did you?"

"No!" Arlen sat back in his chair, looking from one face to another, wide-eyed. "I had no idea – I didn't see anything. Why would I do that?"

"I don't know, Mr. Arlen," Kate said mildly. "Perhaps you were worried about your wife's reputation. You didn't want it known that she'd died of a drug overdose. Perhaps you were worried that your children would come into the room and get hold of whatever was lying around."

Arlen raised a shaking hand to his temple. He was breathing quickly but Kate could see that he was gradually regaining self-control. "I touched nothing, I saw nothing," he said and his voice was quite firm. "You have to believe me. I can't prove it, but I promise you I didn't see anything like that. There wasn't anything like that. And I—" He stopped speaking abruptly.

"Yes?" prompted Kate after a moment's silence.

Arlen dropped his hand back to his lap, limply, as if all the strength had run out of his arm. "I looked," he said simply. "After I realised she was dead. I think I - I think I knew why she'd died, because of the drugs."

Olbeck leaned forward. "You suspected your wife had died of a drugs overdose?"

"I didn't *know*. I just - after I'd caught her that last time... I suspected, that was all. But I promise you this, there was nothing there. I looked around - not very well, I was too shaken up and I knew I had to call an ambulance and stop the kids from seeing her - but I had a quick look under the bed and on the dressing table. There was nothing like that there. No syringes or anything." He looked at them both again and his words had the simple ring of truth. "I found nothing. I saw nothing."

"Very well, Mr. Arlen," Olbeck said. "We'll need to amend your statement with words to that effect."

"Yes." Arlen slumped back against his chair, putting his head back and closing his eyes. "Yes, I understand that."

"Do you have any idea who this person who was with your wife on the night she died might be?"

"I have absolutely no idea.""

"It wouldn't have been a friend of hers? Of yours?"

257

"I can't imagine so. I can't imagine any of our friends being caught up in – in that kind of thing."

"Can you give me a list of your wife's close friends?" asked Kate. "We'll need to talk to them. We've already interviewed Mrs. Mellors but—"

"Oh, it wouldn't have been Kyla," said Arlen, quickly. "She would never do anything like that."

Kate paused. There was something – God, what was it? – in Arlen's tone. Something not quite natural. "You know Mrs. Mellors well, then?" she asked, casually.

When he answered her, Arlen sounded as normal as he ever had. "Yes, very well. She and Trixie and I are good friends. I play golf with her husband sometimes, too."

Kate wondered whether she'd imagined that brief flicker of strangeness in Arlen's voice. It was sometimes too easy to see undercurrents, to see something that wasn't there. She filed the thought away in her head for later perusal.

Arlen scribbled several names down on a sheet of paper, pausing and frowning over each one, before passing it to Kate. She glanced down at the list of five names and rough addresses and sighed at the thought of the time it would take to interview all five women. Still, it had to be done. After making an appointment with Arlen to amend his statement in Abbeyford the next day, they took their leave.

"So what did you think?" Olbeck asked as they drove away. He gave the solitary paparazzi a cheery wave as they drove by him onto the main road. The man scowled and Kate bit back a giggle.

"What did *you* think?" she countered.

Olbeck glanced over at her. "I think he's hiding something."

Kate felt a leap of gladness. It hadn't been her imagination, then. "So do I, funnily enough."

"I don't mean about the drugs," Olbeck went on, flicking on the indicator as they left the village and joined the bypass. "I actually think he's being totally truthful about that. He didn't see anything by Trixie's body that morning because there wasn't anything there to see."

"Yes. I agree." Kate watched the trees on the embankment of the dual carriageway flash by. The leaves were hitting the peak of their autumn colours; a kaleidoscope of copper, amber and auburn splendour. "So what *is* he hiding?"

"God knows. Everyone's always hiding *something* in a case like this. But is it significant or isn't it?"

"I'll do some checking," said Kate slowly, thinking it through. "Work out the timings for what he says he was doing that morning and the night before." Too late, she remembered they hadn't questioned Arlen about the bruising on his wife's arm and cursed. "That was slack of us, Mark," she said, explaining when he looked over enquiringly. "Too much going on at the moment."

"Tell me about it," Olbeck said with feeling. "Anyway, let me know about Arlen. Can you and Theo take the interviews with Trixie's friends?"

"Yep," said Kate, watching as the houses of Abbeyford began to roll into view. "I'm going to see how many stupid children's names I can gather at the same time."

She was rewarded with Olbeck's laugh at they drew into the forecourt of the police station, and she smiled as she bent to retrieve her handbag from the footwell.

Chapter Ten

TRUE TO HER WORD, KATE began interviewing Trixie Arlen's friends the next morning. She and Theo drove down together and worked their way through the list methodically. Kate had anticipated being unable to get hold of several of the people listed – she'd thought that most of them would be at work – but that turned out not to be the case. The five names on the list – Francesca Bolton, Sian Hills, Veronica Tibbert-Jones, Melinda D'Agnew and Carla Denford – all turned out to be women who looked as if they'd emerged from the same cloning laboratory, or perhaps a factory. All five were tall, thin, and well-groomed: all with that indefinable air of polish that only significant amounts of money and equally significant amounts of free time can achieve. Kate, who normally thought she was doing all right, considering how little time she had to spend on her appearance, felt positively scruffy next to them all. Theo, on the other hand, looked as though all his Christmases had come at once.

Not a single one of the five worked outside the home, as far as Kate could ascertain. Melinda D'Agnew did announce proudly that she was starting up her own business – one that Kate dismissively referred to in the privacy of her own head as a 'cupcake-bunting business'. In Kate's eyes, it was clearly a tax fiddle, on behalf of Melinda's husband, but she kept her mouth shut and made appropriate interested noises.

The five women were so alike that Kate had to keep referring back to her notes to see which of them they'd already talked to – she was beginning to get confused. It didn't help that they all looked the same – a mane of long, glossy hair, discreet makeup, all wearing the same unofficial uniform of a striped Breton top and dark, close-fitting jeans. What made it more frustrating was that none of them had anything interesting to tell Kate and Theo at all.

"No, Trixie was fine, she was completely normal last time I saw her," said Francesca Bolton, pouring coffee into fine white china cups. "There wasn't anything worrying her as far as I could tell."

"Trixie and Jacob seemed fine to me." Sian Hills offered them herbal tea and some sort of desiccated 'artisanal' biscuit. "They had their ups and downs of course, like anyone. But I'm sure there was nothing really bad going on in their relationship."

"Trixie? Take drugs? Oh no, you've got to be kidding. Seriously, like, she would never do something like that. God, it's so – so *sad*, isn't it, doing drugs? No one does that anymore." Veronica Tibbert-Jones ran a hand through the long, shiny sweep of her hair, scoffing. "She liked a drink, of course. Wine o'clock and all that. But heroin? Oh my God, no. I can't believe *that*."

Melinda D'Agnew gave Kate and Theo freshly squeezed orange juice. Kate watched her long, slim hands and finely polished nails and wondered just how much, if any, housework Melinda did. "Trixie and I would talk, of course we would. But she didn't mention anything to me that I thought was odd. We talked about business of course – I used to pump her for tips, given she was so successful. She was very generous, you know. A very warm heart. A really genuine person."

By the time Kate and Theo got to Carla Denford, Kate felt as though she'd been talking to identikit Sloanes for most of her adult life. Carla Denford opened the front door to her large, expensive house and Kate bit back a scream of frustration, realising that Carla was, yes, dressed in a navy striped top, grey skinny jeans and had a fall of long, glossy hair. They followed her into the large dining room-cum-play area at the back of the house and Kate braced herself for the offer of more healthy hot drinks.

"Want a drink?" asked Carla. "G and T do you?"

Kate blinked. It was twelve thirty in the afternoon. "No thanks, Mrs. Denford," she replied, glaring at Theo, who looked as if he were about to accept. He shut his mouth hastily.

"Because I get so fed up of fucking *tea*," said Carla with surprisingly bitterness and moved to the enormous SMEG fridge.

Hastily, Kate consulted her list of questions and chose one at random. "How well did you know Trixie Arlen, Mrs. Denford?"

"About as well as I know anyone else here," said Carla, sitting down with a brimming glass. She took a long, thirsty gulp and put it down with a sigh. "Which is to say not at all."

"How do you mean?" Kate realised Carla had probably had one or two drinks already, although her speech was clear enough.

"It's all surface, here," said Carla. Her head drooped towards the table and she put a finger in a spilled droplet on the kitchen table, smearing it in a circle. "The men all work in London in ridiculously well-paid jobs, and the women sit at home in their lovely designer houses, outsourcing their childcare. It's so bloody *boring*; I could just scream sometimes. Instead, well, I..." she gestured to her glass and made a shrugging gesture which was both eloquent and sad.

Kate gave Theo a meaningful glance and, for once, he understood and got up, muttering something about getting something from the car. Once he was out of the room, Kate put down her notebook and leant forward a little, mirroring Carla's position.

"So, it's a bit shit, is it?" Kate said, in a tone she hoped was both wry and sympathetic.

Carla looked at her gratefully. "Oh God, you have no idea. It's funny though, because Trixie was the only one who – she was a bit different. She had a *spark*. A bit of life. At least she'd actually *done* something with her life – before, I mean."

"You said you didn't know her well. Did she ever confide in you?"

"Not really. It was more – I guess I confided in her, more than the other way round. We met at an NCT class—"

"Yes, what *is* that?" asked Kate, unable to help herself.

Carla gave her a slightly odd look. "National Childbirth Trust."

"Oh, right. Thanks."

"Yeah, anyway, we met at the NCT class, caught up with each other a few times after our babies were born—"

"What's your baby's name?" asked Kate, unable to help herself again.

Again, Carla looked slightly surprised. "James."

"Oh, that's *lovely*," said Kate fervently. She got a grip on herself. "So you met up quite frequently after you had your children?"

"Sort of. Occasionally I went to her house or she came here. What they call a 'playdate', around here, which is *ridiculous* because the babies couldn't care less about playing with other babies. Anyway, we did see each other a bit."

"Did Trixie ever seem worried about anything to you? Anxious about anything?"

Carla fell silent, twirling her almost empty glass around in her hand. She appeared to be thinking hard. "There's one thing she said once that I thought was strange," she said, slowly. "It stuck with me."

"What was that?" prompted Kate.

"We were in the kitchen at her place, just chatting, and the radio was on. There was something in the news about – oh, God, what was it? – oh yes, that's right, about a mother who'd been found not guilty of killing her baby. God, *horrible*. Anyway, I said something about not understanding how anyone could do that and Trixie said, in this really sad, slow way, that sometimes people did things that they would always regret, even if they hadn't meant to do them at the time."

Kate paused. "That's it?"

Carla nodded. "Yeah, that was all. She changed the subject the next minute and...I don't know, it was just her voice that got me. Real...real *grief*, kind of dragging through it. It made me shiver."

"She never elaborated on what she meant?"

"No. I remembered it from time to time and thought I'd ask her about it, but I never really felt the time was right. And now I'll never get the chance."

Her voice, finally thickening from alcohol, broke. For a moment, Kate was sure Carla would burst into tears but she seemed to have more self-control than was at first apparent. She took a deep, shaky breath and appeared to compose herself.

There was nothing else that Carla appeared to be able to tell her. Kate eventually gave her thanks and said goodbye. She wanted to say something kind, something that would make Carla feel better, but she couldn't think what. 'Go back to London' was probably not something that would make Carla feel better at all. So Kate said nothing, and smiled and thanked her, and Carla, red-eyed and faintly swaying, just nodded and closed the door behind her in silence.

"Blimey," said Theo as they drove away, Kate taking the wheel for the homeward journey. "Some people don't know they're born, eh? All that money, expensive cars, designer goods and she's still a miserable cow."

"Oh, for God's sake," said Kate, more crossly than she'd intended. "It's not about *money*. Carla's clearly an intelligent woman who feels like a complete outsider here. She's unhappy because she's lonely and bored, that's all."

"Yeah, right," said Theo, looking unconvinced.

"Well, I think that's what's the matter with her," said Kate, more gently. She felt like adding 'I know how she feels', but didn't. What she did ponder aloud was the question, "I wonder if Trixie Arlen felt like Carla did? I wonder that very much."

"Would explain why she was chasing the dragon again," said Theo.

"I think that's *smoking* heroin," said Kate. "Not injecting it. But I see your point." She remembered that she had an appointment with the drug and alcohol counsellor the next day. And the day after that was exam day. She swallowed, queasily. Out loud she said, "Wonder if Arlen's given his new statement yet?"

"Don't know," said Theo, yawning. He settled his head back comfortably against the headrest. "Wake me up when we get back to Abbeyford. Those chicks have worn me out."

"I never thought I'd hear that coming from you," Kate joked. Theo said nothing but smiled lazily as the car joined the dual carriageway that would take them back to their home town.

Chapter Eleven

THE NEXT DAY STARTED BADLY. Kate woke late, after staying up until the early hours trying to cram more knowledge into her head, staring at her notes until they blurred before her. She wasn't sure it had done much good. She was in too much of a rush to have breakfast before she left the house and had to stop off at a service station to grab a cup of coffee and a greasy sausage roll to tide her over.

The sat nav took her into Charlock, the neighbouring suburb to Arbuthon Green, to the modern brick building housing Outreach, the drug rehabilitation service provider. She was due to meet one of the counsellors, Jason Neville, and made the appointment with a minute to spare. Neville turned out to be a man of around Kate's age, with very pale blue eyes and the white skin of a natural redhead. His fox-coloured hair was curly and worn long, tied back into a pony tail. He had the warm, approachable demeanour typical to professional counsellors.

Kate sat opposite him in an office so messy it looked as though it had been burgled. Kate had actually never been in a counsellor's office that was any different; it seemed to go with the job. God knew how they ever found anything. Perhaps there was hidden order amongst the chaos. She turned her eyes from the mountainous piles of paperwork, empty mugs and crumpled food containers on Jason Neville's desk and focused her attention on what he was saying.

"We see all sorts of people here, Detective Sergeant," he said, fiddling with one of the folders on his desk. As he did so, a teetering pile of paper crashed to the floor. "Oh, bugger. Sorry." He began picking them up. Kate bent to help him but he said quickly, "Oh, I'm sorry, these are all confidential. Please don't bother."

Kate could have given him the 'nothing's confidential in a murder case', but she didn't; firstly because they weren't sure whether this *was* a murder case, and secondly, she didn't want to antagonise him. She wanted Mr. Neville to open up as much as he was able to.

"So you see all sorts of people?" Kate prompted, once the papers were returned to even more glorious disorder on the man's desk.

Her eyes fell on a leaflet entitled *Is Your Child a Drug Addict?* In smaller type beneath the flaring headline was a box containing several bullet points. Kate read the first few before she had to bring her gaze back up to Neville's face. *Possible signs of heroin addiction: constricted (small) pupils, noticeable needle 'track marks', hyper-alertness followed by sudden sleepiness...*

Jason Neville was already answering. "That's right. I know there's the public stereotype of an addict – certainly that of an alcoholic – but that's the stereotype, not the reality."

"I'm interested in your clients who are heroin addicts. Would you say they range in type? I know you can't tell me specifics—" she added quickly as he began to frown, "but it would be really helpful to have some sort of guidance."

"Right. Well, we've got people in addiction therapy here from all walks of life. Housewives, builders, professionals. Doctors." He hesitated and then added. "Even a police officer."

Kate was predictably agog. Who was it? Surely not anyone she knew? She filed that thought away for later and merely raised her eyebrows at Neville, who looked at her with a slight touch of defiance, ready to block the questions that he seemed to anticipate coming his way.

When Kate remained silent, he cleared his throat and continued speaking. "We work on a combination of therapies here. We run a methadone clinic, we have several medical treatments that clients can access if we feel it would be appropriate for them. The bulk of our work, though, is psychotherapy."

"I see. Is it the case that most of your patients are dealing with some kind of life trauma – that they're self-medicating with drugs to treat that?"

Neville shrugged. "Sometimes. Quite often they're working through horrendous childhoods, deep-seated emotional abuse, physical abuse, that sort of thing. Or they're unhappy because of something terrible that's happened to them in adult life – a bereavement or a bad accident. Quite a few people self-medicate, as you say, with heroin because it's such an effective pain-killer. Obviously you know that it's a derivative of morphine, which has a wide-spread legitimate use in our hospitals and surgeries."

"Yes, I'm aware of that," Kate said patiently. Briefly, she thought of her mother and how her drinking had blighted Kate's life from childhood. What was her mother dealing with, what trauma from the past was she fighting? Kate's oldest brother had died young, almost too early for Kate to have any memory of him; had that been what started her mother on the slippery slope to self-destruction? Was it something other than that, something earlier and never spoken of in her mother's life? For a moment, Kate wanted nothing more than to run from Jason Neville's room and drive at full speed to her mother's house; she wanted to run through the front doorway and fling her arms about her mother. How long had it been since they last talked? Four years? More?

With an effort, Kate brought her attention back to the present and to what Jason Neville was saying. He was fidgeting with a mug this time and Kate prayed that he wouldn't dislodge another tsunami of paper.

Neville was still speaking. "Of course, once people reach a certain...tipping point, I suppose you'd call it, the problems they're dealing with are all to do with the drug that they're consuming. They behave terribly because they're taking drugs, and then they feel so bad that they have to take more drugs to block out what they've done, and so the cycle just perpetuates. Once we manage to get them into therapy we work very hard on breaking that cycle."

"Yes, I see," said Kate. "What's your success rate?"

"Sorry?"

"Do you have a lot of people who relapse?"

"Yes. Oh, sadly, yes, we do. But then we also have a lot of people who conquer their addictions and go on to live very happy and successful lives."

Kate thought about how to pose the next question. "Would you say that you have clients who might have been clean for years, decades even, and then for one reason or another they go back to using drugs again?"

Jason's pale blue eyes caught her own. There was a long moment of silence. "Yes," he said eventually. "That does happen."

"Why?"

Again he hesitated. "It's difficult to explain, unless you've actually been an addict yourself. There's some research that suggests that once you're addicted to something, you've permanently altered your brain chemistry, and so if you ever begin using again your use spirals out of control very quickly. Whereas a 'normal' person—" he made quotation marks in the air with his fingers, "a normal person can take drugs, even quite regularly, without their use escalating."

Kate frowned. He hadn't actually answered her question. "Yes, I see, but why would someone who's been clean for so long just go back to using drugs again?"

"I don't know," Neville said simply. "Life just gets on top of them. Perhaps they go through another traumatic event. Perhaps they forget just how bad their life was when they were using drugs. Or maybe it's nothing so complicated. Sometimes people just...slip."

LATER, AS KATE DROVE AWAY from the centre, having thanked Jason Neville and made her goodbyes, she found herself thinking of what he had said. What had made Trixie Arlen slip? *Had* she slipped – or was she pushed? Kate reminded herself that they still had to question Jacob Arlen over the bruising on his wife's arm and made a mental note that she would do that tomorrow. Oh God, no, she couldn't tomorrow. Tomorrow was when she would take her exams. Kate swallowed. All thoughts of Trixie Arlen fled, replaced by nerve-grinding anxiety. She wasn't prepared for these exams; she knew she wasn't. Perhaps I should just postpone taking them, she thought to herself, but knew that it would be months before she might get another chance to re-sit them. Months of no career progression. No, no she would take them tomorrow and do her best. Much as she knew that last-minute cramming could be counter-productive, she resolved to spend the evening studying. It'll be fine, she told herself, ignoring the uncoiling worm of uneasiness that writhed in her stomach.

Chapter Twelve

"So how did it go?" asked Theo as Kate slid into the chair of the desk opposite him the next afternoon.

Kate closed her eyes briefly. "Don't ask."

"That bad, eh?" Theo tried to look sympathetic but succeeded only in looking mischievous. "Should have studied harder then, shouldn't you?"

"Shut up!" Kate crashed her chair back from the desk. Theo looked shocked and throughout the office, heads turned. Kate quickly walked to the far side of the room, where the coffee machine was, and made herself a drink with shaking hands, keeping her head down.

The sound of footsteps behind her preceded Theo's quiet apology. "Listen, mate, I'm sorry. I didn't mean to wind you up. Exams are stressful, yeah?"

Kate blinked hard. Theo's apology, on top of the realisation that she really shouldn't have lost her temper in such a childish way, made her feel even worse. "No, I'm sorry," she said, turning round and hoping that her eyes weren't too red. "Sorry. I'm a bit...a bit highly strung, at the moment."

"No worries," said Theo, his cheeky grin bursting out afresh. "Let's have a pint later, yeah? I'm buying."

Kate never drank pints but she appreciated the offer. She returned the grin and they walked back to their desks together. Kate glanced over at Olbeck's office; empty. Never mind, she had dinner with him and Jeff to look forward to tonight, although she hoped she wouldn't have to spend too much time talking about her exams.

They had been as bad as she expected; possibly worse. I've definitely failed, she thought to herself, and the brief lifting of spirits which Theo's kindness provoked flickered and died. She took a gulp of coffee, swallowing past the lump in her throat, and turned her attention to the paperwork littering her desk.

She was halfway through the pile when she came across a copy of Jack Harker's statement about the robbery he'd been victim to. Kate mentally gave herself a shake. It was a measure of her state of mind that she'd almost forgotten that such a thing had happened at all. She made notes to find out if there had been any developments on that case, and whether any more robberies had been reported.

Kate rubbed her temples, feeling overwhelmed. Since her colleague, Rav, had been shot last summer – thankfully not fatally – the team had been one down, with no replacement for him yet in sight. Kate reminded herself that she had to take that up with Olbeck and Anderton. The extra work occasioned by being short-staffed meant that it was more and more likely mistakes would be made. Look at her and Olbeck, forgetting to ask Arlen about that bruising; it was a rookie error, and unforgiveable in officers of their experience.

Kate sighed and added another thing to the mental list of 'stuff to do' she kept in her head – *call Rav*. It had been several weeks since she'd spoken to him and she wanted to know how he was doing. Rav was supposed to be on long-term sick leave, but Kate wondered whether he'd actually ever want to return. It was a shame; he'd been a good officer, as young as he was.

She jumped as Theo flung himself into his chair, making their desks rock. He had the gleeful expression of someone with some serious gossip to imply. "Well, well, well," he said, taking his time about it. "Now we know why the boss has been so distracted lately."

"What do you mean?" asked Kate.

"Dear, dear," said Theo, ignoring her. "I can see why he *has* been distracted. Ooh-wee...."

"What are you talking about?" Kate said it impatiently, but a presentiment of disaster began to filter its way through her. Her heart began to beat a little faster.

Theo finally got to the point. "Anderton's new bird. She's in his office right now. *Hawt!*"

Anderton's new bird. Kate was very aware of her heartbeat now; it rang in her ears like thunder. Her stomach cramped. "What?" she asked, unable to keep her voice steady, but luckily Theo was too busy making lustful noises to notice.

Kate made a mammoth effort and regained control of her voice. "What are you dribbling on about, Theo?" She already knew but she had to hear it again, just to confirm her worst fears.

Theo grinned. "I told you. Anderton's new piece of stuff. She's a lawyer, apparently. Anyway, she's in his office now."

Nobody would ever know what it cost Kate to give a disdainful shrug. "That's nice," she said in a bored tone, keeping her eyes on the screen. She clenched her teeth so hard her jaw hurt as jealousy consumed her. Okay, so she and Anderton had only slept together, once, years ago, but Kate had never given up hope that it would happen again, despite neither of them making any moves towards one another. And now it was too late. Of course it was. You fool, you fool, she told herself fiercely while the blood pounded in her ears and she stared at her computer screen through a mist of tears, utterly unseeing. Why didn't you do something about it when you had the chance? He would have wanted to, you know he would have. What stopped you? Now it's too late. Too late.

She got up abruptly and made her way towards the women's toilets. Her throat was aching with unshed tears. She prayed that no one would be in there, and for once, her prayer was answered.

273

She pushed the button of the hand-dryer and ducked into a cubicle for a few moments, her sobs lost under the roar of hot air. As soon as the dryer switched off, she choked off her tears, biting the back of her hand in an effort to bring herself under control. What a fucking awful day this was turning out to be, she thought. She blotted her face with toilet paper and went out to splash her face at the sink. Luckily she didn't wear much eye-makeup. She made herself stare at the harsh radiance of the overhead strip light in an effort to lessen the redness of her eyes. Then, under control again, she took a deep breath, straightened her back, and left.

She told herself that she would not walk past Anderton's office. She would not. But somehow she found her feet were taking her in that direction, seemingly under no instruction from her brain, as if they'd been bewitched. The blinds in his office were open, and Kate could not have looked away if there'd been a gun to her head. Anderton and a woman were standing quite close together by his desk, laughing about something. The woman was tall and beautiful, with dark blonde hair pulled back into a professional-looking French twist. She wore a very nicely cut pale grey suit and a crisp white shirt, open low at the neck. Kate's bewitched feet slowed and then, as Anderton looked up and their eyes met, Kate found that she could actually walk as fast as she wanted to. She marched back to her desk, her face hot and her heart still pounding as if she had run a race.

SOMEHOW SHE GOT THROUGH THE rest of the afternoon. There was so much to do and nothing she actually wanted to do. Doctor Telling had rung and left her a message asking her to call back when she could, but Kate couldn't quite face doing so, not even for the quiet and soothing tones of the good doctor. I'll do it tomorrow, she told herself, fighting not to put her head in her hands and weep. I'll do it tomorrow when I'm feeling a bit better.

Theo, thank God, kept his mouth shut for most of the afternoon.

At about three pm, he muttered something about a hotel – Kate didn't catch the name – and left the office. He hadn't returned by the time Kate was preparing to leave herself; so much for that pint he'd promised her. She hadn't seen Olbeck all afternoon either, but at about six thirty pm, he appeared in the doorway, looked around and saw her, raising his hand.

"Ready for dinner?" he asked, coming over.

Kate nodded. "Can I just ask that we don't mention my exams? At all?"

"Oh dear." Olbeck looked at her sympathetically. "That bad, eh? Never mind. And no, we won't mention them again."

"Thanks."

"I thought I could give you a lift if you like? Save taking two cars."

"Fine, whatever," muttered Kate. She was beginning to feel very tired. It was too much trouble to work out how she was going to get home or how she was going to get to work in the morning. Who cared, anyway?

She was quiet in the car and it took her a while to realise that Olbeck had that strange, suppressed energy about him again. He was fidgeting a little in the driving seat, tapping the foot not on the accelerator, drumming his fingers on the steering wheel. Despite her exhaustion, Kate wondered what was wrong with him and then realised, as she should have before, that he probably had something important to tell her. She felt a pang of anxiety – what if it was bad news? Like what, she asked herself, and then hurried the thought away before she could clarify what she meant. He didn't seem upset, though; the opposite, if anything. Kate opened her mouth to ask him what the matter was and then shut it again. He'll tell me when he's ready, she thought, realising that she was too wrung out and emotional to be able to take it in properly anyway.

In that, she was wrong. Once they were inside Olbeck's house, he ushered her through to the kitchen. Several pans were bubbling on the stove, and there was an open bottle of red wine breathing on the table. Jeff was nowhere to be seen.

Kate looked around for him. "Where's Jeff?"

Olbeck was almost bouncing up and down on his feet. "He just popped out to get something. He'll be back soon." He opened a drawer, stared blindly into it and pushed it shut again. "I should wait for him to be here before I tell you."

Here we go. "Tell me what?" asked Kate, trying to sound enthusiastic.

Olbeck was silent for a moment. "Oh bugger it, I can't wait," he said, grinning. "I've been keeping this in for so long that I think I'll burst if I don't tell you sooner or later. We're getting married."

Married. Olbeck was getting married. Although she felt as though she'd been kicked in the stomach, Kate managed to stretch her lips into a desperate smile.

"That's great—" she began, but Olbeck was still speaking.

"And that's not the best thing. We've been talking about it and we're pretty sure we're going to look into seeing if we can adopt as well!" he said, clasping his hands together in front of his chest.

The room stilled for a moment. Kate felt the smile freeze on her face as that word echoed around her head. *Adopt. We're going to adopt.* There was a moment of sparkling numbness.

"Are you fucking kidding me?" The words came out in a shriek. Kate could feel her face stretched in a grimace. She was trembling from head to foot.

Olbeck looked at her, his jaw sagging. In a dim and distant part of her mind, she could recognise the hurt that she'd just inflicted beginning to surface on his face, but that was locked away where she couldn't get at it, drenched as she was in shock and furious anger. *Adopt.* Olbeck *knew* how she felt about that, he *knew* what she'd been through, and here he was, all happy and excited; never mind that Kate's heart had just been stamped into a bloody pulp on the floor.

"Kate," Olbeck said quietly. "I know you don't mean that."

"You can't! You can't! If you do that I'll never speak to you again, never, never—" She couldn't say any more; her words were lost in a flood of sobs.

"Kate—" Olbeck tried to speak but she turned and ran from the kitchen. She pulled frantically at the front door. Olbeck called something from the kitchen but she didn't stay to hear what it was; she wrenched the front door open and almost fell over Jeff, who was just outside with a wrapped bottle in his arms. She saw the gold top and knew it was champagne. They actually expected her to *celebrate* with them. By this time, she was crying so hard she could barely see.

"Kate!" Jeff exclaimed in horror. "What's wrong?"

She said nothing but barged her way past him. He gave a shout of surprise and dropped the bottle of champagne. It hit the stone flags of the front porch and exploded in a shower of bubbles and glass, and Kate, by this time at the garden gate, was horribly, viciously glad. She ran down the street towards the main road without a backward glance.

Chapter Thirteen

Trixie Arlen's funeral took place the next day. The weather was suitably funereal; the sky was blanketed with dark grey clouds, and a chill wind whipped the coats and scarves of the mourners as they arrived at the church. The little village of Marshfield, three miles from the farmhouse where Trixie Arlen had died, had never seen so many people. The black limousines of the funeral procession moved slowly through the thronged streets. Cameras and mobile phones were raised high above the heads of the crowds, filming the hearse as it drove by. Paparazzi were clustered around the lychgate to the church, ready to snap anyone who passed through it.

Kate, who'd driven down alone, had to park almost in the next village and walk a mile before she could get close to the church. She was dressed in her black suit and carried another bunch of white roses, just as she had to the funeral of John Miller. What a contrast to this that had been. There must have been three hundred people actually attending the service, not to mention the crowds waiting impatiently outside the church. Kate regarded herself in the rear view mirror for a long moment and then took a pair of dark glasses from her handbag. There was no way she could walk into a church with eyes as red-raw as hers were, even if this was a funeral.

She locked the car and began the long walk to the churchyard, clutching her bouquet. There was an ache in her chest, a physical pain that made her stop once in a while and press her hand against her breastbone. *My heart is actually broken. I've lost my best friend, I've lost Anderton, and I've failed my exams.* Kate stopped for a moment to catch her breath. For a second she felt dizzy and didn't think she could walk another step without falling over. All she wanted to do was go home, hide under the duvet and never leave again; just moulder away beneath the bedclothes until all the pain was gone.

The church was so crowded there was no possibility of getting a seat. Kate propped herself against a chilly stone wall at the back. She was glad that she was wearing a pair of flat shoes, insomuch that she was capable of feeling glad about anything. The coffin was one of those fancy painted jobs, garlanded with roses and strewn with lavender; Kate could smell it even at the back of the church. She found herself wondering what it had cost. All that money for a box that was going to be buried in the ground. Put me in a cardboard box when the time comes, she thought bleakly. Who would come to her funeral? Her brother and sisters, perhaps. They were about the only people in her life she hadn't managed to alienate.

The voice of the vicar droned on. *Eternal life...* the way Kate was feeling, that would be a punishment, not a blessing. She tried to switch her thoughts, tried to find something positive to think about but could think of nothing. To her horror, she felt tears begin to well up again, and she blinked frantically, trying to stop them and realised she couldn't. She felt in her handbag for a tissue. At least at a funeral you didn't need a reason for crying. Restrained sobs and whimpers rose from the packed church. How many of these people had actually known Trixie?

After what felt like several years, the service came to an end. As Kate was near the entrance she was able to leave the church before the masses. She walked over to the churchyard wall, unsure of whether she should wait. She'd caught sight of Olbeck as she arrived and felt a lurch of nausea. The furious anger she'd felt last night had dissipated, just as she needed it. Now all she felt was shame. Olbeck had given her what was probably the happiest news of his life last night and what had she done? Screamed and shouted and abused him. *You're a monster, Kate.* And poor Jeff, as well. They would probably never speak to her again, and who could blame them? All because she had never got over what had happened to her in her teens? Wasn't it time that she did? Wasn't it time she actually grew up and acted like an adult? *You're thirty-one, Kate. Act your bloody age, for once.*

Kate came back to reality with a start. She'd been reprimanding herself in the privacy of her own head for so long that it was quite a shock to realise that most of the mourners had already departed. She could see Jacob Arlen over by the entrance to the church, talking to a tall bald man. Kate looked at the man curiously. He looked vaguely familiar. Was he a celebrity? There had been several at the funeral, gawped at and gossiped about in whispered tones: several television presenters, an actress, a model. Where had she seen him? Kate pondered it a moment longer and then dismissed the bald man from her mind. She had enough to worry about.

She was dreading bumping into Olbeck but he'd clearly already left. He must have seen her standing over by the wall – the way the churchyard was laid out, there was no way of missing her – but he hadn't come over to talk to her. Despite understanding why, Kate felt her heart sink even further. I have to talk to him, I have to apologise, she told herself, and she even got out her phone and brought up his number before putting it away. Not yet. She didn't even know what to say.

Kate looked around for another of her colleagues but couldn't see anyone, not even Theo. She sighed and pushed herself away from the churchyard wall. A long walk back to her car and then a lonely journey back to Abbeyford. Sooner or later, she was going to have to face the reality of work. She was going to face Olbeck – and Anderton. *God.* Kate sighed again and pushed her hands into the pockets of her suit. She began to walk back to her car, head bowed against the spitting rain.

Chapter Fourteen

"Want to hear something interesting?"

"What's that?" Kate had to fight to sound interested. Theo didn't appear to notice her lack of enthusiasm. He was leaning forward over this desk, his dark eyes bright.

"You know that hotel that Arlen was staying in the night of Trixie's death?"

"Do I?"

"You should do. The Granchester. He stays there a lot apparently, the desk clerks all know him."

"Right," said Kate, wondering if there was a point to this.

"*Well*, apparently that night the night porter saw him leave the hotel. About eleven pm."

That got Kate's attention. She sat up a little. "Right," she said again, but more alertly.

Theo's eyes were sparkling. "So, if the night porter's telling the truth – and I can't see why he would lie – then—"

Kate finished the sentence for him. "Then that's Arlen's alibi smashed to pieces."

"Exactly." Theo sat back in his chair and folded his arms. "What if he drove back to his place that night, persuaded his wife to OD – or did it for her – and then pretended to find her first thing in the morning?"

"Yes," said Kate slowly, thinking. "It's possible. But why?"

Theo waved a hand airily. "Oh, motives, motives. I'm not going to worry my head about *why* at the moment. I just want to know if that's how it actually happened."

Kate leapt up. "You're absolutely right, Theo. Let's go, shall we?"

"Hold on a sec. We just need to run it past Mark first."

Kate's stomach clenched. She'd successfully avoided Olbeck all morning, burying her head in paperwork whenever he walked past her desk, refusing to catch his eye when she could feel him staring at her through the glass wall of his office. She wondered whether it was obvious to anyone else that they weren't speaking. During her entire conversation with

Theo, a small part of her had been quite impressed that she'd sounded so normal, considering most of her still felt that death would be quite an attractive alternative to carrying on living.

"You do that," she said hastily. "I'm going to get my coat."

They walked past Anderton's office on the way to the car park but this time, the blinds were closed. Kate wondered whether he was in there with his new woman again. She felt a twist of jealous paranoia and told herself to get a grip. Any more of that and you'll literally go mad, she told herself. Keep a lid on it.

As they waited to join the main road – traffic was always heavy at this point in the morning – Kate let her gaze drift to the newspaper vendor stand on the pavement. The new edition of the Abbeyford Gazette had been published and the large photograph on the front page made Kate gasp.

"Stop! Stop for a minute, Theo?"

"What?" Theo asked, confused.

"Hold on a second." Kate hopped out of the car and ran over to the stand. She bought a paper and brought it back.

"What *are* you doing?" Theo asked.

Kate stabbed a finger at the picture on the front page. "This guy, I knew I knew him. He was at Trixie Arlen's funeral."

Theo looked. "Michael Dekker. Of course you know him. He's about the richest guy in Abbeyford."

Kate was reading the article attached to the photograph. "He's just made a big donation to Outreach. You know, the drug and alcohol charity." She read a few more sentences. "Why would he be at Trixie Arlen's funeral?"

Theo rolled his eyes. "'Cos his son used to go out with her, didn't he? The musician guy. What was his name?"

Kate shrugged. "I don't know. I don't know who you're talking about."

Theo put the car into gear and they finally drove off. "James Gantry!" he shouted triumphantly before they'd gone fifteen yards.

"Oh, *him*," said Kate. "I didn't know that was Michael Dekker's son. Whatever happened to him?"

"He died."

"Seriously? What of?"

"Drugs overdose."

Kate snorted, unsympathetically. "God, how original. Is there a single musician who's managed to off himself or herself in a totally new and thought provoking way?"

Theo didn't dignify that with an answer and Kate, a little ashamed of herself, didn't say anything else for a while.

"Actually," she said after a few minutes of silence. "I might give Michael Dekker a call. It would be useful to talk to someone who knew Trixie Arlen back in the nineties."

"Would it?" asked Theo. Then he cursed and sounded the horn at a black BMW who had cut him up.

"Careful," said Kate. "Yes, I think it would." She hesitated and said "I can't help feeling that Trixie's past is important. I don't know why but...that's what I think."

"Knock yourself out," said Theo.

They finally cleared the clogged streets of Abbeyford and headed towards the motorway. Kate kept checking her phone, thinking she might see a text from Olbeck. Stupid, she told herself, putting it away for the umpteenth time. He's not going to contact me. She closed her eyes briefly, that overwhelming rush of misery engulfing her again. *I have to say sorry,* she thought. *He has to forgive me, because if he doesn't, I don't know what I'm going to do.*

For once, Theo wasn't playing hip-hop or garage at ear-bleeding levels on the car stereo. Instead, there was quite a serious talk show playing quietly in the background. Kate listened with half an ear to the presenter and guest talking about the upcoming films due to be released that month. She and Olbeck used to go to the cinema together quite frequently. *God, this was ridiculous, everything reminded her of her friend. This is worse than a relationship breaking down,* Kate thought.

"You're quiet today," Theo said as they joined the M4, and Kate started guiltily.

"Just got a lot on my mind."

Theo raised an eyebrow. "Who is he?"

Kate half laughed. "There are other things in the world that cause trouble other than sex, Theo. Did you know that?"

"There are?" Theo asked, in mock-shock.

Kate rolled her eyes but she also smiled. After a moment, she pulled her mind back onto the job. "Does Arlen know we're coming?"

"Nope."

"Good," said Kate. "Let's scare him a little."

Theo nodded. "I had the CCTV checked that night at The Granchester. The clerk wasn't lying. Arlen did leave, late. You can clearly see him driving away and he doesn't come back."

"Really? That's excellent, Theo." Kate felt another unpleasant emotion, this time annoyance at herself for not having the idea first. *I've to get a grip,* she admonished herself privately. *My career is all I've got left.* Aloud, she asked "It would be worth pulling any CCTV around the Arlen's farmhouse the night of Trixie's death, wouldn't it? If there is any. Rural places often don't have many cameras."

"Yep," said Theo, moving into the fast lane to overtake a truck. "We'll do that when we get back."

"Are we going to tell Arlen that we've got him leaving The Granchester on camera?"

"Let's see," said Theo. "Let's see what he comes up with before we hit him with the evidence."

They made good time until they reached Putney, where they hit the first of the traffic jams extending from Putney Bridge. Forty minutes later, when the car had advanced all of thirty feet, Kate wondered whether she should suggest abandoning the car and taking the underground.

Eventually they made progress again. Kate watched the glittering surface of the Thames as they drove across the bridge. London had never appealed to her as a place of work or as a place to live. Fine for a visit, but it was too big, too busy; the ancient city took no prisoners. She thought with longing for a moment of the old houses of Abbeyford, the rolling green hills that surrounded the town, the familiar faces that she saw every day. No, she wouldn't want to swap that, not for all the culture, clubs, bars and shops in the world.

Arlen's office on Cheapside was indistinguishable from all the other city offices and financial institutions. Huge walls of plate glass, carefully tinted so visibility from the street was minimal, tight security once you were past the glossy girls of the reception desk. An atrium with a jungle of equally glossy plants, and glass lifts scudding up and down to the many different floors.

Kate watched Arlen's face closely as she and Theo approached. He stared at them as if he couldn't believe his eyes, but she couldn't work out if he was apprehensive that they had come to arrest him or just bracing himself for the anguish of more revelations connected to his wife's death.

"Good morning, Mr. Arlen," Theo said, as Kate shut the door of his office behind them.

"Good morning, officers," replied Arlen stonily. "What can I do for you?"

"I can see you're surprised to see us," Kate said, sitting down opposite him. Theo took the other chair.

"I must confess I am."

Kate and Theo exchanged glances. "Perhaps you'd like to confess to something else as well?" suggested Theo. Kate hid a wince. A bit too obvious, too quickly, surely...

Arlen's frown grew deeper. "I afraid I don't know what you're talking about."

Kate jumped in before Theo could say anything else. "In your statement concerning the night on which your wife died, you stated that you'd stayed the night in The Granchester Hotel on Westbury Street, EC1, and left very early the next morning in order to drive home."

"Yes," said Arlen, clearly realising that Kate hadn't yet finished but just as clearly wanting to say something. "That's ri—"

"You don't wish to amend that statement at all?"

"What do you mean?"

"I mean, do you wish to amend your statement at all?"

Arlen risked a strained smile. "No. No I don't believe so."

There was a moment's silence. Kate hung back, happy to let Theo deliver the blow. He didn't disappoint.

"We have a credible eye-witness, and CCTV footage, that shows you leaving The Granchester and driving from their car park at about eleven pm that evening. Not five-thirty am the following morning, as you said in your statement."

Arlen said nothing. His face remained impassive, but the colour slowly mounted until his entire face turned a dull brick red.

"Do you have anything to say, Mr. Arlen?" Kate asked after a moment.

There was another long silence, and then Arlen spoke in a low voice. "I'm not saying anything until I can speak to my lawyer."

Kate and Theo looked at one another again. Kate was heartened to find that they had shared a flash of unspoken understanding, just as she used to have with Olbeck. The following jab of pain caught her unawares and she broke eye contact.

"We'll continue this conversation down at Abbeyford Station then, sir," said Theo, getting up.

Arlen remained seated. "Is that an order, officer?"

Theo smiled a deceptively charming smile. "No, it's a request. If you refuse that request, however, we will arrest you. Understood?"

Kate saw Arlen's throat ripple as he swallowed. She watched his gaze go to the open plan space beyond his office, the multitude of desks staffed by his underlings and colleagues already casting curious glances over at them. A small sadistic part of her was hoping he would refuse. She would love to slap some cuffs on him and parade him through the goggling crowd of finance workers.

It was not to be, however. Arlen, whatever else he may be, was clearly not stupid. He nodded abruptly and got up without a further word. The three of them walked back across a silent floor but even as the door closed behind them, as they waited for the lift, Kate could hear the whispers begin to start, rising in a slow hissing wave of muted sound.

Chapter Fifteen

MICHAEL DEKKER LIVED IN ONE of the biggest houses that Kate had ever seen. It was beautiful; an isolated Georgian stone mansion surrounded on all four sides by carefully tended and landscaped gardens – grounds, really, *garden* was too reductive a term for something this size. Nestled at the bottom of a hollow, surrounded on all sides by steep green hills and patches of woodland, it didn't seem like a family home at all, but more like something the National Trust might acquire. Kate almost expected to find a ticket booth and a coach car park beyond the high walls that surrounded the house.

Michael Dekker apparently lived in this enormous place alone. Was he married? Kate realised she didn't know anything about him, apart from the fact that he was a philanthropist, whose patronage was particularly aimed at addiction charities, and that he'd had a semi-famous son who'd died young.

A woman answered the door, dressed in a smart black dress. Clearly the housekeeper, she was small, young, with sallow skin and black hair tied back in a neat ponytail. Smiling and silent, she examined Kate's identification carefully and bobbed her head in acknowledgement before ushering Kate through the house, through a variety of enormous, beautifully furnished and appointed rooms, before showing her into a vast orangery that ran half the length of the house.

Michael Dekker was sitting in a white wickerwork chair, staring out through the windows of the orangery at the marvellous view beyond, a panoramic vista of rolling hills, forests and the glittering silver thread of a distant river running through it. Would you ever get tired of that view? Kate wondered. She doubted it. She decided to make that her first question.

"What's that? Oh, no, not at all. Well, you can't blame me, can you, Detective Sergeant? It's sublime." Dekker indicated another wickerwork chair opposite and Kate seated herself. "Can I offer you a drink?"

"I'd love a cup of tea, thanks."

Dekker nodded and raised his eyebrows at his housekeeper, who stood waiting patiently at the entrance to the orangery. She bobbed her head again in understanding and left.

"Now, what can I do for you, DS Redman?" There was a faint hint of a South African accent in Dekker's voice. He was a big man, barrel-chested and bald-headed, with thrusting shoulders and rather pale blue eyes.

"Well, firstly, thank you for seeing me at such short notice, Mr. Dekker. I appreciate you must be a very busy man."

"Well, that's true. But I hope I can help."

Kate tore her gaze from the view with difficulty and shifted in her chair to face Dekker. "I wanted to talk to someone who knew Trixie Arlen, particularly someone who knew her back in – well, in her heyday; I suppose you could call it that. Back in the nineties."

Dekker rubbed his chin. His pale eyes regarded Kate thoughtfully. "Well, I don't know if I can say I knew Trixie well, DS Redman—"

"Call me Kate."

"Very well. Kate. I have known her – I mean, I knew her for years, but I wouldn't have said I ever knew her *well*."

"Well, anything you might be able to tell me could help."

There was a tinkle of china at the entrance to the orangery. The housekeeper had brought an entire tray of tea things: a silver teapot, delicate china cups and a milk jug, a sugar bowl with silver tongs. There was even a plate of expensive-looking biscuits. Again, Kate had the odd impression that she was in a National Trust tearoom, rather than a family home. Perhaps it wasn't a family home, though. She asked Dekker if he'd lived here long.

"Oh, yes. For over twenty years now. My son grew up here."

Dekker's hand trembled a little as he poured the tea. Kate quickly gave her condolences.

"Thank you," said Dekker, emotions under control again. "It's a long time ago now but it still – catches me, I suppose you could say. A child shouldn't die before his parents."

"No, I agree," said Kate, fervently. "Do you have any other children?"

"No. David was my only son. My wife died a few years ago." Dekker passed Kate her teacup and looked around him at all the luxury and splendour. "This place is too big for me, really. I rattle around in here like a...like a bad penny." He gave a short laugh. "I got to know Trixie through David, you know. They were an item for a short while."

"Yes, so I understand."

"She was a very sweet girl, you know. Very lively and vivacious. She and David were very fond of each other for a while, but it didn't last. Perhaps those kind of relationships never do."

"Those kind of relationships?" queried Kate.

Dekker chuckled. "'Showbiz relationships', I suppose you'd call them. Celebrities. David was becoming quite famous for his music when he and Trixie got together. She was the more famous one though, I suppose. At that time. Everyone knew her at that time."

"Why did they split up?"

Dekker shrugged. "I don't think there any particular reason. They drifted apart, or realised they weren't right for one another, perhaps. David never told me anything specific."

"So there wasn't any – animosity?" asked Kate. She'd almost

finished her tea. It was so good she wondered whether she could ask for another cup.

"More tea?" asked Dekker, clearly reading her mind. "Animosity? Oh no. They remained friendly. They were friends right up until David...until David died." Dekker's eyes filmed over and he blinked rapidly several times. "My wife wanted Trixie to read at his funeral."

"And did she?" Kate held out her cup for a refill.

"No. No, not in the end." Dekker dextrously topped up Kate's cup. "I think we both – we all thought that it wouldn't have been a good idea after all. She was devastated by his death – Trixie was, I mean. She said she wouldn't have been able to do it without having hysterics or something. We didn't want to push her."

Kate sipped her fresh tea appreciatively. "I saw you at Trixie's funeral. Do you know her husband well?"

"No. No, not at all. I think that was the first time I'd ever spoken to him. I hadn't really had any contact with Trixie for years, you know. I went to the funeral more out of respect for her memory than anything else. We'd pretty much lost contact over the years. It was a surprise to me to find out that she lived so close. I only realised she'd moved from London when I saw her out and about in the spring this year."

"Did you renew your friendship?"

Dekker shook his head. "No. I think I had thoughts about looking her up and going to see her again properly, but I think – well, I decided that there wouldn't be much point. We were never real friends, you know. We didn't have much in common. David was the only real link between us."

Kate nodded. "I understand. When you knew Trixie back in the nineties, did you – were you aware that she was ever involved with drugs?" Dekker's face flickered and Kate knew that this would probably be a painful subject for him, given his son's death but she had to ask. "I'm sorry, but it could be important."

"That's fine," said Dekker heavily. "I understand. In answer,

I don't know. I don't remember ever seeing her take drugs or even talk about them but then, that doesn't mean that she wasn't involved in some way."

"Did Trixie meet her first husband after her relationship with your son ended?"

Dekker proffered the tea pot again and Kate shook her head with some regret. "Ivo Wright? Yes, Trixie and David and Ivo all knew each other. David and Ivo being musicians, they moved in the same circles. I'm not sure exactly when Trixie and Ivo became a couple but they didn't get married until after David died, I'm pretty sure of that."

Kate carefully placed her empty cup back on the tea tray. She thought once again of how much tragedy Trixie Arlen had experienced in her relatively short life. Perhaps it wasn't so surprising that she'd turned to heroin again – if indeed she had and hadn't had it forcibly injected. Wasn't morphine supposed to be the most effective pain killer? Perhaps I ought to try it, she thought to herself, trying to make an internal joke but instead feeling bleaker than ever.

"Thanks very much, Mr. Dekker, you've been very helpful," said Kate, as she said her goodbyes. In truth, there wasn't much in what he'd told her but she felt sorry for him. He was clearly dreadfully lonely.

"Please do come back if you need to ask me anything else," said Dekker, confirming Kate's previous thought.

"I will indeed. Thank you."

The neat little housekeeper showed Kate to the door and bobbed her head again in response to Kate's thanks. The door shut behind her softly as Kate was halfway down the flight of steps that led to the gravelled driveway. Before she drove away, Kate stood for a moment, looking up at the beautiful façade of the house. A solitary late flower drooped on the stem of the climbing rose that garlanded the front entrance. There was a flicker of movement in one of the windows on the ground floor but the visibility was too limited for Kate to make out who it was. She got into her car and fumbled for the radio, needing to hear something cheerful. All of a sudden, she felt incredibly sad. *I need Mark, I need him to forgive me.* She turned the key in the ignition, blinking hard, and turned the car in a slow circle, leaving Michael Dekker's beautiful, empty, melancholy house behind.

Chapter Sixteen

SHE WAS ALMOST BACK IN Abbeyford when her phone rang; the thing never rang when there was a convenient place to pull over. Cursing, Kate drove on until she found a lay-by and pulled the car in, grabbing for the phone just as it fell silent.

She recognised the number – it was the main number of the pathology labs. With a stab of guilt, she realised Doctor Telling had been trying to get hold of her for several days. Quickly, she redialled the number and was directed through to the doctor's office.

"I'm so sorry for taking so long to call you back," Kate confessed, once she'd introduced herself. "Unforgivable, Kirsten, sorry."

Doctor Telling sounded, for her, rather terse. Kate couldn't exactly blame her. "Yes, I really did need to speak to you quite urgently, Kate. When you didn't call me I contacted DI Olbeck, because what I had to tell you couldn't really wait."

Shit. That was all Kate needed; Olbeck on her case professionally as well as socially. "I'm really, really sorry. What was it you wanted to tell me?"

Doctor Telling wasn't being terse, Kate realised; she was worried. A little finger of apprehension poked her in the stomach. "We've been running some further tests on the samples of Trixie Arlen's blood and also the drug that you found in her bedroom," said Doctor Telling.

"Yes?" prompted Kate.

"As you know, the results of the first post mortem were inconclusive," Doctor Telling continued. "We were waiting for the results of the more detailed toxicity tests before we could confirm the definitive cause of death. We've now received those results."

"Yes," said Kate. That sense of unease was growing.

Doctor Telling's soft voice was not made for drama but what she said next made Kate gasp. "It wasn't the heroin that killed her."

"It *wasn't*?"

"No. There were significant quantities of heroin detected in her blood but we found another chemical composition which was almost certainly the cause of death."

"What chemical?" asked Kate, feeling suddenly cold.

Doctor Telling hesitated. "It's unusual. So unusual that I actually had to consult a colleague who's more of a specialist in biochemistry. He believes it's a derivative of a legal anaesthetic called Sulatenil."

"Right," said Kate, none the wiser. "So what exactly are you telling me? Trixie was injecting herself with something other than heroin? Or taking heroin and this other drug as well?"

"No. Not at all. The heroin that Trixie was using has been mixed with this Sulatenil. Sulatenil causes significant respiratory depression and can cause sudden respiratory arrest in high enough doses. The proportion of Sulatenil in this batch of heroin was very high. Trixie would have died almost instantly after injecting herself."

"I see," said Kate. "Is it – it's not normal to have this Sula-whatsit mixed in with a street drug then?"

Doctor Telling hesitated again. "I'm not a drugs expert, Kate. All I can advise is that I've never come across it before."

"Right," said Kate. "We'll have to look into it. I've got a few people I can consult."

"Yes, I think you should. If I might make a suggestion, I think we should also be testing the blood samples from the other overdose victims we've been examining this past month, to see if there's a connection."

"Yes. Yes, please do," said Kate. That finger of unease had become a fist, pressing hard into her stomach. "If there's a batch of contaminated heroin out there, then God knows how many more people might be affected."

"Yes, I know," said Doctor Telling. "Hence the urgency of my call."

Kate winced, but silently. She deserved that. "Thanks so much, Kirsten," she said, humbly. "If I heard right, you've already advised Mark – I mean, DI Olbeck – of this?"

"Yes, just before I spoke to you."

That meant Anderton would know already. Kate didn't need to call him. Her misery over Olbeck had been so acute she'd almost forgotten her meltdown over Anderton and his new woman. The remembrance caused her a little jab of pain, but that was almost immediately swept aside by the rising sense of urgency. What the hell should she do first, given this news? How many other people were out there, preparing their injections, heating the powder over a flame, drawing up the lethal liquid into the syringe? How many more had actually done so and were now lying undiscovered, cold and still? Kate actually shuddered. She thanked Doctor Telling once more, told her to call her the second they had the results from the tests they were going to run on the other victims, and then said goodbye. She thought for a moment, fighting the urge to put her head in her hands. Her heart was actually thudding. She grabbed up her phone and called Stuart, praying that he'd answer the phone.

"Kate! Hello, sweetheart, what gives? Have I forgotten lunch?"

"No, nothing like that. Stuart, you've taken plenty of drug awareness courses, haven't you? I know you did undercover with a few drug rings."

Stuart sounded amused. "Blimey, that's going back a few years. But yeah, I did. What do you want to know?"

"When dealers cut their drugs, what do they normally use?"

The amusement had faded from Stuart's voice. "This sounds serious."

"It could be. Please, Stuart, I need to know. They normally use, I don't know, icing sugar or something? I don't know, tell me!"

"All right, all right, keep your hair on. Now, what's this all about?"

"I can't go into that at the moment." Kate hated reminding Stuart that he was no longer a police officer but sometimes he needed a little refresher. "All right, specifically, would a heroin dealer cut his drugs using a really strong anaesthetic?"

There was a silence on the end of the phone. Then Stuart said, slowly, "Not usually. The dealers need to cut the smack with something that mimics it in looks and effects. Something that would be water-soluble as well. They might use something that would exacerbate the effects if they could get away with it. Then the punters would think they were getting top-quality gear and come back for more, whereas actually the dealers making even more money by watering down the actual heroin. What's the anaesthetic?"

"I can't remember the actual name," Kate lied. "But we think it's a derivative of a legal anaesthetic."

She could hear Stuart breathing on the other end of the line. "That's really strange, actually," he said in a quiet tone. "Anything like that is going to be expensive. Why would you use an expensive substance to cut another expensive substance, when the whole point is to make more profit?"

"That's what I thought," said Kate. She wondered if Stuart could hear the faint tremor in her voice.

Stuart cleared his throat. "There have been a few cases where heroin has been contaminated with anthrax spores. Several people died last year, do you remember?"

Kate didn't but she made an agreeing noise. "Yes, but anthrax

– that would be a natural contamination, wouldn't it? I mean, someone hasn't deliberately introduced anthrax to a batch of heroin?"

"Oh, no, not at all. The spores might get in through the supply chain at some point but it would be accidental, not deliberate."

"And the victims wouldn't die – well – instantly, would they?" asked Kate. "They would get sick but it would take some time to actually die of anthrax. Is that right?"

"Oh yeah. It could take weeks."

"So in fact, it's nothing like what we've got here then," said Kate, with an edge to her tone.

"Sorry," said Stuart, sounding a little sheepish. "That was the only quick comparison I could come up with. Yes, you're right, Kate. This is something different."

"So what do you think now?"

Stuart hesitated. "I can't say for certain but it may be that this batch of heroin going round has been deliberately contaminated with a lethal substance."

In the silence that followed, Kate could hear Stuart's breathing again, a little faster this time, echoed by the fast beats of her own heart. "Oh, God," she said in a low voice.

"Yeah."

There was another silence and then Kate roused herself from the depths of her anxiety. "Thanks, Stuart. Thanks for your help. I've got to go."

"No worries. Go and do the right thing."

"I will. And Stuart—"

"Yeah?"

"Don't even think of leaking this to the press. I mean it. If you do, I will literally never speak to you again. Ever."

Stuart snorted. "You need the press to be *on* this! You need to get the word out. Otherwise you're going to be knee-deep in dead junkies before the week's out—"

"I *mean* it. We need to work out a media campaign, you *know* that."

Stuart relented. "Yeah, I know. Don't worry. You've got my word."

"Thanks. You're a star," said Kate. "I need to go now but seriously – thanks."

"You're welcome. Keep me posted, yeah?"

"Will do."

After she'd said goodbye, Kate brought Olbeck's number up in her phone. Her thumb hovered above the button, on the verge of pressing it. Then she shook her head and put it away in her bag, clipping her seatbelt back on and flooring the accelerator, leaving the layby with a thin wail of skidding tires.

Chapter Eighteen

As Kate arrived back in the office, she virtually ran into Olbeck as he was walking out into the corridor. They both collided with an 'oof' of surprise and each staggered back a few feet.

"Sorry," gasped Kate automatically. Then reality kicked in. It was the first time she'd spoken to Olbeck since she'd screamed obscenities at him in his kitchen.

He didn't look as though he'd forgotten that. "Kate, I was looking for you."

"You were?" asked Kate, trying to sound unconcerned. The anxiety about the potentially lethal batch of heroin somewhere out in Abbeyford was immediately replaced by the crippling sense of shame she'd carried around with her since she and Olbeck had fallen out.

"Yes," said Olbeck, face impassive. "I've just had a call. I need you to come with me."

Professional curiosity peeked its way above Kate's emotional state. "Don't tell me it's another overdose?" she asked, quickly.

Olbeck looked surprised, and then his face cleared. "Oh, you've spoken to Doctor Telling then? We can talk about that on the way. No, this might be different. I won't know until we've had a look."

"Right—"

"Let's go, then." For a moment, superficially, everything seemed to have gone back to normal. The next second, Kate realised with a sinking feeling that the anger and hurt seemed to still be very much there.

"I must just get my stuff. I'll meet you at the car."

She ran into the office, flipped a hand at Theo and grabbed up her bag. She was still wearing her coat and was aware of the sweat inching down her back beneath the heavy material. It didn't help her feel much calmer.

Driving away from the station, the air inside the car thickened with unspoken thoughts. Kate stared blankly through the windscreen, feeling utterly miserable. This was her best friend, her closest colleague, and the two of them were like strangers. Worse than strangers, they were like enemies. Tears rose in her eyes and before she knew what she was doing, she had turned to Olbeck.

"I'm so, so, sorry. Mark, I'm so sorry. I could cut out my tongue. I'd give anything to take it back, anything—"

To her shame, her voice had thickened so much she couldn't go on. Kate dropped her head, realised that was a mistake when the tears began to drop onto her jeans, and raised it again. She was aware that the tight knot that she'd felt in her chest ever since that awful night had loosened as she uttered the first apology. She made a mammoth effort at control and said it again. "I'm really, really sorry. I don't know how I can make it up to you."

"All right, all right," Olbeck said, and Kate could see the tightness around his jaw loosening a little. He flicked on the indicator and brought the car into the side of the road before pressing the hazard light button on. Then he turned undid his seatbelt and turned to face Kate.

"I'm sorry," she said again. She wanted to say something else but those two words seemed to be the only ones her mouth was capable of forming.

"You really hurt me," Olbeck said softly. They were staring at one another like lovers. Kate could only shake her head and he must have seen the misery in her face because in the next moment,

301

they'd flung themselves at one another and were hugging each other tight.

Kate cried properly then, soaking Olbeck's shoulder. She could feel his unsteady breathing as she held him and knew he was pretty close to tears himself.

They only hugged for a few moments. Then in mutual agreement, they sat back and looked at one another. The tension had eased a little. Kate took Olbeck's hands.

"I don't have any real excuse," she said in a low voice. "All I can say is that you caught me on probably the worst day of my life. No, that's not true. The worst day was when I – you know – when I gave him away."

"I know," said Olbeck. "And *I'm* sorry. If I'd had a bit more tact, I would have realised that you would have found that really hard to hear."

Kate was shaking her head. "No, no, Mark. It's my fault. I have to – I have to get over that. I think you and Jeff will be brilliant parents. *Brilliant*. I just hate myself for what I said. I was just lashing out and it was unforgivable, I'm sorry." Her voice wobbled again and she carried on quickly, before it could break. "I have to apologise to Jeff as well. I'm going to do that straight after work tonight if he'll be in."

"He's okay," said Olbeck. "We were worried about you. It's not like you to be so – so volatile. Not even around that subject."

Kate hung her head. "I know. I don't know why – yes, I do know why. But we'll have to talk about that some other time. All I can say is that I am really, truly happy for you and Jeff getting married and adopting, and I'll spend the rest of my life regretting what I said at first." She looked Olbeck straight in the eye, hoping against hope that he believed her. "Because I didn't mean it."

He said nothing but pulled her back into a brief hug again before releasing her. "Come on, we need to get to the scene."

Kate, unable to stop herself, asked in a small voice. "Do you... can you forgive me?"

Olbeck almost smiled. "You've not murdered anyone, Kate. Of course I forgive you." There was a beat of silence and then he added "You're not invited to the wedding, though."

Kate half-gasped, feeling as though she'd just been kicked in the stomach. Olbeck looked stonily ahead for a moment and then his face broke up. He was actually laughing. "I'm joking, you silly cow. Of course you're invited."

For a moment, Kate thought she was going to burst into tears again. Quickly she rubbed her face, pinching the bridge of her nose hard for a second. "Thank you," she said, her voice almost steady.

Olbeck indicated and steered the car back onto the road again. Kate sat back against her seat, heaving a sigh that seemed to come from the depths of her stomach. She had that empty, hollow feeling that came after a really good cry, which was somehow soothing and relieving at the same time. She and Olbeck were friends again. She didn't kid herself that everything was back to normal again – perhaps it would never be – but they were back on the right track. At that moment, Kate didn't care about dirty heroin, or Anderton's sex life, or her failed exams, or anything else. She had her friend back. That, at that moment, was all that mattered.

"Where are we going?" she asked after five minutes had passed. She realised, after the drama of the last few minutes had calmed, that she had absolutely no idea of where they were heading or what they were going to see.

"A body's been found," Olbeck said. She could hear the relief in his voice and knew that he'd been suffering, probably almost as much as she had. She closed her eyes for a moment, swamped with thankfulness that they'd managed to sort it out. Olbeck went on. "At a house in Mellow Abbot. A neighbour noticed the front door was ajar and went in and found it. According to Dispatch, it's a middle-aged man and it's definitely a suspicious death."

"Okay," said Kate. "There's clearly more. What is it?"

Olbeck glanced at her. "Apparently, he's been tied-up, gagged and killed."

Kate blinked. The robbery report from Jack Harker materialised in front of her eyes. Was this the same thing? "Blimey," she said. "Any ideas as yet?"

"Haven't you been collating a few reports on some similar robberies, recently?"

"Yes. Well, I've been meaning to." Kate found herself wondering what she *had* actually achieved over the last month. She put her hands up to her eyes and rubbed them. I need a holiday, she thought. Perhaps I might try Barbados. It had seemed to work for Olbeck.

The car was slowing. Olbeck had spotted the crime tape that had already been stretched across the driveway of a house up ahead. It was a nondescript semi-detached house, built around the 1930s, with a concreted driveway and pebbledash on the exterior walls.

"Do we know who the victim is yet?" asked Kate, as Olbeck drew the car into the kerb.

"He's not been formally IDed yet but the person who found him told us who he was. Adrian Fellowes, aged forty-eight, lecturer in IT at Abbeyford City College."

"That's the vic?" asked Kate, confused.

"Yes. Sorry, yes. His neighbour was the one who found him, she's still there now. Apparently she noticed the front door was wide open and went on in and found him. Margery Wencleve."

By this time, they had passed through the front door and picked their way through the narrow hallway. Uniforms and white-coated SOCOs milled about. The house was cold, whatever residual heat it had contained leaking out of the front door as it was opened and closed by various officers. It was as nondescript on the inside as it had been on the outside. Cheap grey carpet covered the hallway floor and extended into the living room, which ran down the side of the house. Kate followed Olbeck through the doorway to where the body of the unfortunate Adrian Fellowes could be found.

He was fat, naked and slumped on a cheap and nasty looking sofa piece covered in grubby cream fabric. Kate and Olbeck stood silently, taking in the scene. A man bent over the body and as he straightened up and turned to face the two officers, Kate realised it was Andrew Stanton. Such was her ebullience at having made it up with Olbeck, not even this fact could dampen her spirits. She gave him a big smile and he looked at first shocked and then confused.

"Good morning," said Olbeck. "Anything for us yet?"

Apart from that first glance at Kate, Stanton steadfastly refused to look at her. Kate, still in that strange, reckless mood, had to restrain herself from bounding up to him, pinching his cheeks and telling him to get over it. She bit back an extremely inappropriate giggle.

"There's no obvious cause of death," Stanton was saying. "No stab wounds, no ligature marks, no head trauma."

"Really?" Olbeck asked, surprised.

"Yes, you'll have to wait for the post mortem on this one. I simply can't give you any indication as yet."

Just like Trixie Arlen. "Any sign of drug use? Needle marks, injections, anything like that?" Kate asked.

"No, nothing to indicate intravenous drug use," Andrew said, a little stiffly. "You can see for yourself that he's been indulging in cocaine or amphetamines though. We'll have to run tests to be sure but..."

He indicated the dining table that stood at the back of the room with his head. The top was littered with empty bottles of wine, several glasses with the sticky residue of alcohol in the bottom of them, and what looked like a small bathroom mirror, its surface lightly dusted with white powder.

Kate, having noted this, turned her gaze back to the body. Fellowes' wrists were tied together with what looked like a pair of tights or stockings, his ankles similarly secured. A third stocking gagged his mouth. Kate felt a wrench of pity for him. It was bad enough to die, but to be left in such humiliating circumstances... She wondered whether he had a family and looked around the living room for any photographs, any indication that other people lived here. There was nothing; just an enormous flat-screen television, a pile of computer magazines in the corner of the room, a dusty cactus plant in a chipped blue pot on the windowsill. The room was functional but nothing more, there was no care or attention to comfort, beauty or sophistication.

Olbeck was saying something to her and Kate turned back to him. "What's that?"

"Have a look at him again," Olbeck said. "What's wrong with this picture?"

Kate gave him an old-fashioned look and looked again at the body. "What do you mean?"

"We're assuming this is a potential robbery, right?"

"Yes. Given its similarity to the other cases."

"So, clearly, whoever did this didn't tie him up to make sure he didn't escape. He's not tied to anything, is he? Just – just himself."

Kate nodded. "Yes. But that would fit in with what the previous victim – Jack Harker said. He said he woke up after passing out, or being drugged, tied up."

"Exactly," said Olbeck. "It looks like there's a team or a couple of people out there honey-trapping men into being tied up and then robbed."

"Okay," said Kate. "It's a possibility. But then why kill your victim?"

"Maybe he recognised one of them. Maybe they're getting more aggressive as they go on. Maybe they didn't mean to kill him."

"You don't think that this might be another overdose?" asked Kate in a low voice.

Olbeck looked uneasy. "We won't know until we have the PM results. But it doesn't look like it, does it?"

"No," Kate admitted. Andrew had stated that he couldn't see any injection marks and given that there was clear evidence of cocaine (or similar) use at the scene, it was different to what had happened at Trixie Arlen's farmhouse. All the same... Kate stood and watched the SOCOs at their work, thinking and frowning. There had never been such a spate of potentially suspicious deaths in Abbeyford, not since she'd arrived here. Could there really be no connection between the cases?

She drifted into the hallway again and wandered into the kitchen at the end of the hallway. It was a small, dank room, just as cheerless and as lacking in personality as the rest of the house. Empty pizza boxes and takeaway food containers were stacked messily by the overflowing kitchen bin. The stove top was clean, if dusty – clearly Mr. Fellows was not much of a cook. A small fridge hummed busily to itself by the back door and a narrow gate-leg table was crammed up against its side, its surface littered with flyers, old newspapers and junk mail. Kate stood in the doorway, wondering whether there was any point to what she was doing. She turned and was about to leave when she felt a sudden pull, a little snag of her consciousness, a jab of something significant. Kate turned slowly and regarded the dirty little kitchen again. What had it been? She swept her gaze slowly over the squalor, wondering what it was that she'd subconsciously noticed. Then she saw it, tucked between a packet of sugar and an empty glass jar on the kitchen counter. A small business card, pink with a flowery black logo. *Home Angels, Domestic Cleaning.*

Kate picked it up with gloved fingers and took it back through to Olbeck.

"Look at this."

He glanced at it and then back at Kate, enquiringly.

"It's probably nothing," said Kate "But Jacob Arlen gave me a card for this company when I asked him where I could find his cleaner. She's someone we still need a statement from."

"Right," said Olbeck, not sounding very convinced. "It probably is nothing, like you say."

"I know, but I'd like to look into it, just in case. If the Arlens and Julian Fellowes shared a cleaner, then that's a link between the two cases."

"Fine with me." Olbeck's attention was clearly elsewhere. "I'm trying to find out what's missing. This looks like a guy who was interested in gadgets, right? I can't see anything around here that looks expensive, except for the TV. Let me talk to that neighbour..."

Muttering to himself, he left the room. Kate could have told him he was too late – several minutes ago she'd looked out the window and seen a white-faced middle-aged woman being shepherded into a patrol car - but she let him go. Kate's eyes went to the dining room table. Several empty glasses there... she looked back at the pathetic chubby corpse of Adrian Fellows and thought back to the first person she'd seen at the station wanting to report a robbery, that sad little man who'd changed his mind and scurried off. Who was out there, targeting lonely single men? Was there really any connection to the overdose deaths that had been occurring, or was that just something that Kate's mind was insisting was the case? Kate rubbed her eyes. After the emotional turmoil of the last few days, it was difficult to stay focused on work. She was exhausted. I really do need a holiday, she thought, and vowed that on the completion or winding down of these cases, she would book one immediately. Somewhere hot and sunny and vacuous, where Kate would have to do nothing more taxing than lie on a sun lounger and drink mocktails.

Cheered by the thought, she went to find Olbeck. He was in the one of the bedrooms upstairs, conferring with one of the uniformed officers, who turned out to be Sergeant Bill Osbourne. Bill raised a large, hairy hand in greeting when he saw Kate approaching.

"Bill's just been telling me that everything valuable is gone," Olbeck said as Kate joined them. "Everything valuable that you could carry away by hand."

"So you think they came on foot?" asked Kate.

Olbeck nodded. "Would fit in with our theory that whoever these people are, they're meeting up with their victims for an ostensibly social purpose."

Kate raised her eyebrows. "Like a date?"

"Mmm. Might be a 'chance' meeting though, if they're targeting men they think would be likely to invite them home." Olbeck made speech marks in the air with his forefingers.

Kate tried to force her tired brain to think. "I suppose we should see if this Fellowes was on any dating sites, then. Might be a lead there."

"You'll have a job, lass," rumbled Bill Osbourne. "They've taken his laptop, iPad and tablet."

"I'll put the analysts onto it," said Kate, undaunted. "They might be able to find something."

"Okay, good start," said Olbeck. "We'll have the PM results in the next few days which should give us more to go on."

Kate remembered something. She caught Bill Osbourne's arm. "Bill, have the pathology labs been in touch with you about your case – those two dead drug addicts – Pete and Wayne Thingy?"

Osbourne frowned. "Not that I'm aware. Why?"

Quickly Kate explained, with Olbeck chipping in. Bill Osbourne's phlegmatic face was incapable of showing extreme emotion but he did look unsettled. "Now, there's a thing," he said, once they'd finished. "Contaminated heroin, eh? Nasty."

Kate warned him not to mention it to anyone else. "There'll be a press conference about it any time now, once the info's been primed for the media. But I—" she glanced at Olbeck, "I mean, *we* wondered whether you'd had any more overdoses since we've seen you last?"

Osbourne frowned again, thinking. "Aye. Aye, we have had

one, actually. Totally non-suspicious, another known addict. Last week."

Kate opened her mouth to ask and then shut it again, looking again at Olbeck. He was her superior, after all.

He caught the glance and acknowledged it with a tilt of his head. "Could you send me the PM report and anything else you've got on it, Bill? We'll get the labs to run those specific tests to see if it's connected. It'll all help with making a case against whoever is distributing this batch."

"Aye, I'll do that. No problem."

They conferred for a few more minutes before Kate and Olbeck took their leave. They did a last sweep of the house, sidestepping the white-coated SOCOs and technicians and took a last look at the body; a stretcher and body bag had been laid on the floor in front of the sofa, ready to receive its sad cargo. Kate and Olbeck said goodbye to Doctor Stanton, who was too absorbed in his work to reach his usual level of sniffiness with Kate. He actually sounded rather absentmindedly amiable, which made Kate feel quite cheerful as they left the house, despite the surroundings and the exhaustion which was dragging at her.

She leant her head against the back of the car seat as they drove away and fought not to close her eyes. It reminded her of Theo, as they'd driven back from interviewing all of Trixie Arlen's friends, and that in turn reminded her of confronting Jacob Arlen at his office. She struggled back up to a sitting position. "What happened with Arlen? Did he recant his previous statement?"

Olbeck gave a short laugh. "Not that I heard. His lawyer advised him to say no comment to everything and that's exactly what he did."

"Did you do the interview?"

"No. Anderton and Theo took it."

"Really?" Kate bit back the sharp retort she wanted to make, struggled a little and then temptation overcame her. "What, Anderton actually did some work? You *do* surprise me."

Olbeck glanced at her, surprised. "What is it with you at the moment? You're falling out with everybody."

Kate opened her mouth and then shut it again. "Oh, nothing," she said lamely, after a moment. She wanted to tell Olbeck why, in Anderton's case, she had a personal vendetta against him but decided not to. There was time enough to come clean in the future – she didn't want to rock the fragile equilibrium of the friendship she and Mark had managed to salvage after their row.

"So, we've arrested Arlen, then?" she asked, after a short period of silence.

Olbeck raised one shoulder in a kind of shrug. "I'm not sure. That was under discussion when I got the call about this case."

"Okay. Well we'll know soon enough, I suppose," said Kate, and this time she put her head back against the headrest again and closed her eyes. She was asleep in moments.

Chapter Nineteen

THE NEXT DAY SAW KATE, refreshed after the best night's sleep she'd had in weeks, jumping in the shower at the sprightly hour of six-thirty am without even a muttered protest. She let the hot water ease the night stiffness from her shoulders and thought about her day ahead.

Priority one was to try and track down the mysterious cleaner or cleaning company that was the only known link between the Arlen and the Fellowes crime scenes. Kate twisted the shower control to 'off' and stepped out, reaching for her towel. For a moment, she was assailed by doubt. Was it a lead worth pursuing? Really? There were a hundred other things she could be doing. Should she drop into the office and see if she could sit in when Arlen was interviewed that morning? Jacob Arlen had been formally arrested the day before and the team were going all out to try and get to the bottom of where he had actually been on the night of Trixie Arlen's death. They'd pulled his mobile phone records and the Arlens' bank statements, to see if there was suspicious movement on either of them, but nothing had come up as yet. Perhaps I should try and sit in on that, Kate thought, fingers slipping as she buttoned her shirt in haste. But then, Anderton and Theo had that covered, and she wasn't sure how happy they would be with her if she tried to muscle in at this late stage.

She needed to check with Doctor Telling to see if any other overdose deaths had been attributable to the heroin contaminated with Sulatenil. She needed to check with the analysts to see if there had been a noticeable spike in deaths due to drug use over the past month. When was Anderton planning to do the press conference? Today? Kate pulled on her trousers and zipped them up. God, this was overwhelming, too much to do and not enough time or head space to do it. Think of the holiday, she told herself fervently as she pulled on her shoes and coat. Think of the holiday.

Before she left the house, she tried calling the Home Angels number, to see if she could make herself an appointment with the manager of the firm, but the number just rang and rang until Kate finally hung up. She Googled the name of the firm on her phone but nothing came up in the search results except for the same phone number she'd just tried to call. There was an address on the card that looked to be a unit on one of the industrial sites on the south side of Abbeyford. Kate locked up the house and got into her car, pondering. After a moment's consideration, she keyed the postcode of the business address into her sat nav and turned on the engine.

The satellite guidance system took her to a small industrial estate on the outskirts of Arbuthon Green. Kate drove slowly along the narrow road that led to the address on the business card, which turned out to be a small modern building of maroon brick and white plastic cladding. There were no cars parked on the small forecourt at the front and no lights could be seen behind the plastic blinds at the window. Kate parked the car and got out. There was no answer to her knocks at the door. She tried the handle, just on the off chance, but it was locked. She knocked again, just for luck, but still no one answered. She tried calling the number again and she could faintly hear the telephone ringing inside the office but no one picked up her call.

Well, that was a wasted journey. Kate drove back to the station, trying the number once more just after she locked up her car. No answer. Kate mentally shrugged and made her way to the office.

"Morning," she said to Theo, who was looking through what

looked like CCTV pictures. He gave her a vague wave in response. "Is Anderton still interviewing Jacob Arlen?"

Theo finally looked up. He looked tired, his handsome brown eyes ringed with shadow. "Yeah, he's still at it. We've only got to the end of the day."

Kate nodded in acknowledgement. Once she'd ascertained the interview room number, she made her way there, peeking through the peephole. She could just see the edge of Anderton's shoulder and beyond him, across the table, Jacob Arlen, who looked exhausted. Kate felt a pang of pity for him, which she quickly suppressed. She hesitated, knowing that this might not be a good time to interrupt the interview, but when might she get the chance again? She bit her lip and knocked.

All three men looked surprised to see her. "Sir," she said, for the benefit of Arlen, "Could I have a quick word?"

She meant it for Olbeck but Anderton himself got up and accompanied her outside.

"What's up?" he asked, adding, "Haven't seen you in ages."

He was standing closer to her than he had been for weeks and Kate was disconcerted at the sheer physical response she felt at his nearness. Goddammit, why did she have to find him so attractive? When was she going to get over him?

Trying to keep her mind on the job, she explained as quickly as she could. Anderton raised his eyebrows but made no comment. Instead, he opened the door to the interview room and ushered her inside.

She seated herself next to Olbeck, who obligingly budged his chair over for her. Jacob Arlen looked at her with a frown.

"I've got a very quick question for you, Mr. Arlen," Kate said.

Arlen sighed a long suffering sigh. "No comment."

Kate persisted. "I'm trying to track down someone who might be very important to this case. Could you tell me all you know about your cleaner, Rosa?"

Clearly, whatever Arlen had been expecting Kate to ask, it

hadn't been this. "Rosa?" he asked, cautiously. "What do you mean?"

"I'm trying to find her," explained Kate. "But I'm having a lot of trouble. There's no answer at the agency number and I've got no other way of contacting her."

Arlen glanced at his solicitor, an urbane, white-haired man rather like him in looks. The solicitor nodded slightly.

Arlen turned back to Kate. "Well, I can't help you, I'm afraid. I've got no other contact number for her. Trixie dealt with all of that kind of thing."

"But you have seen her?" asked Kate. "Rosa? You could describe her?"

Arlen looked confused. "Yes, I did meet her, a couple of times, at the house. But I don't *know* her..."

"That's fine," said Kate. "Could you just tell me what she looks like?"

Arlen almost shrugged. "I can't remember exactly – she was dark, long dark hair. Very thin. Young, probably not more than twenty-five."

Kate nodded encouragingly but clearly Arlen had reached the limit of his descriptive powers. "I'm afraid that's all I can remember," he finished.

"Is she English?" Kate asked.

Arlen looked confused. "English? No – no, I don't think she is. Polish or Czech, or something like that. She had quite a strong accent."

Kate nodded. "There's nothing else you can tell me about her? You don't know where she lived or anything like that?"

"No," Arlen said. "I don't know anything more about her. She just cleaned our house." This time he looked at Olbeck and Anderton, as if seeking an explanation for Kate's sudden appearance. They stared back at him, impassive, and Kate felt a rush of gratitude to both of them.

"You don't know if she was married?" she persisted.

"I'm sorry, I don't know," Arlen said with distaste. "I really didn't know her at all well. I don't believe I ever spoke to her."

Clearly that was all he was going to give her. Kate believed him when he said he didn't know anything more. Obviously, to a man like him, a cleaner was so lowly as to be almost beneath his notice. Kate was just grateful that he'd even noticed Rosa at all. She thanked him, nodded to Olbeck and Anderton, and left the room, feeling Arlen staring after her as she closed the door behind her.

She made her way back up to the reception area of the station, walking quite slowly as she thought about his response. As it was, she was almost bowled over as a woman came rushing into the station, in a flurry of windswept hair and a cloud of perfume.

It was Kyla Mellors. She gazed around her in what looked like panic, saw Kate and rushed over to her. "Is Jacob here? I heard you'd arrested him – where is he?"

"Calm down, Mrs. Mellors," Kate said, bringing a soothing tone to the fore. She took Kyla by one slender arm and steered her towards some chairs over by the far wall. "How can I help?"

Kyla looked near tears. "I heard you arrested Jacob. Is it true? It can't be true!"

Kate hesitated before answering. "Yes, Mr. Arlen is currently helping us with our enquiries."

The tears spilled over and ran down Kyla's cheeks. "Is it to do with Trixie's death?" she gasped. "Are you thinking that he had something to do with that?"

"I can't comment on that, Mrs.—"

"Because he didn't," said Kyla, vehemently. "He absolutely couldn't have. It's impossible."

Kate leaned forward a little. "Do you want to amend your statement, Mrs. Mellors?"

Kyla bit her lip and brushed the tears from her face. She glanced around the station and then spoke in a low tone. "Is there somewhere we can talk privately?"

Kate took her to one of the nicer interview rooms and gestured to the one fairly comfortable chair. Kyla seated herself. She had the air of a woman bracing herself for a necessary but unpleasant ordeal. Kate propped herself against the desk and raised her eyebrows in an encouraging way, although she was beginning to have an inkling of what it was that Kyla was about to tell her.

Kyla took a deep breath. "Jacob wasn't anywhere near Trixie the night she died because – because he was with me."

Although Kate half-admired her for coming clean, she wouldn't be human without the opportunity to have one little, very little dig. "By 'with you' I assume you mean..."

Kyla was sitting very upright. A tumble of words practically fell from her mouth. "Yes, with me as in we're having an affair. He stayed the night with me and left very early in the morning." As soon as she'd finished her sentence, she fell back into her seat, as if all the strength had left her muscles. After a moment, she said in a shaky voice, "My God, it's such a relief to finally come clean. I didn't think it would be such a relief." She sat forward then and put her face in her hands.

Kate cleared her throat. "How long have you and Mr. Arlen been sexually involved?"

Kyla sat up again. She looked tearful but in control of herself. "About eighteen months. It was wrong, I know it was wrong but..."

"Does your husband know?" Kate asked after Kyla's voice faded away at the end of her sentence.

Kyla shook her head. "No. No, he doesn't. I'm going to tell him though. Today, I'm going to tell him today. I'm going to leave him. I can't be such – such a coward any longer."

Despite herself, Kate pitied her. "Did Trixie know?"

Again, Kyla shook her head. "I don't think so. I don't think Jacob would have told her." She hesitated and then said in a subdued voice, "They didn't really communicate much. He said that she...with Trixie, it was all surface and nothing underneath." Her eyes met Kate's and she flushed. "All right, I know that's the biggest cliché in the world – 'my wife doesn't understand me'. All I can say is that I believed him. I believed Jacob. I *do* believe him."

Kate nodded. "Is there anything else you can tell me, Mrs. Mellors?"

Kyla looked confused. "About – about the affair?"

"Well..." Kate wasn't exactly sure what she was asking herself. She hesitated and then asked, "What was Trixie like? *Really* like?"

She was hoping that Kyla Mellor's newfound candour would give her some information that perhaps she hadn't had before. But Kyla simply shrugged and said, "I don't know."

"What do you mean? You were friends, weren't you?"

"We thought we were friends. Well, I guess Trixie thought we were friends." Kyla looked down at her hands, at the no-doubt wildly expensive engagement and wedding ring on her left hand. "I wasn't much of a friend to her, was I?" Before Kate could say anything, she looked up at her. "I mean, I really didn't *know* her. It was like Jacob said, all surface. She was nice and friendly and easy to like, but I didn't ever *know* her. She never, ever let me in. Perhaps that's what made it easy, *easier*, to – to do what I did."

Kate shifted a little on the hard edge of the table. "Did you ever take drugs with Trixie?"

Kyla looked shocked. "No. I told you. Never. I wouldn't do that."

"Did you know that Trixie took drugs?"

Kyla's gaze dropped again. "I only know what Jacob told me. He told me about six months ago, that he'd caught her using heroin. Just the once. She swore it was a one-off, apparently."

"Do you think he believed that?"

"I don't think so. We talked about it a couple of times. He said at one point he was thinking about putting a camera in the house, to keep an eye on what she did. I was a bit shocked and I think that put him off the idea. I don't think he ever did it."

Something else that Anderton and Theo could ask their suspect. Except, he wasn't a suspect anymore, was he? Kate found that she believed every word Kyla was telling her. Adulterer he might be, but it looked like Jacob Arlen was nothing more than that.

"Thanks for telling me this, Mrs. Mellors," said Kate. Kyla nodded. She looked worn out but heartily relieved still. "It's a shame you couldn't have been more honest with us at the start of this investigation. You do realise you could be charged with perverting the course of justice?"

Kyla blanched. "Oh my God."

"Yes," said Kate relentlessly. "We don't do this job for fun, you know. Do you know how much time we've wasted already because we weren't given the true facts?"

"I'm so sorry – I just – oh, my God—" Kyla stuttered. Kate continued to frown at her for a moment before she relented.

"The first thing you'll have to do is amend your statement. After that – well, I'll see if I can persuade DCI Anderton not to take things any further."

Kyla nodded and went on nodding jerkily. "Yes of course. Of course I will. I'm sorry."

"Fine. Come with me, then and we'll sort that out now."

Kate got up and Kyla did likewise. At the door, she caught hold of Kate's arm. "I know this is asking a lot, especially after – after what you've just said, but is there – is there any way we can keep this from the press?" she asked, a little desperately.

Kate raised one shoulder in a half-shrug. "I'd like to say yes, Mrs. Mellors, but I'm afraid I can't. These things do have a habit of coming out."

Kyla nodded miserably. Kate was preparing to hand her over to the desk staff when something occurred to her. She took Kyla to one side. "Can I just ask you, did you ever meet Trixie's cleaner, Rosa?"

Kyla blinked but, unlike Arlen, didn't seem to question the relevance of the enquiry. "Rosa? Yes, quite a few times. She was there quite often."

"What was she like? Did you ever talk to her?"

"No. No, I didn't know her to speak to." Kyla was looking a little nervous now. "Is she okay?"

"Rosa? As far as I'm aware. I'm just trying to track her down," said Kate. "Can you tell me what she looked like?"

Kyla hesitated. "Well, she was a bit strange, actually. Really thin. I once thought she might have been quite pretty, if she'd only put on a stone or something. She had long dark hair...I'm not sure what else I can tell you." She paused and then said reluctantly, "There was one thing - she – she had strange eyes. Her pupils were weird, really tiny pupils. Gosh, that sounds really bitchy, doesn't it? I don't mean it like that—"

She was obviously feeling guilty. Kate soothed her and thanked her. Once she'd handed Kyla over to the colleague who would supervise her statement, Kate walked back to her desk, thinking. The description of Rosa, unappealing as it had been, had sparked a memory; some sort of recollection of where she'd heard that description before. The tiny pupils in particular. Kate pondered and then realised with a start that she needed to let Anderton know about Kyla Mellor's confession as soon as she could. She hurried down the steps, abandoning her thoughts about Rosa for the time being.

Chapter Twenty

KATE AND OLBECK ATTENDED ADRIAN Fellowes' post mortem the next day, and Kate was pleased to find that Andrew Stanton, who was performing the operation, had seemingly retained his new-found amiability. He greeted her and Olbeck with every sign of politeness and that awful stiffness that used to accompany his every remark to her had disappeared. In return, she found herself responding in a more natural, friendly way. It was one of the most pleasant post mortems she'd ever experienced.

"Well," Stanton said, once he'd opened up the chest cavity of the unfortunate Mr Fellowes. "Cause of death is plain. Myocardial infarction."

"Come again?" said Olbeck.

Stanton grinned. "Common or garden heart attack. Look here - you can see the severe build-up of plaque in the coronary arteries. A sudden increase in physical activity, not to mention ingestion of cocaine...either of those coupled with a tear in the plaque would have caused a blood clot that would have interrupted blood flow to the heart. Very common."

Kate and Olbeck exchanged glances. "So it's a natural death, then?" Olbeck asked, to be absolutely clear.

Stanton nodded. "Absolutely."

Olbeck blew out his cheeks. "Is it just me, Kate, or do you suddenly find yourself longing for a straightforward, juicy murder?"

Kate couldn't help smiling. "It is a bit topsy-turvy, isn't it? The death we thought was suspicious turns out not to be, whilst all the so-called normal deaths turn out to be anything but."

"Exactly."

"Mind you," Olbeck went on to say to Kate, as they made their way back to the car after the PM. "It's not *exactly* non-suspicious, is it? Okay, so the poor bloke had a heart attack, but the fact remains that someone tied him up and left him there. Do you think they realised he was dead?"

Kate shrugged. "We won't know unless we find them. Have we got any forensics back yet? Fingerprints or anything?"

"Don't know. I don't think so. We'll start leaning on the labs once we get back."

Olbeck was driving again. Kate tapped her fingers on her legs as they drove along, impatient to actually do something. "Can you do me a favour?" she asked, as she saw the sign for Arbuthon Green at the junction they were approaching. "Can we just try the Home Angels office again while we're in the area?"

Olbeck looked surprised but nodded. "Okay. It'll only take a minute."

The industrial estate looked just as deserted as it had the first time, with one exception. There was a large black Range Rover parked outside the Office Angels building. Olbeck took one look at it and drove past.

"What—" Kate began but he gestured at her to pipe down. He drove to the end of the street and pulled into the car park of another building, slowing the car and swinging it around to face the way they came.

"What is it?" whispered Kate, tense in her seat.

Olbeck leant forward, staring at the Range Rover. "I know that car," he said quietly. Then he leant forward even more. "Get down," he said suddenly.

Kate didn't stop to ask why. She dived floorwards, as did Olbeck. They exchanged glances from their crouched position on the car seats. Distantly, Kate heard the engine of the Range Rover start up and then the sound of the engine gradually faded away.

Olbeck cautiously eased himself up in his seat and peered through the windscreen again. "It's okay," he said to Kate and she straightened up. "I just didn't want him to see us."

"Who's 'he'?"

Olbeck looked grim. "Stelios Costa."

"*No*," breathed Kate. "What was he doing?"

"Coming out of your Home Angels office building with a box file."

"No," said Kate again. "The Costa brothers are involved with a *cleaning* company?"

Olbeck pressed the accelerator and the car began to move forward. "If the Costa brothers are involved, it's quite possibly *not* a cleaning company."

They drove back to the office in silence. Kate knew what Olbeck was thinking. The Costa brothers, Stelios and Yannis, were local crime lords. Kate had rubbed up against them in her first case in Abbeyford, the kidnapping of Charlie Fullman and the murder of his nanny. She hadn't relished the experience.

"What do we do now?" she asked as the police station came into view.

Olbeck was indicating to turn into the car park. "I'm going to ask Anderton if we can put a tail on Stelios Costa. We must be able to scrape up something from the budget for that."

Kate nodded. Olbeck parked the car and they made their way back to the office. Kate's head was aching. She felt breathless, as if she was missing something important. So many different things to do and she wasn't sure where to even start. The sudden appearance of Stelios Costa in connection with the Home Angels office was a complication that she hadn't anticipated. Was it possible that Home Angels was actually a legitimate firm? In some ways it must be, given that it had supplied what seemed like a *bona fide* cleaner to the Arlens, and possibly to Adrian Fellowes.

Kate thought back to Adrian Fellowes' house; dusty and musty, and uncared for. Surely he hadn't had a cleaner? Why, then, would he have had that business card? Had he been thinking of employing someone?

By this time, Kate had seated herself at her desk. Theo looked up from a pile of cardboard folders.

"Forensics are in," he said, handing her a couple of the folders. "Take a look at this. Fingerprints found at the Fellowes house match the ones found in the Arlens' bedroom, the ones we couldn't pin down."

"Arlen seemed to think it was from their cleaner, Rosa," said Kate, flipping through the report inside the folder. "I was just thinking that perhaps Adrian Fellows was employing her too, seeing as we found the Home Angels business card at his house."

"Yeah," said Theo. "That's a possibility. But seeing as we haven't even managed to track this woman down, it could be completely wrong."

"I guess you've run it through in case it's on file?"

Theo rolled his eyes. "Uh, yeah – don't you think that's the first thing I did? There's no match. *But*—" he paused, theatrically, "there *is* a match for a second set of prints found at Fellowes' house."

Kate put the folder down. "Yes?"

Theo got up and came round to her desk, propping himself against the side of it. "Yes. A set of female prints all over the living room." He reached across to his desk and yanked over a piece of paper, which he handed to Kate. She looked at it, at the police mug shot of a young, dark woman, scowling at the camera.

"Maria Todesco," she read from the sheet. "Convictions for soliciting, drug offences..." She looked up at Theo. "So Fellowes was using a prostitute? Is that right?" She looked back down at the rap sheet and thought for a rapid moment. "Hang on. What's this got to do with Trixie Arlen? *Has* it got anything to do with Trixie Arlen?"

"I think it has," said Theo. "Forensics found two sets of women's prints all over the living room of Fellowes' house. One of them belongs to Maria Todesco. The other belongs to the unknown woman whose prints we found in Trixie Arlen's bedroom, who we believe to be Rosa the cleaner. Right?"

Kate nodded. "Right."

Theo leaned forward a little. "What if Rosa the cleaner is supplementing her cleaning income with side-work as a prostitute, a prostitute who robs her punters?"

Kate put her head on one side, considering. "Well, I suppose it's a possibility." She looked once more at the surly face of the young woman on the sheet of paper she held in her hand. "I guess the first thing we can do is track down Maria Todesco and see what she can tell us."

Theo pushed himself upright. "Exactly."

Kate got up too. She felt that welcome pulse of excitement, an almost electrical impulse, as things slowly began to fall into place. "Let's re-interview Jack Harker as well – you know, the guy who reported a similar robbery to Adrian Fellowes – see if he recognises Maria as one of the women who robbed him."

They immediately went to Maria Todesco's last known address, a half-way house for women who had recently been released from prison. It was two streets over from the house where the bodies of the two young men who'd overdosed had been found. Kate said as much to Theo as he parked the car.

"Could be a coincidence," Theo said, "but it might not be. Mind you, this is a shit-hole of an area. You've got prostitutes, druggies and dealers all about."

"Yes, I know," said Kate. She put her hands to her head for a moment, rubbing her temples. "What if there is a connection, though? What if every single case we've had in the past month is connected?"

Theo stared at her. "How?"

"I don't know," Kate said frustratedly. "Every time I think I'm getting a handle on it, it slips away again."

"Well, let's just see if we can find Maria to start with," Theo said. He knocked at the shabby front door of number fourteen, Pleasant View Drive. Kate, looking up and down the street, thought it was spectacularly badly named.

The door was eventually opened by a fat, stoned-looking girl, with long greasy hair. Her sleepy eyes widened in alarm as Kate and Theo showed their warrant cards.

"It's all right," said Theo, "We're just looking for Maria Todesco. Does she still live here?"

"Who?" asked the girl, which told Kate all she needed to know. Theo persisted, showing the girl the photograph of Maria's face.

"Oh, her," said the girl. "They, like, threw her out of here. She's a junkie."

"Do you know where she is now?"

"Nah."

"How long ago did she leave?" asked Kate.

The girl shrugged one massive shoulder. "Dunno. Weeks ago."

"Have you heard of someone called Rosa?"

"Rosa? Nah."

She could tell them nothing else. Baulked, Theo and Kate returned to the car.

"Where could she be?" Kate asked, almost rhetorically.

Theo turned the key in the ignition. "She's a prostitute and a junkie. She could be dead. She could be in prison."

"Junkie..." Kate said the word slowly, staring unseeing through the windscreen.

Theo glanced over at her. "What?"

"Trixie Arlen – you said she was a junkie too, remember? When we were doing the search?"

"Yeah," said Theo. "So what?"

Kate raised one forefinger. "Rosa was an employee of Trixie

Arlen. She's also an associate of Maria Todesco, who is apparently a heroin addict."

"Right," said Theo, frowning.

Kate raised her other forefinger and entwined it with her already raised digit. "So, what if Rosa is supplying Trixie and Maria with heroin?"

Theo changed gears with an impatient shove. "So this Rosa is a cleaner, a prostitute *and* a smack dealer? Busy lady."

Kate brushed off his flippant tone. "Don't you think it's possible?"

Theo half shrugged. "I guess so."

Kate opened her mouth to say more and then realised she didn't know exactly what she was going to say. She muttered "We just have to *find* her."

"Yeah, but how? The agency's a dead-end, she doesn't have a record. We don't even know her surname."

"I don't know," said Kate, hearing her own annoyance mirrored in Theo's snappish tone. "Has Anderton done the press conference yet?"

"I think that's going out this afternoon."

Kate tapped her lip with her finger, thinking. "Could we put out an appeal? Anyone with any information on these women contact us in strictest confidence, that sort of thing? Put Maria's details up and say we're anxious to speak to anyone who might know an associate of hers called Rosa?"

In answer, Theo pulled over to the side of the road, pulled on the handbrake and handed Kate his mobile phone. She looked at him, startled.

"It's worth a try," Theo said, simply.

After Kate had spoken to Anderton, they drove to Jack Harker's house. He apparently worked from home as a graphic designer, and his affinity with colour and visual art was clear from the moment Kate and Theo walked through the door of his small terraced cottage. The walls were painted in dark dramatic colours, the floorboards a glossy dark grey, and pictures and photographs were carefully framed and displayed on the walls like an art gallery. It wasn't exactly a welcoming house, but it certainly had style.

Jack Harker received them with his usual aplomb and another lascivious glance at Kate. She could feel Theo bristle on her behalf and wanted to laugh. Coming from him, affront at another man's lustful eyes was pretty rich.

They showed Jack Harker Maria's photograph and asked him whether she was one of the women he believed had drugged and robbed him.

He looked at it for a long moment. "I think so," was all he said, eventually.

"You *think* so?" Theo asked, and Kate saw Jack Harker frown at his aggressive tone.

"It was a while ago now," Harker said in a similarly prickly voice. "I was pretty drunk at the time. Not to mention the roofie they slipped me."

Hastily, before Theo could say anything else, Kate assured him that they were anxious to catch these women. "Anything you *can* remember could help us, Mr. Harker."

"Yeah, I know that. Thing is, I can't remember much at all. They were young, sort of pretty. Eastern European. They both had long dark hair. That really is about all I can remember."

"Did you do any drugs with them when they were here?" Kate asked.

Harker looked uneasy. "Um..."

"We're not going to press any drugs charges—" Kate began and heard Theo mutter *yet* under his breath. She fought the urge to kick him. "Seriously, we've got more important things to worry about than whether you had a joint or a few lines that night. Did you?"

Harker still looked uneasy, but after a moment, he nodded. "Yeah."

"What was it exactly?" Kate persisted.

"Um... both of those. Bit of weed, bit of coke."

"Nothing more? Nothing stronger?"

"Stronger?" Harker looked positively alarmed.

"Heroin," said Theo brusquely. "Do any heroin with them?"

Harker's eyes bulged. "Heroin? Are you kidding? No way. I've never touched that in my life."

"Hmm." Theo looked unconvinced but Kate believed Harker. She shot Theo a repressive look and turned to the other man.

"Thanks very much, sir. If there's anything else you can tell us, be sure to get in touch won't you?"

"WHAT A *WANKER*," SAID THEO explosively, as soon as Harker's front door closed behind them.

"Shhhhh!" Kate flapped a hand at him. They got into the car and Theo started the engine. Kate smiled mischievously. "You're just jealous."

"*Jealous*? Of that prick? I don't think so."

"He's clearly the swordsman that you want to be," said Kate, laughing inwardly. God, it felt good to be able to laugh at something again, even if it wasn't really that funny.

Theo snorted. "Yeah, right. He wishes."

Kate bit down on a giggle. "Anyway," she said, sobering up. "We have a tentative identification of Maria Todesco. Hopefully the press conference might bring in some more info."

As it happened, they arrived back in the office to find Olbeck and Jane watching the tail end of Anderton's address to the media on the office television. Kate felt the familiar pulse of longing at the sight of Anderton's face on screen and stamped it down. That's it, she told herself. I am no longer allowing myself to feel anything towards him. The second I get a hint of it I'm going to – to pinch myself hard. And she did just that while the others had their attention turned towards the screen.

Olbeck turned off the television and swung round just in time to catch Kate wincing. "You all right?"

"I'm fine," said Kate impatiently. "Is Anderton going to debrief us?"

"Yep. He'll be here any minute."

As usual, they heard the human whirlwind that was Anderton approach the room a minute before he crashed through the door. "Hello, everyone. Let's get started, shall we?"

Everyone settled themselves in their usual spots. Anderton began pacing the floor. "Now, I presume you've just seen my ugly mug on the telly." Kate pinched her hand again. "We've put out a request for information about the two women we believe are involved in the robbery and death of Adrian Fellowes – Maria Todesco and Rosa with the unknown surname. We've also now informed the media and the public that there is a batch of contaminated heroin out there that is highly dangerous. Hopefully that might prevent any more overdose deaths but we can't take that for granted."

Olbeck raised a hand. "I guess we've pulled in all the dealers we think might be involved?"

Anderton nodded. "Yep. Nothing from that as yet but you never know. Now, one thing you might not be aware of is the possibility that the Costa brothers may be involved. Well, I'll clarify that. Stelios Costa could be involved – apparently his revolting brother is currently overseas at the moment, Spain to be exact. I've got a tail on Stelios at the moment and he'll report back in a couple of days. Right, what else?"

It was Kate's turn to raise a hand. "Sir, we believe there's a link between Trixie Arlen's death and the death of Adrian Fellows. Rosa's fingerprints were found at both scenes. We know she was the Arlens' cleaner and possibly also for Adrian Fellowes, but it sounds more likely that she was at Fellowes' place as an associate of Maria Todesco."

"Right," said Anderton, pausing by an empty desk and lifting himself onto it to sit, swinging his legs. "You know what I think?" Everyone waited. "I think it's highly possible that Rosa might be the dealer who supplied Trixie with her gear. She may very well be the person who took all the drug evidence from the crime scene."

"So she's knowingly supplying people with deadly drugs?" Theo asked and pursed his lips in a soundless whistle. "No wonder we can't find her. She's on the run."

Anderton shook his head. "We can't know that for certain. But it's imperative that we *do* find her."

Kate had been thinking. She raised her hand again and spoke. "There's one thing I can't work out. Why would you deal drugs which have been contaminated with this deadly substance? I thought the whole point of dealing was to keep your customers hooked so they come back to buy more and more. What's the point of giving them something that's just going to kill them? You're just going to eventually do yourself out of a customer base."

"Exactly," Anderton said, giving her a smile. She couldn't pinch her hand in his full view but she felt like doing so. "That's what doesn't make sense."

"Perhaps – if Rosa is a dealer – she doesn't know her heroin is contaminated," Olbeck suggested. "Why would she?"

Anderton nodded. "Well, almost everything we're talking about is pure speculation. What we need is some evidence. Does anyone else have anything to add?"

Nobody did. Anderton gave them a quick rundown on the findings from the Fellowes post mortem, reminded them to read through the multitude of forensic reports, and brought the meeting to a close.

Kate went back to her desk feeling dissatisfied. It was as Anderton had said – where was the evidence? All they seemed to be doing was scratching around in the dark, scrabbling for clues and coming up with nothing. She began to flip through the pile of reports on her desk but was interrupted by the telephone.

It was Kirsten Telling. She'd rung to tell Kate that the blood samples from the other overdose cases from the last month had now been tested.

"And?" asked Kate, feeling her heart rate speed up a little.

"It's as we suspected," said Doctor Telling's quiet voice. "The samples taken from Peter Hardew, Wayne Potter and John Henry Miller all show high levels of Sulatenil."

It was as Kate had feared. "Right. I understand." She thought for a moment. "Can I suggest you talk to Sergeant Bill Osbourne to see if he has anything else that might need testing as well?"

"Very well. I'll do that."

After she'd put the phone down, Kate told Theo what she'd just learned. He raised his eyebrows. "Just as well we put that appeal out," he said.

"I know." Kate got up and went over to Olbeck's office to pass on the news.

Chapter Twenty One

KATE GOT HOME AT TEN o'clock that night. Exhausted, she made a half-hearted effort to eat something before abandoning her plate of partially eaten toast. She was so tired she decided not to have her usual before-bed shower and was just stripping off her clothes by her bedside, thinking how inviting the bed looked when her phone rang.

Kate cursed and considered ignoring it, but saw Olbeck's name winking from the screen. She cursed again and pressed the 'receive' button in a resigned manner.

"You in bed?" was his opening remark.

"I wish. What's the problem?" Kate could hear the tension in Olbeck's voice and her tiredness began to abate as adrenaline kicked into her system. "What is it?"

"The station just rang me," said Olbeck. "There's a girl in reception who says her name's Rosa Ilenko."

Kate sat down on the side of the bed, winded. "You think it's her? The one we've been looking for?"

"Yes, I do. I'm heading there now."

"Me too," said Kate, quickly. "I'll meet you there in fifteen minutes."

Driving to the station, Kate found herself picturing this mysterious Rosa. Was she a heartless drug dealer? A killer of men? Why had she handed herself in? Kate saw her in her mind's eye: long dark hair, a lean, hungry face. Vampiric. A succubus. A monster.

Yet, when Kate got to the station and made her way to the interview room where Rosa had been taken, she realised she'd been wrong. Here was only a sick and terrified girl.

Rosa was as thin as Kate had expected – thinner, even. Her blotched, grey skin was stretched tight over blueish bones that could be seen beneath their inadequate covering. Rosa was shaking and sweating, her eyes ringed with shadow.

Kate and Olbeck took one look at her and then at each other.

"Doctor," was all that Olbeck said, and Kate nodded and hurried off to make the call.

As was usually the case, the medical attendant for the station seemed to take ages to arrive. Once she did, Kate and Olbeck stood outside the room, shifting from foot to foot and waiting impatiently for the verdict.

Eventually the doctor stepped outside.

"Well?" asked Kate.

Doctor Scofield looked from Kate to Olbeck. "Well, as I expect you've guessed, she's going through quite serious withdrawal at the moment."

"Withdrawal from heroin?"

"Yes. I've given her some methadone which should make her more comfortable. That'll kick in soon and she should calm down a bit. I can leave some anti-nausea medication for her as well."

"Can she be questioned?"

Doctor Scofield nodded. "You'll have to take it easy with her. Keep her warm, make sure she's getting plenty of fluids, some food if she'll take it."

They conferred a few moments longer and then the doctor left. Kate turned to Olbeck.

"Should we proceed?"

"Yes," said Olbeck. He added, a little callously, "It might be useful. Soften her up a bit."

"Come on," said Kate. She opened the door a crack and looked through at the shivering, crying girl perched on the edge of her chair, hugging her arms across her body. "She's in bits anyway."

"We'll go easy on her," said Olbeck. "Come on."

They took her a cup of tea and a blanket. Rosa looked up at them as they entered the room. Tears trickled down her grimy face.

"Here," said Kate, handing her the warm paper cup. "Make sure you drink this."

Rosa reached out a shaking hand for it. She took a sip and then promptly retched, dropping the tea. Warm liquid splashed over Kate's legs, but she barely noticed as she helped Rosa to the wastepaper basket in the corner of the room and held back her greasy hair as she vomited.

Eventually, Rosa straightened up, shuddering.

Kate rubbed her back. "Are you okay now?"

Rosa nodded. "I'm sorry," she gasped, rubbing her mouth.

"Don't worry about it," said Kate. "Now, do you think you're going to be sick again?"

Rosa shook her head. Kate took the blanket that Olbeck was holding out and wrapped it around the girl's sticklike arms, pockmarked with needle tracks. She moved the wastepaper basket to the corridor outside.

"We need to ask you some questions, Rosa," said Olbeck. "Do you think you're up to that?"

The girl nodded, her head hanging forward. "Yes," she said, with a tremor in her voice. "I must talk, I must tell you. I need to talk."

"We'll get the duty solicitor to sit in with you," said Kate, knowing there was no point even asking Rosa whether she had a lawyer. Rosa said nothing, but nodded jerkily.

Once they were all seated in the interview room, Rosa appeared to become a little calmer. She pushed her lank hair back from her face and took a deep breath. "I came here because I was afraid. I'm afraid they will kill me."

"Who will kill you, Rosa?" asked Kate.

Rosa wiped sweat from her forehead with shaking fingers. "The men I work for. They are gangsters. They have girls working for them in a house in Arbuthon Green."

Kate glanced at Olbeck. "When you say 'working for them', how do you mean?"

"As brothel."

Kate nodded. Rosa wiped her face again. "Can you give us the names of these men?"

"One is called John, one is Terry."

"Do you know a man called Stelios Costa?"

Rosa flinched. "Yes. He is boss of the others."

Olbeck leaned forward. "Have these men specifically threatened you?"

Rosa looked frightened. Kate shot Olbeck a look and he leaned back again. Kate used as warm and sympathetic a tone as she could as she continued. "Don't be frightened, Rosa. You can tell us everything. We can help you."

Rosa clasped her shaking hands on the table in front of her. "Can you – please can you get me some gear?"

Kate bit her lip. "No. I'm sorry but no. We can't do that." She hesitated and added "Rosa, if you really want to get off heroin, we can help you with that. We can arrange for you to have treatment, to go to a clinic, anything you might need to help you. But you have to tell us everything you can before we can do that."

Rosa nodded, wincing again. "I am heroin addict. That's how they get me to do everything they made me do. I do it all for the heroin." She began to cry. "My family – my family must not know how I am. They would be ashamed of me. I was not like this back in Romania."

"Is that where you're from?" asked Kate.

Rosa nodded, brushing the tears from her face. "I come here two years ago, to study. But I run out of money and I get in with bad people and all this bad things happen."

"Can you tell us where Maria Todesco is?" Kate asked.

Rosa's pale face became even whiter. Her features seemed to shrink a little. "I think she is dead."

"You think?"

Rosa nodded. "John and Terry took her away. They were angry because of what happened at the man's house."

"What man?"

"I don't know his name. Maria and me go to his house, have sex with him, tie him up. But then he dies and we don't know how to help him. We were very scared. I called Terry and he said to leave him."

Kate found a photograph of Adrian Fellowes in one of the files on her lap. "Is it this man, Rosa?"

Rosa looked and nodded jerkily. "We didn't hurt him. We didn't hurt any of them. They wanted to be tied up, you know, it was like a game to them."

"How did you meet them, Rosa?"

Rosa wiped sweat from her face again. Kate thought that she probably should be offering her some water or tea, but remembering what had happened last time Rosa had had a sip of tea, perhaps that wouldn't be such a good idea. At least the girl wasn't shivering so much.

"The first one came to brothel," said Rosa in a low voice. "He liked to be tied up there as well. When he was paying, John spoke to him and I think he told him that we could come to his house next time. So next time, we go to his house but before we go, John tells us we have to steal all we can once man is tied up."

Kate and Olbeck exchanged glances. "You didn't argue with him?"

"With John?" Rosa's incredulous tone said it all. "Never, never argue with John. You don't understand – Maria, me, we have to do what he tells us. When he tells us. He is the one who gets us gear, you see? And if we argue with him, he beats us. So – we don't argue."

Kate understood. It was funny how she and the rest of the police had been thinking of these two girls as the villains of the piece, when it was obvious that they were as much victims as the men they'd targeted.

"How many times did this happen?" asked Olbeck gently.

"I think three – maybe four times," Rosa said. She rubbed her temples, closing her eyes as if she were in pain. Kate asked her if she had a headache.

Rosa nodded. "Such a pain in my head. My body needs drugs. How can I go without them tonight?" She looked at both of the officers with sudden panic. "I cannot do it, I cannot, you have to help me—"

"All right, Rosa, all right," Kate tried to make her tone as soothing as possible. "We'll have the doctor come and see you again tonight, after we've spoken to you. Okay? She might be able to give you a sedative, or something to help you sleep."

Rosa, having held herself rigid as she pleaded, nodded and slumped back against her chair. Kate waited for the duty solicitor to say something but the grey-haired, portly man was staring at his client with something like disapproval. Kate was conscious of a spurt of anger. Who was he to judge?

"So, let's recap," she said, as nicely as possible. "You freely admit to meeting these three, possibly four, men, tying them up and then taking their possessions." The duty solicitor shifted in his seat but Kate hurried on before he could interrupt. "Did you drug them to make sure they were nice and compliant? I mean—" She substituted another word "Did you give them drugs to make sure they wouldn't fight back?"

Rosa shook her head. "I thought we would have to. But all of them, they wanted to be tied up. For them it was sexy game, fun to do, you know?"

Kate nodded, thinking. Hadn't Jack Harker said he thought his drink had been spiked? But it seemed just as possible that he'd drunk so much he'd passed out.

Olbeck cleared his throat. "What can you tell us about Trixie Arlen, Rosa?"

Rosa's twitching body stilled. She swiped a hand under her nose, her eyes downcast.

"Rosa?" Olbeck prompted.

Rosa looked up. There was a moment's silence. Then she began to speak. "In Romania, when I am little, I want to be a veterinary surgeon. I love animals. I think I will study very hard. If you could have told me then, what I am now, I would not have believed you."

Neither of the officers spoke. Kate, regarding Rosa's thin, haunted face, imagined her as a little girl: dark glossy curls, mischievous eyes, dainty little arms and legs. The contrast to what she could see now was horrible. Pity wrenched at her throat.

Rosa was still speaking. "I come to England three – no, four – years ago. I get work as cleaner, real cleaner, I mean, not cleaner like I am for Home Angels. But I lose my job as they don't want me anymore. When I have no money at all, I become sex worker." Her voice faded out for a moment. "By that time, I am doing heroin. It makes me feel better. Soon, I am doing anything so I can keep taking heroin."

She stopped speaking. After a moment, Olbeck asked her the question he'd asked before. "Can you tell us anything about Trixie Arlen, Rosa?"

Rosa rubbed a tear from the corner of her eye. "Home Angels send me to Trixie's house. I clean for her many weeks, no problems. And then one day, she asks me if I can get her heroin."

"Sorry?" asked Kate. "Trixie Arlen asked you to get her some heroin? Just like that?"

Rosa looked at her, sullenly. "She saw that I am addict. She knows I am. She knows that I have heroin."

Kate and Olbeck exchanged a glance. "She knew from looking at you that you were taking heroin?" Kate asked, to be absolutely sure. Looking at Rosa, she could see how that might have happened.

Rosa nodded. "She sees my eyes, so little, and the marks on my arms, and she knows. She told me her husband was the same."

"When was this?" asked Olbeck.

Rosa shrugged. "I don't know exact time. Maybe six months ago."

"So you got her some heroin?" Kate reiterated.

"Yes. She pay good money. We took it together, that first time."

Of all the things that Rosa had so far said, this shocked Kate the most. The idea of Trixie, the beautiful, famous, wealthy celebrity, injecting heroin with her poor, drug-addicted prostitute cleaner, was both incongruous and sad. That was the reality of addiction, Kate supposed: it made bedfellows of the most unlikely people.

"Did you take drugs with Trixie often?" she asked.

Rosa nodded. "Many times. I would come round at night with the gear and we would do it then. The children were always asleep."

Kate risked a look at Olbeck and saw without surprise that his mouth was crimped with disapproval. She hoped he wouldn't say anything. He didn't.

Kate pressed on. "What about the night Trixie died, Rosa?" She expected the solicitor to intervene at this point but he didn't. Perhaps he considered that Rosa had already gone too far in her confession for his intervention to make any difference at all.

Rosa shut her eyes momentarily. Then she shook her thin shoulders, squaring them as if for an ordeal.

"Trixie text me that afternoon. I go to Terry to get the gear and he give me the bag. I get taxi to Trixie's house like always."

"Wasn't that expensive?" asked Kate. "It's miles from Abbeyford."

Rosa gave her a look that indicated scorn. "She pay for it. Always Trixie pay for it."

Of course. Kate acknowledged this with a raise of her eyebrows and nodded for Rosa to continue.

Rosa dropped her gaze to the table and her thin, shaking fingers clasped together. "When I get there, Trixie is mad. Really mad. She had a big fight with her husband and he shake her. The night before that one, they had a big fight and she is still really mad."

The bruising on Trixie's arm. Kate recalled the post mortem results and realised that at least one part of the mystery was cleared up. Had Anderton and Olbeck ever taxed Jacob Arlen on that bruising? Not that it mattered now, anyway. She turned her attention back to what Rosa was saying.

"Trixie always shoots up first." Rosa gave a one-shoulder shrug. "She have the money so she go first. She had the syringe ready—" she held up her hand, clasping an imaginary syringe. "She looks at me and says 'fuck him if he thinks I'm giving this up for him'." Rosa fell silent for a moment. Again, she brushed a tear from the corner of her eye. "Then she puts it in her arm."

The interview room stilled. Kate could hear the three sets of breathing aside from her own.

"What happened then?" she asked softly.

Rosa's face contorted. "She died. Maybe one minute later. She fell on the bed and died."

"You knew she was dead straight away?" checked Olbeck.

Rosa nodded jerkily. "Her face – her mouth – it was blue. She didn't breathe." She took a deep shuddering breath, as if to remind herself that she herself was still alive. "I was so scared. I – I knew I had to leave her. I got all the drugs and things and I wiped around the bed with a cloth. All that time, I was doing this—" She held her hands out and shook them up and down. "I was scared more than ever before. I left."

There was another short moment of silence.

Then Olbeck asked "You left her dead on her bed and you knew her children were in the house?"

Rosa's face twisted again. She nodded and then burst into tears. "I'm sorry," she gasped. "I'm so sorry for it all. I will pay. I know I will pay. I am ready to pay."

Olbeck nodded. He looked across at Kate, who returned his

nod. "I think we'll leave it there for now," he said and named the time and date before switching off the recorder.

BACK IN THE OFFICE, KATE and Olbeck faced each other across his desk.

"Blimey," said Olbeck.

"Exactly," said Kate. She leant back in her chair and rubbed her eyes. "What the hell do we do now?"

Olbeck leapt up and began pacing around the room, just like Anderton. "We have a confession. We'll have to go through with it."

"I know that," said Kate. "It's just—"

"I know," Olbeck said. "I feel sorry for her too. But she's a criminal, Kate. She might be vulnerable and exploited and fighting addiction, but she's a criminal."

"Yes," said Kate. She leant forward and put her head on Olbeck's desk, feeling depressed. "Do you think she'll get any treatment in prison?"

"I don't know," said Olbeck sombrely. "I'd like to think so."

"She'll probably get worse," said Kate. "You know what the drug situation is like in prison."

"Well, what do you want me to do?" Olbeck almost shouted. "She'll be testifying against some hardened criminals if I get my way. Believe me, heroin or not, she'll be safer in remand."

Kate sat up. "We're going after Stelios Costa then?"

"Are you kidding? The chance to put him away for trafficking – of drugs and quite possibly people as well?" Olbeck grinned tiredly. "Just hold me back."

Kate also smiled reluctantly. "Well, if you put it like that..."

"Come on," Olbeck said. "Let's run it past Anderton. Then we can go home, get some sleep, and go in all guns blazing tomorrow. Possibly quite literally."

Chapter Twenty Two

KATE WAS WAITING ON THE doorstep at five am the next morning. It was pitch black; the sky glittered with stars and the full moon was crossed and re-crossed by wispy black clouds hurrying across the sky. Kate stamped her feet to keep the blood moving, her breath steaming in front of her. Beneath her coat, she felt the reassuring bulk of her anti-stab vest. It was so long since she'd worn one that she'd forgotten the weight of it.

The lights of Olbeck's car appeared at the end of her road and the anxiety and excitement inside her leapt up another notch. She hurried down the garden path and virtually jumped into the passenger seat.

"You're keen," said Olbeck, grinning. "Here, I got you a coffee."

Kate eagerly grasped the warm paper cup with her cold fingers. "Thanks. So, are we raiding first?"

"You bet."

"Shame," said Kate. "I could just do with hauling Stelios Costa's arse out of bed and bundling him out of the house in his boxers."

Olbeck laughed. "Well, Anderton and Theo have that pleasure. You can sit in on the interview later if you like and give him evil looks across the desk."

"I don't want to sit in," said Kate. "You know what he'll be like. He'll just 'no comment' himself to death."

"True." Olbeck hunched forward a little in his seat, peering through the dark windscreen. "It should be up here, I think."

They parked some way down from the house they'd come to enter. As Olbeck switched off the engine, Kate could see the others had already arrived: a team of uniformed officers, their colleague, Jane, wrapped in a voluminous puffa jacket, her face still smeared with sleep. There were two women there that Kate didn't recognise, both smartly dressed in black suits. No press, thank God; too early for them. Kate climbed out of the car and shut the door quietly, shivering as the cold enveloped her.

"Morning," Jane said, yawning. Several red curls could be seen peeking out from beneath her woolly hat, in jaunty contrast to her pale skin. "We're just about to go in."

Kate could see several of the officers readying the device that would force the door open. Kate had used one several times when she was on the beat and felt a flash of envy for a moment. Detective work was all very well, but sometimes all a girl wanted to do was bash down doors…

The two women came over and shook hands. The older one introduced herself as Karen Elliot and her companion as Sarah Grange. They were attending at Anderton's request, seconded from the civil service.

"We work for the Modern Slavery helpline," Karen Elliot explained, shivering a little in the cold. "DCI Anderton thought we might be able to assist."

Kate nodded. "We don't know for certain that any of these women are actually trafficked," she said. "It seems that at least a couple of them were able to freely come and go as they pleased."

Karen Elliot frowned. "Not all slaves are kept chained up, Detective Sergeant. Psychologically, whilst they might physically be able to leave their place of work, they're unable to actually go far because they've been so brainwashed."

Kate was getting impatient. "I realise that, Ms. Elliot. Perhaps we could talk about specifics in more detail after the raid?"

"Yes. Yes, of course. I'm sorry."

The woman's penitent tone made Kate feel bad. She was only trying to help, after all. Kate hastened to reassure her.

"Okay, we're off," Olbeck said, gesturing at them both to be quiet. The three women fell silent. In the quietness that followed, Kate heard rather than saw the crash of the battering ram, followed immediately by the splintering of wood and the shouts of the officers who crowded through the door.

Kate and Olbeck waited tensely. This was always the worst time. What were the officers going to find behind the door? A bunch of terrified women or a furious man wielding a weapon? Kate found herself clenching her fists and made herself relax her hands.

They waited one, two, three agonised minutes, straining their ears. Then Olbeck glanced at Kate. "Okay. Let's go. Ladies—" he nodded at the government workers, "please stay here until we let you know it's safe for you to join us."

The three officers hurried to the front door of the house, which was now hanging by one hinge. A splinter of wood from the shattered lock scraped against Kate's coat as she crossed the threshold. The house was cold and it stank: of blocked toilets, of unwashed human flesh, of rotting food. Trying not to grimace, Kate followed Olbeck through the hallway. All the overhead lights had been switched on but as they were red and purple light bulbs, visibility was poor. Red light bulbs in a brothel... Kate shook her head at the cliché.

There were shouts in the room ahead of them and a crash. Kate and Olbeck froze and then jumped back against the corridor wall as a gaggle of four burly uniforms appeared in the doorway ahead, carrying a struggling, handcuffed man between them. He was bowled along past them and out the front door, no doubt to be slung into one of the vans that were parked out of the front.

"A punter?" asked Kate quietly.

"Not this early in the morning, surely?" replied Olbeck. "We'll ID him back at the station."

They cautiously walked further into the building. The room which had disgorged the struggling man was obviously a kind of sitting room, last decorated sometime in the early eighties from the looks of the swirly-pattern carpet, pockmarked all over with cigarette burns. A filthy sofa stood against one wall and on it were four women, huddled together and shivering. There were two more women slumped against it on the floor. All were thin and shaking and terrified. Several female officers were already attempting to talk to them, offering blankets and soothing words.

Kate and Olbeck wordlessly surveyed the room for a moment. Kate wondered whether she should be talking to the women as well, to see if they could tell her anything more than Rosa already had. She even took a step forward before changing her mind. These poor girls were in no fit state to be questioned as yet.

"Come on," said Olbeck. "We need to find the drugs."

It was a struggle to get the gloves over cold fingers. Kate could feel the tip of her nose going numb as she and Jane followed Olbeck out of the room. What must it have been like for these women here, being raped and abused, spending their days naked and shivering? No wonder they turned to drugs – or, as was more likely, were deliberately given them to ensure their compliance. What kind of man would voluntarily want to actually have sex with these emaciated, strung-out, blank-eyed girls? A bad one, Kate told herself as she turned to follow Jane into another small room. A bad man. One who saw women as commodities, nothing more than that – a product to be exploited and then tossed aside when they had finished.

As it turned out, the heroin was easy to find. Upstairs, in a filthy bathroom, Olbeck pulled away the side of the bath to reveal two black rucksacks, each containing several pounds of brownish powder, some already divided up into individual plastic bags. Olbeck looked up from his search at Kate and Jane. "Not the brightest tools in the bunch, are they? Talk about a crap hiding place."

"They probably thought they were being really original," said Jane. "Stupid bastards."

"There might be more," said Kate, crouching down. She hefted one of the bigger bags in her hand. "Do you think this is the Sulatenil stuff?"

"No idea. I won't be injecting it to find out. We'll have to wait for the test results," said Olbeck.

Kate grinned. She heaved herself to her feet. "Are you going to tell Anderton?"

Olbeck got up, groaning a little. "God, my back. Yes, let's get back to the station while SOCO get to work here. Anderton's going to be a very happy man."

"Let's see Stelios Costa 'no comment' his way out of this one," Kate said vindictively, as they made their way back to the car.

WHEN THEY ARRIVED BACK AT the station, Olbeck sprinted off to the interview room where Anderton was enclosed with Stelios Costa. Kate decided to check on Rosa. As she peered into the holding cell through the peep-hole, she braced herself. But Rosa was sitting up in bed quite calmly and quietly, clasping her hands over her knees.

Relieved, Kate pushed open the door. "You're looking better, Rosa," she said, sitting down at the other end of the narrow bed.

Rosa didn't exactly smile but her face relaxed a little. "I feel better. I feel as if I was in a dark cloud and now it is starting to break, a little."

"That's good to hear," said Kate. "I'm glad because I need you to come with me for a moment. There's something you can do for me."

Immediately, Rosa tensed. "What?"

"Nothing bad," soothed Kate. "We've arrested several people who were present at the building that you indicated was a brothel. You remember you gave us the address?"

Rosa nodded cautiously. "You have arrested them? For Maria's death?"

A little taken aback, Kate shook her head. "Not specifically for that, no. We're still gathering evidence. What I need you to do is identify the two men that we currently have in custody. Can you do that for me?"

Rosa's sense of calmness was rapidly disappearing. "What if they see me? They will hurt me, I know it."

Kate hastened to reassure her. It was only after several minutes of persuasion that Kate was able to get the girl to go up to the interview room floor with her and an accompanying officer, where the man who'd been arrested at the brothel was currently under surveillance in the room with a one-way mirror on the wall.

"Here, Rosa," said Kate, gently positioning the girl so she could see into the room. "Can you identify this man?"

Rosa gazed through the glass, her thin, grubby fingers at her mouth.

"Is Terry," she said eventually.

Kate nodded. "Thank you." She left Rosa in the care of the PC who'd accompanied them up to the viewing room and quickly ran to the interview room where Anderton and Theo were. She knocked.

"Detective Sergeant Redman has entered the room," said Anderton. All four men in the room looked at her: Anderton and Theo inquisitively, Stelios Costa and his lawyer with a frown. Kate murmured her request in Anderton's ear and although he looked surprised, he nodded.

"Two minutes, Kate," was all he said. Happy with that, Kate straightened up and left the room, shutting the door firmly behind her. Hopefully her little intervention would at least have given Stelios Costa a few minutes' worry if nothing else came of it.

Back in the viewing room with Rosa, Kate watched Terry being removed by several officers. The door of the room shut and then opened again and Stelios Costa was ushered in. Anderton and Theo remained by the door.

She saw Anderton's mouth move as he gave an instruction and Stelios turned to face the mirror. Kate saw him smile as he looked straight ahead and was momentarily disconcerted. It was as if he could actually see them.

She could feel Rosa begin to tremble beside her. "It's okay," she said. "Don't worry, he can't see you. Can you identify this man, Rosa?"

Rosa was breathing fast. After a moment, she said in a voice so small, it was barely audible, "It is Costa, his name is Stelios Costa."

"Thank you," said Kate. A positive identification at least. Now they just had to make sure that Rosa would testify as a prosecution witness, and then finally they might be able to jail one Costa brother for good.

"He is such a bad man," said Rosa, still in an almost whisper. "I always think his face is like a shark."

Kate looked at Stelios, looking at them. She knew what Rosa meant – it was something in his eyes; a blankness, a void, nothing behind the flat black gaze.

"He can't hurt you here," she said, anxious to reassure Rosa. "You're perfectly safe."

Rosa stood still, hugging her thin arms across her body. "I know he does bad things but I never see him angry," she said. Then she looked up at Kate. "Only when the bald man comes once. That was the only time."

"Sorry?" asked Kate. "What bald man?"

Rosa shrugged, turning back to look at Stelios again, who was being ushered out of the door by Theo. "I don't know. He came one, two times. Last time Stelios was very mad." She relaxed a little as the viewing room door shut. "I am very tired now."

"I'll take you back to your cell," said Kate, nodding at the PC. They walked slowly back down the corridor, Rosa and the PC in front of Kate, who was puzzling over what Rosa had just told her. Was it significant?

It wasn't until they reached the cell floor that things began to fall into place. As Kate realised the significance of what she'd just been told, she stopped dead, as if she'd just walked into a heavy, immovable object. Surely – was she wrong? She *had* to be wrong – but what if she wasn't?

"Take Rosa into her cell," she asked the PC. "I'll be back in a minute."

Kate sprinted back up the stairs to the office floor, wondering what the quickest way of obtaining the photograph she needed would be. After a moment of hesitation, she went over to the paper recycling box by the window and dug through it. Would it still be here? Just as she was asking herself the question, she spotted it and pulled out the crumpled paper with a cry of triumph. Then she wheeled around and ran back down the stairs again.

"Can you let me in?" Kate asked the PC, who was just turning to go. He looked surprised but nodded, reaching for his keys.

Rosa had sat back down on the edge of the bed and was biting her nails. She looked up in surprise as Kate came in.

Kate held out the paper with its front page photograph. "Is this the bald man you saw with Stelios Costa?" she asked, puffing slightly.

Rosa looked at the spotted, creased paper for a long time, frowning slightly. Then she nodded, a quick bob of her dark head.

"You're sure?" persisted Kate.

"Yes, it was him."

"Good girl." Kate turned to go, anxious not to delay even for a moment. Then, at the cell door, she turned round. "Rosa, for what it's worth, I think you're an extremely brave person. You really are."

Rosa finally smiled, a little wanly. Kate smiled back in response and then she was out the door and across the floor to the stairs, running as fast as her tired legs would carry her.

Olbeck was back in his office, thank God. Kate almost fell through the doorway, still clutching her paper. He looked up, surprised. "What's up?"

"I'll tell you in the car," said Kate. "We need to go. I'll drive."

Chapter Twenty Three

THEY APPROACHED THE HOUSE JUST as the sun was starting to set. The reddish light blazed off the autumn colours of the trees as they drove slowly down the winding driveway, gradually descending into the hollow of the valley. The beautiful, lonely house was before them. It had a blank, closed-in look, as if nobody lived there.

Kate parked the car and they rang the doorbell. Kate was expecting the small, dark-haired housekeeper to answer the door, but nobody came. She looked at Olbeck, raising her eyebrows.

"Try again," he said. "This house is so massive, it might take ages to get to the door."

Kate rang the bell again and knocked for good measure. There was no answer. "Well..." she said, stepping back a little. "Do we force it?"

As she spoke, Olbeck tried the door handle. It moved easily in his grasp. "It's open."

They stepped into the house, announcing their presence in muted shouts. Kate expected to see either the housekeeper or Michael Dekker himself appear, alarmed at their sudden entrance, but again, nobody came. The house felt empty. Their footsteps sounded inordinately loud as they crossed the marble floor of the hallway and passed into the rooms beyond.

Kate walked towards the orangery at the back of the house, merely to ascertain that it was empty. But seated in the same chair as he'd been sat in when she'd visited before was Michael Dekker.

For one frozen moment, she thought he was dead – he was so silent and still, staring out at the view beyond the window with glassy eyes. She and Olbeck stopped and she almost jumped when Dekker spoke.

"Come in, Detective Sergeant. Do sit down."

Kate and Olbeck remained standing, watching Dekker, who hadn't taken his gaze from the window. He looked diminished; smaller, somehow, than he had at their last meeting. There were grey shadows beneath his pale blue eyes. His hands were folded together in his lap and his legs were tucked under a tartan blanket.

"Won't you sit down, officers?"

"Do you know why we're here, sir?" asked Olbeck.

At last Dekker moved his gaze to look at them. He smiled a little. "I saw on the news you'd arrested Stelios Costa. I guessed it wouldn't be long before you paid me a visit."

"We need you to accompany us to the station, Mr. Dekker."

Dekker smiled again. "Would you mind if we spoke here, just for now?" He looked at them directly again. "I'll tell you everything again later, at the station. I've got nothing to hold back now. But if we could talk here...?"

Olbeck hesitated. Then he nodded. "Very well, Mr. Dekker." Kate and he moved further into the room as he spoke the words of the caution. Dekker said nothing for a moment, but Kate saw him close his eyes briefly as the charge of murder was mentioned. Then he opened them again and an air of calm resignation touched his features.

Kate and Olbeck seated themselves in the two armchairs that faced Michael Dekker's seat. He continued to look past them, staring into the distance. Once they had settled themselves, he turned his gaze back to their faces.

"Do you wish to have legal representation?" asked Kate. Something about his stillness, his aura of fatalism, was making her faintly uneasy, without her being able to put a finger on exactly what it was.

Dekker shook his head. "Not just now. Perhaps later."

"What did you want to tell us, Mr. Dekker?" asked Olbeck.

"Everything," said Dekker, simply. "Everything. I'll start by telling you about my health. About a year ago, I was diagnosed with an inoperable, incurable cancer." He tapped the side of his bald head. "Up here. The doctor told me that I had only months to live."

"I'm sorry to hear that," Olbeck said, frowning a little.

"It's probably why I decided to finally act," said Dekker. Then he shook his head, as if dislodging the thought. "No, no it's not. I know why I decided." He shifted a little in his chair, unclasping his hands. "I saw Trixie Arlen earlier this year. I think I told you so before. I almost bumped into her, but as it happens, she didn't see me. It was the same day as the anniversary of David's death. I couldn't have had a clearer sign than that."

"A sign to do what?" asked Kate gently.

Dekker looked at her in surprise. "To kill her, of course. To kill her. I should have done it years ago."

"You admit to killing Trixie Arlen," Olbeck said. "Is that right? Why?"

Dekker looked at him as though he were stupid. "Do you have children, Detective Inspector?"

Olbeck shifted a little in his seat. "Not yet."

Don't ask me, prayed Kate. But Dekker's attention, for the moment, was entirely on her partner.

"I think if you had children you might understand. Trixie Arlen was not the golden girl, the nation's sweetheart that she liked to be seen as. She was a monster."

Dekker's gaze had somehow narrowed and sharpened. Despite his illness, for a moment, he pulsated with real energy. It was hate, Kate realised. Strong enough to kill.

Seeing that the detectives weren't going to say anything, Dekker continued. "Trixie Arlen killed my boy. She murdered him as surely as if she plunged a knife into his heart. She killed her first husband too, and the baby that she lost. All of them."

For the first time, Kate began to doubt his sanity. She looked anxiously over at Olbeck but he was staring at Dekker steadily.

Dekker carried on speaking. "I can see you don't believe me. Trixie's own mythology was quite seamless. Of course, she told everyone that her first husband, Ivo Wright, was the one with the drug problem. Would you believe me if I told you that it was Trixie who introduced *him* to drugs? Within a year of meeting her, he was a hopeless drug addict. She did the same to David."

Kate didn't want to interrupt him but she couldn't quite let that go. "Don't you believe that people make their own choices, Mr. Dekker? Didn't your son decide to take heroin of his own free will?"

Dekker look at her, smiling gently. "Addicts don't have free will, Detective Sergeant. The first time David took heroin was the start of his addiction. He didn't realise it then, of course. Trixie lied to him, as she lied to everyone else. She lied to the entire country about who she was."

This time, Kate didn't speak. She realised that further interruptions would be futile. This man had a story he wanted to tell, probably a story that he'd wanted to tell for a long time. All she and Olbeck had to do was listen.

"Everyone was so sorry for her," Dekker was saying. His mouth twisted a little. "The poor young widow who then lost her baby. You know *why* she lost the baby? She was still taking drugs, of course. She cared so little about the life of her unborn child that she continued to take drugs during the pregnancy and then, of course, the baby died."

"How do you know this, Mr. Dekker?" Kate hadn't wanted to interrupt but she couldn't help herself.

"David," said Dekker, simply. "David told me everything the night before he died. After he told me, he went home and injected himself with an enormous quantity of heroin. I think he wanted to die. His life, by then, was such a source of misery to him that I think he didn't want to carry on."

There was a moment's silence. Dekker raised one trembling hand to his eyes and brushed away what could have been a tear.

He started to speak again. "I don't know why I didn't kill her the second I realised what she was. When David died I was – I was so – I couldn't function. I could barely live, let alone plan. So...so time went on and Trixie still lived, and I went on doing what I did, but I never forgot, you see. You never forget. They say time heals everything but that is nothing but a lie, I'm afraid. You never forget. Every morning on waking – every morning – I have a couple of seconds of pure happiness, did you know that, Detective? Just a few seconds before I remember, and then it's like reliving the day he died, over and over again."

Dekker's voice had grown hoarse. He stopped speaking for a moment, clearing his throat, before he began again. "When I saw Trixie that day, I knew I had to act. At first I thought of killing her myself. I wanted to do it. I wanted to see the fear on her face. But when I began to think about it, I realised I could do society more than one service. I could remove Trixie Arlen from the face of this Earth and in doing so, get rid of as many drug addicts as I could at the same time. Let Trixie kill herself as I knew she would one day. There was as certain poetic justice in it that appealed to me."

Again, he stopped speaking. After a moment, Olbeck leaned forward. "It was you who organised for a shipment of heroin to be contaminated with Sulatenil?"

Dekker nodded. When he spoke, he sounded almost proud. "When you're rich, Detective Inspector, you can do pretty much anything. You can arrange for chemists and manufacturing laboratories and whatever ingredients that you need. All you need is money. Did you know that?"

"No," said Olbeck. "I wouldn't know."

"Well," said Dekker. "Now you do."

Outside, the sun had almost set. Shadows were creeping across the marble-tiled floor of the conservatory, entwining Dekker's blanketed feet in darkness. Kate could see the blood-red clouds on the horizon as the last of the daylight began to slip away.

Dekker was still speaking. "I went to Stelios because I knew he was exactly the kind of man who would do as I asked. He was surprised, of course. I think he thought when I first made the appointment that I wanted to do something with his legitimate business interests." Dekker chuckled. "He soon came round to the idea, though. He could see the profit in it. And no doubt he also thought it would also make excellent blackmail material if it ever came to that."

"Did he realise that you'd contaminated the heroin with Sulatenil?"

Dekker looked surprised. "Of course not. Where would be the profit in that for him? No, Stelios thought he was distributing heroin in the 'normal' way. I knew he would be able to ensure that Trixie Arlen was given the drugs that would kill her, without realising what he was doing." He was quiet for a moment. "Of course, when people began dying, he realised something was wrong. But by that time, I'd achieved what I set out to do. I didn't care much about the rest of it anymore." He paused again and then said, "I don't care anymore. I can't really bring myself to care that much about anything."

Olbeck and Kate glanced at each other. They waited for Dekker to go on speaking but it seemed that he'd come to the end of his confession. The silence stretched on and on, as the room gradually darkened.

Eventually Olbeck stood up. "Mr. Dekker, you'll have to accompany us to the station now."

Smiling again, Dekker shook his head. "I don't think so."

"It's not a request, sir."

Dekker was still smiling. "I won't be going anywhere."

"You—"Olbeck began, but that was all he had time to say. Dekker's hand slipped down to the blanket on his lap. It delved beneath the tartan fabric and came up swiftly, holding something. For a frozen moment, Kate thought it was a gun and she was on her feet before she realised it was a syringe. Before she could say or do anything, Dekker had plunged the needle into his thigh, stabbing himself through the blanket, and depressed the plunger.

Rosa had said it had taken Trixie Arlen a minute to die. Michael Dekker didn't even have that long. In the twenty seconds it took Kate and Olbeck to reach him, to pull the syringe from his leg, a spurt of blood coming with it, he was dead. He sagged against the back of the sofa, his head rolling to one side.

Olbeck dropped the syringe and it fell to the hard floor, rolling away beneath the sofa. Kate stood trembling, looking down at Dekker's blue-tinged mouth and half-open eyes.

"Oh God," was all that Olbeck said, in a low, aghast tone. Kate said nothing but she groped for his hand as the last of the sunlight finally slipped below the horizon.

Chapter Twenty Four

"Wow, you look like shit," was Theo's heartening remark as Kate flopped into her chair the next morning.

"Gee, thanks. Hardly surprising is it?" countered Kate. She put her handbag under the desk, noticing a brown envelope on her desk as she straightened up. Frowning, she got up to make herself and Theo a coffee.

"Thanks," said Theo, as she handed over a brimming cup. "You know we charged Stelios Costa with everything we could throw at him?"

"I heard," said Kate. "Fantastic. Let's just hope we make it through to the trial."

"Well, yeah." The two of them were silent for a moment, remembering the other times they thought they'd had the Costa brothers firmly in their sights only for them to slip away under the instruction of their highly paid and ruthless legal representation. Theo brightened a little. "Still, fairly watertight case, this time round. Particularly if it really is true that Maria Todesco is dead."

Kate yawned. "Do we have any evidence of that? They might have just moved her to another brothel."

"Let's hope so," said Theo. "Let's really hope so."

There was a short silence. Kate looked at the pile of reports that needed attention, squared her shoulders and pulled the first one towards her.

"So, did Dekker really just kill himself right before your eyes?" Theo asked suddenly, leaning over the desk.

Kate flinched. "Can we not talk about it right this second, thanks?"

"But did he?"

"Yes. And there will probably be hell to pay. That's why I don't want to talk about it. Okay?"

Theo said nothing. Instead, he sauntered round to Kate's side of the desk and gave her cheek a hearty smacking kiss. She reared back in amazement. "What the hell are you doing?"

"You'll be all right," Theo said, grinning. "You'll be just fine."

He wandered off, whistling a little tune. Kate looked after him with raised eyebrows. Then, shaking her head and smiling despite herself, she turned back to her desk.

She sipped her coffee and picked up the brown envelope, turning it over in her fingers. She had a nasty feeling she knew what was inside it. In an act of cowardice unlike her, she opened her desk drawer and dropped the envelope inside it, shutting it up out of sight.

The day passed slowly in a blur of paperwork, phone calls and many cups of coffee. Towards the end of the day, Kate found her gaze being drawn back to the closed desk drawer. She tried to ignore it, turning her attention to the final report that she'd planned for the day. Once that was signed and complete Kate sat back, tapping her pen against her jaw. Leave it for today, she told herself. Wait until you're not quite so knackered and burned out. She switched off her computer and stretched, easing the ache in her neck. Then, in a rush, she pulled open the drawer, yanked out the brown envelope and quickly slit the back of it with a trembling finger.

She read the first line *we regret to inform you that in your recent examinations for the position of Detective Inspector...* and slumped back in her chair, closing her eyes. Bitter regret surged up her throat. If she'd just worked harder, studied harder, spent more time actually focusing on passing the exam... Kate leant forward, pressing her fingers into her eye sockets, dangerously near to tears. What an *idiot*. She'd applied for the exams in such confidence – *I'll breeze through them* – and to realise that she had, in fact, failed was a bitter pill to swallow.

She soberly folded the letter back into its envelope, not wanting to read it here in the office, and put it away in her handbag. Looking up, she realised she was alone in the office – just as well, as she felt as if she were about to burst into tears at any moment – but at the same time, she felt a sharp surge of loneliness. Slowly, she got up, pulling on her coat.

As she turned to leave, Kate's gaze fell on the neat pile of reports she'd completed during the day. She remembered Rosa, so scared but so determined to do what was right. She thought about all the women who'd been in that stinking house, and what their lives must have been like. Really, when you thought of it like that, what did a silly exam really matter? You're good at your job, Kate, she told herself. You can retake them. In the grand scheme of things, it *really doesn't matter*.

Feeling a little more cheered, she marched out of the station and stopped on the top steps. There, standing side by side, with their hands in their pockets were Olbeck and Jeff. They looked up at her and smiled a greeting.

"Were you waiting for me?" Kate asked, feeling a burst of happiness at the thought.

"Who else?" said Olbeck. He extended his arm as Kate came down the steps and she took it, hooking her other arm under Jeff's. "We thought we'd go for tea and cake. We need to talk *weddings*."

"Oh God," said Kate. "That sounds ominous."

"You're our best woman, darling," said Jeff as they began to walk down the street. "You can't get out of it now."

Kate squeezed his arm. "I know, I'm joking. I'm thrilled." They walked a few more steps while she wondered whether to say anything and decided that yes, she would. What were best friends for, if not to listen to your troubles? "I failed my exams."

"Oh bugger," Jeff said, just as Olbeck said over the top of him.

"That's a shame but don't worry about it, just retake them. You'll ace them next time."

"Yes," said Kate stoutly. "I'm sure I will."

Their six feet shuffled through a rustling pile of autumn leaves. The daylight was fading and a chill wind made them all huddle into one another as they walked. Kate could feel the warmth of Olbeck and Jeff on either side of her and she sighed with deep thankfulness that despite everything else, she still had her friends. That was all you needed, really, wasn't it? When you got right down to it. That was all that really mattered.

They turned the corner of the street and Kate could see the welcoming lights of the tearoom up ahead.

"Come on," she said, "I'm buying. It's the least I can do."

"Nice one," said Olbeck and they walked up the steps of the tearoom together.

THE END

Echo

A Kate Redman Mystery: Book 6

Prologue

FOR THREE WEEKS IT HAD rained every day. For those past three weeks, daybreak was a gloomy affair. The skies gradually moved from a thick blanket of dingy white clouds to the deepest shade of grey, peaking here and there in ominous black thunderheads. The rain came down hard in rippling sheets, or softly, insidiously; pattering onto land already sodden, into rivers which threatened to break their weakening banks, onto roofs which leaked and dripped and twice collapsed under the sheer weight of water.

Munford Gorge was a local beauty spot nine miles from the West Country town of Abbeyford. A large lake at the bottom of an encircling bracelet of hills, their steep sides comprised equally of moorland and deciduous forest. On a sunny summer's day, the sandy shore of the lake was swamped with picnicking families, small children running and splashing in the shallow edges of the water, bolder souls venturing out onto the depths on canoes and flotation-devices before their anxious parents called them into shore. On warm summer nights, teenagers built campfires, smoking weed and taking pills, losing their virginity to the lap and swell of the lake waters breaking in wind-ruffled wavelets upon the little beach.

Now, in February, nobody went there. No one save a few hardy walkers, braving the torrential rain, trudging along the shoreline before taking the footpath that led up across the moorland and over the escarpment of the first hill. Now, at midnight, no one went there at all. The wind pushed the surface of the lake into foam-frilled waves which crashed against the wet sand of the banks. Rain poured down relentlessly, hissing against the saturated ground. Puddles became ponds, streams became rivers. Up on the far shore of the lake, as the ground inclined steeply towards the brow of the hill, subterranean groans became louder and louder, until, with a dull roar, a section of the hillside gave way. Mud, rocks and stones rushed downhill in a landslide. The shattered surface of the lake became even more turbulent, as the hillside cascaded into the water.

The rain eased a little, then slackened completely. After the thunder and crash of the last few minutes, the countryside by the lake grew quiet once more, the plink plink of falling drips the only sound to be heard other than the slap of the waves as they broke against new piles of mud and stone where the land had collapsed. Eventually the black clouds above were chased away as the wind strengthened. A thin sliver of moon cast a faint, tremulous radiance over the devastation below it. Even so, there was not enough light to bring a glimmer to the bones that could now be seen, poking out from the tumble of mud, tree-roots and stones that the landslide had brought to the surface.

Old bones are not white. The twisted remnants of what had once been a hand were brown; as brown as the earth that surrounded them. Even if a human observer had been there to watch, they would have seen nothing in the faint light of the moon. The bones stretched forward in darkness, in silent, unseen supplication.

Chapter One

"Okay," Detective Inspector Mark Olbeck said. "So what about *this* one?"

He regarded himself in the mirror anxiously. Such was his focus on the suit he was currently modelling, he failed to notice that his companion had slithered from her chair and was engaged in hiding her head underneath a pile of velvet waistcoats.

"Mark," Kate Redman said, her voice muffled. "It's a grey suit. It's nice. It's as nice as the fifteen other grey suits you've tried on. Can we please just pick one now and go and get a coffee or something?"

"Mmm," said Olbeck, continuing to stare into the mirror. "I don't know about the lapels, though. I mean, they're seventies, but are they too seventies? I don't want to look like an ABBA tribute act or anything."

Kate, head still buried, suppressed a scream. Then, taking a deep breath, she pushed herself out from under the waistcoats and sat up. "Seriously, I had no idea you were going to be such a *girl* about this. Can't you, you know, ask Theo about this? Ask Jeff? Please?"

Olbeck caught her eye in the mirror. "Sorry. Am I being a pain?"

"Yes. Seriously, I know it's your wedding and all, but...Mark, it's a suit. It looks great. Please buy it. Please. Then we can go and do something else. Anything else."

Chuckling, Olbeck turned the collar up and then down again. "Okay. You've persuaded me. I'll buy it."

"Thank God." Kate pretended to swoon in relief.

"Who are you bringing?" Olbeck asked as they made their way to the exit of the department store. A grey and white striped bag with ribbon handles hung from his arm.

"What?"

"Are you bringing anyone to the wedding?" Olbeck asked patiently.

"Oh, God, I don't know," said Kate. They'd reached the pavement outside by now and both grimaced as the rain hit them. Kate fumbled for her umbrella and Olbeck flipped up the hood of his coat. "Stuart, maybe. If his new girlfriend lets him come."

"Are you mad?" asked Olbeck. "We've sent Stuart his invitation already. He's *bringing* his new girlfriend."

"Oh, bollocks," said Kate. "Oh well. Do I actually have to have an escort? Can't I come on my own?"

"Yes, of course. I just thought you might like to bring someone along, you know, for company."

"Well, thanks," muttered Kate. "I'm sure I'll manage to scrape someone up. Besides, I know loads of people going. I'm sure I'll be fine."

"Mmm." Olbeck paused at the kerbside, hesitating. The rain was coming down so hard, it was difficult to see across the street. "God, this weather. Has it actually stopped raining this *year*?"

Kate said nothing, engaged as she was in crossing the road without being hit by flying sheets of water from passing cars, but she agreed with the sentiment. Had there ever been such a wet start to the year?

They made it to the multi-storey car park where they'd both left their cars. They reached Kate's little Ford first and she fumbled in her handbag for her keys.

"Listen, I need to talk to you about the speech—" she began, before both her and Olbeck's mobiles started to ring at the same time. They shared a glance of mutual apprehension before answering their calls.

"Hello, sir—" Kate heard Olbeck say before she heard a familiar voice on the end of her phone line.

"What's up, Rav?"

"Oh, hi, Kate. Did I interrupt you?"

"Only doing some shopping. What's the problem?"

"I'm with the chief now—" Rav began, and as Kate listened, she could hear Olbeck listening to Anderton's voice on his phone in a rather eerie tandem effect, as both men were clearly calling from the same location.

"I'll be right there," Kate heard Olbeck say, just as she was saying, "Fine, Rav, I'll be there as soon as I can."

Olbeck and Kate both terminated their respective calls and turned to one another.

"Here we go again," sighed Olbeck.

"No rest for the wicked," agreed Kate. "That was Anderton, yes?"

"Yes. He's at Munford Gorge, with—"

"Rav," finished Kate. "They've found a body?"

"Yep. That's it."

"Right," said Kate. "So I'm following you, yes? I don't know the way."

It was slow going making their way out of Abbeyford. Kate's windscreen wipers struggled to clear the lashing rain from the glass and, more than once, she lost sight of Olbeck's car as other vehicles overtook her. Eventually, she managed to find her way to the dual carriageway that ran from Abbeyford towards Bristol. She had a vague idea that Munford Gorge lay on the west side of the town, but where, exactly? She caught sight of Olbeck's car up ahead, parked in the layby, with yellow hazard lights flashing, and breathed a sigh of relief. She pulled in behind him and tooted her horn.

Once out of the city, the traffic eased a little. Kate saw Olbeck's yellow indicator begin flashing and a moment later, saw the brown road sign for Munford Gorge. The two cars drove slowly down a smaller road and then turned again into an unsurfaced track that ended in a small car park. It was full of police vehicles, the white vans of the scene of crime officers and the ambulance that would eventually transport the body to the mortuary to await the post mortem examination.

Kate struggled to pull her already wet coat on. The rain hadn't eased at all – it still fell relentlessly from the sky. Rivulets of muddy water were already flowing across the stony, rutted surface of the car park from the slightly raised ground that lay to its rear. Kate thought of all the trace evidence that was being washed away, even as she and Olbeck made their way to the scene, and frowned. She said as much to her companion.

"I know," said Olbeck. "But what can we do? Let's just hope there's *something* left."

They reached the lakeside and walked towards the bustle of activity at the far end of the lake. Kate spotted Rav and waved. She was still unused to seeing him back at work. The thought made her smile; she was so pleased that he'd managed to make it back. Rav had been terribly injured in the course of duty two years ago, and Kate knew he'd sometimes wondered whether he would be able to come back at all.

SOCO had already erected the white tent that hid the body from public view; not that there was any public to screen it from – the hissing rain meant that the only people here were professionally involved. Kate, Rav and Olbeck ducked through the entrance flap of the tent and straightened up. Kate's eyes immediately went to the tall figure of Detective Chief Inspector Anderton, who stood looking down at the body. Her first feeling was one of surprise. She'd expected to see a *body* but here, amidst the tumbled earth, was just a sad collection of bones. For a moment, she was reminded of something else, something quite innocuous, but the exact memory eluded her. Then it came to her: a trip to London and to the British Museum, looking at the exhibition of the body found in the peat bog, thousands of years old and still perfectly preserved.

Anderton looked up as they approached. "Morning," he said. "Something slightly out of the ordinary here."

Olbeck crouched down to look more closely. "This is *old*. Isn't it? We're talking years, here."

"Mmm." Anderton made a noise of assent. "I would have thought so."

Kate recollected her first impression. "I suppose it *is* a suspicious death, sir? It's not actually an archaeological find?"

Anderton looked at her briefly and smiled. "I admit the thought did cross my mind, Kate. It's not as if this area isn't thick with historical artefacts – and bones. But, look here—" He crouched down beside Olbeck, pointing, and Rav and Kate leant forward to see. "Look here." His pointing finger indicated a fine metal chain around the base of the skull, too clogged with mud to make out any fine details. "That's modern jewellery. Twentieth century, at least. No, I think we're definitely looking at a job for the team."

Kate ran her gaze over the rest of the body, what she could see of it. Half of the torso was still buried in mud. Now she was closer, she could see slimy scraps of cloth adhering to some of the bones. Was it a man or a woman? An adult at least, she thought, with an inner shiver of something like relief.

"Excuse me, please." They all turned at the sound of the voice. A burly middle-aged man stood behind them, white-suited.

Anderton raised his eyebrows as he rose to his feet. "And you are?"

"Ivor Gatkiss. Pathologist."

"Oh, right." Anderton made a sweeping gesture with his arm

towards the rest of his team. "All right, guys, move back. Let the doc get to work."

They reconvened by the entrance to the tent, nobody suggesting moving outside into the pouring rain. Kate could already see water beginning to trickle under the edges of the tent, running towards the slight hollow in which the skeleton rested. The techs would have to work fast to preserve the scene, she thought. A drop of water fell on the exposed skin on the back of her neck and made her shiver.

"Right," said Anderton. "Now, there's not a lot we can do with this one until we know a bit more about the body. There's no point going back and pulling MISPER records until we know when he or she died, who they might possibly be... you get my drift. Someone needs to stay to see if the techs can give us anything immediate to go on. You never know, there might be a wallet or a handbag buried underneath that lot." He gestured to the sea of mud that surrounded the bones. "Always think positively. So, who's going to stay?"

There was a moment's silence. Kate could feel her own reluctance echoed in both Rav and Olbeck's demeanour. The tent was cold and draughty and her feet were starting to become uncomfortably wet.

"I'll stay," Rav said, after the silence stretched on for an uncomfortable minute too long.

"Oh, no, don't worry. I'll do it," said Kate immediately. Rav still looked so frail she couldn't bear to think of him standing about in this miserable place.

"Well done, Kate," said Anderton, who had clearly been thinking along similar lines. Kate smiled a little, warmed by his approval.

"Thanks," Rav said gratefully. She said goodbye to the three of them and watched them leave. At least I'm in the dry, she told herself, trying to make the best of it. Another drip fell on the back of her neck and she shivered again.

The work inside the tent went on. Kate watched, shifting from numb foot to numb foot, wondering whether there was really any point her being there. She stared at the brown bones protruding from the earth, wondering who they belonged to. The jewellery suggested that the body was female, but not necessarily. How long had it been here? Could it conceivably be a natural death? But then, how had the body been buried? Kate mused, pacing up and down and stamping her feet.

After half an hour, she moved over to where Doctor Gatkiss was still examining the body.

"I don't believe we've met before," said Kate. She was tired of standing about silently.

Doctor Gatkiss looked up and just as quickly looked down again. "No, I don't think we have. I haven't been working at the labs that long." He had a quiet voice and a shy manner that Kate found rather endearing.

"Are you Andrew's replacement? Sorry, Doctor Stanton's replacement, I mean?"

Doctor Gatkiss nodded, with another quick look at her, before turning back to his work.

"How's he getting on?" Kate persisted. She knew Andrew had taken a bit of a career swerve, leaving the pathology labs for a stint on a team with Medicin Sans Frontieres, working in Sierra Leone to try and halt the current Ebola epidemic. Kate and Stanton's relationship was long since over but she couldn't help still worrying about him a little. Kate had finally – reluctantly – joined Facebook and occasionally saw a picture from Andrew's timeline; smiling children in African villages, happy faces under intensely blue skies, but nothing more than that.

"I – I think he's fine. I'm sorry, detective, would you mind – I just have to concentrate—"

"Of course. Sorry." Kate stepped back and let the doctor get back to work. She pushed her cold hands deeper into the pockets of her coat and felt a faint buzz under her fingertips. Her mobile phone, set to vibrate. Clearly it was Anderton or Olbeck wanting an update. She groped for her phone, grabbing it just as it fell silent. Kate pulled it from her pocket and looked at the screen to see who she'd missed.

Doctor Gatkiss concluded his examination and got to his feet, ineffectually trying to brush the mud from the knees of his protective suit. He turned to see Kate staring at her mobile phone screen as if turned to stone, finally frozen into immobility by the biting cold.

"Detective?" he asked tentatively. "Detective?"

Kate gave a start and snapped back to attention. She put the phone back in her pocket and turned her gaze on him, forcing a rictus smile. "I'm so sorry. You wanted me?"

She could see that Doctor Gatkiss had an inkling that her full attention was not immediately on him, but he obviously decided to speak anyway. "I've finished the preliminary examination. I'm afraid that I can't give you any firm indication on cause of death yet. I believe the body to be that of a young woman, possibly late teens, early twenties, but there will need to be a post mortem before I can give you any other information." Kate nodded, unsurprised. Doctor Gatkiss continued. "You may actually need the services of a specialist forensic anthropologist. These remains have been here for years. Most probably decades."

"Right," Kate said. The small part of her mind that was always focused on her work came to the fore, leaving the rest of her brain in utter turmoil. "Thanks very much. We'll speak later, I'm sure."

She watched the pathologist leave the tent, the movement of the entrance flap momentarily showing the driving rain that still continued to pour down outside. Kate stared blindly after him for a moment and then turned back. She conferred briefly with the senior investigating officer, Stephen Smithfield, going through the motions, working on autopilot. Then she left the tent herself, slogging back to her car through the mud and the rain, head down, almost oblivious to the discomfort.

Once she was in the driving seat, her wet coat flung into the back of the car, the engine running and the heater turned up to full, Kate drew her phone from her pocket again and stared at it. She hadn't been mistaken, then. She hadn't hallucinated it. *Mary Redman*, the screen said, showing the telephone number from which the call had been missed. Kate looked at her mother's name, the words blurring a little as her hand shook. She hadn't spoken to her mother in almost five years. She looked at the name a moment longer and then tossed the phone in the back seat, clamping her teeth together as she put the car in gear and prepared to drive away.

Chapter Two

INCREDIBLY, THE NEXT MORNING WAS a sunny one. The rainclouds temporarily vanished and the sky stretched across the horizon like a gauzy blue blanket, fuzzed here and there with wispy white clouds. Kate sat eating her breakfast in dancing sunbeams, occasionally deliberately moving her head forward so that the dazzle forced her to shut her eyes. She moved her face from side to side in the unexpected warmth, knowing that it wouldn't last.

Her mobile phone lay beside her plate. Every so often, she picked it up to look again at the list of missed calls. *Mary Redman.* Kate read the name and then placed the phone back down on the table with an exclamation of annoyance. What did it mean? Why was her estranged mother trying to call her?

Could it have been a mistake? Mary's phone tumbled about in the bottom of a handbag, unlocked, Kate's number accidentally pressed? It was that thought that stopped Kate doing the obvious thing and ringing her mother back – that and the realisation that she had absolutely no idea what she would say. What could you say to a mother who hadn't wanted to talk to you for half a decade? Put like that, Kate's mood dimmed further, despite the cheerful sunshine. She put the phone in her handbag and sat back down at the kitchen table, chewing her toast moodily.

The squeak and crash of the cat flap, recently installed in the back door, heralded the arrival of the newest occupant of Kate's household, padding over the kitchen tiles before appearing with a leap into Kate's lap. Merlin pushed his big black head up under Kate's chin insistently, until she gave in and began stroking him. Soon, he curled himself into a comma shape on Kate's lap, purring in satisfaction. He was so big that he drooped over each of her legs, but it didn't seem to bother him.

"Don't get comfortable," Kate warned him. "I've got to leave for work in five minutes." Merlin gave a lazy flick of the ear in response.

"You do realise you've become the biggest cliché in the book?" Kate's brother Jay had told her, a grin in his voice, when she'd told him she'd got a cat. They were talking on the phone at the time so Kate was forced to actually *tell* him she was giving him the finger in response, which somewhat robbed the gesture of its power.

For a moment, Kate thought of ringing Jay there and then, to see if he'd heard from their mother or if he knew why Mary Redman had inexplicably decided to ring her. But as she brought up his number, she reconsidered. He'd be on his way to work right now which meant he'd probably be underground, stuck on a tube train somewhere in West London, and out of mobile signal. And what if it *had* been a mistake on her mother's part? No, best to leave it.

Kate thought of her little brother as she started the car. Jay and his long-term girlfriend, Laura, had moved to London last summer, having both managed to obtain quite impressive jobs in media and in finance respectively. Kate was proud of Jay – she was proud of them both – but she missed them. Until last July, they'd only been a ten minute drive away. Now she didn't have any family left in Abbeyford at all. Inevitably, her thoughts snapped back to her mother's phone call. At the same time, she became aware that the sunshine had gone, the blue sky blotted out by ominous looking black clouds. As Kate drove within sight of Abbeyford Police Station, the first few drops of rain began to fall, spattering her windscreen.

Kate paused in the doorway to the office, as she tended to

these days. It was still something of a shock, but a pleasant one, to see Rav back at his desk. And of course there was the new DC, recently arrived from Cheltenham. Felicity Durrant. "Call me Fliss," was the first thing she'd said on arrival, with the kind of ringing self-confidence you'd expect to find in a baronet's daughter, not a recently qualified detective constable. Kate liked her – you couldn't help *liking* her – but found her rather annoying too. Keep a grip on it, Kate reminded herself. She knew she had a tendency to take against people far too quickly – look at how she'd first reacted to Stuart, for example, and now he was one of her closest friends. At least this time she was more aware of the fact, and was able to pull herself up on it, every time she felt as if she were falling into bad habits. She didn't think Fliss (stupid name!) had noticed. She wasn't the sensitive type.

"Morning, Kate," Fliss sing-songed across the desk as Kate sat down. "Shame about the sunshine. Still, it was nice while it lasted. I heard about the body at Munford Gorge, that's a bit of a turn-up for the books, isn't it? Jane said it was ancient. I suppose we'll hear about it from the boss today. Can I get you a coffee?"

Kate thought longingly of the days when Theo used to sit across from her and the only greeting she'd get first thing was a comment when she looked particularly haggard. She glanced across to where Theo sat now, three desks over. He and Rav were looking at something on Rav's phone, laughing. "That would be great, thanks, Fliss," she said, finally, trying to sound grateful.

She turned on her computer and began the process of easing into her working day, checking her emails, listening to her voicemails, riffling through the paperwork that needed her attention. Fliss's hand appeared in front of her suddenly, bearing a steaming cup of coffee and making Kate jump. "Here you go!"

"Thanks," Kate muttered. She took a sip, burning her lip, and put the cup down hurriedly. Behind her she heard the office door crash back against the wall and realised Anderton, her boss, had made his characteristic entrance.

"Morning, team. I hope you're feeling mean and keen and ready to get on with some work?"

"I'm definitely feeling mean," said Kate, turning around.

Anderton grinned at her. "Glad to hear it, Kate. Hope you didn't catch cold from your vigil yesterday."

"I'll survive—" Kate began and was surprised by an enormous sneeze.

Anderton raised his eyebrows. "Oh, dear. Get yourself a hot drink." He glanced at the steaming mug beside her and added "Oh, you have. Well, never mind."

By this time, everyone had turned from their phones, computers and newspapers and were facing their boss, who began his usual pacing up and down the room as he began to recap what they knew.

"Now, unusually," Anderton began, "we don't actually have a starting point for this investigation yet. Without knowing the age, sex or ethnicity of the victim, we're a bit stymied on moving forward." He looked hopefully at Kate. "Anything you can enlighten us on, Kate?"

Kate sneezed again. "Sorry. Yes, there is some preliminary data. The doctor thought the victim was female and young, late teens or early twenties. That was about all he was able to tell me."

"No idea how long she'd been in the ground?"

Kate shook her head. "He didn't say. I guess we'll know more after the PM."

Anderton nodded. "Indeed. That's taking place tomorrow. Kate, could you be our representative?"

Kate groaned. "Why is it always *me* who has to do the PMs?"

"Because you love them," Anderton said, grinning.

"That's totally untrue. You make me sound like a complete ghoul."

Fliss looked back and forth between Kate and Anderton, as if she couldn't quite believe her ears. She was still treating the DCI with the hushed reverence of a lowly cleric for the head bishop, or perhaps the Pope. Kate smiled inwardly.

Anderton rubbed his chin. "All right, you're off post mortem duty. Theo, you do it."

"Oh, *cheers*," Theo said.

"It's all right," Rav said. "I'll do it. I need to get back into the swing of things."

"Good lad," Anderton said. "All right. We'll see what the PM throws up, if anything. We might need a specialist, a forensic anthropologist or something similar. Felicity, that's a job for you. Could you do some research and get me a few names? The path labs will be able to advise." Fliss virtually stood to attention, which made Kate smile again. "Kate, it might be worth you going through the MISPER files for young women who've been reported missing."

"No problem," Kate said. "But do we know the date range? I mean, how far back do you want me to go?"

Anderton shrugged. "Your guess is as good as mine. Why not start with this year, and work backwards as far as you can by the end of the day? Tomorrow we might have a better idea of when our victim was actually killed."

"If she *was* killed," said Olbeck.

"True. But natural deaths don't tend to end up with the bodies being buried in out of the way beauty spots. She didn't dig herself into the ground."

Kate watched Anderton as he paced up and down. She tested herself for romantic feelings towards him and was pleased to find that they'd reduced to a mere glimmer. Was she finally free of her attraction to him? Was she *finally* free? She took a deep, relieved breath. One less complication in her life, at least. Now she could reap the benefits of finally controlling her feelings. It had been hard – so hard – to suppress what she felt for Anderton, but she'd fought it every step of the way and now it seemed it had been a battle worth winning.

She returned to her desk as the briefing broke up. The sight of her handbag on the floor by her chair recalled the missed telephone call from her mother and her high spirits suddenly fell. Why had her mother called her? She scrolled through until she found the missed number. I'll call her later, she thought, putting off the evil deed, wondering whether she'd actually go through with it.

She began working through the reports of missing young women. It was a quicker task than she'd anticipated. This year, in Abbeyford and its surrounding districts, only five young women had been reporting missing. Two were assumed to be runaways from a local care home. The other three seemed equally straightforward – one was a young woman with a history of mental health problems, last seen in the vicinity of the Severn Bridge, a notorious suicide spot. Kate sighed. The other two young women who'd been reported missing had both been found safe and well. She finished reading and shuffled the papers into a neat pile. It didn't seem likely that the body would belong to someone who'd only gone missing in the last year. Surely the bones would have had to have been buried for much longer? How long did it actually take for a body to become a skeleton? Kate tapped her pencil on her chin and thought for a moment, reaching for her desk phone a moment later.

"Hi, Steven. It's Kate Redman. Could I ask you a quick question?"

One blessing, when it came to the senior investigating officer of the local SOCO team, thought Kate, was that he was never fazed by any question to do with forensics. Steven Smithfield simply assumed that you felt the same keen, some might say slightly worryingly, obsessive interest that he had for his subject.

"It varies completely," was his answer to Kate's question. "Dependent on a multitude of factors. How wet the ground was, whether there was any insect activity, you could have saponification, adverse weather conditions, all sorts of things might affect the rate of decay."

"Fine, fine," said Kate, rolling her eyes. "But could you give me a ballpark figure? I mean, are we talking weeks? Months? Or would it take years?"

"Totally depends on the conditions," said Steven. "Could be three months, could be three years. I couldn't say."

How helpful. Kate sighed and was about to terminate the call when Steven spoke up. "Is this about that body we found at Munford Gorge?"

No, I routinely ring up to ask about the skeletonisation of a human body, Steven. Just for kicks. Kate thought it but didn't say it. She answered his question in the affirmative.

"Well, if it's *that* one we're talking about, we're definitely looking at years. What did I say earlier? Three years? I'd take that as a starting point. Three years or older."

Kate clenched a fist in triumph but kept her voice level. "That's great, Steven, thanks. Really helpful."

"You're welcome."

Three years or older. Well, that was a start. Kate fired up the database again and began to check reports from three years ago. Perhaps she ought to do two years ago, just in case she missed something important. She went and got herself another coffee and sat down to her desk again, feeling re-energised. Absorbed in her work, her mother's missed phone call went totally out of her head.

Chapter Three

"WHO'S THAT FROM?"

Kate looked up at the sound of Theo's voice. "What's that?"

Theo pulled Fliss's empty chair out from under her desk and sat down opposite Kate. "Your card. Who's it from?"

Kate's glance fell to the flowery card in her hand. She smiled. "It's from Rosa. Remember her?" Theo looked blank. "From last year. You know, the drugs case?"

"Oh, yeah. She's writing to you?"

"We write to each other, occasionally. I just like to – to keep her spirits up."

Theo looked unconvinced. "Oh, yeah?"

Kate looked down at the card and the hesitant writing inside of it. "She's doing okay. In an open prison now and she's gone through rehab. Hopefully she'll make it, once she gets out."

"Yeah," said Theo once more, with finality. He was clearly sorry he'd asked. "Anyway, what's happening today?"

"Rav's at the PM so hopefully he'll come back with a bit more info. I'm still going through the missing persons reports. Not sure it's really worth my while until we get an actual date of death."

"True." Theo yawned. "Why do I get the feeling that this is going to be one of *those* cases?"

"What do you mean?" asked Fliss, who'd just returned to her desk with a steaming mug in her hand. Courteously, Theo stood up to let her sit down.

"Oh, you know. One of those cases that drags on and on and *on* and we never find out who did it or even who the vic was."

Kate spluttered. "We've never even had *one* case like that here, Theo. What are you talking about?"

"There's always a first time," Theo said darkly.

Felicity was looking puzzled. "Didn't you have an unidentified body last year?"

Kate nodded. "Yes, the body we found in a derelict cottage. Badly decomposed – we had to go on dental records and DNA. But we found him all right. John Henry Miller. We had to do some digging to identify him but we *did* identify him. Just as we're going to do on this case." She shot Theo a glance, daring him to disagree, but he was already making his way back to his desk, his back turned. Felicity nodded, a serious look on her face, before she turned her attention to her own computer screen.

Gradually, quiet settled over the room as they all began to work, the silence punctuated at intervals by ringing telephones, the buzz and whirr of the coffee machine and the click and squeak of the office door as people came and went. Kate finished checking her emails and looked over at Theo.

"By the way, are you taking anyone to Mark's wedding?"

"Huh?" Theo asked absently, intent on his work.

"Are you taking anyone to Mark's wedding?"

Theo looked up. He smiled. "Oh, that. Well, I've narrowed it down to a choice of three. Still deciding."

Kate snorted. She might have known. "Right you are."

"Why?" asked Theo, still grinning. "Want me to be your date?"

Kate flicked a rubber band at him. "No. I just wondered if I was going to be the only one going on my own."

"I'll be your plus one if you like," said Fliss, with rather too much enthusiasm for Kate's liking. "We could make a girls night of it!"

Kate forced a smile. "That's something to bear in mind. Thanks, Fliss."

"It's *no* problem."

Oh, God. Kate slumped over her keyboard, moodily clicking the mouse. She found Fliss particularly irritating this morning. Her innate sense of fair play meant she was also irritated with herself because she was being rather unfair. Fliss wasn't doing anything wrong. She couldn't help being so damn annoying.

Kate got up and made herself another coffee. Glancing at the clock on the wall by the water heater, she realised that the post mortem on the remains would now be underway. Despite her protests to Anderton yesterday, she thought then that she would rather have attended. At least then she'd know more before anyone else and perhaps have some idea as to how they could progress the case further. Theo's doom-laden sentiments reoccurred to her. *One of those cases...* Kate dismissed such gloomy thoughts. They had the sex, the rough age, presumably a full set of teeth with which to compare dental records. There was that necklace that Anderton had noticed. Other identifying objects may have been buried with the body, not to mention the possibility of clothes and shoes. They had plenty to be going on with, Kate told herself as she sat back down. Plenty. She kept glancing at the clock, despite those sentiments, wondering when Rav would be back.

As it turned out, it was past lunchtime when Rav finally returned from the post mortem. Anderton joined the rest of the team in the office while Rav gave them a rundown of what the pathologist had told him. "There's no discernible cause of death, apparently. No obvious knife damage to the bones, nothing left behind that could have been a weapon."

Anderton paced his usual pathway from the whiteboards to the nearest desk and back. "That's not surprising. Anything else?"

Rav flipped the pages of his notebook over and scanned his writing. "Strangulation is a possibility but again, only a possibility. The bones had been tumbled about in the landslide so damage to the hyoid bone could have been caused by that, rather than by human activity."

Anderton nodded. "Again, not a surprise. Any form of identification found?"

"There were some scraps of clothing but most of it had rotted away. We might be able to trace the manufacturers of the underwear. That was synthetic and seems to have stood up to the elements a bit better than her outer clothing. There'll be photos in the main report."

Kate raised a hand. "What about the necklace, Rav?"

Rav smiled. "Now that is the one bit of good news. I took a copy of the photo of the necklace. Here you go—"

He handed it to Kate first who took a good look. Cleaned of the clotting mud, she could clearly see the metal lettering that formed part of the gold chain. "Jonie?," she murmured, almost to herself, reading it.

There was a subdued buzz of excitement. People crowded around the photograph, looking at the necklace which spelt out a girl's name.

"Now *that* is a big step forward," Anderton said. "Possibly. Of course, we're jumping to conclusions that 'Jonie' is the name of the victim. Most people who buy a necklace that spells out a name buy one that spells out their own name, don't they? But not necessarily. It might be the name of our victim's mother, or daughter, or friend."

"Or lover," Olbeck said.

Anderton acknowledged the suggestion with a wave of his hand. "Indeed. Anyway, it's something to go on. We need to try and trace the manufacturer. Fingers crossed it was a bespoke necklace. That really *would* be a stroke of luck..." He trailed off, rubbing his chin. "Rav, what about the age of the bones? That's going to be crucial."

Rav looked a little uncomfortable. "Sorry, guv, they couldn't tell. Doctor Gatkiss said it was a job for a specialist. They're going to send them off to the Centre for Human Anatomy and Human Identification. You know, CAHID, up in Dundee."

"When will they have the results?"

"Not sure. Within the week, I think he said."

"Fine. Keep on at them. Without a definite date, it's going to be ten times harder to ascertain identity." Anderton stopped pacing. "Right, we've got a bit more to go on. Kate, can you narrow down your database searches for anyone with the name 'Jonie' or variations thereof. Different spellings, you know the sort of thing. Abbreviations. Try 'Joan' as well."

"Of course," Kate said.

"Fliss, can you start digging into possible manufacturers for that type of necklace? Anything you can pull up on possible designers, sellers, anything really."

"Yes, sir." Fliss sat up so straight she almost vibrated. Kate hid a grin.

"Rav, keep me posted on updates from the path labs, will you? Chase them if they start slacking off. Mark, have you got five minutes for a quick chat?" Olbeck nodded. "Great, let's wrap it up for now."

The office door crashed shut behind Anderton and Olbeck as they left the room. Kate turned back to her desk and then noticed that Theo, Fliss and Jane were still poring over the picture of the necklace. She went over and joined them.

"People don't wear this kind of stuff now, do they?" Theo mused. As one, they all looked at Fliss as the youngest member of the group.

"Well, *I* wouldn't wear it," she said brightly.

"But would your friends?" asked Kate. "I mean, it's not fashionable to wear name necklaces now, is it?" She was suddenly acutely aware that she sounded middle-aged and out of touch. "It's not, is it?"

Jane was shaking her head. "I used to have one, back in the nineties. It was around the time of *Sex in the City*, remember? Carrie Bradshaw used to wear one."

"Who?" asked Theo. The two older women exchanged amused glances.

"Never mind," said Kate. She looked again at the photograph. "Were necklaces like that around before the nineties?"

Nobody knew. There was a moment's silence and then Theo handed the picture to Fliss. "Here you go."

They drifted back to their respective desks. Kate fired up the database that she'd been searching before and began typing in 'Jonie' with renewed enthusiasm. Theo's previously Cassandra-like proclamations began to fade away in her memory. Perhaps this would be an easy case after all.

Chapter Four

KATE OPENED HER FRONT DOOR that evening to Merlin's frantic mews. He immediately began curling himself around her ankles like black smoke. He was clearly, in his own mind, in imminent danger of starving to death.

"Oh, calm down," said Kate, bending down to stroke him. "Stop panicking."

How nice it was to have someone to greet you when you got home, she thought as she opened a tin of cat food. Even if that someone had four legs and a tail. *I should have got a pet years ago.* Perhaps they should be standard issue for all new police officers – especially single ones.

She put a frozen pizza in the oven to cook, showered, changed into her pyjamas and settled onto the sofa with a newly satiated Merlin curled up on her lap. Kate was tired but not tired enough to go to bed yet. She thought about ringing Jay and then about ringing Hannah, her best friend, and dismissed both ideas – too late. She'd try them tomorrow. The sight of her mobile phone on the coffee table brought her mother's missed call to her mind and as she picked up the phone she realised she'd missed another call. This time, she didn't recognise the number. Could it be her mother again, calling from another line? Did she think that Kate was screening her calls? Kate hesitated, her finger on the redial button. It was probably nothing to do with her mother. A wrong number, perhaps. Kate heard the beep of the oven timer go and got up, carefully dislodging Merlin. Oh well, she wouldn't be calling anyone back tonight, it was almost eleven o'clock. Far too late for making phone calls.

Perhaps it was the pizza, eaten too hastily, or perhaps the puzzle of the mystery mobile number, but whatever it was, Kate slept badly. She woke to the blare of her alarm clock with a curse and stumbled into the bathroom. She was due to pick up Rav on her way to work – he was still not able to drive himself – and she knew she'd be late. She sent a quick and apologetic text before hurrying to get ready.

When she drew up outside of Rav's flat, he was waiting on the pavement, an umbrella over his head to fend off the inevitable raindrops.

"You idiot, why didn't you wait inside?" Kate asked as she opened the passenger door for him.

"Oh, it's all right. I get fed up being indoors, to be honest. I was stuck in there for so long without being able to get out." Rav settled himself carefully into the seat and winced minutely as he reached for the seat belt.

"You okay?" Kate asked anxiously.

"I'm fine," Rav said impatiently. Kate was reminded of her own recovery from an injury, years ago now, and how irritating she used to find everyone's concern.

"Sorry," she said. They drove in silence for a few moments.

"I've got physio later," Rav said after a minute or two. "You remember the physiotherapist? Gill Becker?"

Kate grimaced. "The memories are burned on my brain."

Rav grinned. "She said to say hello, last time I saw her."

"Hmmm." Kate drew up to a T-junction and waited for a gap in the traffic. Rav's mention of his physio session had reminded her that she had her own appointment to go to that week. She had her monthly session with Magda booked in for Friday evening and hoped that work would allow her to attend it. She'd missed a few sessions lately, and Magda had told her that kind of thing wouldn't help her therapy. Apparently the sessions were very carefully structured.

Once they got to the office, Kate familiarised herself with the reports she'd printed out yesterday. She'd gone through the entire list of missing females from the last twenty years, checking for the name 'Jonie' or variations of the same, looking at the names, the ages and the gender. So far, she'd not come across one exact match – there wasn't anyone called Jonie reported missing in the area from the past two decades. Kate shuffled the papers into a neater pile, thinking. What if the body had been brought from another county? Another country, even? Thinking of it like that, it did seem like a rather hopeless task. Kate mentally squared her shoulders and bent to her keyboard again.

She heard the muffled buzzing of her phone in her bag and groped for it, reaching it just as the ringing stopped. She looked at the call display – again, it was an unfamiliar number. As Kate frowned, thinking, the little icon that denoted a voicemail waiting popped up on the screen. She dialled in to her mailbox and listened. A man's voice, unfamiliar to her. "Hi, Ms. Redman, this is Tin Johnson. You won't know me but I'm a freelance journalist and I'm working on a story that I think you might be able to help me with. I'm also calling on behalf of your mother, Mrs Mary Redman. It's probably easiest to talk about this face to face, or at least on the phone, so do you think you could give me a call back when convenient? Thanks very much." His voice went on to leave a mobile number, repeated twice. Then he said, "Thanks again, goodbye," and there was the click as he disconnected the call.

Kate blinked. She listened to the call again. What the *hell*? She listened to the call once more, from the beginning. There were so many questions she wasn't sure which one was most pertinent. Who was this Tin – *Tin*? Surely she'd misheard, it must have been Tim – Johnson. A journalist? What story? And what the hell was he doing calling on behalf of her *mother*? Kate slowly put her phone down on her desk, staring at it, unseeing, while a thousand different thoughts flew round her head. She thought of the other men her mother had been involved with. Was that what Tim Johnson had meant? He was in a relationship with her mother? What the hell...

Kate slowly became aware that someone was speaking to her. She looked up with a start to see Fliss standing by her desk, patiently repeating herself for what was possibly the fifth time.

"What's that?"

"Do you want another cup of tea?" Fliss asked.

"Um. No." Kate got up and grabbed her phone off the desk. "Thank you," she added, belatedly.

She walked back through the station, out through the main reception and onto the steps outside the main entrance. For once it wasn't raining, although the sky sagged with heavy grey clouds. Kate stood for a moment, irresolute, and then walked quickly down the steps, following the road until she came to the little park five minutes away. She passed through the gateway and kept going until she found a bench towards the middle of the park. The traffic noise was muted there and there was no one else around, no one in the park at all, in fact. The bench was soaking wet, bejewelled with fat beads of water. Kate propped herself against the damp bark of a beech tree and took a deep breath. She dialled the number Tim – was it Tim? – Johnson had left her.

He answered almost immediately.

"Ms Redman? Hi, thanks for calling back."

"No problem," said Kate automatically. "I'm a bit – I don't really know how I can help you."

"Yes, I know my message was a bit mysterious," Tim Johnson said cheerily. He had a nice voice, warm and friendly, and cultured without being what Kate, despite herself, would have called 'posh'. "It's probably easiest if we do meet face to face but I'll fill you in as best I can."

"You were calling about my mother—" Kate began.

"Yes, I understand that you haven't had much contact with Mary over the past few years." He managed to sound sympathetic without sounding patronising, quite a difficult feat. "It's not my business to go into why that is but all I can say to start with is that she would like to see you. I think – did she try and call you?"

"Yes," said Kate. "But I missed the call. I wasn't sure – I wasn't sure whether it was a mistake or not." Why was she telling this complete stranger this? She closed her mouth over the rest of the words that she wanted to say.

"Yes, I can see that. I've been – Mary and I have been collaborating on a feature I'm working on, about the Marhaven care home, the unmarried mothers' home? You know, in Bristol?"

"Sorry," said Kate, at a total loss. "I'm not sure what you mean—"

"Never mind, I can understand you're not familiar with it. Listen, could we actually meet up? It would be much easier to talk in person, explain everything if you see what I mean."

"Okay," said Kate rather feebly. She felt dizzy. It was easiest just to agree.

"Oh, great. How about tomorrow night? Would that suit you?"

"Um. Yes."

"Great. How about we meet at The Black Cat? You know it? It's on the high street, a nice quiet bar so we can talk and it does good food. How about eight o'clock?"

"Okay," said Kate. She had a feeling she should be saying something else but couldn't think what.

"Great. I'll look forward to it. You've got my number so if anything comes up just send me a text and we can rearrange, okay?"

"Great," said Kate in a whisper. Tim Johnson said a cheery goodbye and the line cut off.

Kate pulled the phone away from her head and stared at it blankly. What on Earth had she just got herself into? Who was this Tim Johnson anyway? What feature? What did it have to do with her mother? Kate pressed her clenched fist against her forehead. This was all she needed. Why the bloody hell had she called him back? What was this all *about*?

She made a mammoth effort and brought her fizzing head under control. A few deep breaths, that was the thing... There was no point stressing over what on Earth this was all about when she would find out tomorrow anyway. She was meeting him in a public place, so she wasn't so worried about her personal safety. She might do a quick search on his name when she got back to the station - just to be on the safe side. Should she ring her mother and find out more? No, Kate told herself decisively. *You'll find out tomorrow. Wait until then and then you can decide what to do.*

She turned slowly and made her way to the exit. It had begun to rain again, lightly and then with increasing force, the drops pattering down, adding to the already large puddles. Kate hunched her shoulders against the rain, almost oblivious. Despite her best intentions, she was still thinking about the phone call.

Chapter Five

KATE HAD NEVER BEEN TO The Black Cat before. She didn't really go to bars, not being much of a drinker. Slanting her umbrella back so she could check she was at the right place, she caught sight of the sign; the lettering in a vintage-type font, the black cat of the name painted in a stylised manner, its long tail curving to underline the words. Momentarily, the cat reminded her of Merlin. The Black Cat was a small place, situated in one of the older buildings on the high street. Black-framed, many-paned windows shone with a warm golden light, and inside Kate could see a variety of comfortable looking sofas as well as a small restaurant section. What did this Tim Johnson look like? Kate put down her umbrella and stepped into the foyer of the building, furling the dripping umbrella and shaking out her hair. She'd come straight from work and was dressed in her usual black suit. She was glad, as it felt like armour.

The bar wasn't busy. Kate swept her gaze over the room. There were a few small groups of people, several couples and a few men on their own, reading newspapers or peering at their phones. Kate wondered which one was Tim Johnson. I should have asked him to wear a red carnation, she thought and, despite the tension, grinned to herself.

A tall man with a rugby player's build turned and caught Kate's eye. He raised his eyebrows in a questioning kind of way and came towards her.

"Kate?"

"Yes," said Kate confusedly. She hadn't expected him to be black. Why not, Kate, she asked herself. A secondary thought came that she also hadn't expected him to be quite so good looking. She took a grip on herself. "Hi. Is it Tim?"

"Tin, actually. It really is Tin." He smiled as she stuttered out an apology. "Don't worry, everyone gets it wrong. Seriously, everyone. It's short for Tindebaye, so you can see why I use an abbreviation."

They made their way to the bar and Tin turned to her to ask what she wanted to drink. He asked for her lemonade without comment and ordered a glass of red wine for himself. Kate waited with him, feeling pleasantly dwarfed. She liked tall men. *Get a grip, she ordered herself. Don't forget what you're here for.*

"'Tindebaye'?" Kate asked as they seated themselves near the fireplace. It was a real fire, another point in this bar's favour. Kate thought she might come here again, it was so nice.

"My mum wanted me to have an African name. I like it, actually, I just got tired of having to spell it out all the time." Tin took a sip of his drink and then sat forward. "Thanks so much for coming to meet me. It must have been a bit confusing for you."

"Well, you could say that."

Tin nodded, looking serious. "As I said, I'm a journalist. Freelance, now. I've worked for some of the nationals but I also do quite a lot for the local papers in the South West." He reached into the back pocket of his jeans and extracted a card which he held out to Kate. "Those are my other contact details and some links to my articles, if you want some more reassurance."

Kate took the card and turned it over in her fingers. There was a QL code on the back and a list of email and social media addresses. She didn't mention that she'd already searched for his name on both the public search engines and various police databases and found nothing alarming. "I'm sure I'd be satisfied with your *bona fides* but..."

"'But what's it got to do with you?'" Tin smiled again. He had the kind of smile that lit up his face. Kate found herself smiling back, unselfconsciously. "Good question. I take it from our phone call earlier that you haven't heard about the Marhaven care home? No?" Kate shook her head. "No, well, most people haven't. Anyway, it's due to be demolished in a couple of weeks, and I pitched the idea for a feature about its history to the editor at the Western Telegraph. She liked it so I started chasing up some details." He paused and gestured to Kate's empty glass, which she had emptied in nervous gulps. "Can I get you another one of those?"

"My round," said Kate. She went and fetched them both another drink and sat back down again.

"So anyway, the Marhaven home has quite a history. It was originally built as a school back in Edwardian times, but in the seventies it was a care home for teenage girls, girls who were what they used to call 'unmarried mothers'. Not just pregnant teenagers, actually, some other girls who were in care, orphans, foster children, that sort of thing."

"Right," Kate said, feeling that she should be making some sort of contribution.

"I put an ad out asking anyone who'd been at the home or who knew anything about it to get in touch and that's when your mum contacted me."

"My mum?" Kate said, blankly. "What's it got to do with her?"

Tin gave her a strange look, half disbelieving, half sympathetic. "Well, she was there, of course. In the home. When she was a teenager. Did she never tell you about it?"

Kate dropped her gaze to the shimmering surface of her glass of lemonade. Her face felt hot. No, her mother had never mentioned anything to her about being in a care home. Being in a care home as a teenager, no less. Kate sifted back through her memories, to her childhood; there had been her older siblings – half siblings – Terry and Amanda, but they'd been removed into care themselves before Kate was born. After that, their contact with Mary had been sporadic and Kate had grown up never really knowing her older brother and sister. Terry had been killed in a motorbike accident at eighteen, and Amanda – Manda, they always called her – had long since moved away. She lived up north now, Kate recalled, and was married with several children. Kate hadn't seen or heard from her in years.

She came back to reality with a start, realising she'd been silent for a good few minutes. Tin was looking at her with a sympathetic look on his face.

"Sorry," said Kate. "You've probably already guessed that my family and I aren't that close. Well, I mean, I'm not that close with some members of it." She thought of Jay, and Courtney and Jade, with affection. "If you've been in contact with my mum, no doubt she's given you her side of the story."

Tin was twirling his half empty glass between his fingers, the liquid within rocking gently up the curved sides of the bowl. "You might be surprised," he said. "But we can talk about that later."

Kate looked at him, curious. "What's she been saying about me?" Then she realised she didn't really want this handsome man to have to repeat what was bound to have been unflattering. "Never mind. I'd rather not know." She took another sip of her drink. "So is there a story around the care home or are you doing a historical piece? Or something else?"

Tin's cheerful face suddenly looked a little grimmer. "Something else, all right." He put his glass down. "I don't know if you've been following the news lately?"

"When I can."

"You probably know that the digging up of historic abuse cases is the hot topic in journalism right now." Tim paused for a moment and half smiled. "Hot topic or hot potato, I'm not sure which. Anyway, in the light of stuff like Operation Yewtree, Rotherham, etcetera, there's been quite a lot of interest from editors in chasing up stories that might be along a similar line."

Kate was conscious of a slow, sinking feeling. "You're telling me the Marhaven care home was – that there was abuse going on there?"

Tin shrugged. "That, Kate, is the story. Was there? Or wasn't there? There's nothing but rumours and innuendo. Nothing but gossip. The few people I've tried to talk to about it insist they don't know anything – either that or there's nothing there to know. Every time I think I'm getting somewhere I keep coming up against a dead end."

"Okay," Kate said slowly. "So why bother pursuing it?"

Tin sat forward. "*Because* I keep coming up against a dead end. I don't know, call it a hunch, call it intuition, call it sheer bloody-mindedness, but I think there's something there. No one will talk to me, I can't seem to get any further forward, but – I don't know – I don't want to give up just yet."

Kate was thinking. "I thought you said that no one was talking to you. What about my mother?"

"She's talking to me," said Tin.

"Why?" demanded Kate. "What's so different about her? Why is she talking and yet nobody else is?"

Tin sat back again, looking slightly uncomfortable. "Well – special circumstances. It's a bit difficult – I mean, perhaps you should hear it from her."

"Hear what?" asked Kate.

Tin's gaze moved from her face to glance up, over her shoulder. "Perfect timing. You can ask her yourself."

Kate froze. Behind her, over the subdued hubbub of the bar, she could hear the squeak of the main door as it opened and a waft of cold night air as it shut. There were hesitant footsteps behind her that faltered to a stop. Kate hadn't yet looked around.

"Hi, Mary," said Tin, slightly too heartily. "Come and sit down."

Kate remained seated and facing forward. She felt as if she'd frozen in that position, doomed to remain there forever. There was a rustle of clothing and a harsh cough and then Mary Redman sat down at the table, next to Tin and opposite Kate.

Kate looked up and received her second major shock of the evening. What had happened to her mother? Mary Redman was desperately thin, almost skeletal, just a jumble of skin-wrapped bones in her winter coat. There was a bright blue scarf wrapped around her throat and the colour seemed to do something dreadful to the skin of her face, draining it of colour, casting grey shadows underneath her eyes. Kate hadn't seen her mother for almost five years but surely that length of time was not enough to lay such waste to her physically? Kate swallowed hard, knowing that the first flinch when she'd seen her mother had been obvious to both Mary and to Tin.

The silence stretched on. Eventually Mary coughed again, covering her mouth with bony fingers, and then smiled tremulously.

"Sight for sore eyes, aren't I?"

Kate was still staring. From somewhere deep within, she managed to get a grip on herself and pulled her horrified gaze from Mary's ravaged face. "Hi, Mum," was all she could manage to say, and that in a feeble whisper.

"I'm going to get another drink," Tin said tactfully and stood up. "I'll be up at the bar so you two can have a few moments. Mary, your usual?"

"Yeah, thanks, love." Mary's voice had a new hoarseness to it that Kate didn't remember from before.

Once Tin had walked away, the silence between the two women grew again. Kate, morbidly fascinated, couldn't stop herself from staring at Mary. Five years with not a hint of contact from her mother, not a call or a letter or a text, nothing...and then this shock meeting. Kate's thoughts flew to Magda and for a moment she wondered wildly about getting an emergency appointment, before bringing herself back to reality.

"Hello, Kelly," said Mary, eventually. She held her handbag on her lap like a shield, and her thin fingers fumbled inside it for what Kate guessed was a pack of cigarettes.

"You know you can't smoke in here," she said. Her voice sounded angry, more hostile than she intended and she saw Mary flinch.

"I've given up," said her mother.

Kate's eyes bulged. "You've *what*? Since when?"

Mary looked away. "Few months now."

Kate sat back in her seat, a little winded. Her mother had smoked like a chimney since before Kate was born. Seeing Mary Redman without a cigarette in hand was incongruous, as if she were half-dressed or something equally ridiculous.

"Well, congratulations," said Kate and cringed inwardly at the jeer she could hear in her voice. What was wrong with her? Everything was coming out wrong.

Tin's hand appeared before Mary, holding a glass with what looked like a triple whisky.

"Here you go, Mary." Mary took it from him, looking up at him with a shaky smile. "What about you, Kate? Another lemonade?"

"No, I'd like a gin," said Kate, surprising herself. "A large gin with very little tonic. Please."

"Okay. Coming right up."

In any other situation, Kate would have felt a bit embarrassed about demanding an expensive drink just like that from a comparative stranger. As of now, though, she didn't care. Underneath the shock, she was beginning to feel the first stirrings of anger towards Tin Johnson and his surprises. She shoved those feelings back down and faced the more immediate emotions that facing her mother across the table engendered.

"So, how are you, Kelly?" asked Mary.

"It's Kate," Kate said automatically.

Mary dropped her gaze and said, "Oh yes, sorry. I keep forgetting."

Kate's eyes narrowed. Her mother had never accepted her name change, way back in her teens, and had continued to call her Kelly whenever she could. Why had that changed? Briefly Kate thought back to being Kelly Redman. How long ago it seemed now. Why, she was a totally different person.

Tin came back to the table with Kate's drink, a tall glass packed with ice, tonic and a throat-flaming amount of gin. Kate took a deep swallow, fought not to do the 'drinking spirits face' that she always did, and put the glass back down on the table with something that was almost a bang. She could feel the gin making its way to her stomach in a long, burning trail.

"What's going on?" she asked, emboldened.

"What d'you mean?"

"Oh, come on, Mum." The word was out again and the two of them waited to see how the other would react.

Mary coughed again, harshly, the spasms shaking her thin body. After a few minutes, she sat back, wheezing and looked at Kate through watering eyes. "Nothing's going on. I don't know what you mean."

"What are you doing here?" Kate had to fight quite hard against the unexpected pity that was welling up inside her. Her mother looked so frail and vulnerable. She looked so *old*. Her hair was an unnatural coppery colour and hung in harsh strands around her thin face. It didn't look like her real hair. In fact, nothing about this woman looked like the mother Kate remembered at all. She had to stamp down on a sudden sense of paranoia that in fact this wasn't Mary Redman, that the woman was an imposter brought here to meet her for unknown purposes. Kate told herself not to be so ridiculous and took another large swallow of gin.

"I wanted to see you. I tried to call you but you didn't call me back..." Her mother was fighting back another cough. Kate waited impatiently for the coughing fit to end, but once her mother could draw breath again, it seemed as though she had run out of things to say.

"I saw your number. I didn't call you back because—" It was Kate's turn to pause. Why hadn't she rung back? "I didn't know whether you'd meant to do it or not. It's not like I'd heard from you lately. For Christ's sake, Mum, you're the one who told me to get lost, remember?" Kate was crouched forward now, talking in a furious, hissing whisper. "You told *me* to fuck off, remember? Slipped your mind, had it?"

Mary, who had normally been so quick to anger, now seemed to shrink beneath Kate's angry onslaught. She was shaking her head. "I was wrong to say that. Don't you think I don't know that, Kelly? All these years I wanted to see you, I wanted to say sorry, but I don't know – I just couldn't make that first step." Her voice was shaking now, the hoarseness gathering. Kate could see her fighting off another cough. "I just wanted to see you to say sorry."

"Fine," said Kate, some small mean part of her unable to forgive that quickly. "So why now? What's changed?"

Mary coughed, brought her thin, shaking hands to her mouth, coughed again. Kate could see her forcing herself to breathe normally by sheer effort of will. Mary looked up at her with streaming eyes. "I wanted to see you before it was too late."

Kate felt her heart beat suddenly, beat in thuds that she could feel throughout her ribcage. "What do you mean, before it's too late?" she asked, through numb lips.

"I mean I'm dying," said Mary Redman. "And I wanted to see you, to say sorry, before it was too late."

Chapter Six

"You all right?"

Kate looked up at the sound of Olbeck's voice. "What's that?"

Olbeck sat down on the corner of her desk. "Are you all right?" he repeated in the loud, slow voice of someone talking to an idiot.

Kate pulled herself together. "I'm fine," she said impatiently. She wasn't, of course; she was a long way from being *fine*, but there was no way she was going to discuss everything with Olbeck in the middle of a busy office. "Just thinking about things."

"God help us," said Olbeck, getting up. "You don't want to start *thinking*. Where would we be then?"

He winked at her and moved away, towards his office. Kate forced a smile and then turned back to her computer. Immediately, her thoughts reverted to her mother and the conversation they'd had in The Black Cat last night. Conversation was a misnomer. Kate had sat in frozen, silent horror whilst her mother had falteringly described her diagnosis, the treatment, the treatment she'd had after the first treatment had failed, the consultant's gentle but relentless prognosis – *he said six months, maybe longer if the chemo keeps working* – the pain, the sickness, the increasing frailty, the breathlessness, the fear...

Eventually, when Kate could bear it no longer, she managed to say "Okay, Mum, please stop. Please just let me—" and then her voice had failed her and she clamped her lips together, blinking hard. Taking in deep breaths, determined not to break down.

"I know it's a lot to take in," Mary had said, in her new, humble voice, and that had almost pushed her over the edge.

Tin had clearly noticed the jagged emotional tension emanating from their table and after a few minutes, he'd walked back to them, looking anxiously from one face to another.

"Everything all right?" he'd asked, tentatively.

Kate had welcomed the enormous surge of anger she'd then felt. Displacement, she knew that, but it had meant she didn't dissolve into a sobbing heap in public. She'd shot him a glance of fury that had made him step back a little and then turned to her mother who was sitting, still clasping her handbag as if its gaudy leather would protect her from anything that might assail her.

"Mum, I have to go now," Kate had managed to say, as gently as she could. "I'm not running away—" A lie and they both knew it. "I just need a bit of time... I'll call you tomorrow or in a couple of days. That's a promise. Or you can call me. But we'll speak again – we'll see each other again very soon. I promise."

She'd almost run to the door of the bar. Tin Johnson had clearly thought better about following her, proving he was quite intelligent after all. Kate, in the bustling office at the police station, didn't like to think about the ten minutes that followed, once she'd reached the comparative safety and privacy of her car. She looked down at her hands, probing at the tenderness along the sides of both with a wince. Her steering wheel wasn't designed to be pounded hard with clenched fists.

Kate sighed from the depths of her being. She'd checked her phone several times already that hour, but she found herself digging back into her handbag, bringing out her mobile. Three missed calls from Tin Johnson and two voicemails. A text from him too. *Please, Kate, could you give me a ring? I just want to be sure you're okay.* The *nerve* of the man... Nothing from Mary. Kate sighed again and put the phone back in her bag.

She squared her shoulders and straightened up from her

slumped position. Aware that Rav was waving at her from across the room, Kate made her way over to his desk. "What's up?"

Rav looked pleased. He, at least, was looking a little more robust – his physiotherapy was obviously working. "I've heard from CAHID. They've got a definite date on the bones."

"Really?" asked Kate, feeling a welcome surge of excitement. Something to take her mind off everything else. "That's excellent. So what year are we talking?"

Rav paused dramatically. "Are you sure you're ready for this?"

"Yes," Kate said. "Don't drag it out."

Rav exhaled. "Nineteen seventy three."

"Seriously?" Kate was impressed and somewhat aghast. "That long ago? Jesus."

"I know. I wasn't even born then."

"Me neither."

They both looked at one another. Kate sat down on the edge of Rav's desk. "Blimey, this could be a bit more complicated than I thought. Did CAHID give you anything else?"

"Oh, yeah, of course. Got the whole report here."

He handed her a cardboard folder. "Thanks," Kate said. "Mind if I give it a quick once-over?"

"Be my guest. I'm off to update the boss."

Kate almost ran back to her own desk and opened the folder. As she began to read it, she marvelled at the scientific techniques that now allowed such a long ago crime to be investigated. Was it a crime though? Of course it was, she told herself. Bodies didn't bury themselves.

She read on. The bones belonged to a young woman, probably between sixteen and twenty one years of age. The centre had been thorough in their investigation. The woman had been Caucasian, her height estimated at between five foot two and five foot five, her weight approximately eight stone. The right humerus revealed an old fracture, probably sustained when she was a child, and she'd had two wisdom teeth removed. Kate re-read that paragraph.

That could be really useful when checked against dental records. She made a few notes. What about DNA? They could check for matches against the National DNA Database. What about also checking for partial or familial matches? Kate scribbled her thoughts down as they occurred to her.

Intent on her work, she eventually sat back, easing the ache in her neck and back. For a blissful hour she hadn't thought about her mother – or Tin bloody Johnson – once, but, of course, the moment she relaxed, it all came flooding back. Kate jumped up, gritting her teeth, and made herself go and drink a glass of water before sitting back down again. As she did, she saw Theo walking across the office, past the window that faced the high street. She saw him glance casually out of the window, do a double take, and then stop and look. He started laughing.

Jane, who sat near the window, looked up at the sound. "What's up?"

"There's a bloke outside holding up a sign," said Theo, still chuckling. "What's he playing at?"

By now, everyone was looking. Kate began to get up.

"Look," said Theo, pointing him out to Fliss and Jane, who'd joined him at the window. "That black bloke there, with a sign saying 'sorry'."

Kate shot up from her seat and hurried across to the window. Surely not... But yes, there he was, Tin Johnson, holding up a hand-lettered sign and wearing an apologetic grin.

Kate made a strangled noise. The others looked at her.

"Don't tell me he's something to do with you," said Theo. His smile grew wider and more mischievous. "You're *joking*. Kate, what's he done? Kate?"

But Kate had already left the room at a run. She thundered down the stairs, out through the station reception, and hurried down the steps to the pavement.

"What are you playing at?" she hissed at Tin. She was conscious of a chorus of muffled cheering coming from the office window above her.

"Well, you wouldn't answer my calls," said Tin. He handed her the piece of paper with 'sorry' written on it. "So you forced me to take direct action. Here you go."

Kate took it, crumpled it into a ball and threw it on the ground. Then, because not even in extreme anger was she able to drop litter, she stooped and picked it up again. "I do not *believe* you." She began to walk quickly away. "Come on!" she threw back over her shoulder at Tin, who jumped and then hurried to keep up with her. She waved an extended middle finger in the vague direction of the crowd at the office window.

Once they were out of sight of the station, Kate came to a sudden halt and whirled around, hands on hips. "You're sorry? Really?" She put her hands up to the side of her head in a gesture of resignation and then dropped them. "You really thought it would be a wonderful idea to spring my dying mother on me?" Angry tears came to her eyes and she turned away, folding her arms.

Tin had stopped smiling. "I really am sorry," he said quietly. "I had Mary asking me to do it, and I didn't – I didn't know how to refuse her. Like you said, she's dying." Kate flinched and he went to put a hand out to her before drawing it back. "I'm sorry. I shouldn't have made it such a surprise. No wonder you got upset."

"Yes," Kate said, not trusting herself to say any more. Her throat was aching.

There was a moment's silence. Then Tin asked, still in that same quiet voice, "Are you going to call her?"

"That's none of your business," Kate said. Then she relented, a little. "I will talk to her. In my own time, and when I'm good and ready."

"All right," Tin said. "You're right, it's none of my business really. But – don't leave it too long. Please. She doesn't – Mary doesn't really have much time left."

Kate felt the tears brim over and swiped angrily at her face. She was still turned away from Tin but after a moment, his hand appeared in her peripheral vision, holding a clean tissue. She took it with a muttered thanks.

"Listen," said Tin. "You're right to be angry with me. I want to make it up to you. Can I buy you dinner?"

"I don't know," said Kate, snippily. "Can you?" She took refuge in sarcasm when upset, it wasn't one of her best traits but right at this moment, she didn't care.

Tin smiled sheepishly. "All right, Miss Pedant. *May* I buy you dinner?"

Kate sighed. She suddenly felt very tired. "Okay."

"Tonight?"

"I've got to work."

"Tomorrow?"

Kate considered refusing again. Why make it easy for him? But she was conscious that, despite her anger and upset, quite a big part of her really did want to have dinner with Tin Johnson. "Okay," she said in a tone that she purposefully made slightly more bored than she felt.

"Shall I pick you up from the station?"

"No. Just tell me where to go and I'll meet you there. And now, if you'll excuse me, I have to get back to work." With that, she turned smartly on her heel and walked away without a backward glance. She felt a twinge of anxiety as she turned the corner. Had she been a bit harsh? Too late now, if she had. Kate walked back up the steps to the station entrance, bracing herself for the storm of questions and teasing that was about to engulf her.

Chapter Seven

"I'll give you this," said Kate as she sat down in the restaurant Tin had chosen and looked about her. "You don't half know some nice places to eat."

"Well, I try," Tin said modestly. "It all stems from my days of having expense accounts. Sadly gone."

"But I bet that knowledge still comes in handy."

"It doesn't hurt," said Tin.

"Wine and dine a lot, do you?" asked Kate ironically.

"Oh yes. I'm out with a different woman every night, me. 'Shagger Johnson' is what they call me." He caught Kate's eye and laughed. "Oh, come on. What will you have to drink while we're waiting to order?"

Kate relaxed back into her chair as Tin went to fetch the drinks. Looking around the room, she was reminded of being out with Andrew – he'd had a penchant for fine dining but to be honest, this nice little bistro was probably a little too casual for him. Andrew had liked white linen tablecloths and hovering, deferential waiters, and Kate – well – hadn't. She liked places like this, where you could relax and enjoy the food without worrying about which fork you were supposed to use.

"I called my mother," Kate said as Tin sat down at the table again. She surprised herself – she hadn't meant to say that. Was she hoping for Tin's approval or something?

He raised his eyebrows. "That's good."

"I didn't actually get through. But I left her a voicemail." Kate wondered why she was continuing with this. "Anyway, not that it matters..."

The waiter approached their table and there was a necessary lull in conversation as they placed their orders. When the waiter had left, Tin leaned forward a little. "I was really glad you took me up on my offer. I wouldn't have blamed you if you hadn't."

"Well, that's very gentlemanly of you," said Kate, sarcasm dripping from every word. "I mean, why on Earth would I have been upset to have suddenly been confronted with a parent I'd been estranged from for half a decade?"

Tim looked sheepish. "How many times am I going to have to say I'm sorry? This isn't the best start to a new relationship, is it?"

Kate looked at him, startled. He didn't exactly blush, or if he did it wasn't apparent because of the tone of his skin, but there was an air of embarrassment about him, as if he'd suddenly been caught out in something he hadn't quite meant to say.

Kate wavered. Half of her wanted to take him up on the phrase 'new relationship', probably with an added side extra of sarcasm to boot. Half of her wanted to pretend he hadn't said it. She dropped her eyes to her menu, running her gaze over the printed dishes without seeing them.

The waiter brought their food and the moment itself fell away. They both chatted fairly easily about other things for a while: the weather, the various items of news that were currently hitting the headlines, their plans for the week ahead. Kate was surprised at how easy it was to talk naturally to Tin – after all, she barely knew him.

After their main course plates were cleared away, they both sat back a little, full of food and more relaxed than perhaps they had been at the start of the meal.

"So what made you become a cop?" Tin asked.

"'Cop'?" Kate tutted. "This isn't America, you know."

Tin's grin grew wider. "So, why you Babylon, innit?" Kate almost choked. "That any better?"

Kate laughed, despite herself. "That only proves you are definitely not down with the kids, Tin. *Babylon*. No one has said that since the nineteen eighties."

She liked the sound of his name, it sounded natural and easy. Perhaps the same thought had occurred to him because he just chuckled at her admonishment and said "Tell me about it. I'm almost forty."

Kate raised her eyebrows. He looked a good ten years younger than that. "When's the big day?"

"April the seventeenth. Why? Will you come to the party?"

"If I'm invited," Kate said demurely.

"Oh, I think that's a given," Tin said. "Anyway, you're prevaricating. Why did you become a police officer?"

Kate dropped her gaze to the table, to the half empty wine glass which gave off a subdued sparkle in the candlelight. She'd been meaning to answer him in the same half-jokey fashion with which she'd been parrying most of his questions. Now, she didn't want to do that. She wanted to take him seriously and for Tin to take her seriously too.

"I wanted...order," she said slowly. "I wanted rules. I spent my childhood in utter chaos – there were no rules, or if there were, they weren't ever...enforced. I wanted – God, I just wanted the world to be...tidy."

Tin nodded as if he understood.

"How much have you talked to my mother?" Kate demanded. "What's she said about it? About what it was like bringing us up on her own?"

Tin shrugged. "She gave me the impression that it was pretty hard work. She told me she'd already had two children taken into care when she was pretty young."

Kate nodded. "Terry and Manda. My older brother and sister. I never knew them."

"You don't see them now?"

Kate's gaze dropped to her wineglass once more. "Terry died when he was eighteen – a motorbike accident. I think Manda lives up north, somewhere. I think she's married, had a couple of children, but I don't ever see her. She probably barely knows I exist. They were both fostered from quite a young age, I think." She was silent for a moment and added, "Mum couldn't cope." The bitterness in her voice surprised her and she tacked on another sentence. "She couldn't cope with much, ever."

The warm and friendly atmosphere that had once existed between her and Tin seemed to have evaporated. Kate wondered whether he was condemning her for her hard words. What exactly had Mary told him?

"You probably think I'm very judgemental," she said, after a silence that seemed to grow too deep for comfort.

Tin shook his head. "You know what I think? I think you are but the person you judge the most, that you judge the hardest, is yourself."

Kate stared at him. To her horror, she felt tears begin to sting her eyes and looked away sharply, blinking hard. What a strange evening this was turning out to be – and there she'd been at home, getting ready, with Merlin twining around her ankles, thinking that she was going to enjoy it, that it was simply ages since she'd been on a date.

"Are you okay?" Tin asked, still in that warm and sympathetic voice. Perversely, she disliked him for it then – she didn't want him to pity her, she wanted him to admire her.

"I'm fine." She picked up her wineglass and emptied in it three swallows. "I hope you don't mind but I really do have to go now. I've got a very early start in the morning."

It was there, just for a flash – the look of disappointment. Kate didn't know whether she was sorry or glad. She didn't say anything but sat waiting for him to say something in return.

"Okay," Tin said eventually. "Can I give you a lift back?"

"No, I'll get a taxi," said Kate. She could hear the coldness in her voice and felt a horrid jab of despair, anger and frustration. It was all going wrong and she was making things worse. "Thank you for dinner," she said limply and Tin laughed, not very cheerfully.

"I'd be happier if I thought you'd actually enjoyed it," he said.

They both paused by the entrance to the restaurant. Kate pulled on her coat and felt another surge of those uncomfortable feelings at the bleak tone of his voice. Why did I ever think that this was a good idea? She asked herself, catching sight of her unhappy, taut face in the mirror that hung by the wall by the door.

On impulse she put a hand on his arm and the warmth beneath her palm seemed to melt away the anger and hostility that she was inexplicably feeling. "Tin," she said, and at last her voice had lost that hard edge. "I'm really sorry. I'm feeling – I'm all mixed up and I seem to be taking that out on you. I don't know why. I'm really sorry."

They stood very close together. Tin's face moved a little closer to Kate's and she thought, with a leap of the heart, that he was about to kiss her. He didn't though, but he put a finger to her mouth and then took it away.

"You don't have to apologise for anything," he said, very softly. "I just – if I can help, you only have to let me know."

Kate's mouth felt as if it were on fire, just from that gentle touch. She was lost for words for a moment and could only nod, dumbly. Then Tin stepped back a little and the charge between them dissipated.

"I'll buy dinner next time," said Kate. "If there is a next time."

"I'd like there to be," said Tin. "Just let me know."

Kate nodded. Then she said goodbye and turned and left. She walked away down the street towards the taxi rank and didn't look back, but she was conscious of Tin watching her as she walked away, and suddenly she felt happy.

Chapter Eight

"So, Kate, how have you been?"

Magda always opened their counselling sessions with those words and Kate always replied in the same way. "Oh, I'm fine." Then she would reflect on how she was really feeling and go on to qualify her statement, just as she did today. "Actually, it's been a bit of a stressful week."

"Why don't you tell me about it?"

So Kate did, relaxing back into the green velvet sofa that her back and bottom had come to know intimately over the past few months. Kate had decided to seek some counselling last year, having been horrified by some of her behaviour – most notably to Olbeck during a very stressful case. She had cringed at the thought of talking to a perfect stranger about her problems but once she'd met Magda, and begun her treatment, she could feel it doing her good. She felt smoothed out, all those tangled threads and rough edges gradually beginning to unravel. She and Magda had worked their way through her childhood, through the events of her teens that had caused her so much anguish, right through her career as a police officer, her romantic attachments, the problems and regrets and mistakes that made up much of her life. And Kate, as she gradually untangled her emotions and feelings and decisions, found that she was being easier on herself. She had always taken pride in her work but she now found she could take pride in something else too – being strong enough to face up to where she'd gone wrong in the past and to take those lessons with her, into the future.

Tin's words from the dinner the previous night recurred to her as she talked to Magda. *The person you judge the most, that you judge the hardest, is yourself.* He was right, she realised. Perceptive guy. She found herself wondering when she could introduce him to Olbeck, to see what her best friend thought of him. She shook herself internally, bringing her focus back to the room and to what Magda was saying to her.

"So, how do you feel about re-establishing a relationship with your mother?" Magda asked.

Kate shrugged. "I'm not sure how I feel about it, to be honest."

"Well, that's understandable. Can you elaborate on your feelings? What's the uppermost one, the dominant emotion?"

Kate sat up a little. "You know, I hate to say it, but it's – it's anger. I actually feel furious at her. Seriously, I could call her up right now and scream at her. That's awful, isn't it?"

Magda shook her head. "I'd say that was completely normal. You've not only got a huge amount of unresolved tension between you, not to mention your history, but anger can be a very normal reaction to news that someone is terminally ill. Death is such a big thing to confront that your mind almost wants to deflect it. You become angry at the person because you don't want to have to think about what's going to happen to them."

"Yes," Kate said. "I suppose so."

"If your mother were here now, and you could express how you were feeling towards her, what would you say?"

Kate shrank back against the chair. "No, I don't want to."

"It might help."

"No. No, I really don't want to."

Magda hesitated for a moment and then said, "That's up to you, Kate, of course. But I'd be cautious about repressing what you're feeling. You know we've talked about that before. You can't keep it down forever."

Kate sighed. "I know."

"Why not give it a try?"

Kate wavered, torn between knowing the truth of Magda's words and between feeling stripped raw, emotionally vulnerable. "Okay," she said eventually, reluctantly.

"Fine. Just imagine your mother is sitting across from you and just let yourself talk to her, naturally. Close your eyes if it helps."

Kate did so. She began to speak, feeling ridiculous. "Mum... hi, Mum. I wanted to talk to you the other day at the restaurant but I couldn't trust myself. I just couldn't believe that was you, after so many years. And I wanted to ask why it took you dying to come and find me." She stopped speaking for a moment, feeling the ache building in her jaw. "Why did you leave it so late? And you haven't said sorry, not once, not once for being such a shit mum all those years. And now you want my forgiveness? Just so you can die happy? Well, tough because it's too little, too late. I don't think you even care about me and how I'm feeling at all." Her voice broke then and she put one hand up to her mouth, her fingers trembling.

After a moment, Magda prompted her gently. "Did you want to carry on, Kate?"

Kate shook her head, unable to speak for a moment. After a few minutes, she put her hand down from her mouth and said hoarsely, "I don't want to do this anymore."

"All right," Magda said, just as gently. "We can leave it there if you want."

Later, as Kate closed the door of Magda's house behind her and walked down the four steps that led to the garden gate and the pavement beyond, she could still feel that tightness in her jaw. She understood what Magda was trying to do, and with the logical side of her mind, Kate could see the point. Therapy had taught her that the most painful things to confront were often the things that could make the biggest difference, if addressed. Kate knew all that – but she still didn't like it. She reached her car and unlocked it. She turned the heating up to full – somehow, she was always cold when she'd had a session with Magda. The blow of warm air on her face and hands was very comforting. She always sat for a moment, collecting herself, before trusting herself to drive.

By the time she arrived back at the station, Kate felt much more in control of herself. She had to spend the afternoon running data through various databases in an attempt to find a match with the information that the CAHID report had given them. She raised a hand to Olbeck as she walked in and saw him beckoning.

"What's up?" Kate asked, leaning on the doorframe of his office.

"Nothing work-related. Just wanted to know how your speech is coming along?"

"Sorry?" asked Kate, nonplussed. Then she realised. "Oh, um, it's fine. I haven't finished it yet."

"No worries – it's just that we've got the rehearsal coming up in a fortnight and you'll need to have done it by then."

"I'll do it," said Kate, slightly annoyed. "You're turning into a right Bridezilla, did you know that?"

"Am I?" said Olbeck, shocked. "I'm not, am I?"

Kate relented. "No, not really. I guess you only get married once, you want it to be just right."

"I *hope* it's only once." Olbeck pushed his chair back from his desk and got up. "Anyway, moving on. Any further on an ID for our young woman?"

Kate and he walked back to Kate's desk, discussing the CAHID report. "I've asked to have it run through the DNA database, see if there's a match, obviously, but also if there's a partial match," Kate said.

"Good idea. God, the time lag makes such a difference.

Nineteen seventy three – what are the chances of routine DNA collection then? Did that even happen?"

Kate shrugged. "Don't ask me."

Fliss leapt up. "I could find out. Do some research?"

Olbeck smiled at her. "That would actually be helpful, thanks, Fliss." He flicked the pages of the report back and forth. "Anyone got any other ideas?"

"Cold cases," said Theo, leaning back in his chair. "I thought of this last night. Why don't we cross check against the cold cases from that sort of era, see if there's anything that comes up? I mean, our vic's young, female – she might be a forgotten victim of a serial killer, or something like that."

"Yep," Olbeck said absently, head bent to the report again. "Another good idea."

Fliss had been busy typing at her computer. "The first conviction involving DNA profiling was in nineteen eighty six," she said, reading aloud from the screen.

"Right," said Olbeck. "Well, that helps. Has anyone checked the dental records yet?"

"Waiting to hear back," Rav said, smartly. "Although again, the time lapse might mean we get nothing. Do dentists normally keep records for forty years?"

As one, they turned to Fliss who smiled and reiterated her previous remark. "Leave it with me," she finished.

After that, they all separated, moving back to their individual desks. Kate pushed up her sleeves, pulled her chair in tight to her desk, and turned to her computer screen, determined to track down the young woman in the missing persons database. Wouldn't it be great, she thought, if I get a match straight away? But as she tapped keys and read, she had an inkling that it wouldn't be that straightforward.

It wasn't. After several hours of searching, Kate knew that there was nothing to be found. She'd expected it, but it was still frustrating. She sat back, easing the ache in her shoulders from where she'd been sitting hunched forward – a very bad idea, she reminded herself; she really should have known better. She got up and stretched, looking over to where Theo was doing what she'd just chastised herself for.

"Oi, straighten up, Theo," she called over. "Remember your posture."

Theo looked at her, startled. "What?"

"Oh, never mind." Kate wandered over to his desk and perched on the edge of it. "Guess what?"

"What?"

"There's no missing persons match."

Theo's face flickered for a moment, then cleared. "Well, I can't say I'm surprised. What about DNA?"

Kate shook her head. "Nothing's come back. However, I might just have one more trick up my sleeve."

"Oh yeah?"

Kate pushed herself upright. "I read up on it last night. There was a case – funnily enough in 1973 – where three young girls were raped and strangled in South Wales."

Theo grimaced. "Nice."

"Well, eventually – years and years later, in the noughties, I think - someone did develop a DNA profile from the crime scene samples. Enough to run through the national database."

Theo raised an eyebrow. "And they found a match?"

Kate shook her head. "Nope. No match. But about a year later, the investigating officer decided to search for partial matches – basically looking for a family connection. And guess what? He found one. Some car thief had had a DNA swab and that was a fifty percent match to the crime scene DNA. And that's how they tracked the killer down."

Theo nodded. "And you're telling me this rather than searching the records because...?"

Kate grinned. "I just wanted to tell you because it makes me sound rather clever to have thought of it, don't you think?"

Theo snorted. "Makes you sound like a nutter, more like. Come back and tell me when you've actually found something."

"Oh, Theo," Kate said, mock-sorrowfully. "You're no fun." She dodged the paperclip he threw at her with a giggle and went back to her desk.

Habit made her check her phone before she got back to work. The smile was wiped off her face when she saw she had a text from her brother, Jay. *What's up, sis? J x.* Kate had called him last night and left a voicemail that she needed to talk to him. Why hadn't he just called her back, rather than texting? Perhaps he couldn't talk, she told herself. It was the middle of a working day, after all. But what if he hadn't called her because he knew what it was she wanted to talk to him about, and he was actually avoiding her?

Such paranoia, Kate. She texted Jay back *Will call you again later x* and turned back to her work.

She got home that evening early enough to make that phone call possible. She drew out a portion of home-made lasagne from the freezer and popped it into the microwave to defrost and cook. One of the ways in which she was trying to be a bit nicer to herself, on Magda's advice, was to feed herself healthy, home-cooked food rather than relying on ready meals and takeaways. It had been hard at first – Kate got home so exhausted some nights that even heating a pizza up was beyond her – but she'd learned to plan ahead, make a big batch of freezable food and portion it up to eat at her leisure. As the microwave whirred, Kate keyed in Jay and Laura's home number and prepared herself.

Laura answered and Kate had a few minutes of pleasant small talk with her before she asked to speak to Jay. It could have been her imagination, but Kate thought that there was the slightest hesitation in Laura's voice as she answered "Of course, I'll go and get him. He's glued to the X-Box at the moment."

"Thanks," said Kate. She pressed the phone to her ear, trying to hear Jay and Laura's conversation but nothing could be heard except vague, low murmurs. Eventually Jay came onto the line.

"Hi, sis. How you doing?"

He sounded normal as ever, but was there just a slight wariness, just a shade of constraint in his tone? Again, Kate told herself not to be paranoid.

They chatted about inconsequential things for a few minutes: work, the weather, Jay and Laura's upcoming holiday to Spain. Then Kate girded her loins. "Have you spoken to Mum, lately?"

There was a short silence although Kate could hear Jay's faint breathing on the other end of the line. "Why?" he asked, eventually.

"Come on," said Kate, an edge to her tone. "I think you know why. You know, don't you?"

There was another pause, and then Jay sighed. "Yeah. I know."

"Why didn't you tell me?" Kate burst out, louder than she'd intended to. She could hear a tremble in her voice.

"Kate, come on. I wanted to tell you, of course I did, but Mum told me not to. She said she wanted to see you herself, tell you herself. She totally *forbade* me to say anything. What was I supposed to do?"

Kate struggled against another burst of anger. She knew it was mainly against herself. Of course Jay couldn't have gone back on a promise to their mother. It was her news to tell. Kate knew that – but still... She swallowed hard, biting back the words she wanted to say but knew she'd regret if she did.

"You should have told me," was all she said limply, after a moment. Jay said nothing and the two of them breathed down the phone at each other for another minute or two.

"How are you feeling about it, anyway?" Jay asked quietly.

"I'm fine," Kate said, her automatic response to anything uncomfortable. She paused, remembered that this was her brother she was talking to, the relative she was closest to. "I'm a bit shocked, actually. A bit shaken. She just looked so – so *ill* when I saw her."

"Yeah. Poor Mum, she's not looking too clever."

Kate thought back to her mother sitting across the table from her, her thinness, the shadows on her face, the strange coppery hair that sat slightly wrongly on Mary's head. A wig, Kate only now realised. Of course it would be a wig, what with the chemotherapy and everything.

She steeled herself and asked him the question that she really wanted the answer to. "How long do you - do you think she's got?"

"I'm not sure," said Jay. His voice was almost steady. Kate suddenly had a vision, as clear as if she could see down the phone line: Laura sat close beside Jay on the sofa at their flat, while he talked to her, her hand on his arm, warmth and love in her touch. Kate closed her eyes briefly, conversely warmed and saddened by the sight. Thank God Jay has someone to care for him, had someone on his side. *But what about me?* Kate pushed the thought away with an effort.

"The hospital said six months to a year," Jay was saying. "But from what I've been reading and hearing about, that doesn't really mean anything. In fact, it could well be an overestimate."

Kate again closed her eyes briefly. She remembered Tin saying something similar to her, that afternoon in the park. *Don't leave it too long. Please. She doesn't – Mary doesn't really have much time left.* The jab of pain caught her unawares.

"You okay?" asked Jay.

"I'm fine." Kate straightened up and pushed her hair back from her face. She and Jay talked a little more, skirting around the edges of the conversation both of them were aware that they should be having, but neither of them quite able to breach the conversational gap. In the end, talk about Mary petered out and they were left to say their goodbyes.

"Let's catch up soon," said Kate, more sincerely. She missed her brother.

"Yes, we must. When we get back from Spain."

Once Kate had put the phone down, she stared ahead of herself for a moment. Then she brought Mary's number up on her mobile screen. Her thumb hovered above the 'call' icon, but she somehow wasn't able to bring herself to press it. Tomorrow, she promised herself. I'll call her tomorrow.

Chapter Nine

KATE WOKE THE NEXT MORNING to something that had almost become a novelty – bright sunshine. She pushed the bedroom window curtains aside and looked out onto a flawless morning, the sky a bright blue, the pavements dry. With delight, she noticed that the tree outside her house was finally budding. Eagerly, she got up and dressed and made breakfast for herself and Merlin, eating it standing by the back door and looking out onto the sunny garden. It was incredible how a bit of sun could make her feel a hundred times better.

Buoyed by the good weather, Kate grabbed her mobile phone and, without hesitating, rang her mother. She waited, listening, telling herself not to tense up. It was something of an anti-climax when the phone call went to voicemail. Kate pulled herself together and left a message for her mother in a tone that was as steady and as cheerful as she could make it, suggesting meeting for tea and cake at a time that would suit Mary Redman. She signed off by saying "Take care, Mum," and hung up, feeling that sense of relief that comes from finally tackling a much-hated job. Why had she procrastinated for so long when actually, when it came to it, the task wasn't so bad after all? Kate stroked Merlin on his black, glossy head in goodbye and headed out the front door.

Even the sight of the piles of paperwork on her desk didn't daunt her. Kate squared her shoulders and sat down, pulling her chair closer to her desk. After a moment, she realised Rav was waving at her across the room.

"What's up?" she asked, making her way over to him.

Rav looked excited. "We've got a DNA match."

Kate was conscious of a jab of annoyance, even under her exclamation of happy surprise. She'd wanted to be the one to find it – she'd worked so damn hard on sifting through all that data – but even she couldn't keep working through the night on it. She told herself it didn't matter. Surely the important thing was that they finally had a match.

"That's great," she said, leaning forward to look at Rav's computer screen. "That's brilliant. A full match?"

Rav shook his head. "Nope, not that good. Partial only, so it must be a family connection. Here, I've printed it out for you. I know you've been working really hard on this."

"Oh, thank you," said Kate, grateful that her efforts had at least been acknowledged by one person. She patted Rav on the arm affectionately and made her way back to her desk, clutching the sheaf of papers he'd given her.

The DNA profile from the bones had been partially matched to another profile on the database. Kate looked at the name and age. Kayla Tripp, aged twenty-five, arrested for assault. Kate read through the details, frowning. Could this Kayla be the daughter of the woman whose bones had been found? Kate did some quick mental arithmetic. If Kayla was twenty-five, then she would have been born in nineteen ninety. That meant it was impossible for her to be the daughter. So what was the connection?

Kate went back over to Rav's desk and told him what she thought.

"Yeah, I'd worked that out too," Rav said. "The dates don't match, not even close. But there must be a connection."

"A niece, perhaps. Can't be a sister, can it?"

"Nope. We should talk to her though, eh? This Kayla Tripp."

"Absolutely."

Rav and Kate both looked at the address details on the report sheet and groaned in unison.

"Sheffield! Bloody hell..." said Rav.

Kate smiled. "I'll drive."

"We can't get there and back in a day, surely?"

Kate pondered. "No, probably not. Besides, we might need to talk to other members of her family." She jumped up. "I'll just run it past Mark and we can get going."

Olbeck approved the trip, and Kate and Rav were soon in the car and on their way to the motorway. Kate tapped the steering wheel in time to the music, glad to be out of the office and finally doing something constructive. She said as much to Rav.

"God, I know. I was starting to think we were never going to get anywhere with this case."

"Me too." Kate adroitly steered the car into the inside lane. "Still, there's always *something*, isn't there. That's what Anderton says. You always get some sort of a break." She considered for a moment and added, "Not necessarily in time, though, it has to be said."

The traffic, for once, was quite light and reasonably fast moving. Kate and Rav made good time and found themselves on the outskirts of Sheffield by late afternoon. Kate, having not visited the city before, was thankful for her sat nav. The traffic gradually got heavier as the offices, schools and other places of work closed for the day and the rush hour began. It was an hour and forty minutes later when they finally drew into the crowded car park of the Holiday Inn where they would be staying for the next few days.

Rav had attempted, whilst en route, to contact Kayla Tripp but without success. He and Kate conferred in the reception area of the hotel once they'd checked in.

"We've got a last known address," said Kate. "That's got to be our first port of call. If not, there's another contact number here for her next of kin, her mother." She scanned the page again and frowned. "Maybe we should try her mother first, actually. After all, if it *is* a family connection, time-wise, it's more likely the mother might know more about it than a twenty-something."

Rav walked abruptly to a nearby seat and sat down. Kate looked at him sharply. "You all right?"

Rav had one hand to his stomach. "I'm all right," he said with an effort, after a moment. "Sitting for hours in the car with that seat belt against me wasn't that good."

Kate bit her lip. "Maybe you should go and rest. I can do this."

"No. I'm coming." Rav took a deep breath and struggled to his feet. "Otherwise what's the point of me being here?"

"Uh-huh." Kate put a hand on his shoulder and gently turned him around. "Go on, go and lie down for a bit. Did you bring your painkillers?"

"Yes."

"Well, take a couple, get some rest and I'll report back soon. Besides, you could try and track down some more of the Tripp family, see if there's anyone else around that we could talk to."

Rav wavered for a moment and then gave in. "Yeah, I guess I could do that."

"Want me to help you up to your room?"

"No," Rav said impatiently. "I'm fine. I'll just – lie down for a bit and start looking through some more data."

"Okay." Kate made herself step back a little and watched him make his slow and faltering way to the lifts. Rav had never been what you'd call robust, but since the incident and his recovery he'd grown so thin he was almost child-like in stature. Kate had to force herself not to go over and put her arms around him, helping him along. He wouldn't like that. She made herself give him a cheery smile and wave as the lift door shut and she caught his eye and he grinned in return, just before the closing doors cut him off from view. Kate dropped her hands to her sides and exhaled. Then she checked the report again to see where it was she had to go.

Despite the satellite navigation, Kate still got lost twice

looking for Kayla Tripps's address. As she finally pulled into the side of the correct street, she heard the buzz of her mobile phone as a voicemail alert came through. She'd missed another call from her mother, but at least this time Mary had left a message. Kate listened, wincing inwardly at the hoarseness in her mother's voice. She sounded worse than she had the other night. Surely she sounded worse? Kate pressed the 'repeat message' button and listened again. Mary had agreed to meet her on Friday, in the tea room that Kate had suggested. Kate felt an absurd surge of panic at the thought of facing her mother again, despite the fact that she'd suggested it. She stamped down on the feeling, told herself that she was being ridiculous, and conjured Magda's calm and soothing tones in her head, thinking over all the times she and her therapist had discussed her mother. After a moment, she felt more in control. Even so, she didn't call her mother back but instead sent a text confirming the meeting on Friday. She dithered over ending the text with a kiss. She put one in and then deleted it again. Her mother's wasted face facing her over the table at The Black Cat came to mind again and Kate, shaking her head impatiently, added the kiss again to the end of her message and sent it.

She got out of the car, stretched and looked about her. Whittington Road was a nondescript street, lined end to end with small, terraced red brick houses, thrown up in their thousands, perhaps millions, during the Victorian and Edwardian eras. Kate could see little, brave touches here and there – a freshly painted door, a window box with some early daffodils – but the overall impression was of poverty and making-do and tiredness.

She found Kayla Tripp's last known address and knocked at the house. Nobody answered. Kate knocked again, tried the (broken) doorbell, knocked and waited once more and then retreated to the car, wanting to get out of the cold wind. So, no luck with Kayla. The only contact number they had for her wasn't working or had been cut off. Kate looked at the only other name on the sheet, a Jackie Tripp, Kayla's mother. She keyed the address into her sat nav, turned the car around, with some difficulty in the narrow street, and set off to find her. It was worth a try at least.

As it turned out, Jackie Tripp lived in an almost identical house, in a very similar street, some two miles away. There were limp, yellowed net curtains at the windows that gave it a bleary, run-down look. Jackie Tripp had much the same look, Kate thought, as the door opened and a faded, middle-aged woman stood there, blinking in the light as if she'd just emerged from a dark tunnel.

"Jackie Tripp?"

"Yes," the woman said, looking at first puzzled and then apprehensive. Kate hastened to reassure her and explained why she was there. It was an explanation that necessarily took a little while, and even after she'd given it, Jackie Tripp stood looking at her with very little comprehension.

"You what, love? DNA sample?"

Kate patiently explained again, finishing by asking if she could come in for a minute. Jackie nodded, still obviously confused, but stepped back to allow Kate to step over the threshold.

It was a house where the front door led straight into the living room. It was a small room, cluttered with too much furniture. A large black cat lay curled in front of the gas fire. Kate thought for a fanciful moment that it could be Merlin's brother, it was so like him. A secondary thought occurred to her that she needed to text Olbeck, to see if he'd remembered to pop in and feed Merlin, as he'd promised.

"I've got a cat just like him," she said, pointing, hoping a little small talk would ease the look of worried confusion on Jackie Tripp's face.

Jackie said nothing in response but nodded, a little warily. "Sit down, love," said Jackie, indicating a sagging settee covered in magazines, tabloid newspapers, crumpled tissues and a pile of clean but unfolded washing.

Kate perched on the few clear inches towards the arm of the settee.

"I'm sorry, love, I don't quite understand what you're here for," said Jackie, once more. "It is something to do with our Kayla? Is she in trouble again?"

"No, it's nothing like that, Mrs Tripp. I appreciate it's quite confusing. I'm from Abbeyford CID, that's a town in the West Country, near Bristol?" Kate leant forward a little, hoping she wasn't going too fast. Jackie nodded tremulously. Kate went on to explain the discovery of the long-buried body, the fact that the DNA profile they'd been able to take had matched, in significant proportions, the DNA sample that had been taken from Kayla Tripp. She spoke as slowly and as clearly as she could, trying to keep the jargon to a minimum. "Is that clear to you now, Mrs Tripp? We believe that the body we found in Munford Gorge is in some way related to Kayla. I understand you're Kayla's mother?"

Jackie nodded at this, a little more emphatically as though that, at least, was something that she was sure of. Kate took a deep breath and went on. "That's very helpful to know, Mrs Tripp, because – and I hope this isn't too distressing for you – because that also means that the remains that we found recently are in some way related to you."

Jackie received this news in silence. Kate could see her digesting the information and braced herself for some sort of emotional outburst as the news sank in. But there was nothing, nothing except a faint expression of puzzlement on Jackie's worn face.

"Has there ever been anyone reported missing in your immediate or close family? Someone who may have gone missing as long ago as nineteen seventy-three?"

There was a flicker on Jackie's face and Kate sat forward a little. But then Jackie shook her head. "No. No, love, I can't think of anyone."

Kate sat back again. "No one at all? No one in the wider family?" she persisted.

Jackie Tripp was rubbing her hands together nervously. "I can't think – I don't think so."

Tamping down her frustration, Kate tried to think of the best way to frame her next question. She was beginning to doubt herself. Could the DNA be wrong? Had there been some cross-contamination somewhere? It did happen. If that was the case, then she was wasting her and Jackie Tripp's time.

"Is there anyone in the family that you haven't heard from for a long time?"

Jackie's face flickered again. Kate could see her beginning to shake her head and her lips to frame another negative sentence. Then she stopped.

"There was me sister, Jean," said Jackie. "I haven't heard from her in years. But she went abroad, love. She sent me postcards."

Kate sat forward again. "Your sister? Kayla's aunt?"

"Yes. But it can't be *her*. She went to Spain."

Kate took a deep breath. "Can you remember exactly when you last saw Jean, Mrs Tripp?"

Jackie's nervous hands continued to rub together as she thought. "Oh, it were years ago. She was older than me. Always a bit wild. Ended up going down to London, thought she was going to be one of those models. She was pretty, though, I'll give her that. Maybe she did end up being a model."

Kate controlled her impatience. "When did Jean go to London, Mrs Tripp?"

"Oh, I can't remember exactly. How old was I? Ten, I think. Jean was older, five years older, so she would have been fifteen. So when would that have been?" She paused, clearly calculating in her head. "It's funny, love, but I think that *would* have been the early seventies. Maybe nineteen seventy-two. God, it seems so long ago..." Her voice drifted off and Kate waited until it became clear that Jackie wasn't going to say anything more.

"Mrs Tripp, you've been really helpful, but I just need to clarify a few things. You had a sister, an older sister called Jean, who left for London at the age of fifteen? And you think this was in the early nineteen seventies?" Mrs Tripp nodded. "And you haven't heard from her since?"

"No, no that's not right," Jackie said emphatically. "She sent us postcards, at least two postcards from Spain. Said she was living there. I remember, because I got quite excited at the thought of visiting her. I'd never been to Spain. Never been abroad, then."

"Do you still have the postcards, Mrs Tripp?"

Jackie laughed nervously. "Somewhere, love, but look around you." She gestured at the mess and clutter. "It would take me all day to find them."

Kate nodded in understanding. Long experience had taught her that it was no use offering your help in the search. "Can you tell me if the postcards were in your sister's writing? Or were they typed?"

Jackie looked confused once more. "I can't remember, love. It were so long ago. I just remember Mum telling us we had a postcard from our Jean one morning. Maybe it was only the one that came."

"It would be really helpful for our investigation if you could find those cards, or that card if there was only one. Not now, I don't mean that, but if you could have a look over the next day or so and give me a call." Kate handed over her own business card. "Do you know if a missing persons report was ever filed for Jean? Did your mother ever report her missing, that you know of?"

Mrs Tripp took the card nervously from Kate and held it carefully in both hands. She was shaking her head. "She was never missing, she just left home. She didn't come back again but she weren't *missing*."

Kate tamped down the feeling of impatience that these answers were inducing. She wondered how she could tactfully ascertain whether Mrs Tripp's mother was still alive and able to be questioned. "So, as far as you know, Jean was never reported missing?"

"No. She wasn't."

Kate took the bull by the horns. "Would it be possible for me to speak to your mother directly, Mrs Tripp?"

"She died last year."

Kate had been expecting something of the kind, but she nodded and murmured something sympathetic. Quickly she glanced down at her notes, wondering if she'd missed anything. Oh yes, there was that...

"I'm sorry if this sounds like a strange question, but would you remember if Jean ever broke her arm as a child?"

Jackie Tripp was frowning. Kate had the impression that her confusion was now bordering on bewilderment and told herself to slow it down, take it easy. She was an experienced interviewer, after all; she should know how to reset the tone of the questions if it looked as though they were becoming distressing.

"Broke her arm? What do you mean? I don't know, I'm sure – I can't remember..." Jackie was finally beginning to look a little tearful.

Kate hastened to soothe her. "You've been very, very helpful, Mrs Tripp – I'm really so grateful. I know it's not always the easiest of things to undergo, particularly after such a long time."

Jackie blinked and managed a tremulous smile.

"There is one other thing you can do for me, which would really help," said Kate, rather hesitantly. "Would I be able to take a DNA sample from you? It's completely painless, it's just a mouth swab, that's all."

Jackie looked worried. "Oh, I don't know about that. What would it – would it—"

"It would be really helpful to us," said Kate quickly, talking over her. "We could then match it against the DNA we have already. I promise you it doesn't hurt – and we wouldn't store in the National Database or anything like that. It would just be for the purposes of this investigation."

Jackie acquiesced, rather hesitantly, and Kate took the swab and sealed it in an evidence bag. "Thank you so much, Mrs Tripp. That will be really useful."

As she said goodbye to the older woman at the door, Kate could feel and hear her mobile ringing in her pocket. She smiled a last goodbye at Jackie Tripp and turned away, striding down the street before answering the phone. It was Rav.

"God, I'm so sorry I haven't called before. I just woke up. Did you get anything?"

"Yes, and I'm on my way back. I think we might be able to get an ID but it depends on how quick I can get this sample to the labs." Kate explained where she had been, talking rather breathlessly as she walked quickly towards her parked car.

"I'll get the hotel to organise a courier," said Rav. "We can get that sample biked over and get the express turnaround."

"Fabulous. See you soon." Kate hung up, flung the mobile on the passenger seat along with the evidence bag and gunned the engine, impatient to get things started. As she drove away, the lowering grey clouds were pierced by a shaft of golden sunlight and she chose to interpret that as a good omen. It seemed they were finally making some headway after all.

Chapter Ten

THE NEXT AFTERNOON SAW RAV and Kate back at the Abbeyford station, after a long and tiring drive back from Sheffield that morning. Both were waiting impatiently for the call from the National DNA Database to confirm whether or not the sample from Jackie Tripp matched the DNA sample from the body. Kate kept looking towards her telephone, thinking perhaps if she willed it hard enough, the phone call might come through, forced into being by her mind. It didn't, of course. She kept jumping up to make cup after cup of coffee, each one abandoned to go cold after she'd drunk half.

When at last the telephone finally rang, Kate actually jumped. She was so eager to pick it up that she almost dropped the receiver in her haste to answer it. At first, she was almost disappointed to hear Jackie Tripp's tremulous voice on the other end of the line. "I've remembered, love, about Jean's arm. You asked me about it yesterday?"

Kate tamped down her impatience and disappointment at the call not being from the laboratory. "Oh, yes, I remember."

Jackie went on, sounding a bit surer of herself. "Well, it's funny that I forgot about it but you know, love, Jean did actually break her arm when she was a kiddie. I remember because she let me draw a flower on the cast. I must have only been about eight. She came off her bike coming down the hill and went into someone's car door."

Kate sat up straighter at the leap of excitement. All right, so it wasn't definitive proof but it was another piece of the jigsaw puzzle. "That's so helpful, Mrs Tripp. Can you remember which arm it was that Jean broke?"

"Her right one. I remember because she couldn't do any school work for a month because she couldn't write. Not that Jean was ever much good at that sort of thing."

"That's brilliant." Kate scribbled down as much detail as she could. "Would you remember the name of your family doctor, Mrs Tripp, by any chance? I know it's – oh, Doctor Gregson, you say?" She wrote the name down. It might come in handy for comparing X-rays and medical notes. "Thank you so much for letting me know. I don't suppose you've been able to find that postcard that Jean sent to you?" She very nearly said 'supposedly sent to you' but managed to restrain herself. As it turned out, Mrs Tripp hadn't found it. Kate thanked her anyway and said goodbye.

The phone rang almost immediately after she put the receiver down. Kate lunged for it again and this time it was the laboratory with the results of the DNA test. Kate listened to what they had to say, suppressed a whoop of joy, thanked them for their time and put the phone down. Then she ran across the room to Rav's desk and virtually threw herself on it.

"It's a match?" he said breathlessly. Kate nodded, grinning. Rav let out a shout of "Yes!" that turned heads across the office.

"Close familial match to the DNA from the bones. Closer than the match with Kayla Tripp. This is it, Rav. We have an ID."

Kate bounced back upright. Rav was beating his hand on the edge of his desk in a victory tattoo. "This is too cool for school," he said, his face alight. "We've only gone and bloody got an ID."

"I'll tell Mark and Anderton," said Kate. "Our victim is Jean Tripp, never reported missing."

"You know what this means?" asked Rav.

"What?"

"We'll have to go up to bloody Sheffield again."

Kate shook her head, grinning. "Don't care. We got a match!"

She bounded her way across the office to Olbeck's office. He'd been alerted already by Rav's shout and Kate's general demeanour.

"That's brilliant," he said once she informed him of what they found. "Come with me and we'll tell Anderton together."

It was on the short walk to Anderton's office that Kate's elation began to cool. It was good, obviously, that they'd finally been able to identify the body but where exactly did that get them? If Jean Tripp had been missing for over forty years, what was the likelihood that they would be able to identify her killer? She hadn't even been reported missing by her family. If she had indeed gone to London, and met her killer there, how on Earth were Kate and the team going to be able to track him or her down?

"Oh, nil desperandum, Kate. Nil desperandum," Anderton said cheerfully as she unloaded her worries before him as she and Olbeck took seats at his desk. "Don't go looking for trouble, that's my motto."

"Yes, you thought we might not even be able to get an ID at one point, didn't you?" asked Olbeck. "But we did."

"Exactly, Mark," Anderton said. "So let's have no more of this pessimism. We're a gigantic step forward and we've just got to think of where we move to from here."

"I guess re-interviewing Jackie Tripps is a priority," Kate said. "Poor woman, we've got to break the news to her that her long-lost sister is dead."

"Well, perhaps the intervening years will soften the blow," Anderton said. "Kate, are you able to go back to Sheffield to do that tomorrow?"

Kate opened her mouth to say yes but realised that she'd already arranged to meet her mother the following evening. For a second, she thought about cancelling the arrangement and then realised that she wouldn't be able to. She couldn't prioritise work over her family, not this time, much as she wanted to.

She explained, reluctantly, why she couldn't go and Anderton, who knew something of her relationship with her mother but not of her mother's illness, nodded. "Theo and Rav can go," was his only comment.

Olbeck looked at Kate with some surprise. She realised she'd hardly had a chance to talk to him about anything recently: not about her mother, or Tin, or anything that wasn't to do with his and Jeff's upcoming nuptials. She felt a stab of guilt at the realisation that she hadn't even started writing her speech.

Anderton was still speaking. "We need to build a picture of Jean Tripp's whereabouts when she left Sheffield. Where did she go in London? Did she ever reach London? Kate, if you're office-bound, can you start doing some digging on her name, anything you can pull up – medical records, arrest records, even newspaper articles? Just see if you can find anything that will give us a clue as to where she might have ended up."

Kate nodded. The three of them spent some time discussing questions to be put to Jackie Tripp and other members of Jean Tripp's family up in Sheffield. Then, with a repetition from Anderton that they were not to lose hope on getting anywhere with this case, Olbeck and Kate made their way back to their office.

Kate worked as hard as her tired brain would allow her that afternoon. She made telephone calls, trawled through databases and scribbled notes but without making much progress. One thing she was able to track down were Jean Tripp's medical records, from her old doctor's surgery. The surgery, now a much bigger medical centre for that suburb of Sheffield, apparently had archives of their patients' medical records dating back to World War Two. Kate obtained a promise, from the clerk at the storage facility, that Jean Tripp's medical notes would be sent on by courier. She looked down at her list of things to do and made a large, bold tick against that item. One down, many more to go. She stretched and yawned, wondered about pushing on for another hour with the help of several strong coffees but rejected the idea. Merlin would need feeding and she desperately needed some sleep. Besides, she had to strengthen herself for the meeting with her mother tomorrow. *And* she had to write that bloody wedding speech. Kate sighed and got up, picking up her bag, and walked towards the exit, mentally writing and rewriting lists in her head.

Chapter Eleven

THE TEA ROOM WHERE KATE had arranged to meet her mother was one she frequented regularly. As she climbed the few steps to the front door of the café, Kate could see through the window that her mother was already there, seated with her back to the window. She had a moment's regret that she'd suggested this place. It was a place of happy memories, of afternoon teas with Olbeck and Jeff, of quiet mornings on her own, with a steaming pot of tea and a plate of scones, the Sunday newspaper on the table in front of her. Now, all that was probably going to be tainted.

Oh, stop being so melodramatic, Kate, she told herself and pushed open the door. She wasn't sure whether to kiss her mother or not, and they both settled for an awkward sort of half-hug. Kate sat down opposite Mary Redman. She looked worse than she had when Kate had first seen her at The Black Cat. She looked as though she were slowly fading away. Kate tried not to show her distress.

"How are you, love?" Mary asked, in a voice that was surely even hoarser than it had been two weeks before.

"I'm fine," said Kate, hastily. "And you?"

Mary shrugged. "About the same."

"Right." Their tea came and Kate busied herself with pouring cups, arranging cakes on plates, handing over a napkin. After the bustle of that, silence fell.

"Coppers treating you all right, are they?" Mary asked. She

had always used to ask that, whenever she saw Kate, and Kate always answered in the same way, as she did now.

"Fine, thanks."

They both looked away and sipped their tea. A lengthier silence fell. Kate kept her eyes on the shimmering brown surface of her tea cup, thinking how excruciating this was.

"You spoke to Tin recently?" Mary said eventually.

Kate gave a non-committal nod. She didn't want to tell her mother that she'd arranged another dinner date with him for the following night.

"Handsome lad, in't he?" Mary had put down her cup and was dabbing the napkin around her mouth like a lady. "You could do a lot worse there, Kel – Kate."

"Yes, all right," said Kate, more testily than she'd meant to. "There's nothing like that going on." Well, she reasoned with herself, there wasn't at the moment. Despite herself, she felt a leap of excitement at the thought of what might happen tomorrow night. Aloud, she said, "I understand you've been talking to him about your experiences of the Marhaven care home." She noted with her police officer's eye the slight flinch that Mary gave at the mention of the home. "Is that right?"

Mary coughed and cleared her throat. It was Kate's turn to wince at the thick rattle of phlegm. Mary coughed, coughed again and wiped her mouth with the napkin. "Yeah, I've been talking to him," said Mary. "I want to set the record straight before I – before I go."

"What is there to tell?"

Mary looked at her with watering eyes. "There were bad things going on at the care home. People got away with stuff for far too long. Now it's time to put things right, as much as I can, while I still can."

Kate leant forward a little. "What kind of bad things?"

Mary dropped her eyes. She was quiet for a moment and then said, in a hoarse, low voice "Bad things. Girls given out to people, to men. It was a *care* home, there were girls there who were children. They were supposed to take care of us."

Kate was silent for a moment, thinking. "Are you saying this happened to you?"

"Sort of." Mary coughed again, wiped her mouth again with the sodden tissue.

"Let me get you a fresh one," said Kate, trying to hide her disgust. She delved in her bag for an unopened pack of tissues and gave it to her mother. "What do you mean, sort of?"

Mary slit the plastic of the tissue packet and extracted a new one. "A few things happened that shouldn't have happened. Touching and stuff. But I was never shared out, not like the others. Well, I was heavily pregnant by the time I got there, they wouldn't have wanted me."

Kate stared at her. "You were pregnant with Terry when you were at Marhaven?"

"No." Mary was shaking her head. "Not with Terry."

Kate was lost. "What do you mean – you mean you had another child before Terry?"

"He died." The words rang out with finality. Kate and Mary stared at each other across the table, steam rising from the teapot between them.

"You had another baby and he died?" Kate checked. Why had Mary never told her this before?

"He died when he was born," Mary said, almost to herself. She broke eye contact with Kate, looking away and off into the distance, clearly reliving her memories.

Kate shook her head, helplessly. "Mum, tell me about it from the beginning. You're saying you went to this children's home, this care home – why? Because you were pregnant?"

"Yeah. The social workers put me there, I didn't have anywhere else to go. I was only fifteen."

"It was one of those places where they used to put unmarried mothers?"

"Yeah, but not just that. They had other girls there too, runaways and orphans, people like that." Mary reached for her teacup and Kate tried not to notice her hand shaking or the stick thinness of her fingers. "Vulnerable girls. They knew nobody would believe them."

"So what are you saying happened, exactly? Sexual abuse?"

Mary flinched again. "I reckon. Something like that. Girls used to come in and every so often they'd be taken away in a big car. Someone told me that they used to get driven to a hotel and men would come to – you know..."

"Who told you?"

"Another girl at the home. Can't remember her name now, but she was there before I got there. She ran away though, one night. I guess she couldn't stand it anymore."

"You don't have any other evidence?" Kate could hear herself, sounding as though she was conducting a police interview, but she couldn't seem to stop herself. "Just the word of this other girl, this runaway?"

Mary dropped her eyes again. "I don't know – there was other stuff – it's hard to say what it was now though, but I remember feeling something was wrong, really wrong there."

She trailed off. Kate waited and then prompted her. "Like what?"

"I don't know," said Mary, looking close to tears. "There was something wrong there. But I was in a mess after the baby died, I didn't know whether I was coming or going. But there were other girls there who knew what was going on, they were all involved but no one believed them. We were helpless, no one wanted us. We tried to stick together, we wanted to be brave, but it's so hard when you've got no one on your side." Her voice sank and she muttered something else to herself, something that sounded like *Boudicca*.

For the first time, Kate found herself wondering about her mother's mental stability. Half of what Mary was muttering to herself seemed like a nightmare, a mish-mash of memory, fantasy and hallucination. She tried to get Mary to explain further but her mother shook her head, insisting that she couldn't remember any more. Eventually Kate gave up and poured her mother the last of the tea in the pot. Did it really matter, anyway? There was no evidence of a crime, nothing more to go on than a dying woman's memories which might be totally fabricated anyway. Kate winced at the brutality of her thoughts, but it was true, wasn't it? She had enough to worry about without wondering about a long-ago crime that may or may not have happened.

"I'll talk to Tin about it," she told her mother. "I'm sure he'll be able to explain better – I mean, I'm sure he'll be able to explain it all to me."

The conversation, such as it was, died after that. After the last drops of tea were drunk, both Kate and her mother began to make their excuses, talking over the top of one another.

"I've really got to get back—"

"Thanks for the tea, love but I've got to go—"

At the door to the tea room, Kate hesitated after helping her mother on with her coat. Then she made herself lean forward and kiss her mother's bony cheek. The flesh was cool beneath hers.

"I'll be in touch, Mum," she said. "Take care of yourself."

"You too," said Mary Redman. She turned and began to walk carefully down the steps to the pavement. "But then you always did that, didn't you? Always made sure you were okay, never mind anyone else."

She was gone before Kate could respond. Kate was only able to stand there on the top steps, with her mouth open like a fish, before anger and guilt began to mix in her stomach like a poisonous cocktail. Kate shut her mouth and began to walk back to where she'd parked her car, clenching her jaw all the way.

Chapter Twelve

THIS TIME, KATE PICKED THE restaurant for her dinner with Tin. As she walked through the door of The Boathouse, an Abbeyford pub that stood by the Avon River as it wound through the town park, she was assailed by doubt. It wasn't quite as nice as she remembered. How long had it been since she last came here? Kate thought back and realised it was probably over a year ago, when she and Olbeck had come here for a working lunch.

"Sorry," she said to Tin as she came up to him at the bar. "I remember this place being a lot nicer."

"It looks fine to me," said Tin, who was already perusing the menu. "They do steak and kidney pie. That's all I care about."

Kate grinned and ordered some drinks. They made their way over to the window seat, which did at least have a fine view of the Avon slipping past the terrace below. Kate watched the brown surface of the river twist and ripple with competing currents. A trio of mallard ducks floated by, almost in formation.

"The river's dropped a bit," Tin said, following her gaze. "Don't you think? We haven't had so much rain recently."

"Thank goodness." Kate looked up as the waitress approached with their starters. She was surprised at how easy it felt to be sat across from Tin, almost as if she were with a friend she'd known for years. All that marred the sense of comfortable familiarity were the butterflies that sparked in her stomach every time she caught his eye.

They chatted about the weather for a few moments longer. Kate mentioned that her best friend was getting married in a month's time and he was hoping for glorious sunshine. "Some hope," she said, spooning up some more risotto. "Still, if he and Jeff will insist on getting married in March, what do they expect?"

There was a flicker of surprise on Tin's face, quickly suppressed. "I've never been to a gay wedding before."

"No?" asked Kate, in a rather prickly tone. Surely he wasn't homophobic? She was mollified a second later when Tin added, "My gay friends aren't exactly the settling down type."

They concentrated on eating their meals for a few minutes. Kate was wondering where to begin in her questions. As it happened, Tin pre-empted her. "Mary said you two caught up the other day."

"Yes."

"She said you had some questions about Marhaven."

Kate wiped her mouth with her napkin and sat back. "That's putting it mildly."

"What has Mary told you?"

Kate recapped what her mother had said to her in the tea rooms the other night. She ended by asking, "She kept going on about these girls and being brave but nobody believed them. I couldn't make head nor tail of most of it, to be honest. What does she mean by that?"

Tin's normally cheerful face darkened. "Long story. I'll start at the beginning." He lined his cutlery up neatly in the middle of his plate and pushed it away from him. "Marhaven was built in the early nineteen twenties as a village school. It was a school up until the Second World War, when it remained empty for some years before being acquired by a church-funded charity group in the late nineteen sixties. They turned it into a care home for what were then termed 'unmarried mothers', although by the seventies, they were also taking in non-pregnant girls, a mixture of care-home cases, runaways and other children who needed to be cared for." He looked up at Kate. "Stop me if this begins to sound like a lecture."

"Stop," said Kate, unable to help herself. "No, I'm joking. Go on."

Tin did stop for a moment although he didn't smile. Instead he reached down to the rucksack he'd brought with him and brought out a thick manila folder. "These are some of my notes and research."

"Bloody hell," said Kate, taking it from him and weighing it in both hands. "You're quite thorough, aren't you?" She handed it back to him and said, joshingly, "Bit strange, though, bringing it all along on a date."

"Oh?" said Tin. "Is this what this is?"

There was a moment of silence as their eyes met across the table and Kate realised later that that was when the evening could have changed into something more...*interesting*. At the time, though, she was conscious merely of the usual pull-me-push-you sensations that she got when mixing business with pleasure. Half of her wanted to say 'sod the job' and merely please herself, move closer to Tin and throw caution to the wind. The other half, the half that never really gave up on the job, was shouting in her ear for her to stop mucking about and get on with what could be important professionally.

"What this exactly is, hasn't been ascertained yet," said Kate hastily but with a smile that was as flirtatious as she could make it. Tin returned it in kind. There was another charged moment and then Tin seemed to recollect himself, dipping his head towards the folder and placing it on the table in front of him. He's focused, thought Kate, recognising the same strength of purpose in Tin that she knew in herself. She didn't know whether that insight made her feel better or worse. He's ambitious, she told herself and something about that rang a faint warning bell. She sat back in her chair, business-like once more.

"Anyway," said Tin, clearly recollecting himself as well. "In the early nineteen seventies, two young girls, teenagers, made two separate accusations of sexual assault against the manager of Marhaven, Godfrey Peters. He and his sister, Melanie Peters, ran the care home together, under the auspices of the church charity."

"Okay," said Kate, feeling a little less giddy. "Do you have the reports there?"

"Somewhere. I'll dig them out in a second. Anyway, there were no charges brought in the end."

Kate rolled her eyes. "Okay."

Tin continued, "There was also a much more serious accusation levelled against the managers of the home by another girl a year or so after the first two reports. She accused Godfrey Peters of keeping her as a sex slave and essentially pimping her out to his friends."

Immediately Kate remembered her mother at the tea rooms the other night. *A few things happened that shouldn't have happened. Touching and stuff. But I was never shared out, not like the others...* She repressed a shiver. "Go on," she said in a low tone, when Tin showed no signs of continuing.

Tin cleared his throat. "Pretty horrible accusations, as you can see. However, the problem here is that the accuser was clearly very mentally unwell. After she reported those claims to the police, she was immediately sectioned, or whatever the nineteen seventies equivalent was. She remained in the mental hospital for several years after that."

"What was her name?" asked Kate.

Tin consulted his notes. "That girl was Jane Moor. The other two girls who reported the alleged sexual assaults were called Tina Fetterton and Sarah Smith."

"And where are they all now? Have you talked to them?"

"I've tried to talk to Sarah Smith. She lives up north. She wouldn't say anything about Marhaven, or what might or might not have happened there. Just didn't want to know."

"And the others?"

"They're both dead. Jane Moor died of complications of pneumonia in nineteen ninety-five – she was an asthmatic – and Tina Fetterdon fell into Clifton Gorge in nineteen seventy-five."

Kate raised her eyebrows. "*Fell* into Clifton Gorge?"

"Well," said Tin. "Let's just say the coroner recorded an open verdict but everyone else seemed to think it was suicide. She was a very troubled young woman, apparently."

"Not surprising, really, is it?" said Kate. "If those accusations were true and nobody believed her?"

Tin sat forward again. "Exactly," he said with an urgency that surprised Kate. "That's what I'm talking about. That's what I'm investigating. What if those claims were true and yet no one did anything about it? What if Jane Moor's claims were true but no one believed her either, because they thought she was mad?"

"I know," said Kate slowly. "But where do you start? It's all so long ago."

"I know, and no one who was there is talking to me either." Tin rubbed both sides of his nose with his fingers, closing his eyes. He slumped back in his chair. "Oh, I don't know what I'm doing sometimes. Maybe it is pointless."

Kate felt a sharp surge of sympathy for him, knowing the feeling. "Don't give up yet," she said as encouragingly as possible.

"Yeah, I know," said Tin. "Anyway, if this really is a date, maybe I've talked enough about unpleasant things such as the Marhaven. Why don't I ask you a few more pertinent questions?"

"Such as what?" asked Kate, smiling.

"I'm going to get another drink and think of some really good ones," said Tin. "What can I get you?"

"Same again, thanks. Will you excuse me for a moment?"

Tin nodded as Kate got up. What was the etiquette for saying you needed the loo on a date? Kate wondered as she made for the stairs that led down to the toilets. Should she just have been bold and said 'I need a wee'? Or would that be a bit off-putting? It was so long since she'd been out with a man she couldn't remember what was done and not done on a first date.

Don't be ridiculous, she told herself, washing her hands. Her gaze was drawn to a poster stuck on the wall by the mirror, advertising a local club night. On the poster, the outline of a woman was drawn, raising her hands to the night sky beyond her. Kate stared at it. The outstretched tips of the woman's fingers reminded her of something. Should she ask? It would be such a long shot... She climbed the stairs, slowly, thinking.

"I've thought of one!" said Tin, waiting for her back at the table with two full glasses. "When—"

"Sorry," said Kate, interrupting him. "Can I just ask you something first? It's still about Marhaven, unfortunately."

"Sure."

Kate sat down. "Was there ever any record of a girl called Jean Tripp at the home?"

"Spelling?" asked Tin, reaching again for his folder. Kate obliged. Tin ruffled through various pages. "No – no, there wasn't."

"Oh well," said Kate. "It was a stupid idea anyw—"

"Wait, sorry – there was." Tin pointed to a line of text with his fore finger. "Sorry, she was known to the others there by another name, that's why I didn't pick her up immediately."

"*What*?" Kate was on her feet, transfixed. "Seriously? There was a girl at the Marhaven home called Jean Tripp?"

Tin looked up at her. "Yes. Yes, she's mentioned in statements several times. But she liked to be called Jonie, that's why I didn't immediately make the connection."

Jonie. The necklace. Kate sat back down abruptly, feeling as if all the strength had gone out of her legs.

"Why?" asked Tin.

Kate opened her mouth to tell him and shut it again abruptly. *He's a journalist, remember.* She thought he might actually make the connection, knowing the case that she was probably working on and given her obvious excitement. She forced herself to look cool and unruffled.

"Oh, it's just the name of someone who might be connected with a case I'm working on," Kate said casually. "Nothing serious. It was just a shot in the dark, really."

Beneath her calm exterior, she was fizzing with excitement. The fact that she was on a date with Tin was momentarily forgotten. At that precise moment, all Kate wanted to do was call Olbeck. Could she get away with saying she had to make a phone call? She picked up her drink and took a long sip, thinking.

"What's going on?" asked Tin, his eyes narrowed. She might have known he'd be too intelligent to be fooled for long. Kate decided to come clean.

"Tin, I'm really sorry but there's a call I have to make. In fact, I've got a really early start so perhaps I should be making a move."

"Now?" Tin looked unconvinced. "Are you going to tell me why you're really going?"

Kate wavered. She really liked him, she didn't want to hurt him but... But sometimes work had to come first. "I can't explain right now. It's nothing to do with you – I mean, it's nothing that you've done. It's just – oh, I'll have to tell you later. I'll get this," she said, indicating the empty plates and glasses.

Tin snorted. "That's hardly the point. I thought we were going to start to get to know one another?"

"I know. I'm sorry. And we will. It's just – I do really have to go." Kate was immediately transported back to numerous scenes with Andrew Stanton: having to placate him for being out at work when he wanted her to be at home with him. Oh God, was this what all her relationships were going to be like? Do all men have this problem, she wondered. Probably not.

She forced herself to sit back down. After a moment, she reached over to take Tin's hand. The warmth of his fingers and the strength of his grip surprised her and once more she wavered. Did she really need to go tearing off to alert the team? Could she not just sit and enjoy the rest of the evening and not think about work for once? Kate considered it and rejected the idea. The fact was, excitement over Tin was one thing but excitement over a breakthrough in the case was another.

Tin still looked rather thunderous. Kate, on impulse, leant over the table and kissed him.

His mouth was stiff under hers for a moment and then relaxed. In a moment, they were kissing, really kissing, like schoolchildren who'd just discovered it for the first time. For a moment, the hubbub and swirl of the pub faded away and it was just the two of them, joined at the mouth and lost in one another.

Kate pulled back and they looked at one another. "I really do have to go," said Kate, somewhat breathlessly. "But I just – I just wanted..." She trailed off, her heart thumping.

Tin looked at her, with a tiny spark of amusement glimmering in his dark eyes. "Go on," he said eventually. "I'll take that as a positive sign."

"Do," said Kate. She kissed him again, more briefly this time but conscious of feeling it right down to her toes. "See you soon."

She grabbed up her bag and coat and turned, making her way to the exit. It was cold outside, a chill night wind blowing, but she didn't feel it at all, wrapped in warmth all the way back to where she'd parked the car, walking along on feet that seemed to float, only barely touching the pavement.

Chapter Thirteen

"WHAT ARE YOU SMILING AT?"

Kate, caught out in a dream, re-running that kiss through her memory over and over again, started. "What's that?"

"You're grinning at nothing like a complete nutter," Theo said. He threw a plastic folder over the table at Kate who barely caught it in time. "What have you been up to?"

"What do you mean?"

Theo grinned. "I know that look. It's the one you get after a damn good seeing to." He smirked and then added, "All my ladies get it."

Kate became aware that she was perilously close to blushing. "Oh, sod off, Theo. When are you actually going to grow up and have a proper relationship, not just a load of friends with benefits?"

She became aware that she sounded a lot more defensive that she had planned to. Theo grinned even more. Kate added, "How many 'lay-dees' are you up to now, anyway?"

Theo looked smug. "About four on the go."

Kate rolled her eyes. "I don't know where you find the energy."

"Four what?" Fliss asked cheerfully, as she walked up to the desks with a pile of paperwork in her hands.

"Don't ask," said Kate. "Theo's just showing off, as usual." She picked up the plastic folder he'd just thrown at her and looked at it. "Have you actually been doing some work for once? What are these?"

"Read 'em," Theo said, picking up his empty mug and getting up. "Statements from Jackie Tripp for starters. Rav and I have been busy up in Sheffield while you've been getting lucky." Kate threw a paperclip at him and he ducked and grinned, sauntering off towards the coffee machine.

"Cheeky bastard," muttered Kate, bending her head towards the statements. Something to read through now while she waited for Olbeck. She looked up to check his office once more, but it remained stubbornly empty. Where was he? Had he told Anderton yet?

"You might also want a look at these," said Fliss, holding out another bunch of folders.

"What are they?"

"Medical records for Jean Tripp. They were couriered down this morning."

"Thanks, Fliss." Kate thought of the thousands – millions – of words she'd have to wade through today and suppressed a groan. "Better get started, I suppose."

Fliss offered to make her a coffee and Kate accepted gratefully. She was beginning to warm to the newest member of the team. For one thing, Fliss at least was not about to boast of her many sexual conquests, or Kate didn't think so. Dismissing the irrelevant musings, Kate forced herself to concentrate on the mountain of paperwork before her.

She began with the medical records. Jean Tripp had been born in nineteen fifty-eight, the third daughter of parents who were approaching middle age when she was born. The usual childhood illnesses were documented, as was the fractured arm that Jackie Tripp had mentioned and that the post mortem had found. There was nothing much untoward in the records until Jean reached the age of twelve. Then a note of discord could be ascertained, creeping into the official jargon of the doctor's notes: bruising from a fight in the school playground, several urinary infections, a prescription for sleeping tablets. Kate read on, frowning a little.

After a while, she looked through the paperwork that Rav and Theo had managed to track down from Jean's old secondary school. As she read through it, a definite picture emerged; of a troubled girl, who could be violent, a girl who up until the age of twelve seemed to have had a normal, happy, untroubled childhood. So what had happened? The onset of puberty? Getting in with a bad crowd? Drug use or alcohol abuse? Kate riffled through the remaining pages. The signs were there but what did they point to, and who could they ask now? She got up, stretched and sat back down again, reaching for Jackie Tripp's statement.

Jean was my older sister by four years. Our parents were Doreen and Stanley Tripp, who were married in 1949. Our father worked in Benson's, the local paint factory, up until his death from lung cancer in 1965 and our mother married again two years later. Jean didn't get on with our new stepfather, John Billson, and they would have frequent arguments. Jean would sometimes run away but would always be brought home again by the police. In 1971, when she was fourteen, she left home without telling our parents but she told me before she left she was going to London to try and become a model. She had always had an interest in acting and singing. After that time, I did not see her again but some years later, possibly in 1973 or 1974, a postcard arrived from her, typed but with her signature at the bottom, telling us that she was moving to Spain and would try and visit us before she went. Jean never did visit us and there was no more communication between us.

Was that it? Kate turned the page over to see if there was anything on the back and was met by blank space. She sighed and looked up at Theo. "Is this really all that Jackie Tripp could tell you?"

Theo looked up from his report. "Listen, it was an effort even to get her to say that much. She's not exactly the sharpest knife in the drawer, is she?"

"No," Kate admitted. She looked again at the few paragraphs of type. The mention of the stepfather was interesting. Kate worked out the dates in her head. If Doreen Tripp had remarried when Jean was eight, that would explain the gradual decline in her behaviour, if Jean and her stepfather had been at loggerheads. But was that all it was? Kate read through the medical notes again, her eye snagging on the record of several urinary infections. She bit her lip. That could suggest something much worse...

She caught a flicker of movement out of the corner of her eye and looked up. Olbeck was back and he and Anderton were both beckoning her from the office doorway. Kate shot out of her seat.

"My office," Anderton said and wheeled around. Kate and Olbeck hurried after him.

"So," said Anderton, when they were all seated in his office – or rather, Kate and Olbeck were seated and watching their boss pace up and down. "How the hell did you manage to track that little piece of info down, Kate?"

"A journalistic contact," said Kate, loftily. She thought that might sound a bit more professional than saying 'from a bloke I really do quite want to sleep with'.

Anderton raised his eyebrows. "And this contact is legit?"

"I think so. Obviously we're going to have to corroborate the evidence."

Anderton continued his pacing. "Well, I can't imagine that would take much time. Perhaps we need to start looking a bit more closely at this so-called care home. It's not still in use as that sort of facility, is it?"

"I don't think so," Kate said, wishing she'd asked Tin that very question.

"Okay. Well, that will do for starters. Find out everything you can about it. Talk to your journalistic contact." Kate met Anderton's eye and fought not to blush. "Presumably they'll have plenty of information on it. See if you can pull any records relating to Jean Tripp and any known contacts. Try and talk to someone who might have known her, if there is anyone. Find the people who ran the facility, if they're still alive, and question them." He finally came to a halt and threw himself into his desk chair, churning his thick grey hair with one hand. "That's all I can think of for now but if anyone else has anything to add...?"

"I'll talk to Kate back in my office," said Olbeck, getting up. "I know you've got stuff to do."

"Never busier. Okay, I'll talk to you both later."

Kate and Olbeck were almost at his office door before Anderton added "I'm sure you're aware of this, but keen as I am to get this case closed, be aware that I don't have an unlimited budget."

Kate turned to stare at him. He shrugged, looking a little uncomfortable and said "I just had to point that out. You of all people, both of you, know how stretched we are."

Olbeck and Kate exchanged a look. "We understand," Olbeck said a moment later.

"Good," Anderton said, dismissing them with a wave of his hand. "Off you go."

"What was *that* all about?" Kate said, once they were back in Olbeck's office with the door shut.

"God knows."

"We're always on a limited budget," Kate said. She wandered around the office, looking out onto the busy floor through the glass walls. "Why did he feel he had to point that out?"

"Kate, I don't know." Olbeck seated himself at his desk and clicked the mouse to bring the computer screen to life. "Maybe we're on more than a usually restricted budget."

"Maybe," Kate said. She frowned and said, "It was almost..."

"What?" prompted Olbeck, as she trailed off.

"I don't know. Almost like he was warning us off."

Olbeck gave Kate a puzzled look. "I think you might be reading a little bit too much into it."

"Maybe," Kate said, once more. Then she shrugged and said "I'm going to make a start, anyway."

"Nice one." Olbeck rolled his chair nearer to his computer. Kate gave him a casual salute in farewell and was almost out the door before Olbeck said "Oh, by the way, have you done your speech yet? It's just that Jeff keeps nagging me—"

"Almost finished it!" Kate lied smartly. "I'll run through it with you tomorrow. No, maybe the day after tomorrow."

Hastening back to her desk, she groaned inwardly. That bloody speech: She'd have to make a start on that tonight, exhaustion or no exhaustion. Feeling tired at the very thought, she sat back down again at her desk and bent her head towards the many folders, determined to make a dent in the paperwork.

Later that evening, Kate put down her empty dinner plate on the living room coffee table, pushed Merlin away as he went to investigate the leftovers and pulled a notepad and pen towards her. She wrote 'speech' in large letters at the top of the page, underlined the word several times with vigour, sat up straighter with pen poised in her fingers – and then collapsed against the back of the sofa, groaning aloud.

Think, Kate, think. *I first met Mark when...* no, too clichéd. *I knew Mark and Jeff would be a happy couple when...* when what? Grimacing, she scrolled through her memories, trying to find the one definitive recollection that would kick-start her speech, leaving people hanging on to her every word and not doing what most people normally do during the wedding speeches, which is surreptitiously drink more and pray for them all to be over.

After fifteen minutes, the sum total of which yield three stilted sentences, Kate flung her pen down, swearing. Then she picked it up and wrote 'DO IT TOMORROW!' in flaring capital letters, picked Merlin up and went up the stairs to bed.

Chapter Fourteen

THE PILE OF PAPERWORK FOR the Jean Tripp case seemed to have tripled overnight. Kate, Theo, Jane and Fliss shared it out between them and sat back down at their desks, with the grim demeanour of those who knew a decent lunch break would be a distant dream.

Kate opened the first report, which turned out to be the victim statements from the two girls who had reported Godfrey Peters for sexual assault back in the seventies. The foremost one was the report from Tina Fetterdon. Kate read through it carefully, noting the accusations: touching her breasts, touching her genitals, forced fellatio. Kate grimaced, looked at Tina Fetterdon's date of birth and worked out Tina would have been fourteen at the time she accused Godfrey Peters. Briefly, Kate recalled an earlier case she'd worked, another abuse case culminating in the deaths of two people. From there, her mind skipped back to Jean Tripp's medical reports. What if Jean Tripp's stepfather had been abusing her? Was that why she ran away from home?

Kate read on, working her way through the report from Sarah Smith. Much the same as Tina Fetterdon's accusations. Why the hell hadn't it been properly followed up? Two girls reporting the same person for the same crimes – surely that warranted a decent investigation at least? It was the seventies, Kate reminded herself, thinking about all the hideous things several famous men had done at the time to hundreds – if not thousands – of children. People got away with things.

She looked at the name of the officer who'd filed each report. The first, a Kevin Doherty, drew a blank, but the second made her frown. Norman Chambers. Now why was that familiar? Kate sat, thinking for a moment before she realised. Why of course, Norman Chambers, a detective sergeant at the time of the report, had ended up being Detective Superintendent Chambers. She'd even met him once, when he visited her in hospital when she'd been recuperating from the attack that nearly killed her, three years ago. He'd retired soon after that, but he was still seen at the yearly Abbeyford Police fundraiser and occasionally in the office. Kate could recall him now, a rather lantern-faced man, with tufty white eyebrows and equally white hair arranged in a patrician crest.

She shook herself mentally and brought herself back to the present. Would it be worth trying to get an interview with Norman Chambers, to see if he could remember anything about the interviews with these girls? Kate knew Anderton and he were friendly; Chambers had once been Anderton's direct superior, if she remembered correctly. Kate made a note to ask Anderton whether he thought it was a good idea.

Okay. One thing to do. Kate scribbled notes as other ideas occurred to her. The first was one that she almost discounted out of hand, purely because of her emotional reaction to it. Then she told herself not to be so ridiculous. She would contact her mother and see if Mary could recall anything, anything at all about Jean Tripp – Jonie.

Kate put her pen down for a second, realising she'd not moved from her desk in over an hour. She stretched, groaning, catching Theo's eye.

"Anything, mate?" he asked.

Kate always found it rather endearing when he called her mate. "A few leads." She explained about Norman Chambers, ending with the question, "Think he'd talk to us about what happened?"

Theo's dark eyebrows rose rapidly. "Hmm... well, worth a try, maybe." He was silent for a second and then added "We might be just a little bit too low down on the scale, though."

Kate frowned. "I'm not going to *interrogate* him, just ask him if he remembers anything."

"It's over forty years ago. I'd hazard a guess he'll remember the sum total of fuck all."

Kate blew out her cheeks. "Yes, well. You're probably right." She stood up, stretched again and asked "So, what about you? Anything?"

"I think we should be interviewing Melanie Peters. If she's still alive and *compos mentis*."

Kate immediately thought of Tin and how he'd tried to do exactly that. Mind you, she and Theo had the might of the law on their side. "Yes, that's probably a good idea."

They both returned to their desks and bent over the folders again. At lunch time, Fliss offered to go and do a McDonalds run, for which Kate, much as she deplored fast food, could have kissed her. She remembered being the newly qualified rookie in Bournemouth; all those endless rounds of tea-making and sandwich buying, hoping to find her place in the team, hoping to be accepted. A secondary thought was that, to date, she hadn't really made much effort to be friendly to Fliss, to be inclusive and welcoming. *Bad Kate.* She made a resolution that that would change.

Buoyed by her good intentions, Kate called her mother. The phone went to voicemail again so Kate left what she hoped was a friendly, casual sort of message, that nevertheless implied that Kate would really like to talk to Mary again soon. Of course, she didn't mention Marhaven or anything like that. Putting her mobile down, she tapped a pen against the side of her jaw, thinking. What next?

Her thoughts were interrupted by the crash of the office door being flung back on its hinges as Anderton strode into the room.

Olbeck came to the door of his office, obviously in enquiry. Kate and the rest of the team turned their chairs to face their boss.

"Nothing to panic about, people," said Anderton. "But the identification of Jean Tripp goes public today. It'll be in the national and the regional press, so be prepared for a deluge of calls from people claiming they knew her, that they know who killed her, how she was abducted by aliens who then buried her – you know the drill."

Kate smiled reluctantly. Anderton raised a hand and said, "That's all, folks. We'll catch up later," and began to walk back to the corridor. Kate jumped up and followed him out.

"Hello," he said, as she caught up with him. "What's up?"

With Anderton, Kate was never quite sure whether he meant that question as a personal or a professional enquiry. Consequently, she never quite knew how to answer him. She mumbled something as they went into his office and both sat down. Kate, looking at him across the table, wondered whether he was still seeing the beautiful blonde who'd visited the office all those months ago. How that had hurt at the time. She was pleased to realise that now the thought didn't give her more than a moment of uneasiness. Relaxing a little, she smiled at him across the desk.

"I've got a quick question," she said.

"Yes?"

Kate explained about the reports and the fact that Norman Chambers had been the officer on the record at the time of the accusations. "So, I was wondering if you think it would be a good idea to talk to him?" she finished, leaning forward a little in her chair.

Anderton was still for a moment, obviously thinking. Kate, practiced at reading his face, could have sworn that, just for a second, there was something like a flash of uneasiness. Just a second's worth of anxiety. It was gone in an instant, fast enough for her to have doubted that she'd seen it.

"Yes, sounds like something worth doing," Anderton said, after a moment.

"Great," Kate said. "Could you give me his address?"

"There's just one thing," said Anderton. "It might be easier if I do it. I mean, no offence, Kate, but this is a highly decorated former officer we're talking about. And he's a friend of mine."

Kate frowned. "I only want to talk to him, briefly really – see if he remembers anything."

"I know, I know. But you know how it is – hierarchy and so forth. He'll probably be a lot more receptive to having a chat with me."

Kate swallowed. What Anderton was saying made sense, of course it did, but... There was something underneath it all, just a finger of uneasiness that nudged her. It was too nebulous a feeling for Kate to truly be able to identify just what it was that made her uneasy.

She brushed it aside. "That's fine," she said breezily. "I understand. No problem."

"It'll be a good chance to catch up with the old bugger, actually," Anderton said, sitting back in his chair. "Haven't seen him for months. Leave it with me and I'll see if I can see him sometime this week. How are things going, anyway? Anything else to report?"

Kate sat forward again, taking Anderton through her list of things to do. He listened with his usual attention and Kate spoke quite normally but, underneath it all, she was still aware of that faint hint of uneasiness, like a cold draught, a tiny stream of cool air from a source that was undetectable.

Back at her desk, she tried to shake the feeling off. She had two missed calls on her mobile, one from her mother and one from Tin. Kate hesitated and listened to the voicemail from her mother first. Mary Redman, voice huskier and weaker than ever, left a hesitant message saying that she would be in hospital for treatment for the next couple of days but would like to talk to Kate again anyway. Kate frowned. Which hospital was it? Surely she should go and visit her mother, if she had any compassion, after all. I must call Jay, she thought, and the others, and see what they think. Then she brought up the missed call from Tin and dialled into the voicemail he'd left her.

"Kate, it's me." Had they reached such terms of intimacy already? Kate was both pleased and alarmed by the thought. She listened further. "Could we meet up again? Not just because you owe me a decent dinner." Kate smiled reluctantly at that. "I've got some info that might prove...fruitful. Hell, I just want to talk it over with someone, really. No, that's not true. I want to talk it over with you. Let me know where and when, okay? If they do a decent steak and kidney pie, that's a bonus."

Kate smiled again and pressed the button to end the call. There was something to be said for mixing business with pleasure, she mused, already wondering where she could suggest for dinner. She tried to ignore the tiny voice that piped up that she didn't really know the man from Adam, and the fact that he was an investigative journalist meant that she really ought to be going into this with her eyes wide open. *Oh, sod it.* Kate dialled Tin's number, got his voicemail and left him a message telling him that she'd be free for a sumptuous dinner that evening at The Black Cat, if he was free. She put the phone down, fighting down a smile that wanted to become a beam.

TIN WAS WAITING FOR HER as before, thankfully this time unaccompanied by Kate's mother. He caught sight of her as she came through the doorway and waved. Kate walked up to him rather self-consciously. Was she supposed to kiss him? There was an awkward moment of hesitancy and then Tin leant forward and pecked her cheek. "Hello."

"Hello." Kate threw her hair back in apparent unconcern and sat down. She was remembering the kiss they'd shared at their previous meeting. Had Tin thought that that had been a mistake?

Was he cooling off? Get a grip, she told herself – not for the first time.

"You look good," Tin added.

Kate struggled not to show how pleased that remark made her. "Thanks," she said, coolly, and added, "so do you." Their eyes met once more, and Kate felt very surely then that Tin was in no danger of cooling off.

She forced herself to drag her gaze away. "What was it you wanted to talk about?"

Tin seemed to recollect himself too. "I see you've released the name of the victim in the Munford Gorge case." He held her gaze for a beat and then added, "What a coincidence."

Kate was too old a hand at this to blush. "Well, I have to thank you for an excellent lead. It really brought things forward."

Tin half-laughed. "I'm starting to think you're just meeting up with me for my journalistic skills."

"That too," said Kate and winked at him. "Seriously, though, I couldn't mention it to you then. I can't talk about the case now, so if that's why you wanted to meet me, then I'm afraid we're going to have to call it a night right now."

"All right, all right," said Tin, sounding a little offended. "God, I never knew you coppers were such hard work."

"Now who's getting defensive?" said Kate, conscious of a spurt of annoyance. They both realised they'd gone from doe-eyed looks to glares across the table and both looked away. Kate felt suddenly quite depressed. Why was she never seemingly able to make a relationship work? Not that this one had even so much as got off the ground... She stared down at the table for a moment before realising that Tin was asking her if she wanted a drink. "Okay, then," she said and then pulled herself up with a jerk, realising how sullen and grudging she sounded. She looked up at him again.

"Look," she said. "This hasn't gone according to plan, and it's probably my fault. I'm sorry." There you go, Magda, she thought.

All that hard work was finally paying off. *I'm finally able to admit when I'm wrong.* "Perhaps we shouldn't talk about Marhaven, or anything else to do with the case. Perhaps we should just talk about – oh, I don't know – about normal things. The sort of things everyone else talks about when they meet up for a drink."

Tin had listened to her speech with an impassive face which gradually softened into something approaching his normal, cheerful demeanour. Once she'd finished speaking, he said "Well, you're probably right. Let's have a drink and be normal for once."

"Right!" said Kate, sitting back in her chair. She watched Tin go to the bar and order the drinks, forcing herself to relax back into her seat, trying to get herself into a 'normal' frame of mind. The trouble was, as she became acutely aware, that she realised she really did want to know what it was he had to tell her about the case.

Tin sat back down again with their drinks and Kate, unable to help herself, said "Look, I know we just agreed not to talk about it but what was it that you wanted to tell me?"

Tin burst out laughing. "You're unbelievable, you are. I thought I was wedded to my career, but you're even worse."

Kate laughed despite herself. "Well, at least you're getting to know this up front. No hidden surprises further down the line."

Tin gave her an amused glance. "Well, as it happens, I also want to talk about it, but being too much of a gentleman, I had to wait until you gave me the option." They both exchanged smiles that acknowledged their mutual weakness. "Now," said Tin, becoming business-like. "Like I said, you've named the victim of the Munford Gorge case as Jean Tripp, right?"

"Right."

"Well, a day after that became public knowledge, I had a call from a guy who used to be a journalist for the Abbeyford Gazette, years ago. He's retired now, but he used to cover quite a lot of reporting for them and for some of the other regional newspapers."

"Okay," said Kate, taking a sip of her drink.

Tin continued, "This guy – his name's Tom, Tom Marks – he told me that he'd been contacted by Jean Tripp in the early seventies because she wanted to give him an exclusive on some big scandal involving the Marhaven home. Apparently she didn't want to go into details over the phone but she sounded legit enough, so he arranged to meet her in a few days' time in person."

Tin stopped talking for a moment to gulp his drink. "And?" prompted Kate after a moment.

"Well, that's just it. Apparently Jean Tripp never turned up. Tom Marks knew that she was living at the Marhaven care home, and after a few days he made some discreet enquiries and was told that Jean had run away. That was apparently that."

"And?" said Kate, sensing there was more.

"You'll have to meet this guy, Tom, and you'll see what he means. Apparently, he didn't like it, this supposed run-away. Something about it just didn't quite sit right, he said. So he started doing a bit more digging, trying to talk to a couple of the other girls there, that sort of thing."

"Why hasn't he come to us?" demanded Kate.

Tin looked uncomfortable. "Well, he had his reasons. Like I said, it's probably best if you contact him yourself. He may or may not tell you what he told me."

Kate sat back and stared at Tin. "Are you being deliberately obtuse? Why the big mystery?"

Tin dropped his gaze to the beermat he was turning around and around in his hands. "There's no mystery," he said after a moment. "It's probably best if you talk to him yourself, that's all."

Kate set her teeth in annoyance. Then she sat forward and said abruptly, "All right."

"Okay," said Tin "So if I—"

"Let's go," said Kate. "We'll go and see him now."

Tin's eyes bulged. "What? Now?" He risked a look at his watch. "It's almost ten."

"So call him and tell him we're on our way. I assume he lives locally?"

"Yes, but—" Tin looked up at Kate as she stood up and began gathering up her things. "Seriously? You want to talk to him now?"

"Yes, I do. And seeing as you're the one who brought him to my attention, it's probably best you come along too."

"Blimey, I..." Tin trailed off and then seemed to collect himself, getting up and pulling on his coat. "You don't mess about, do you?"

"Not in things like this." Kate stood back to let him move past her. "I'll drive if you'll show me the way."

Chapter Fifteen

TOM MARKS LIVED IN A small terraced house on the outskirts of Abbeyford. He seemed unsurprised to have two relative strangers arriving on his doorstep at ten fifteen in the evening, but Tin had managed to talk to him as they drove towards his house and give him a little bit of warning. Kate had said nothing as she listened to their conversation, but she'd heard enough to hear a faint nervousness in the disembodied voice of Tom Marks as it was heard issuing from Tin's mobile.

Tom Marks was a small man, thin but wiry, with a pair of black-framed, John Lennon glasses. He was totally bald and wore a grey cashmere sweater and a pair of dark denim jeans. He obviously lived alone, in a house stuffed full of books, papers, pictures and plants that was nonetheless homely and comfortable.

He shook Kate's hand and glanced at her warrant card, which she presented as a matter of course. She was aware of Tin's swift glance at it too. "Pleased to meet you," Tom Marks said, adding, "that's not something I thought I'd ever find myself saying to a police officer, to be honest."

Kate said nothing but noted the remark. They moved into a small front room, with a fire flickering cosily in the brick grate. Tom seated himself in a brown leather chair, clearly the one he used every day, and left Tin and Kate to find themselves a seat on the small sofa. Kate glanced at Tin, hoping to indicate that she would lead the talking and after a moment, he raised his eyebrows and sat back in acquiescence.

"I understand that you were contacted by someone you believed to be Jean Tripp, Mr Marks? When exactly was this?"

Tom Marks didn't reply for a moment. He leant forward, poked the fire and then said, with his face turned away, "Is this off the record?"

"You're not under caution, Mr Marks."

He nodded, apparently satisfied. "It's probably best if I tell you what happened from start to finish. Then you can question me further if you think it necessary."

"As you wish," said Kate, shifting a little on the sofa to face him more fully.

Tom Marks added another log to the fire and then sat back himself, crossing one neat leg over the other. "It's been so long since it happened, it's almost a lifetime ago. But it's funny, as soon as I heard her name I was transported straight back there, almost as if the intervening years had never happened. I suppose it was because it was the first time in my life I'd been truly frightened. The first time in my adult life, I mean." He was silent for a moment and then continued. "I was working for the Abbeyford Gazette at the time. It was nineteen seventy three, I remember that distinctly. As soon as I heard you were coming over, I looked up my notebooks from that time. I always kept them – like I said, it made a great impression on me."

"Why did you not come straight to us, Mr Marks?" said Kate, unable to help the question.

He glanced at her and frowned. "That will be made perfectly obvious as I go along. Please, let me continue."

"Sorry," said Kate. "Please go on."

He inclined his head in acknowledgement of her apology. "Like I said, I was working at the Abbeyford Gazette at the time. I was their crime correspondent, for what that was worth – we hardly had a lot of serious crime then, or so you would think." He thought for a moment and then went on. "I'm sure there was just as much evil and depravity in the world then as there is now, but it was far more hidden. People got away with things then."

Kate's thoughts exactly. She leaned forward a little, intent on Tom Mark's words.

He went on. "Jean Tripp rang me one day, in June, I think it was. She was quite distressed, quite upset but very – how can I put it – very earnest in what she was saying. Very sincere. She told me that she had certain knowledge of a very serious crime taking place at the Marhaven care home and that she wanted to talk to me about it, to 'get it all out in the open before it was too late'. Those were her exact words, I remember them as if it were yesterday."

Tom Marks again fell silent. Kate wondered whether she dared interrupt him but this time, Tin did it for her.

"What exactly were her accusations?" Tin asked.

Tom Marks didn't answer for a moment. Then he said with sadness in his voice "She told me that the girls in Marhaven care home were used as sex slaves and pimped out to different men in a kind of paedophile ring. She didn't use that term, I'm not sure it was even in common knowledge at that time, but looking back, that's what she meant. She said that the men that used the girls were from some of the most respectable places in Abbeyford, teachers, lawyers, etcetera. Godfrey Peters, who ran the home, would arrange for the girls to be delivered to special parties at secret locations. Jean told me that she was one of these girls and that she'd been raped and abused at these parties by men who were otherwise pillars of the community. I'm paraphrasing, of course, but that's what it came down to."

Nobody said anything. After a moment, Tom Marks began to speak once more. "I believed her. Or, let me be clearer, I was sufficiently concerned as to want to talk to Jean further. So we arranged to meet in a few days' time. I asked her to meet me in a coffee bar in Abbeyford, but she didn't want to, she said she was scared of being followed, so we arranged to meet somewhere in Bristol, a pub near the docks."

Unable to help herself, Kate interrupted. "She said she was scared of being followed?"

Tom Marks nodded. "She was quite scared, quite paranoid. There may have been a good reason for that, as I found out later, but it could have been because she truly was afraid that someone was following her. Anyway, we arranged the meeting, and on the day I went to the venue we'd decided on and waited. And waited and waited. She never turned up." He turned to poke the fire once more and they all watched the orange sparks flower up into the darkness of the chimney. "I didn't have a contact number for her but I knew she was living at the Marhaven home. I waited to see if she would contact me again, but a week went by and there was nothing." He paused once more and said "To be honest, at first I thought she'd got cold feet. That Jean had been lying about what she'd told me and she'd got scared of the repercussions."

There was a short silence. Kate cleared her throat and asked "But something must have made you start looking for her? Tin—" She gave him a glance and he returned it, half-smiling. "Tin said that you made some enquiries at the home?"

Tom Marks nodded. He'd been sitting hunched forward in his chair, as if cold and needing the warmth of the fire. Now he sat back, easing his shoulders as if they were stiff and painful. "After a few weeks, I started to get a bit worried. It was her distress, you see, when she called me. She sounded – I don't know, desperate. And if what she had told me was true, then it was possible that she was in some danger. So I thought about it and after a while I decided to see if I could find her."

"How did you do that?" asked Kate.

Tom gave a grunt of a laugh. "I posed as a documentary film maker. I went to see Godfrey Peters and his sister and told them I was making a Christian documentary on the wayward youth of today."

"They believed you?" asked Tin.

"Apparently. They certainly weren't worried about telling me that they had several 'problem girls' at the home and one of them had recently run away."

"Jean," Kate said; a statement rather than a question.

Tom nodded. "They told me it wasn't the first time. Apparently she was a runaway from her family home and had ended up at Marhaven having been on the streets. They told me she had drug and alcohol problems, which they were trying to arrange for her to have treatment for. I asked if they'd reported the fact that she was missing to the police and they told me they had."

Kate, listening intently, frowned. If what Tom was saying were true, then the Peters had been lying, about that if nothing else.

Tom was still speaking. "I talked to some of the other girls there, or I tried to. I left my contact number for several of them and told them that Jean had talked to me and to get in touch with me if they had anything to tell me. I told the Peters that it was because I might need to interview them for the documentary."

"Did any of them get in touch?" asked Kate.

Tom shook his head. "No. No, they didn't." He looked again into the depths of the fire once more and then turned back to face them. "Would anyone like a drink?"

Kate and Tin both declined but Tom went on to say "Well, I'll go ahead and have one, if you don't object. I could do with one, for this part of the story."

Kate and Tin both murmured something along the lines of that being no problem. Tom left the room for a moment and came back after a few minutes, carrying what looked like a glass of whisky. He sat back down again, sighing.

"Hardly drink spirits these days," he said. "Not like in my reporting days. My God, we used to throw it back then. Amazing I'm still here, really." He took a sip, grimacing, and then a longer one, swallowing the liquid down as if it were medicine. Then he put the glass down and leant forward. "It was about a week after I'd been to Marhaven and talked to the girls. I was coming back from town, quite late – I think I'd been reporting on a traffic accident or something like that. I was just outside of Abbeyford – I lived in Cudston Magna then, right out in the middle of nowhere. So I'm driving down these dark country lanes and suddenly there's a flashing blue light in my rear view mirror."

The fire had died down once more. The room seemed to gather shadows, the warm light from the fire dimming so that Kate found it suddenly hard not to shiver.

Tom went on, glass in one hand. "Once I'd pulled over and wound my window down, this officer appeared. I didn't recognise him but he was a big chap, broad-shouldered. I didn't think to look at his badge number or anything like that, you just didn't think about those things in those days. It was dark, anyway, pitch black with no streetlights. He said something like 'Going a bit fast for these roads, weren't you, sir?'" Tom stretched his shoulders back again and went on. "Of course, I hadn't been. I knew how dangerous those roads could be, especially at night. I said something to that effect and that's when it stopped being a nuisance and started being something that I thought could – could escalate. He ordered me to get out of the car and stand with my hands on the bonnet and then he started searching the car, all the while telling me to shut up, because, of course, I was protesting at this point, because as far as I could see I'd done nothing wrong." Tom lifted up the glass to his lips and drained it. Coughing, he went on. "It seemed to go on for ever. It was cold, I remember that, for a summer night. I remember feeling my fingers go numb on the metal of the car. Eventually, the officer came up to me and held something in my face, a small plastic bag full of white powder and he said, something like, 'What's all this, then?'"

Kate leant forward herself, watching Tom closely. "What was it?"

Tom shrugged. "I presume it was cocaine, or something like

that. Whatever it was, it certainly didn't belong to me. The closest I ever got to narcotics was marijuana. Anyway, the upshot of it was this officer was going to charge me for possession. For something that wasn't even mine."

There was another moment of silence.

"Are you saying you think he planted it on you – in your car?" asked Kate, just to be sure.

Tom seemed to shake himself a little, as if waking himself from a dream. "Well, it's the only explanation that fits, isn't it? It wasn't mine and none of my friends would have dreamt of leaving something so incriminating in plain view. But what really made me realise what had happened was that the policeman used it as a threat. He was ranting about court and prison and things like that – I remember the clouds of steam puffing into the air as he yelled at me - but then he calmed down and told me that he could find a way to let me off – if I learnt how to behave myself. And that meant keeping my nose out of things that didn't concern me."

Tin leant forward. Kate saw the pink tip of his tongue moisten his lips and wondered if his mouth was as dry as hers. "Did he mention Marhaven specifically?" Tin asked.

Tom shook his head. "No. No, nothing that specific. To be honest, at that point, I was so shaken I wasn't really thinking about anything like that. I just wanted to get home without being arrested." He sat back in his seat with a sigh. "Anyway, eventually he let me go, once I'd grovelled enough. I drove home very slowly. I was shaking." He looked down at his hands, clutching one another. "The next day I thought it over and I wondered what was going on. Had I just run up against one bad apple, or was I poking about in things that were too dangerous to go on investigating?"

The three of them were silent once more, looking at the sunset glow of the fire.

"So did you drop it? Like he told you too?" Kate asked eventually.

Tom looked grim. "I tried contacting some of the girls at

Marhaven once more, just once. Then I woke up one morning to find all my tires slashed. I got the message after that. I left it all well alone." He shifted in his seat. "I kept trying to tell myself that it could have been due to something else – I was reporting on several cases that year, at least one of which was gang-related – but – I don't know – it just left a nasty taste in my mouth. It haunted me, you might say. That's why, when I heard that the body you'd found was Jean Tripp, I knew I had to tell *somebody*. But you can see why I didn't – I don't – want to go to the police."

"You can't surely think..." Kate trailed off. She was thinking back herself, back to that faint sense of uneasiness that she'd recently felt pervading the case as she worked. What was wrong? Was it... There was nothing she could put her finger on, nothing concrete; it was all too faint, a cobweb of doubt.

"Did you ever find out who that officer was?" asked Tin.

Tom nodded. "Naturally. That was almost the first thing I did. His name was Kevin Doherty." Kate gave a small start of surprise and she saw that both Tin and Tom had noticed. Neither asked her to explain though. Tom went on. "Let's just say I followed his career from then on, with interest, you could say. He was not a pleasant man."

"What happened to him?" asked Kate, knowing she'd have to look into this herself.

"He was dismissed from the force in nineteen eighty because of an accusation of sexual misconduct with a suspect. No charges were actually brought." Tom paused and then added, "He died in a hit and run accident that same year. They never found the culprit."

Kate wondered whether she could ask him to elaborate but decided against it. It would be something to investigate at work tomorrow. The thought of work made her realise quite how late it was, past midnight. They'd been sat here for hours. She glanced at Tin, hoping to make him understand, indicating with a nod of her head her wristwatch. He nodded.

"Mr Marks, you've been so helpful," said Kate, "but it's getting late and I think we're going to have to call it a night. There's just one thing." She hesitated, unsure of the reception her question would receive. "Would you be willing to make a statement to the effect of everything you've just told me – us?"

Tom looked at her without speaking for a moment. She could see his eyes behind the glass of his spectacles, dark and watchful. "Well, I suppose that depends, doesn't it?"

"Depends?" asked Kate

He looked directly at her. "Depends on who's in charge."

They said goodnight soon after that, and Tin and Kate walked back to the car. Both were silent. Kate turned the heater of the car up to full as she pulled away from the kerb, hunching herself back into her seat. She felt colder than the night's temperature warranted. "Where am I dropping you?" she asked Tin, the first words either of them had spoken for ten minutes.

She could see Tin looking at her and she wondered whether he'd expected to be invited back to her place for the night. Well, if he had, he'd be disappointed. She was far too tired and emotionally wrung out from the night's conversation to even think of anything amorous.

"You can just drop me back at my car," said Tin, quite coolly, as if she were a vague acquaintance.

Kate was conscious of a feeling of sadness, of another wasted opportunity, but she was just too limp with fatigue to do anything about it. She thanked him for his help colourlessly, and he answered her in much the same tone. She pulled up beside his car parked near the restaurant, where the evening had started off so promisingly, but their goodbyes were the cold, polite farewells of virtual strangers.

Chapter Sixteen

KATE SAT DOWN AT HER desk the next morning with a notebook full of scribbled memos, all of which seemed equally important. She started with Keith Doherty, checking back that his was the name that she'd seen on the victim statement from Tina Fetterdon. She hadn't been mistaken – he'd been the investigating officer on that case. Kate put the report down slowly, thinking. Then she brought up a search engine on her computer and typed in *Kevin Doherty*, along with various combinations such as *police officer, scandal, death*. She soon found the newspaper reports of his dismissal from the Abbeyford force and read through each link with increasing concentration. Detective Sergeant Kevin Doherty had been accused of sexual involvement with a female suspect in a burglary case. The case had eventually collapsed due to the unreliability of several key witnesses but, by that time, Doherty had already been dismissed from the force.

Kate re-read that part. He'd been dismissed, not resigned. She looked at the photographs accompanying the article. Doherty had been a big man, bull-necked and thick shouldered. He looked like a dangerous thug, which, from reading between the lines, he probably had been. She searched again for articles on his untimely death, of which she also found plenty. Doherty had been found dead by the side of a lonely country road in the early morning of a Saturday in October, nineteen eighty. His injuries were consistent with being hit by a car but despite an investigation, no suspect was ever charged with his killing. Kate read through several more reports, noting that Doherty had also been linked to some rather dubious people, most notably a well-known criminal gang operating from Bristol at that time.

Kate looked at the photograph of the road where Doherty's body had been found; a small country road overlooked only by fields and hedges. Had he been run down deliberately? Or was it a genuine accident? Kate didn't suppose she would ever find out. Did his death have anything at all to do with the Marhaven care home or was it because of his involvement with another crime?

She sat back, easing the stiffness in her neck that came from reading hunched forward over the keyboard– so much for setting a good example for Theo – and looked up to see Anderton waving at her through the corridor window. She got up and made her way over to him.

"Just thought I'd let you know that I dropped in on Norman Chambers last night," Anderton said, as they got to his office. He gestured to Kate to take a seat and shut the door. "I was over that way anyway so I thought I might as well kill two birds with one stone."

He sat down in his chair, facing Kate over the desk. "Yes?" asked Kate. "Did he have anything to say about the two reports?"

Anderton tousled his hair for a moment. Then he sat forward, clasping both of his hands together. "I have to say that he didn't, really," he said. "It's not very surprising, it was so long ago. But he did promise to have a think and to see if he could recall anything about the girls and anything else that might help."

It was no more than Kate had expected but she was aware of a jab of disappointment. She murmured her thanks and went to get up – and then sat back down again. "Actually, if there is a chance to speak to him again, I'd like to know if he could tell me anything about Kevin Doherty."

Anderton's brows drew together. "Kevin Doherty? Now, why on Earth would you want to know about him?"

"You knew him?" asked Kate.

"Unfortunately, yes. We worked together on the same team for a few years – that's when Norman was my SO. He was for both of us. Doherty was... Well, let's just say *you* wouldn't have liked him."

Kate raised her eyebrows. "It doesn't sound much like you did either."

"I didn't," said Anderton. He sat back again in his seat. "He was a bigoted idiot with some very questionable views towards women. Getting rid of him was the best thing Abbeyford ever did."

Kate nodded. "So what do you think happened? His death, I mean."

Now it was Anderton's turn to raise his eyebrows. "Incredibly suspicious, I'd say. He was a man who liked to keep his friends close and his enemies closer. Perhaps they were one and the same, in this case."

"Right." Kate was silent for a moment, thinking. She was just opening her mouth to ask another question when Anderton said, "Anyway, Kate, I just thought I'd bring you up to speed. I'll let you know if I manage to speak to Norman again or if he has anything that can help us."

Kate knew a dismissal when she heard one. She gave her thanks again and got up.

"Oh, I'll be doing a debrief later," Anderton said just as she was leaving. "Warn the troops, will you? About three o'clock." Kate nodded. "Good stuff. I'll see you later."

Kate went back to her desk. Files and folders seemed to have bred in the short time she'd been away. Sighing, she tried to shuffle them into some sort of order, noting that there were at least three new cases vying for her attention. She flicked through them quickly. A sexual assault, a robbery, a suspicious death. Her gaze went to the fat folder on Jean Tripp. There were only so many hours in the day, and how many of them could she devote to this one case anymore? Sighing again, she pulled her chair up to her desk, picked up her pen, and got back to work.

She'd almost forgotten about Anderton's debrief that afternoon and had entirely failed to warn anyone that he'd be doing that, so it was lucky that all the team were coincidentally in the office when their boss came crashing in in his usual inimitable style. Kate waved frantically to Olbeck to attract his attention, guiltily aware that she'd forgotten to warn even him.

"Afternoon, team," Anderton said. "Just a quick update on where we are. Now, I know that most of you have been working very hard on the Munford Gorge case, and you've done well with it so far. But time is ticking on and the high-ups have just let me know that as from today, we'll be scaling back our time on that particular case. We're not closing it, don't get me wrong, but we're being snowed under with other work and I need to reallocate some resources."

Kate was aware of the faint feeling of surprise in the room, emanating from the others, as they digested what Anderton was saying. It wasn't the first time that investigations had been abruptly scaled down – there were only so many people and so much money, after all – but it hadn't happened for a while. Surprise was too mild a word for what Kate was feeling. Shock would have been a better choice of description. *He's lying*, she thought to herself, and was shocked again at the thought. *Why are we really pulling back on this case?*

Anderton was still talking, taking the team through the workload up ahead with the new cases that had come in. Theo and Jane were directed to the sexual assault case, with Fliss and Kate working with Olbeck on the others. Kate scarcely heard him. She was wondering what exactly she was going to ask once he'd stopped talking. How could she openly question his judgement without, well, questioning his judgement?

Anderton paused for breath and Kate shot her arm up into the air. "Yes, Kate?" asked Anderton and she could have sworn there was a tiny undercurrent of resignation in his voice, as if he'd been expecting her to make a fuss.

"What's going to happen with the Jean Tripp case? Sir," she added, after a moment.

"Management want it moved to Cold Cases. I should say that they've been asking for this for a while now and so far I've resisted."

"But you agree with them now?"

Anderton met her gaze steadily. "Yes, Kate, I do. We're being flooded with other cases just as much in need of our attention – probably *more* in need of our attention."

Kate lowered her arm, unhappy with the answer but knowing this was not the time to start arguing. She let the others ask questions and Anderton answer them, all the while drumming her fingers moodily on the edge of her chair.

Eventually, the debrief was over, and people began to move back towards their work. Kate waited until Anderton had waved a hand in farewell and begun to walk back towards his office. She hurried after him but was briefly detained by running into Theo, who was moving with determination towards the coffee machine. Once they'd untangled themselves – *sorry, sorry mate, after you* – Kate walked as fast as she could towards Anderton's office. The door was firmly shut and Kate knew as well as anyone that that meant Anderton was not to be disturbed. She bit her lip, shifting from foot to foot outside the door. To hell with it. She raised her hand and knocked.

"What is it?" Anderton asked, once she'd peered around the door in answer to his "Come on in then, Kate. If you must." How had he known it was her?

"What's going on?" was what she asked, once she was inside with the door shut behind her.

"What do you mean?"

"You know what I mean." This was skirting dangerously close to being disrespectful but at the moment, Kate was angry enough not to care. "Why the hurry to close this case?"

"We're not *closing* it, like I said. It's moving to Cold Cases. It's no longer top priority, that's all."

Kate sat down with a thud. "Why's it not top priority?"

"Oh, Kate." Anderton sighed. "Because this department doesn't have an unlimited personnel budget? Because we don't have an unlimited budget, full stop? Because I've got cases queuing up that involve people suffering here and now, not forty years in the past? That enough for you?"

Kate bit her lip. "We were making good progress—"

"I know that," Anderton interrupted, but in a gentler tone. "Your hard work hasn't gone unnoticed, believe me. I know you like to see things through to the bitter end but believe me, Kate, sometimes the decision is just out of my hands. I'm sorry."

"But—" protested Kate, unsure of what else she could say.

"Kate," said Anderton with finality. "I understand your disappointment but it's out of my hands. I need you to get started on the new cases, right now. Can I ask you to do that?"

Kate swallowed down her annoyance. "Yes, sir," she muttered, after a moment of seething silence.

"Good." Anderton looked down at his cluttered desk and sighed. "Was that all?"

"*Yes*," said Kate, trying to infuse that one word with all her anger and resentment. She wasn't sure it had worked.

"Right. Off you go then."

Kate walked back to her desk, doing her best not to stamp. She flung herself into her chair, clicking her mouse moodily. What the hell was wrong with Anderton? She tried telling herself it was nothing, going over all the reasons he'd given her for the reallocation of the case, but it didn't work. The same phrase repeated itself again and again in her head. *He's lying. He's lying.*

"Cup of tea, Kate?"

Kate barely heard Fliss's offer. When it was repeated, she looked up and muttered something, a yes, a no, she didn't really care. The file for the new case was already on her desk, placed on top of the bulging folder that contained all of Kate's work on the Jean Tripp case. Kate looked at the new folder and then pushed it aside, petulantly. Then she took the Jean Tripp file and walked over to the storage room with it.

"Sorry, Jean," she muttered as she locked the file away in the cabinet. What was Anderton's phrase? "It's out of my hands."

She heard her mobile ringing as she was walking back to her desk and ran to answer it. It was Jay.

"What's up?"

"It's Mum." Kate's heart gave a massive thump but Jay was already speaking as if he could hear her reaction. "Listen, don't panic, don't worry, but you know she's been in hospital?"

"Yes – I was going to visit her." Kate was conscious of a spurt of guilt, realising she hadn't even bothered to find out which hospital Mary had actually been admitted to.

"Well, they've moved her out of there into some sort of hospice. They didn't say as much but I think she's taken a turn for the worse. Me and Laura are going down there tomorrow to see her. Will you come too?"

Kate suddenly realised she was standing stock still in the middle of the office floor. People were looking at her with concern. Turning away and heading for the corridor, she said "Yes. Yes, of course. Where is it?"

Jay named a suburb on the outskirts of Bournemouth. Kate agreed to meet them there tomorrow at eleven, adding "Can you text me the details, Jay? I haven't got a pen on me." She felt so flustered and upset she knew there was no hope of her mind retaining the details.

They said goodbye and she trailed back to her desk, slumping down in her seat. She could see Fliss giving her worried looks across the table and straightened up, wanting to deflect any questions. She reached for the folder on the new case, opened it and began to read, but the words could have been in an unknown language for all the sense they made.

Mum's dying. That was the first time that Kate had truly taken it in. *She's dying.* She could feel her eyes begin to burn and, not wanting to cry at her desk, jumped up and hurried for the ladies', where at least she could sob in a modicum of peace.

When she got home that evening, the first thing she did was to pick Merlin up and bury her face in his soft black fur. She sat down on the sofa, hugging him against her until he squirmed out of her tight grip and ran away towards the kitchen. "Stupid cat," muttered Kate. In a minute, she would get up and feed him, would start to think about making dinner, would hang out the washing and take the rubbish out – all the chores that kept the house running – but just at that very moment, all she could do was lie on the sofa and stare up at the ceiling, thinking of her mum and of Jean and of what the hell she was going to do.

Chapter Seventeen

THE BAD WEATHER FINALLY BROKE the next day. Kate drove along the motorway in a blaze of spring sunshine. She could see patches of snowdrops on the banks of the dual carriageway with a cheerful burst of yellow daffodils here and there. Perhaps Jeff and Mark would have sunshine on their wedding day, she thought sentimentally and then cursed as she realised she still hadn't done that bloody speech. Tonight, I'll do it tonight, she promised herself, knowing full well that she would probably forget again.

The hospice where Mary Redman was staying was a modern brick building, set in some landscaped grounds, all one storey. Kate assumed that was to make it easier for patients to be transported around; no worries with stairs and falls if everything was on the ground floor. She saw Jay and Laura getting out of their car as she pulled into the car park and waved, feeling a burst of happiness at the sight of her brother that not even the anticipation of the grimness of this particular visit could dim.

"You're looking well," she said to Laura as they walked towards the entrance.

"You're looking knackered," said Jay, peering at her face. "Are you working too hard?"

Kate couldn't help but laugh. "When aren't I working too hard? You know how it is."

They made their way inside the building. Directed by the woman at the reception desk, they found Mary's room quite easily. Jay knocked and they all heard Mary's breathless voice telling them to come in.

As shocked as Kate had been by the first sight of her mother, all those weeks ago, that was nothing to the shock she felt now, looking at the woman who lay on the bed before her. Mary was skeletally thin, the bones of her skull protruding from the almost translucent skin that overlaid them. She lay almost lost in the hospital sheets, wearing a cotton nightgown that echoed the colour of her skin; white, with an undertone of grey. Mary still wore her coppery wig, and there was something so brave and yet so pathetic about the sight that Kate felt her throat closing up. Blinking, she followed Jay and Laura's example and kissed her mother hello, trying not to tighten up her face as their cheeks made contact.

She let Jay and Laura do most of the talking, finding herself a seat that was furthest from the bed. Laura asked some gentle, appropriate questions about how Mary was feeling, like the thoughtful, considerate girl that she was. Kate sat back and listened, letting her eyes roam about the room. It was quite a nice room, the walls painted in a peaceful grey-blue, a framed painting of an impressionist print over on the far wall. The owners of the hospice had obviously tried to make it seem as little like a hospital room as possible, but you couldn't escape the oxygen tanks, the medication on the side table by the bed, and the bed itself, which could be raised or lowered as needed. An oxygen mask lay beside Mary's limp hand and every so often she would lift it to her face and gasp weakly.

At last, Jay and Laura began to make tentative noises about leaving, and Kate jumped up, trying not to appear too eager to leave. Again, she kissed her mother's cheek and said something cheerful and fatuous about being back soon and was at the door when her mother said, in the strongest voice that Kate had heard today, "Kelly. Wait."

Jay and Laura turned enquiringly to Kate. She herself turned back to her mother, eyebrows raised, hoping she didn't appear too impatient. "What's wrong, Mum?"

Mary took a gasp of oxygen. "I want to speak to Kelly – to Kate – alone."

Kate sighed inwardly. "It's okay, I'll see you guys later," she said. "Don't wait for me." After exchanging hugs with them both, she saw them both out of the door and then returned to the bed, trying to keep her face neutral. "What is it, Mum?"

She was bracing herself for a bollocking, a diatribe on her real or imagined failings, although she couldn't quite pinpoint what it was Mary thought she'd done. It was just the low-level, permanent miasma of guilt she carried about with her, that's what it was. Kate sat down again, this time nearer to the bed.

Mary looked at her from over the black rubber rim of the mask, the clear part of the plastic clogged with spittle. Kate looked into her mother's eyes. What she saw surprised her. There was no anger there, but there was an unmistakeable appeal. "What do you want, Mum?" she asked again, more gently.

Mary tore the mask from her face. "I want to make a statement," she said, once she was able to talk again. "I want to make a statement about my time at Marhaven and what happened."

Kate's heart thumped. "About Marhaven."

Mary nodded, struggling either for breath or through the grip of strong emotion. "I've not got much time left, but I need to do it. It's important. They shouldn't get away with it, it's been too many years but we can put it right, Kelly, you and me. But you've got to help me."

Kate leant forward and took her mother's bony hand. "I'll help you. Just tell me why you want to do this now?"

Mary gave a hoarse cough and Kate flinched back a little until she realised that her mother was trying to laugh. "'Cos I'm *dying*, Kelly, aren't I? I want to set things right before I go. God knows I was always a useless bloody mother, but this is my chance to do something right for a change. I want to make a statement, I need to tell someone what happened at Marhaven. As much as I know."

"Okay," said Kate, "That's no problem. We can—"

Mary interrupted her, both in voice and with a hand that clutched back at hers with desperate strength. "I can't tell you everything but there were others there. They'll tell you too, once I've got things started. That's how it always works, doesn't it, other girls come forward. There was two, two who knew stuff that went on. Sarah, that was one of them. Talk to Sarah. Tell her to be brave and tell someone too." Mary coughed and fastened the mask to her face. Kate stared at her as she gasped in the oxygen, willing her to be able to carry on. At last, Mary pulled the mask away from her face. "Sarah always said she was a warrior. Said she wanted to be that one, the one who fought the Romans, the woman chief."

"Boudicca?" asked Kate, doubtfully.

"That's it. Tell Sarah to be Boudicca. It's not too late. Tin'll help you if you ask him. But I need to make my statement, and soon, Kelly – Kate."

Transfixed by her mother's gaze, Kate nodded slowly. "I can't take it myself, Mum," she said. "But there's several people at work who can do it. I'll get one of them down here tomorrow. They've been trained for it, for this kind of thing. Tomorrow, you have my word."

Mary nodded. She held the mask up to her face again briefly before seeming to shrink back on the pillows. Her eyelids fluttered. "I'm tired," she said after a moment. "Worn me out, that has. You go now, Kelly. Go and sort it out for me."

"Yes. Yes, I will. Try and rest now, Mum. I'll have an officer here first thing tomorrow to talk to you and you can take all the time in the world."

Mary smiled. Her eyes closed and she murmured something, so that Kate had to lean in to hear. "That's what I haven't got."

"Well..." Kate stood up, preparing to go. Then she leant down and hugged her mother, properly, feeling the bones of her mother's chest and shoulders beneath her arms. "Well done, Mum," she said, equally as quietly. "We'll sort it out together."

"Good girl." Mary turned her head and fastened the mask back onto her face, dismissing her. Kate looked at her for a long moment and then left, shutting the door gently behind her.

Chapter Eighteen

THE SECOND THING THAT KATE did the next morning on reaching the office was to call her mother. Unable to reach her by mobile phone, Kate redialled the hospice reception and informed them that someone from Abbeyford Police Station would be arriving that morning to take a victim statement from her mother. She gave the details of her colleague, Jane, to the receptionist, hearing the undercurrent of surprise and curiousity running beneath the receptionist's usual bland tones. Finally, she asked if her mother could call her back when she was able – if she was able to – and said goodbye.

Right. One job done and ticked off the list. Kate jumped up and headed for the file storage room. She planned to look through the Jean Tripp file once more, to cross-check against what her mother had told her. Surely there must be another lead there, something that might bring this case forward, back into the remit of Kate's team?

The Abbeyford CID team kept their case files in a secure room, able to be entered only through a door protected by a key code. Kate punched it in and pushed at the heavy door. The room beyond was small and windowless and always slightly too warm (it was amazing how much overdue filing got done on cold winter days). Kate went to the filing cabinet, slid the drawer out with a metallic clang and then stopped dead.

The file was missing.

She could see that straight away, the emptiness of the cardboard hanging file which had held the manila folder. She could see that, but still she searched the files before and after it, right to the end of the drawer. Then she slid out the one below and searched that, and then the final drawer nearest the floor. Nothing.

Kate slowly slid the metal drawers back into the cabinet. She was aware of her heart beating just that little bit faster. Don't panic, she told herself. Chances are it's already gone down to Cold Cases. Don't panic – yet.

She shut the door of the storage room firmly behind her and walked over to Theo's desk.

"Um, did anyone from CC come up and get the Jean Tripp file yet? That you know of?" she asked, in as casual a tone as possible.

Theo looked up from his report. "Nope. Don't think so." He shouted Fliss's name across the room. "Fliss! Anyone come up to collect that Jean Tripp file?"

Fliss was shaking her head. "No. No one. Why?"

"Oh, doesn't matter," said Kate, trying to smile. "It's not important."

"Because they wouldn't have the codes to the storage room without asking us, would they?" asked Fliss. She got up then and moved closer. "Is something wrong?"

She was clearly worried that she was in trouble for something. Kate forced herself to smile properly and say, "No, no, don't worry. I think I know where it is, anyway. Seriously, Fliss, it's fine."

Mollified, Fliss took herself back to her desk. Kate sat down opposite her, trying to breathe and act normally. The office hummed about her in its usual state – telephones ringing, photocopiers whirring, people talking – the normal, everyday sounds of a workplace. But Kate couldn't relax, couldn't stop thinking about what the missing file might mean. She knew she had put it there the night before last, she knew it. Stop panicking, she instructed herself once more. Olbeck's probably got it – or Anderton.

At the thought of Anderton, her heart gave another great thump. There *had* been something odd about him, she couldn't escape that. Why had he shut the investigation down so suddenly? Kate hunched forward, her forehead propped against her hand as she stared down at the surface of her desk, thinking. Could he have taken the file? Why?

She jumped up again and made her way over to Olbeck's empty office. She marched in purposefully and took a quick scan of his desk, the top of his filing cabinet, the pile of files on the carpet. Nothing there that looked like the Tripp file. Where was he, anyway? She suddenly realised he had the morning off – more wedding stuff with Jeff, no doubt. Should she call him and see if he had the file? But how could he, when any file that had to be taken out of the office had to be logged and signed out and there was nothing in the log book for the Jean Tripp file since last night?

All right then. Kate took a deep breath and went to Anderton's office. The blinds were down and the door closed but she knocked anyway, holding her breath for the sound of his voice curtly telling her to come in. There was nothing but silence. Kate hesitated for a moment. Then, looking up and down the corridor and seeing that no one was in sight, she opened the door to Anderton's office and quickly slipped inside, shutting it behind her.

I'm just having a look, she told herself, heart thumping once more. She checked the surface of his desk, looked underneath – nothing there but a large black gym bag – and quickly scanned the rest of the room. She couldn't see it anywhere. Biting her lip, Kate listened out once more. Hearing nothing, she took a quick, guilty glance at the door and then, before she lost her nerve, opened the drawers to his desk one by one.

If anyone caught her doing this, she would be in so much trouble it wasn't funny. *Stop this, stop this*, she screamed at herself, but somehow she was still doing it, still searching through the cupboards and filing cabinets, blood pounding in her ears. She was holding her breath but even over the thump of her heartbeat, she became aware of the sound of footfalls in the corridor outside, growing louder. Almost slipping in her haste, Kate dashed back round to the other side of Anderton's desk and flung herself in a chair, just as the door handle clicked and the door opened.

"Kate," said Anderton a moment later, surprised by the sight of her. Kate pinned a smile on her face. She hoped she wasn't too obviously red-faced. "What can I do for you?"

Kate's mind went blank. She groped for a second. "I just wanted to know if you had five minutes. Not now. Later," she added, terrified that he'd ask her to tell him all about whatever was bothering her that very moment.

"What about?"

Again, Kate's mind went blank. "Um – um – I'd rather not go into it right now," she said after a moment. She unconsciously wiped her sweating palms on the sides of her thighs. "If that's okay. I'll bring you up to speed fully later."

Anderton was looking at her slightly oddly. "Okay," he said in a voice that didn't sound too convinced. "I'll give you a shout when I'm free."

"Great," Kate said, overcompensating. She fought down a blush. "I'll be around. Thanks. Thanks very much."

She scuttled back to her desk and collapsed in her chair. What the hell was going on? She tried to think back to whether a file had ever been lost before. It must have happened, human error was always a possibility but...

After a moment, Kate got up and went back to the storage room. While she was waiting for Anderton, she decided to go through every cabinet in that room – just in case.

It was getting on for six o'clock when Anderton finally reappeared. Kate sat at her desk, staring blankly at her computer screen. Across from her, Fliss was chatting continuously about her plans for the evening, about one word in ten of which was penetrating Kate's consciousness.

"Kate." Anderton appeared behind her shoulder with suddenness, making her jump. "When you're ready, I am."

Kate got up and made to follow him. He shook his head minutely at her and leant forward, close enough to whisper something before moving away, heading back out of the office door. Kate stared after him. Had he just said 'get your stuff'?

Heart beginning to speed up a little, Kate gathered her coat and bag, said goodbye to Fliss in a mutter and hurried out. She nearly ran straight into Anderton who was waiting for her in the corridor.

"My car. Come on. Right now."

What the hell? Kate hurried after her boss, bag slipping in her sweating hands. Oh God, was she about to be fired? Had he seen her searching his room? Swallowing hard, Kate almost ran after his swiftly striding figure, hurrying behind him down the stairs and through the echoing metal doors to the underground car park, all the way over to Anderton's car, parked at the far edge of the grounds.

Kate was buckled in and they were speeding away from the station before Anderton spoke.

"Sorry about that... abruptness. I thought we'd go for a drink. That okay with you?"

"Sure," said Kate, so worried and confused she hardly heard herself. What the hell was going on? She was driven inescapably back to that time, years ago now, when she and Anderton had had a one night stand. Was this – was this – did he mean to finally make a move? Not *now*, surely? Oh God, it can't be that, thought Kate. I'm in trouble here, big trouble. She said nothing else for the duration of the drive, waiting and worrying until Anderton drew into the car park of a pub unknown to Kate.

Inside the pub, it was nice – open fires and fairy lights strung along the wainscoting, a decent countryside sort of pub. Anderton ushered Kate through the building to a little snug at the back, where there was only room for one settle and a table.

"Bit easier to talk here," said Anderton. Kate subsided on to the seat feeling as if she were trapped in some kind of dream. "What will you have?"

While he was at the bar, Kate tried to collect herself. Don't admit to anything, don't do anything rash, she told herself, wishing she felt calmer. She thought of Magda and the breathing exercises she'd taught her and tried to do some of the more unobtrusive ones, stopping as Anderton came back into the little room with their drinks.

"Now," he said, sitting back down and taking a hearty pull of his pint. "Sorry about all that cloak and dagger stuff."

Kate gathered her courage. "What's going on?"

Anderton looked into the golden depths of his drink for a moment. "Has it struck you – do you think that there's something a bit funny going on at work?"

What exactly did he mean? Kate wavered for a moment and then bit the bullet. "Yes," she said bluntly. "I do. For a start—" she stared him straight in the eye. "The Jean Tripp file has gone missing."

"No, it hasn't."

Kate was almost winded. "What? Yes it has. I looked for it everywhere today, nobody's seen it, nobody's logged it out—"

"It's not missing. Or if it is, it's gone missing in my gym bag."

Kate thought for a moment she'd misheard. "What?"

"Shh," Anderton said, leaning in a little closer. "I said, I've got it."

Kate's eyes bulged. "You have? Why?"

Anderton sat back again and took a gulp of beer. "Because I didn't want it to go missing *permanently*," he said, putting his glass back down again.

Kate drew a breath in through her nostrils. "Okay," she said, after she'd calmed down a little. "What's going on?"

Anderton leant forward again. "Something bloody odd is going on, that's what I think," he said quietly. "That's why I wanted to come here, so we couldn't be overheard. Something definitely dodgy is going on."

"So, what?" Kate asked, equally quietly.

"I've thought it ever since I went to see Norman. He didn't seem that surprised to be asked the questions that I asked him. Now, why would that be, seeing as the events I was asking him about happened almost forty years ago?" Anderton glanced around as if expecting to see someone eavesdropping. "He was – he was as normal as he could be but – I don't know – there was something. He was lying to me, about something."

Kate slumped a little in her seat, almost weak with relief. There she had been, thinking that Anderton had been the one putting the spoke in the wheels, trying to shut down the investigation when that wasn't the case at all. Although... she felt a sudden jump of paranoia. Had he purposefully asked her here and told her this in order to keep her on side?

"When I asked you about Kevin Doherty," she began, cautiously. "You were the same. You didn't even ask me why I wanted to know about him, someone that you can't have even thought of for decades."

"That's why," Anderton said grimly. "I'd already started to get suspicious. I went to question Norman, question him about something that should have been quite innocuous. A couple of days later, I'm told that I'm to shunt the case over to Cold Cases, it's not top priority anymore. You can imagine that didn't sit well with me."

"You still did it though," Kate said, resentment still present in her tone.

Anderton gave her a look. "Kate, believe me, I had no choice. Besides..." He lowered his voice. "If you're thinking what I'm thinking, then the worst thing to do is start hurling accusations around before we've even got any evidence."

Kate then took a look around the empty little snug herself. "What are we thinking?" she murmured.

Anderton took another bracing pull of his pint. The glass was almost empty and Kate spared a thought, a minor worry, about how she was going to get back home. "We're being told not to take an interest, in so many words," Anderton said. "I don't like that. That doesn't sit well with me. There were always rumours about Doherty but nothing – nothing concrete. He was a dodgy bugger, though. What if he had something to do with this case? That's corruption at the highest level, Kate. Cover ups. Whitewashing. We've seen it happen recently, in Rotherham, with Savile. All those people who let those things happen or turned a blind eye."

Kate was hanging onto every word, almost breathless. The momentary paranoia she'd had, that Anderton was just out to trip her up, dissipated. Sincerity rang in his every word. "So, what do we do?" she asked.

Anderton sighed. "I need another drink for this."

Kate folded her lips together for a moment. I can always get a cab, she thought and got up, offering to get them this time.

She ducked back into the corridor that led back to the main bar. Waiting there, she felt a blast of cold air as, behind her, the door to the road opened. Kate looked into the mirror that ran the length of the bar and straight into the reflected eyes of Fliss, who had crowded into the pub with what looked like about ten other girls.

Fliss saw her and immediately smiled and waved. Kate, after a moment, did the same. She didn't turn, but saw Fliss approaching her in the mirror, and only as she saw her arrive just behind her did she swing round.

"Hi, Kate," said Fliss. "What a coincidence! We're having a bit of a pub crawl. Want to join us or are you here with someone?"

"I'm – well, I'm—" began Kate before, to her horror, she saw Anderton appear in the corridor doorway to the bar. Too late, she drew her gaze back from him as if he were red hot, but not before Fliss had looked herself and seen him.

"Oh!" Kate heard the exclamation and cringed. Then Anderton was coming over, smooth as you like, hailing Fliss and chastising Kate for the lateness of their drinks order.

He, Fliss and Kate chatted for a few excruciating minutes before

Fliss excused herself and with a rather strained 'goodbye' and left to go and join her friends who were gathered in a noisy circle in the corner of the main room of the pub. Kate and Anderton took their drinks back to the snug in silence.

"Well," said Kate, unable to help herself, as they sat back down. "That's torn it."

"Oh, don't worry about it," said Anderton, breezily. "She'll just think we're having an affair," he added, causing Kate to spit her drink out across the table.

"Bloody hell," said Kate, as they mopped up. "Sorry. But, honestly."

"Seriously, don't worry about it. We've got more important things to worry about." Anderton pushed the little pile of soggy paper napkins to the side of the table and folded his hands on the table. "So, this is what I was going to suggest. Do some investigating on your own. Take some time off and go and see what you can dig up." He caught sight of her face. "What's the matter? Not keen?"

"It's not that," said Kate. "I'm just as keen to see this one through as you are. But why—" She hesitated for a moment. "Why can't we do it officially? Blow the whole thing open and start another investigation?"

Anderton didn't reply for a moment. "We don't have the evidence," he said eventually.

"Oh, come on," Kate said. "We've got a dead body, a statement from someone who was at Marhaven with the victim, we've got the names of the other girls who were there." She stopped, wondering whether she should mention Tom Marks and his story. "What's stopping us?"

Anderton sighed. "Kate, it's – it's difficult. Take it from me, they wouldn't make it easy. It could be a big mistake to go any further officially without some *serious* evidence."

Kate eyed her boss for a long moment, conscious of a sinking feeling in her stomach. "Why won't you do it?" she demanded after a moment. "What's the real reason?"

"I've told you."

Kate scoffed. Then, as realisation dawned, she said, unable to stop her lip curling. "Oh. *I* see."

"What?"

Kate folded her arms. "What have they got on you?"

"I don't know what you mean."

"No?" Kate tried to keep the anger out of her voice and failed. "What have you done that gives them such a hold over you?"

Their eyes met for a long, charged moment. Then Anderton broke the contact, looking down at the table. "This isn't to go any further."

Kate rolled her eyes. "Naturally."

There was an edge to Anderton's voice. "Nobody's perfect, Kate. Not even you." Their eyes met again and this time Kate flushed, partly from anger, partly from memory of their brief affair. Anderton went on, looking away. "I – I slept with a suspect. She – she didn't take kindly to me breaking it off once I realised what a stupid thing it was I was doing. Made a complaint against me. It was dropped for lack of evidence but – it's still there, in the records. It could make life very difficult for me if, *by some coincidence*, it was made public knowledge."

Kate stared at him. "Does any of this sound familiar? What were we just talking about?"

"Exactly!" Anderton leant forward again. "That's why I think there's a cover-up going on. Someone has something on someone very senior. That's why we can't let this lie, Kate, as much as they want us to. But I'm not risking my job without being damn sure of a conviction. I'm sorry, but that's that. No arguments."

For a moment, Kate thought about protesting. But she could see the sense in what he was saying. If Anderton's seniority wouldn't be enough to save him, then where did that leave her? Out in the cold, that was where. Slowly, she nodded.

"Good," said Anderton. "Now, drink up and I'll drop you home.

Don't look like that—" He added, seeing Kate's significant glance at his empty glass. "I've only had two pints. Now, I'll sign you off on holiday from tomorrow. See what you can dig up. Didn't you say your mother had made a statement?" Kate nodded. "Great. That's a good start. Plan your action and keep me posted."

Kate threw him an ironic salute. "Aye-aye, captain."

Anderton smiled and for one moment, there was just the slightest hint of the possibility of something more between them. Kate turned her face sharply away, breaking their gaze. Don't start that again, she told herself. They walked towards the exit of the pub and Anderton and Kate both waved to Fliss, who returned it rather uncertainly. Kate worried about how she was going to handle the inevitable questions at work tomorrow before realising that she wouldn't be there and her spirits lightened. On the way home she sent a text to Tin apologising for her silence and asking him just one question. Then she put the phone away, answered Anderton's small talk as best she could and inwardly, made her plans.

Chapter Nineteen

"THANKS FOR COMING," SAID KATE, glancing over at her passenger.

"Humph," said Tin, sounding a little cool. "I surprise myself, sometimes."

Kate glanced over at him once more and was relieved to find that he was half-smiling. She faced the road again and checked the sat nav. Half an hour until they would reach their destination.

"So, tell me as much as you can about Sarah Smith," she said. "I know she lives in Haworth, that she was at Marhaven, that she was one of the girls who accused Godfrey Peters of sexual assault. What happened to her after that?"

Tin leant his head back against the head rest. "She left the country," he said. "Not long after she made that accusation."

"Seriously?" Kate raised her eyebrows. "But she was – wasn't she underage? Although—" She considered for a moment. "If she'd travelled with someone, an older person for example, that might not have flagged up any concern."

"Exactly," said Tin. "She was reported missing by the Marhaven home not long after that accusation was made. No one was really concerned – she was a habitual runaway, a troubled, argumentative little madam, according to those who remember her. Anyway, I managed to trace her movements into Spain, then I think she went to Australia and was out there for years. She only came back to the UK a few years ago."

"Have you managed to talk to her before?"

Tin shook his head. "Wouldn't even open the door to me. I had the devil's own job trying to actually find her here. She must have changed her name more than once, got married maybe."

Something that Tin had said had rung a faint bell with Kate. She frowned, trying to pinpoint what it was, but it slipped away from her. Never mind. It would come back.

They were approaching Haworth now. The drive had been a pleasant one, winding their way through the calm, green hills of the Yorkshire dales, the grassy flanks of the hills criss-crossed with the grey lines of the drystone walls and dotted here and there with grubby looking sheep. Kate drew the car into a layby for a moment at the top of the road into the town and they looked down at the valley, the stone cottages and winding streets, and up on the opposite hill, the building made famous as the home of the Bronte sisters. Kate felt a fleeting disappointment that they wouldn't have time to go and have a closer look.

"You're sure that's her address?" she asked Tin.

"Unless she's moved in the two months since I tried to talk to her."

"Okay." Kate put the car in gear and pulled back onto the road. "Let's do this."

The street on which Sarah Smith lived was a typical one: rows of little stone cottages with doors opening directly on to the cobbled streets. Kate found a parking space at the end of the road and shut off the engine.

"Shall we both go?" she asked Tin.

"Not to start. Let me try again. I can tell her that things have moved on in the investigation. Talk to her about Jean Tripp. That might work."

Kate nodded slowly. "Okay. If you don't get anywhere, come back and I'll have a go."

She watched Tin walk towards the house in her rear-view mirror and was momentarily side-tracked in admiring his rear view. Recollecting herself, she put the time to good use in trying to find them both somewhere to stay for the night. She found a likely looking hotel, made the booking there and then and was just trying to check her emails when the car door opened and made her jump.

Tin got in, grim-faced. "Nothing. She won't even open the door."

"But she's in?"

"Yes. I saw the curtains move in the front room."

Kate considered. "All right. Leave it for now. I've found us a hotel, so let's check in and we'll come back after lunch." She thought, but didn't add, *if she continues to refuse, I'm pulling out my warrant card*. Hopefully it wouldn't come to that.

The hotel actually turned out to be a local pub, the accommodation rather basic but at least clean and comfortable. Kate had hesitated but in the end had booked two rooms adjoining one another. She was starting to think that her fledgling relationship with Tin had crossed the line from romance to business-like friendship. *I'm not going to worry about that now*, she reminded herself. *Keep your mind on the job, Kate.*

They had lunch in the pub. Kate could see Tin attracting some curious but not hostile glances from the locals at the bar and felt cross for him. He was eating his steak and kidney pie, seemingly oblivious to the attention, and after a moment Kate shrugged off her anger and turned her attention to the excellent food.

After coffee, the two of them faced each other across the table.

"We're trying again?" asked Tin.

Kate nodded. "It's my turn now," she added, as they made their way to the door.

Sarah Smith lived behind a door that was covered in peeling red paint, as if the wood was afflicted with some kind of skin disease. Kate knocked using the dull metal knocker, rang the doorbell, knocked again. Nothing. She leant forward, almost certain she could hear the woman breathing, standing behind that implacable door like a statue.

505

"Ms. Smith," Kate called, as quietly as she could but still hopefully loud enough to be heard. "Ms. Smith, don't be alarmed but I really need to speak with you. Can you hear me? Can you open this door?"

She did hear it then, a distinct intake of breath. Kate leant ever closer and carried on with her pleas. "Ms. Smith – Sarah – I need to talk to you. I don't mean you any harm, in fact, I'm here to help you. Can you let me in? Please?"

Nothing. Silence. Baulked, Kate stood back for a moment, cast a frustrated glance at Tin who was hovering several feet away and then leant back towards the door.

"Sarah, my name is Kate Redman. I'm a—" She stopped herself finishing the sentence. *I'm a police officer.* That would probably not help her case at all. Going blank for a moment, she then remembered. She leant forward again. "Sarah, I'm Kate Redman. I'm Mary Redman's daughter. She was with you in the Marhaven home in the seventies. Do you remember? I think you were friends. Mary Redman. She said I had to talk to you."

Nothing still. In increasing desperation, Kate pressed herself onto the peeling paint, ignoring the curious looks from passers-by. "Sarah," she said, her mouth at the keyhole. "Mary told me to talk to you. She said to be brave. She said to be Boudicca." Kate could feel the cold metal of the keyhole against her mouth. "Be Boudicca," she repeated, desperately.

There was a sudden click, as of a bolt drawing back. Kate drew back from the door, holding her breath. The door swung inwards by a few inches and Kate could see, framed in the gap, the face of Sarah Smith.

"Sarah?" she asked, tentatively. There was a small nod from the woman standing in the doorway.

"You can come in," said Sarah in a low voice, that still carried a slight Australian twang. Then, as Tin made a move towards the door, she pulled it back towards her until only an inch of space showed. "Not you. Just her."

"Go on," said Kate to Tin. She handed him the car keys. Then, as Sarah drew the door open again, just wide enough for Kate to slip through, she entered the house.

The door opened straight into the living room, as was customary with these old houses. The room was dark, curtains pulled against the daylight, and warm – the central heating was obviously on. Kate and Sarah stood silently regarding each other for a moment. Sarah was a tall, heavy woman, with rather beautiful thick, blonde hair. Crows-feet cut sharply into the skin around her brown eyes and her face was spattered with freckles.

"Wow," said Sarah after a moment. "You do really look like Mary. I haven't seen her in so many years but looking at you... Wow. It brings it all back."

Her face clouded. Moving further into the room, she turned back to Kate to ask a question. "Do you want a drink?"

"Tea would be lovely—" Kate began before realising that Sarah was reaching for a bottle of red wine that stood on the sideboard. "Oh, no thanks," she added hastily. "I'm fine."

"I don't normally drink during the day," said Sarah. "But I think I might need one now." Kate was reminded of Tom Marks. Sarah poured herself a generous glass and sat down on one of the two armchairs in the room. Kate sank back into the other, facing her.

There was a short silence whilst Sarah drank her wine. Kate studied her covertly. She probably hadn't ever been pretty but there was both strength and character in her face. No wedding ring. She was dressed in comfortable, drab clothes; loose grey tracksuit trousers and a baggy grey jumper. She was probably the same age as Mary Redman but she looked younger. That wasn't hard, Kate thought, feeling a pang at the thought of her mother.

As if Sarah had read her mind, she looked up. "Why does Mary want you to talk to me? All that stuff that happened was so long ago. Why does she think we can do anything about it now?"

Kate leant forward clasping her hands and wondering how to

begin. In the end, she decided to tell the truth. "Mary – Mum – she's got terminal cancer. She's dying." Sarah said nothing but winced a little. "She's already given a statement to the police about what she saw at Marhaven, the sexual abuse allegations. She wants to bring it all to light before she – before she dies." Kate felt her throat close up at these words and stopped speaking abruptly.

Sarah hadn't taken her eyes off Kate's face. Something in her own face reflected Kate's anguish for a moment. "Mary was always brave. She's the one who taught me about Boudicca. She was sort of a heroine to us both. We needed a role model in that place, by God we did."

Kate cleared her throat. "So, tell me about it."

Sarah was silent. Then she jumped up and poured herself another glass of wine, a bigger one this time. Then she sat down again.

"It's all right," she said, catching Kate's glance at her brimming glass. "I won't have any more. I won't be drunk if that's what you're thinking." She took a sip, put the glass down on the coffee table in front of her, and sighed. "I haven't talked about this in years. I thought I'd almost managed to forget about it. I've had so much therapy, you wouldn't believe... It did work, mostly. It got me through. I mean, I'm still here, aren't I? Not like the other one who came with me to the station, what was her name?"

"Tina Fetterden," said Kate.

"Yeah, her. Jesus, it took us such a lot of... I mean, trying to get the courage up to report *him* and his dirty little secrets. And then nothing ever happened. I started getting worried though, especially after Jonie said she was going to the papers—"

Kate didn't want to interrupt her but she had to. "Who's 'him', Sarah?"

"Mr Peters. The guy who ran the home, him and his weird sister."

Kate nodded. Sarah went on speaking, haltingly but without

stopping. "He was a paedophile. It was the perfect job for him, wasn't it, in charge of all these young girls, these young troubled vulnerable girls, who nobody was going to believe when they tried to tell someone about what he did. He used to pimp us out, you know." Sarah looked up at Kate through a curtain of blonde hair. "He used to lend us out to all his rich and powerful friends. A taxi would come and pick us up and take us to this hotel in Bristol. The hotel owner was one of them, one of the men. They'd give us drugs and alcohol and take it in turns to rape us." She was shaking now, what was left of the wine sloshing dangerously in her glass. Gently Kate reached out and took it from her, putting it down on the coffee table. Sarah carried on speaking. "There were all sorts of men there, doctors and lawyers and police. I should have known not to bother going to report him."

Kate's skin was prickling. "There was a police officer there? Did you know his name?"

Sarah clasped both of her hands together. "I didn't at first. Then Jonie found out. That's what she said she was going to tell the journalist she went to."

Kevin Doherty. Kate was dying to mention his name but she knew she mustn't lead the witness. "What was his name, Sarah?" she repeated, gently.

"I don't know his first name. But he was there all the time. Chambers, that was it. Someone Chambers."

For a second, Kate thought she'd misheard her. She swallowed. "Chambers?"

"Yeah. Him and that other copper used to come. The big one, he was awful. I thought he'd killed Tina once, he was so rough." Sarah looked down at her clasped hands. Kate thought she saw a tear fall from behind that blonde curtain of hair. "He had an Irish name, the big one. Kevin something."

Kate's heart was thumping so loudly she was surprised Sarah couldn't hear it. *Chambers.* She could feel her hands begin to shake. If Norman Chambers had been part of a paedophile ring...

Kate took a deep breath and then another. What the hell was she going to do now?

"Can you tell me anything more?" she asked Sarah, hoping her voice wasn't trembling too much.

Sarah unclasped her hands and wiped the palms along the sides of her tracksuit trouser, leaving a faint grey mark. "It started not long after we arrived at the home. He used to touch us, that Peters, and make us do things. He'd give us stuff afterwards, fags and sweets and stuff like that, but he made it pretty plain that nobody would believe us if we told anyone, and if we told anyone, we'd be out of Marhaven and then where would we go? We were in the last chance saloon there. I don't know why I didn't run away sooner, to be honest. I suppose – Tina being there, and Jonie and Mary – it was the first time I'd ever had any real friends. I didn't want to leave them."

Kate felt her eyes stinging and blinked. "So what made you go to the police when you did?"

"Jonie." Sarah cleared her throat. "Jonie arrived. She was different. She'd been abused back at home, and she knew what Peters was doing was wrong. She persuaded us to go to the police." Sarah made a small choking sound that could have been a laugh. "Chambers took my statement and I think Doherty took Tina's. We didn't know them then, but it wasn't long after that that we started getting shipped out to the hotel. I recognised him then, all right." She took a long breath in and sighed it out. "I got scared then. I knew if he was that sort of man, and he knew I'd reported Peters for abuse, then he was bound to tell him. Tina knew it too. That Doherty – he was scary. We used to see him parked outside the home sometimes, watching. Just watching."

Kate didn't think she had breathed through the whole of Sarah's speech. "What happened then?"

Sarah cleared her throat again. Her voice had grown thick, as if she had a cold. "I was all for skipping out there and then but Jonie said not to. She said she was going to the papers, she'd already contacted a journalist and she was going to meet him and give him the whole story. Then we'd be safe, because they couldn't sweep it all under the carpet anymore." She was silent for a moment and then said, with difficulty. "She said she'd spoken to him, this journo, already, and she was meeting him in two days' time. She – the next day, she'd gone. Just gone. We were told she'd run away."

"You didn't believe that?" asked Kate, who didn't believe it either.

Sarah shook her blonde head. "Of course not. Jonie wouldn't just have gone and left us all in the lurch. She had a plan, she was going to get us out of there. She said that after she'd done the interview, she was going to leave and go somewhere, somewhere where they'd never find her. And of course I said that was impossible. But she said she'd do it and fool them. She gave me a postcard to send her family, said I should post it from somewhere so they wouldn't worry."

Kate blinked, knowing that *that* was what had bothered her about Tin's conversation earlier. "Sarah, did you send that postcard that Jonie gave you when you got to Spain?"

Sarah half-smiled. "I thought that would be a good enough place." Her face clouded again. "When I got there, I don't know – I thought, how weird if Jonie actually *did* get to Spain. I was almost fantasising about it, whether I might run into her accidently or something. But I knew I wouldn't. I knew something had happened to her. She wouldn't have gone without saying goodbye, I know she wouldn't."

Kate was silent. Someone had got wind of Jonie's – Jean Tripps's – plan for exposure. Who? Godfrey Peters? Norman Chambers himself? She would put money on Kevin Doherty being the person who'd actually disposed of Jean and buried her body.

She leant forward, fixing Sarah with her eyes. "Sarah, would you be prepared to make a statement?"

Sarah looked at her with puzzlement. "What do you mean? Like Mary?"

"Yes." Kate could see that she was going to have to come clean. Bracing herself, she went on. "Sarah, I am Mary Redman's daughter, that's the absolute truth. But I will tell you something else. I'm also a police officer."

She saw the recoil, the flash of anger. Sarah was on her feet, her posture half aggression, half fear. "A police woman? What the hell do you think you're doing? I told you everything because you said you were here from *Mary*."

"I am. I am here from Mary. I'm actually here off the record." Kate got up herself and moved backwards out of Sarah's space, holding her hands out in a reconciliatory fashion. "Sarah, listen. I'm here because the detective chief inspector of Abbeyford CID believes you. He sent me here to talk to you, to see if we could persuade you to make a statement, to see if we could help you to put these bastards behind bars. He *believes* you, and so do I. We're here to help you." Sarah was still glaring at her, one hand raised half to provoke, half to protect. "Sarah, we believe you. Help us. Help us get you the justice you deserve, that Mary – that Mum – deserves."

Kate stopped, panting.

Sarah regarded her with what looked like a slight cessation of hostility. "I want to believe you," she said, after a moment, in a low voice.

"Please, *do* believe me. I'm telling you, we're going to win this one. I give you my word. Whatever it takes, we're going to see that all those people who hurt and abused you and robbed you of your childhood, we're going to see that they pay for it. I give you my word. Whatever it takes."

Sarah stepped forward slightly. She sat down, fixing her gaze on Kate. "You'd better mean that."

"I give you my word," Kate repeated.

Chapter Twenty

THE DOOR, WITH ITS PEELING red paint, shut behind Kate and she stood for a moment in the sunshine, tipping her face up to the warmth. She felt as if she'd just emerged from underground, like some sort of tunnel-dwelling creature, as yet unused to bright light.

Shaking her head, she walked towards the car, where she could see the back of Tin's curly black head through the rear windscreen. This time, it was Kate's turn to make him jump as she opened the car door suddenly.

"Well?" asked Tin, putting his iPad away.

Kate said nothing for a moment, sliding into the driver's seat. She reached for the car keys and then stopped. She couldn't face driving just yet – her mind was fizzing with what Sarah had told her – she wouldn't have the concentration that driving a car demanded.

"Well?" prompted Tin again.

"Give me a moment," Kate said, slowly. She was thinking furiously. There was no way that she was going to be able to tell Tin about Sarah's allegations, particularly the ones regarding Norman Chambers, not until she talked to Anderton about their next steps. She had meant every word of her impassioned speech to Sarah, but here, sitting in the car, she was coming up with a whole host of arguments as to why pursuing this was going to be a very bad idea. No. No, she was not going to let that poor woman down. If it meant that she, Kate Redman, would risk her job, then so be it. Kate heaved a big sigh and looked over at Tin. "Okay, you're not going to like this," she said.

Tin's face flickered momentarily. "Yeah?"

"Sarah made a statement, or at least she told me what had happened. But—" Kate inwardly braced herself. "I can't share that with you at the moment. I'm sorry."

"Oh, for God's sake." Tin threw his hands up in the air and flung himself out of the car in one swift movement. Shocked, Kate froze in her seat for a second before she got out herself.

Tin was standing a few feet away, his hands in his pockets, angrily rocking back and forward on the balls of his feet. Kate walked up to him warily.

"I'm sorry," she said quietly. "I wish it could be different. But I have a job to do, Tin, you know I'm constrained by that."

Tin looked at her for a long moment, his face clearly expressing what he was thinking. Then he took his hands out of his pockets and lifted them in a gesture of resignation. "I need a bloody drink," he said and turned on his heel, making for the pub on the corner of the street.

Kate trailed after him a little uncertainly. As Tin reached the door of the pub, she became aware of her mobile ringing. She pulled it from her bag, looking at the screen. Jay's number was displayed. Kate hesitated for a moment – was it worth answering when she and Tin appeared to be in the middle of a row? – and then lifted the phone to her ear.

"Hi, Jay."

At first she thought the line was bad, the reception terrible. She could hear nothing at first but the odd muffled word. "Jay – you're breaking up—"

The line seemed to clear. Kate heard her brother's voice clearly, his tear-filled, choked, heartbroken voice. "Kate. Mum's died."

There was a second of blankness as Kate took in the words and then she was suddenly on the pavement, all the strength running out of her legs. She could hear Jay talking to her, words interspersed with sobs but she wasn't able to talk back, she couldn't say anything. Grief had lain her to waste.

Suddenly Tin was there, his arms around her, helping her up. She felt him take the phone from her hand, heard him talking to Jay, explaining who he was. She heard it all as if she were behind a sheet of thick glass, hearing it from afar. She was crying so hard she could barely see. Then Tin picked her up bodily and carried her back to the car. She felt him put her in the passenger seat and fasten the belt around her and then, though her eyes were closed, her hands hiding the world from her view, she felt the car move as Tin drove them away.

Looking back on the time between that phone call and the time where she lay on her hotel bed, crying, Kate realised that she must have moved, must have walked from the car, through the pub and up the stairs to their rooms, but she couldn't remember it. It had been erased from her memory as if a giant hand had wiped it away.

Kate lay on the bed and cried, and Tin lay beside her and held her. He didn't say anything, no platitudes or hurtful, thoughtless comments, for which she was grateful. He just lay and held her, and gradually the storm of tears stopped and she was able to lie there, her chest hitching in the aftermath of her crying fit, until the windows of the room darkened as night drew in and eventually, lulled by the warmth and nearness of Tin, worn out by emotion, Kate fell asleep.

WHEN SHE WOKE IN THE morning, Tin was still there. It seemed the most natural thing in the world to reach for him, seeking comfort. He didn't resist but whispered to her "Are you sure?" and Kate nodded, wordlessly.

Afterwards, they lay together in each other's arms. Kate could feel the sadness beginning to gather again, grief building and building in a relentless wave before she started crying again, softly this time. *Poor, poor Mum.* All the bitterness and resentment from her childhood was washed away for the moment, and Kate could only mourn for the relationship they might have had, for the few fond memories she did have of her mother. She remembered their last meeting, the final hug goodbye although she hadn't known it at the time and was glad that, at least, their final words had been those of love and tenderness.

She rang Jay, who sounded just as wrung-out and drained of tears as she herself was. She spoke to her sisters, Jade and Courtney, who were staying with Jay and Laura until the funeral. The funeral – Kate felt herself tremble at the thought of it. She supposed that she should be the one to organise it, but Jay reassured her that he and Laura would take care of the arrangements. Kate gave way, gratefully, and not for the first time thanked God that her brother had such a wonderful fiancée.

Tin had tactfully absented himself as Kate made her phone calls but he came back into the room, freshly changed and showered. Kate sat on the edge of the bed, slumped over, and Tin came and crouched down between her legs, putting one hand on each knee.

"Okay?" he said. There was so much concern in his voice that Kate almost started crying again but managed to control herself.

"I think so," she replied, with a watery smile. They both looked at each other. The usual slight awkwardness that might be felt after a first shared sexual experience was conspicuous in its absence. Kate felt – *safe*, that was the word. The uncertainty, the anxiety that she was used to feeling at this tentative early stage in a relationship was gone. She sighed deeply and leant forward resting her head on Tin's broad shoulder.

"Could you eat something?" he asked. "It's no problem if not..."

"No, I could," said Kate, surprised to find that she was actually hungry. She pushed herself off the bed, wobbled a little and added, "I think I really *do* need to eat something."

They made their way down to the restaurant section of the pub and found a table right at the back. Kate let Tin order for her. She was undergoing what every recently bereaved person experienced – the surprise and the anger that the world was going on much as it always had, despite the earthquake that had just taken place in her life.

She thought of what Sarah had told her yesterday and felt nothing. She knew that soon, that would change, but at that very moment, the thought of actually having to do something about it was too much. She couldn't do it. But Mary had been so brave, had been so insistent that the two of them do something about it. How could Kate let her down now? *I'm sorry, Mum*, she said to Mary in the privacy of her own head. *I won't let you down. Just let me have this one day to grieve, and then I'll carry on.*

Plates of food arrived in front of them and Kate ate what was there mechanically, tasting nothing, re-fuelling. Afterwards, the two of them went back up to Kate's room. This time there was no love-making. Kate didn't even need to say anything. Tin just laid her down on the bed, curled himself around behind her and let her drift off to sleep again, warm and comforted.

Chapter Twenty One

KATE KNOCKED AND OPENED THE door in answer to Anderton's shout.

"Kate," he said in surprise as she entered his office. "I thought you were – aren't you on compassionate leave? I was really sorry to hear about your mother."

"Thank you," murmured Kate, the usual colourless rejoinder that she'd been forced to make day in and day out for the past week. "I am but I came in because I needed to talk to you."

"Take a pew," Anderton said, indicating the chair opposite him.

"Privately," Kate said, remaining standing.

There was a moment's silence. Then Anderton said "Ah," nodded to himself and got up, reaching for his coat.

They didn't speak for the whole time they were walking to Anderton's car, or for the whole of the journey to the quiet county pub that they'd been to before, the night that Fliss had surprised them. How long ago it seemed, Kate thought, as Anderton drew the car into a parking space at the back of the pub. How much had happened since then. She shut the car door and followed Anderton's broad back into the pub, pulling her coat more tightly around her. Despite the gradually warming spring weather, she always felt cold nowadays. Shock and emotional strain, Tin had said. Thinking of him, Kate checked her mobile almost as a reflex and looked at the last text he'd sent her, first thing that morning. No words but just a line of kisses.

Comforted slightly, she made her way to the snug at the back of the pub whilst Anderton got their drinks. A small part of her was dreading the upcoming conversation, but most of her just felt empty. Empty, sad and lost. Magda had told her that was normal, that there were distinct stages of grief to be worked through, but at the moment, Kate felt like she didn't have the energy for working through anything. The one thing that was keeping her going was the promise she'd made to Sarah Smith and to the ghosts of her mother, Jean Tripp, Tina Fetterden and Jane Moor.

"So," Anderton said. "How are you? The funeral's on Friday, isn't it?"

Kate nodded. "Would you mind very much if we didn't talk about that, sir?"

Anderton looked slightly uncomfortable. "Of course, of course." There was a short moment of silence whilst he sipped his pint and Kate tried to gather the energy to speak. "So...?"

Kate drew a deep breath. "I managed to make contact with one of the girls who made an accusation of sexual abuse against the manager of Marhaven, Godfrey Peters. Her name is – well, was, she's changed it several times since then – was Sarah Smith."

Anderton nodded. "Yes, I remember."

Kate continued. "She opened up to me because I'm - I *am* Mary's daughter." She managed to hide the jab of pain that speaking her mother's name brought her. "She trusted me enough to tell me all about what used to go on at Marhaven." She explained to Anderton some of the accusations that Sarah had made, the sex parties with underage girls, the sexual abuse at the home itself. At that point, she didn't mention any names.

Anderton listened to it all. "Is she credible?" was his first question, when Kate paused for breath.

Kate nodded. "Yes. Yes, I believe so. She's very suspicious, very hostile to the police because of what happened—" She stopped herself for a moment. "I'll get onto that in a minute," she said, a trifle awkwardly. "But despite all that, I think she'd be prepared to make a statement, to testify in court if there's a chance of a conviction."

Anderton raised his eyebrows. "So she's named a suspect, or several suspects, who are still living?"

Kate nodded, swallowed to try and get some moisture into her dry mouth. "Yes. Yes, she has." She paused, gathered her courage together with both hands. "One of the suspects she's named as complicit and involved in a paedophile ring operating at the time, in the seventies, is – is known to you already." She heard the dread in her tone, saw it mirrored in Anderton's apprehensive face. "It's Norman Chambers."

In the echoing silence that followed, Kate kept her eyes fixed on Anderton's face. She saw something there, just a flash of an emotion that, when the full impact struck her, she gasped in horror. Anderton – some small part of Anderton— was not surprised. Kate raised a shaking hand to her mouth. "You knew," she said, through paper-dry lips.

Anderton leant forward and grabbed her arm, shaking his head. "No. No! I did not *know*." She could see him trying to recover his poise and winced beneath the tightening hand on her arm. "You just gave me a hell of a shock, that's all." He caught sight of Kate's increasingly pained expression and snatched his hand back from her arm with an exclamation. "Sorry. It's just – my God, Kate. Norman Chambers." His voice dropped almost down to a whisper.

Kate sat back, keeping her eyes fixed on his face. She knew she hadn't misread that first flash of emotion. "You weren't surprised. Not really surprised. Are you really, honestly telling me that you didn't know what he was like?"

Anderton eyed her. "I'd be bloody careful about what you're implying, DS Redman," he said, in a not very friendly voice. "Yes, I'd just tread a wee bit carefully with what you're implying."

If he was trying to frighten her, it wasn't working. Dimly, Kate thought that she was too wrung-out emotionally to be bothered about being frightened. "I'm not implying anything. All I'm saying is that when I mentioned his name, in connection with a *paedophile ring*, for a second, you looked as though it wasn't news to you. Are you telling me I'm wrong?"

Anderton sat back too, mirroring her posture. His eyes never left her face. "You don't just go and accuse the former chief superintendent of this county of paedophilia, Kate."

"Oh, don't I?" said Kate, sarcasm dripping from every word. "Why not, if that's what he is?"

They eyed one another for a long moment. Then Anderton sighed and broke the eye contact. He seemed to sag a little in his seat. "There was nothing concrete," he said, quietly. "Nothing but rumours. And not many of those. Just a few jokes flying around, you know, when I first joined, that he liked them young. It was the eighties, Kate, people made jokes about sexy schoolgirls and things like that." Kate rolled her eyes in disgust and Anderton held up a hand. "All right, it was wrong. I get that, I'm not denying that. But when you asked me if I knew, then if what is being alleged is true, then of course I bloody didn't. What do you take me for? I've got three daughters of my own, you know. Do you think I relish the fact that, if this *is* true, one of my long-term colleagues, former boss and family friend is that sort of man? Do you?"

"No," Kate said. "Of course not. I'm not stupid. But given what we know, what else can we do?" Anderton looked away, into the depths of his pint. Kate repeated "What else can we do?"

There was another long moment of silence. Then Anderton cleared his throat and spoke. "We could – we could do nothing."

Kate felt the bottom of her stomach drop, as if she were standing in a plummeting lift. "What?"

Anderton didn't answer for a moment. "If we go ahead, this is going to bring up one hell of a shit-storm, Kate. Do you know how many cases we'll have to re-examine if it turns out that Norman is – is guilty?"

"*If*?" said Kate, trying to moisten her dry mouth.

Anderton took no notice. "All these things have been buried for so long. Do we – do you want the responsibility of raking it all up again?"

Kate clasped her shaking hands together in her lap. "I can't believe I'm hearing this. Are you seriously saying we should just forget it? Just let it all – just rake it under the carpet again?"

Anderton was still refusing to meet her eye. "All I'm saying is that perhaps we should think about what we'd be doing. Whether it would actually be for the best."

Kate sat still, clasping her hands and staring at nothing over the table. Her heart thumped. She thought of her mother, looking at her over the rim of the oxygen mask, the frantic appeal in her eyes. She thought of her mother's bravery; in choking out her statement, struggling against her failing lungs because she knew that she had to do it. Giving that statement had probably hastened her death, Kate realised. She sat up a little straighter and drew back her shoulders.

"Sir," she said. "I gave my word to the victims of the Marhaven home that I would see this case through until justice was done. Now, I want that justice to be achieved through our investigation."

"Right," said Anderton. "But—"

Kate went on, talking over him. "If you won't help me on this, if you refuse to see it through, then I'm afraid you leave me no choice."

Anderton's eyes narrowed. "*Meaning*?"

Kate swallowed. "I will take all the evidence I've gathered so far and I will take it to the press."

There was a moment of silence. The hubbub from the public bar out in the corridor seemed to fade away for a moment. Kate could feel the small hard semi-circles of her fingernails digging into the palms of her hands.

Anderton spoke then, quite softly. "You realise that if you did that, it would be the end of your career in the police force?"

"I'm aware of that fact," said Kate, trying not to let her voice tremble.

"You'd risk that?" Anderton's eyes searched her face. "You'd throw away all those years of sacrifice and hard work, for crimes that were committed forty years ago?"

Kate squared her shoulders. "Yes. I would. Because it's the right thing to do." She looked him in the eye and although she spoke softly, the passion in her voice made it vibrate. "Because if we turn a blind eye now, what happens forty years into the future? How many children are out there *now*, being abused and not being believed? Throw the historic cases open, make it known, and perhaps we can stop it from happening again. Can't you see that?"

They both regarded each other in silence. Kate held her breath. Then Anderton shook his head slowly, with sadness. "I can't, Kate. We don't have the evidence."

"Oh, *bollocks*." Anger finally made itself felt. Kate leant forward and smacked one fist against the table top. "We've got credible victim statements, we've got the journalist who was contacted by the murder victim, we've got *plenty* of evidence. Put an appeal out for other victims and people will come forward. Set up a report line for victims to contact us. You *know* there's more out there, you *know* as soon as one person comes forward and breaks the silence, others will follow. There'll be plenty of people out there who knew what went on at Marhaven, so don't tell me that we don't – or we won't – have the evidence." She breathed in sharply and sat back, flexing the hand that she'd banged on the table. She looked Anderton straight in the eye. "You're just too much of a bloody coward to see it through."

She pushed her chair back from the table, snatched up her bag and turned to go, sick at heart. What the hell – she was fired anyway. She was at the doorway when Anderton spoke.

"Kate. Kate."

She stopped but didn't turn around. She heard Anderton get

up and walk towards her but kept her face turned away until he appeared around the corner of her vision, moving around until he was facing her and blocking the doorway.

"Was your mother proud of you?" he asked.

"I don't know," said Kate, tightly. "Probably not."

"Well," Anderton said. "She should have been."

Kate blinked away the tears that rushed to her eyes. She stood, clutching her arms across her body, knowing that she should say something, but for that moment, she was just clean out of words. They were all gone, swept away by the rush of emotion.

"Come on," Anderton said. "Sit back down. Let's discuss what we're going to do first."

"First?" asked Kate, finally daring to look at him. She thought of industrial tribunals, getting a lawyer, finding out who her union representative should be.

"Yes," Anderton said. "We should probably start with setting up the help line, like you said. And after that, proceeding with the interview, under caution, of Norman Chambers. Don't you think?"

Chapter Twenty Two

ON FRIDAY MORNING, KATE REGARDED herself in the mirror of the women's toilets at Abbeyford Station. She looked horribly pale, she thought, but then top-to-toe black never had suited her. She pinched her cheeks, trying to get some colour back into them, and smoothed her hair back for the fifteenth time that day. Displacement activity, she knew that. She straightened the lapels of her jacket, took a deep breath and turned away from the mirror.

"Why are you going into work *today*, of all days?" Jay had asked her that very morning. Kate had muttered something about needing to check on the investigation but she didn't really know the answer herself. There was some comfort in being back here, that was the sad thing. She'd seen the new bank of telephones and the specially trained staff who were seated by them, ready for the calls. Kate looked in again as she passed the room where they were situated. One of the women was already talking to someone on the phone. Kate nodded in quiet satisfaction and made her way to the station exit.

She had to pass through the canteen on the way and found her gaze drawn to the television that hung on one wall. It was always tuned to one of the twenty-four hour news stations. Kate passed it and stopped suddenly, hearing what they were currently reporting on. She stood watching the screen, clutching her elbows across her body.

The reporter was a young woman, barely mid-twenties, with a fall of long, glossy chestnut hair. She was standing outside of the

Abbeyford County Court building – Kate recognised the entrance. She concentrated on what the young woman was saying – it wasn't news to her, but it was the first time she'd seen it reported in the press.

"Former chief superintendent of the North West Somerset Police Force, Norman Chambers, today appeared in court charged with the possession of over a thousand images of child sexual abuse. The pictures were found on his home computer after police raided his house in connection with Operation Echo, the ongoing investigation into the historic abuse cases, centred around the Marhaven care home in the nineteen seventies and eighties…"

Kate blew out her cheeks. She watched Norman Chambers being handed into the back of a police car, on his way to – where? Home? Prison? The latter, probably. Kate hoped so.

"North West Somerset Police have confirmed that several historic cases will be re-opened, given the involvement of Chambers and his deputy, disgraced ex-officer, Kevin Doherty. Doherty, who died in nineteen eighty, is implicated in the murder of teenager Jean Tripp, who was also a ward of the Marhaven care home—"

Kate shifted from one foot to the other. She knew she should be going but there was something grimly fascinating about seeing everything play out on the small screen in front of her. She glanced at her watch, caught her breath at the time.

The young reporter was still speaking. "Police have set up a victim support help line in connection with Operation Echo, for anyone who might have something to report in connection with the cases under investigation. The number is—"

Kate finally turned away. Holding her bouncing handbag against her, she ran through the station and out the front door, emerging into sunlight so brilliant that for a moment she stopped, dazzled. Once she'd blinked her way back to clarity, she saw Tin behind the wheel of his car, waiting for her at the foot of the steps, the engine idling. She raised a hand and saw him smile in return, a more subdued smile than his normal wide grin, fitting with the solemnity of the day.

There were a lot of people standing about on the pavement. As Kate made her way down the steps, she recognised them, all of a sudden, stopping dead and blinking. There was Anderton, in black, and Olbeck next to him, and Rav and Theo and Jane and Fliss...

"What's going on?" asked Kate, staring at her colleagues.

"Well, you didn't think we'd let you go to the funeral on your own, did you?" replied Anderton. He tugged at the lapels of his black jacket, straightening it.

"Don't be silly," added Olbeck. He reached Kate's side and pulled her into a hug, kissing the top of her head.

Kate swallowed past the huge blockage in her throat. "Thank you," she said, in a watery voice, once she was able to speak.

"So, we're following you, yeah?" asked Theo, twirling his car keys around one long forefinger. Jane and Fliss were obviously travelling with him. Rav and Olbeck arranged themselves behind Anderton.

There was a subdued shout from Tin, who had got out of the driver's seat. "What's the hold up? Oh—" he said, once he'd realised what was going on.

Kate gave Olbeck's arm a squeeze as she walked past him on her way to the car. "I've finally finished the speech. I hope it's okay."

Olbeck gave a short laugh. "My God, Kate, you don't think Jeff and I are worried about that now, do you?" He moved aside to let her past him. "But, thank you," he added. "I'm sure it'll be great."

Kate gave him a relieved smile. She slid into the passenger seat beside Tin, and he leant over and kissed her. "All right?" he asked, with obvious concern.

"I'll be fine," said Kate. She glanced in the rear view mirror and saw her colleagues getting into their own vehicles, ready to follow her. "I'm sure I'll be fine."

Tin said nothing but he gave her leg a squeeze before putting the car in gear. The vehicle moved off from the kerb, followed by the two others behind it; driving off towards the funeral, through the golden morning sunshine.

BACK AT THE STATION, IN the room where the telephone bank stood, the phones continued to ring. One of the operators picked up the receiver and spoke in her calmest and most professional tone.

"Operation Echo Reporting Line. How may I help you?"   .

A woman's voice on the other end of the line, hesitant. The operator listened, spoke gently in reply, made notes on her writing pad. Around her, the lines trilled and voices rose into the air like smoke.

"Operation Echo—"

"Operation Echo Reporting Line—"

"Hello, you've reached the Operation Echo Reporting Line. How can I help you?"

THE END

Enjoyed this book? An honest review left at Amazon, Goodreads, Shelfari and LibraryThing is always welcome and really important for indie authors. The more reviews an independently published book has, the easier it is to market it and find new readers.

Want some more of Celina Grace's work for free? Subscribers to her mailing list get a free digital copy of Requiem (A Kate Redman Mystery: Book 2), a free digital copy of A Prescription for Death (The Asharton Manor Mysteries Book 2) and a free PDF copy of her short story collection A Blessing From The Obeah Man.

Requiem
(A Kate Redman Mystery: Book 2)

WHEN THE BODY OF TROUBLED teenager Elodie Duncan is pulled from the river in Abbeyford, the case is at first assumed to be a straightforward suicide. Detective Sergeant Kate Redman is shocked to discover that she'd met the victim the night before her death, introduced by Kate's younger brother Jay. As the case develops, it becomes clear that Elodie was murdered. A talented young musician, Elodie had been keeping some strange company and was hiding her own dark secrets.

As the list of suspects begin to grow, so do the questions. What is the significance of the painting Elodie modelled for? Who is the man who was seen with her on the night of her death? Is there any connection with another student's death at the exclusive musical college that Elodie attended?

As Kate and her partner Detective Sergeant Mark Olbeck attempt to unravel the mystery, the dark undercurrents of the case threaten those whom Kate holds most dear...

A Prescription for Death
(The Asharton Manor Mysteries: Book 2) – a novella

"I had a surge of kinship the first time I saw the manor,
perhaps because we'd both seen better days."

IT IS 1947. ASHARTON MANOR, once one of the most beautiful stately homes in the West Country, is now a convalescent home for former soldiers. Escaping the devastation of post-war London is Vivian Holt, who moves to the nearby village and begins to volunteer as a nurse's aide at the manor. Mourning the death of her soldier husband, Vivian finds solace in her new friendship with one of the older patients, Norman Winter, someone who has served his country in both world wars. Slowly, Vivian's heart begins to heal, only to be torn apart when she arrives for work one day to be told that Norman is dead.

It seems a straightforward death, but is it? Why did a particular photograph disappear from Norman's possessions after his death? Who is the sinister figure who keeps following Vivian? Suspicion and doubts begin to grow and when another death occurs, Vivian begins to realise that the war may be over but the real battle is just beginning...

A Blessing From The Obeah Man

DARE YOU READ ON? HORRIFYING, scary, sad and thought-provoking, this short story collection will take you on a macabre journey. In the titular story, a honeymooning couple take a wrong turn on their trip around Barbados. The Mourning After brings you a shiversome story from a suicidal teenager. In Freedom Fighter, an unhappy middle-aged man chooses the wrong day to make a bid for freedom, whereas Little Drops of Happiness and Wave Goodbye are tales of darkness from sunny Down Under. Strapping Lass and The Club are for those who prefer, shall we say, a little meat to the story...

Just go to Celina's blog on writing and self-publishing to sign up. It's quick, easy and free. Be the first to be informed of promotions, giveaways, new releases and subscriber-only benefits by subscribing to her (occasional) newsletter.

http://www.celinagrace.com

Twitter:
@celina__grace

Facebook:
http://www.facebook.com/authorcelinagrace

More books by Celina Grace...

Hushabye
(A Kate Redman Mystery: Book 1)

ON THE FIRST DAY OF her new job in the West Country, Detective
Sergeant Kate Redman finds herself investigating the kidnapping
of Charlie Fullman, the newborn son of a wealthy entrepreneur
and his trophy wife. It seems a straightforward case... but as Kate
and her fellow officer Mark Olbeck delve deeper, they uncover
murky secrets and multiple motives for the crime.

Kate finds the case bringing up painful memories of her
own past secrets. As she confronts the truth about herself, her
increasing emotional instability threatens both her hard-won
career success and the possibility that they will ever find Charlie
Fullman alive...

Hushabye is the book that introduces Detective Sergeant Kate
Redman. Available as a FREE download from Amazon Kindle.

Imago
(A Kate Redman Mystery: Book 3)

"They don't fear me, quite the opposite. It makes it twice as fun... I know the next time will be soon, I've learnt to recognise the signs. I think I even know who it will be. She's oblivious of course, just as she should be. All the time, I watch and wait and she has no idea, none at all. And why would she? I'm disguised as myself, the very best disguise there is."

A known prostitute is found stabbed to death in a shabby corner of Abbeyford. Detective Sergeant Kate Redman and her partner Detective Sergeant Olbeck take on the case, expecting to have it wrapped up in a matter of days. Kate finds herself distracted by her growing attraction to her boss, Detective Chief Inspector Anderton – until another woman's body is found, with the same knife wounds. And then another one after that, in a matter of days.

Forced to confront the horrifying realisation that a serial killer may be preying on the vulnerable women of Abbeyford, Kate, Olbeck and the team find themselves in a race against time to unmask a terrifying murderer, who just might be hiding in plain sight...

Buy Imago on Amazon, available now.

CELINA GRACE'S PSYCHOLOGICAL THRILLER, **LOST Girls** is also available from Amazon:

Twenty-three years ago, Maudie Sampson's childhood friend Jessica disappeared on a family holiday in Cornwall. She was never seen again.

In the present day, Maudie is struggling to come to terms with the death of her wealthy father, her increasingly fragile mental health and a marriage that's under strain. Slowly, she becomes aware that there is someone following her: a blonde woman in a long black coat with an intense gaze. As the woman begins to infiltrate her life, Maudie realises no one else appears to be able to see her.

Is Maudie losing her mind? Is the woman a figment of her imagination or does she actually exist? Have the sins of the past caught up with Maudie's present...or is there something even more sinister going on?

Lost Girls is a novel from the author of The House on Fever Street: a dark and convoluted tale which proves that nothing can be taken for granted and no-one is as they seem.

Currently available exclusively from Amazon.

THE HOUSE ON FEVER STREET is the first psychological thriller from Celina Grace.

Thrown together in the aftermath of the London bombings of 2005, Jake and Bella embark on a passionate and intense romance. Soon Bella is living with Jake in his house on Fever Street, along with his sardonic brother Carl and Carl's girlfriend, the beautiful but chilly Veronica.

As Bella tries to come to terms with her traumatic experience, her relationship with Jake also becomes a source of unease. Why do the housemates never go into the garden? Why does Jake have such bad dreams and such explosive outbursts of temper?

Bella is determined to understand the man she loves but as she uncovers long-buried secrets, is she putting herself back into mortal danger?

The House on Fever Street is the first psychological thriller from writer Celina Grace - a chilling study of the violent impulses that lurk beneath the surfaces of everyday life.

Shortlisted for the 2006 Crime Writers' Association Debut Dagger Award.

Currently available exclusively from Amazon.

EXTRA SPECIAL THANKS ARE DUE TO MY WONDERFUL ADVANCE READERS TEAM...

THESE ARE MY 'SUPER READERS' who are kind enough to beta read my books, point out my more ridiculous mistakes, spot any typos that have slipped past my editor and best of all, write honest reviews in exchange for advance copies of my work. Many, many thanks to you all. Special mention goes to Margaret Gardiner, June Donnelly, Gina, Bonnie Bunge, Helen Drye, Deanne Wimberley, Marian Grandy, Beth Bruik, Alan Pease, Kathleen Charon, Valerie Cobbs, Shannon Watz, Rick Felix, Alexandra Ragle, Fleur Wilkinson, Verlie Williams, Roxanne Loveday, Janet C Clarke, Anne Dannerolle, Denise Grzesiak, Alan Pease, Rosemary Earl, Maureen Vincent-Northam, Karen Ford, Teresa Jones, Cathy Rock, Marianna Roberg, Margie Nelson, Sue Reid, Dave Floyd, Shauna Taylor, Myra Duffy, Andrea T, Caithlin Barry, Patricia George-Lezama, Michelle Judge, Denise Zendel, Jacky Montgomery, Kim Davy, Donna Wolz.

If you fancy being an Advance Reader, just drop me a line at celina@celinagrace.com and I'll add you to the list. It's completely free, and you can unsubscribe at any time.

ACKNOWLEDGEMENTS

MANY THANKS TO ALL THE following splendid souls:

Chris Howard for the brilliant cover designs; Andrea Harding for editing and proofreading; Kathy McConnell for extra proofreading and beta reading; lifelong Schlockers and friends David Hall, Ben Robinson and Alberto Lopez; Ross McConnell for advice on police procedure and for also being a great brother; Kathleen and Pat McConnell, Anthony Alcock, Naomi White, Mo Argyle, Lee Benjamin, Bonnie Wede, Sherry and Amali Stoute, Cheryl Lucas, Georgia Lucas-Going, Steven Lucas, Loletha Stoute and Harry Lucas, Helen Parfect, Helen Watson, Emily Way, Sandy Hall, Kristýna Vosecká, Katie D'Arcy and of course my wonderful and ever-loving Chris, Mabel, Jethro and Isaiah.

Printed in Great Britain
by Amazon